ABSOLU

Sally's Secret Mind
There it was, a spider thing with six eyes. All
of the eyes were looking at the children.

Our Kronos Kids are getting out of hand, said
the Mastermind. It glared into every corner of
their minds with an odd mixture of suspicion
and contempt. It found nothing to warn it of
danger or betrayal, but that only made it
more suspicious.

Sally's Secret Mind rode piggyback over the
Mastermind, an unsuspected parasite. *Kronos,*
it remembered, *who ate his children.* Every
time Sally heard that name, she saw the illustration by Goya that went with it. Her Secret
Mind saw the Mastermind perching on the
child-eater's head, its six eyes glazed with a
hunger that more than matched his.

The Three knew perfectly well what role they
played in the painting. One would have thought it
would shame them.

Instead it pleased them.

Now, commanded the Mastermind, *where is
Olympus?*

THE
KRONOS
CONDITION

EMILY DEVENPORT

A ROC BOOK

ROC
Published by the Penguin Group
Penguin Books USA Inc., 375 Hudson Street,
New York, New York 10014, U.S.A.
Penguin Books Ltd, 27 Wrights Lane,
London W8 5TZ, England
Penguin Books Australia Ltd, Ringwood,
Victoria, Australia
Penguin Books Canada Ltd, 10 Alcorn Avenue,
Toronto, Ontario, Canada M4V 3B2
Penguin Books (N.Z.) Ltd, 182–190 Wairau Road,
Auckland 10, New Zealand

Penguin Books Ltd, Registered Offices:
Harmondsworth, Middlesex, England

First published by Roc, an imprint of Dutton Signet,
a division of Penguin Books USA Inc.

First Printing, February, 1997
10 9 8 7 6 5 4 3 2 1

 REGISTERED TRADEMARK—MARCA REGISTRADA

To Christopher Schelling and Martha Millard,
who took a chance on a new Kid.

and
To Jennifer Smith and Amy Stout,
who helped me through two books that are
very important to me.

FOREWORD

I'm going to go out on a limb and run the risk of alienating some of my readers at this point by stating that I think telepathy and telekinesis as I have presented them in this novel are pure fantasy.

That may seem like a contradictory thing to say; but I can explain. I think these concepts are fantastical, and that makes them excellent material for fiction. In fact, I'm going to be even more political at this point and state that I think if science fiction and fantasy have a purpose other than entertainment, it is to examine the human condition from odd angles that would be impossible using the medium of regular fiction. (Generally speaking, anyway, since I've noticed that "our" genres have begun leaking into "their" genres lately. Contagious, aren't we?) Telepathy and telekinesis are fascinating fictional devices when viewed in that fashion; but I didn't decide to use them just because they are "fascinating." I'm never that rational when I decide to write a book.

To give you an idea what I mean, I will try to explain how this book came to exist.

Three years ago, when I was working as a sweeper at a local grade school, the lady who worked in the section across from me was murdered along with her entire family, including her five-year-old son. She was a kind and outgoing person, the sort who makes you enjoy coming to work every day. When she was murdered I would have been less surprised if she had been struck by lightning. One question I couldn't avoid asking myself over and over, as the dreadful days came and went, was this: How can a human being kill a family and not be horrified by what he is doing? How is his brain different from mine? Is it very different, or just a little different? How do you quantify that sort of thing, anyway? And if you could quantify it, what could you then turn around and do about it?

As you might expect, this line of questioning did nothing to soothe the horror I was feeling. (I still feel it. By the time you read this book, it will have been over three years since my friend was murdered, and not one day has gone by that I haven't thought about it.) But I can't help pursuing it. My nonfiction reading at the time consisted largely of books on neurology and animal behavior because of another fiction project I was pursuing, a book about intelligent, nonhuman animals. This subject matter led my thoughts into odd, sometimes disturbing territory.

Along about this time, Octavia E. Butler's wonderful novel *Mind Of My Mind* was rereleased. When I had read it several years ago, it was the first novel I had ever encountered that portrayed telepaths as people who might be capable of extraordinary (but utterly human) cruelty. Back then I had been horrified and thrilled by it. This time around, it struck an even deeper chord.

The night after I finished *Mind Of My Mind,* I had a nightmare. I dreamed that I was Sally, the main character of *this* novel. I was on a bus with some other children, waiting to be murdered. The people who were going to kill us could read our minds, so we couldn't let them know that we knew. We were driving to the edge of the Grand Canyon, but we weren't there yet. I was trying to think up a way to save our lives without actually thinking about it. This is just the sort of nutty, impossible reasoning that only makes sense in dreams (and in fiction). Whenever I have dreams of this sort, I usually lie awake for a couple of hours afterward, thinking things over. This time was no exception.

Finally I asked myself: If telepaths like the ones in my dream existed, then what would be the neurology of telepathy?

I don't believe that such people exist, but you have to understand that writers (especially those of us who work in the fantastic genres) can't help trying to bring the impossible into the real world. We are crazy wizards, and though some of us truly do strive to write fiction about solid scientific principles, I can't claim that I always have anything in common with these hard-science fiction writers except for curiosity and a desire to get things right.

This was a challenging project, involving a lot of research and soul-searching. I think I understand more about the human mind, not to mention the various theories of the evolution of the human mind, than I did before. But do I understand the guy who killed my friend? Do I know how his mind differs from mine?

I have a few theories; but they don't comfort me, much. My friend is still dead, and guys like the one who killed her will probably still continue to be with us for as long as we continue to be the human race, whether we understand them or not. We may never figure out how to spot them, or what to do with them once we have.

And for now, that's what we're stuck with.

We, we fragile human species at the end of the second millennium A.D., we must become our own authorization. And here at the end of the second millennium and about to enter the third, we are surrounded with this problem. It is one that the new millennium will be working out, perhaps slowly, perhaps swiftly, perhaps even with some further changes in our mentality.

—Julian Jaynes
The Origin Of Consciousness
in the Breakdown of the Bicameral Mind

𝔛

Sally's Secret Mind was listening to the opera inside Ralph's head. It was Puccini's *La Bohème,* and the soloist was Leontyne Price. Sally didn't remember that herself; Ralph did. Ralph knew every composer, every musician, every soloist who had ever been recorded. He even knew some who had *never* been recorded.

Timothy was helping Ralph, as usual. He was a fine-tuner. The two of them sat four seats up on the opposite side of the bus from Sally, Timothy resting his smooth, black hand on top of Ralph's pale pink and white one, reassuring him, easing away the rattle and sway of the old bus, keeping all of Ralph's physical functions stable and well within the comfort zone so that Ralph could just work on his music.

After fourteen years of being raised with him, Timothy didn't have to help Ralph focus his special talent at all. All he had to do was keep out the distractions.

Sally gazed at their motionless heads, knowing, with admiration, what was going on inside of them. They might be her favorite brothers. They loved each other, but without all of the petty jealousies and quarrels brothers always had. Timothy was as moved by the music as Ralph was (as Sally and her Secret Mind were); they were together always, except when Timothy was being appropriated for other matters.

Like the search for Olympus.

That was what they were supposed to be doing. In

fact, in one way or another it was what they had always done. Six children on a bus built for twenty. Six talents, all sitting alone except for Ralph and Timothy; Caitlin up front, Sally in the middle, Joey and Jim bringing up the rear. Their energies were always supposed be focused on Olympus, either the concept or the reality.

But no one could concentrate *all* the time, and for the moment everyone was being left to his or her own devices. For the next few precious minutes, it wasn't necessary to think about details.

For instance, they didn't know their *earthly* destination, except that they were somewhere in Arizona, going toward Globe. And they didn't know how hot it was. Marc was regulating the temperature inside the bus, keeping it at seventy-seven degrees Fahrenheit. The children were all hungry, but that could wait. Sooner or later Marc would decide to feed them.

Sally was content to listen to Ralph's music, to let the world slip by and not worry about threats and eventualities. It was safer to listen to Ralph. He didn't mind if you listened, just as long as you didn't disturb him when you came in. Most of the others would have reacted in some way.

Especially Caitlin. Caitlin was sitting on the very front of the bus, on the right, like she always did, her copper-red hair the barest hint of the fires that raged inside her. No one ever dared challenge Caitlin's place on the bus. If Caitlin suspected Sally was trying to enter her mind, she would try to kill Sally. Sally would have to defend herself, and that would alert The Three.

Marc . . . Ted . . . Susanna . . .

A highway patrolman had noticed that the bus, and the Volvo that was following it, were speeding. He took off after the Volvo, seeing two heads in the front seats. Sally felt a pang of anxiety for him. He couldn't know that it was Ted and Susanna he was following. But it was better he didn't know, because that's why Ted didn't take him as a threat. Ted simply reached into the patrolman's mind and changed it. Now it looked like they were *not* speeding. So the patrolman broke off his chase and pulled over again, forgetting them.

Ted did that a hundred times a day, changing people's minds, covering up the crimes of The Three, large and small. Ted could get away with anything. Absolutely anything.

No, Sally never, ever wanted to alert The Three. That would be frightening, and her fear might give her secret plans away. It might even reveal her Secret Mind.

So Sally stopped thinking about it. She looked out her window and saw a roadrunner. It wasn't running like the one in the cartoon who could go faster than a train. It wasn't smart, either. It was scared of the bus, confused by the noise and the smell. It almost ran right into the wheels.

Sally gave it a gentle nudge in the other direction, out of the path of danger. She memorized its genetic code, its internal organs and brain waves. It was very interesting. In the meantime, her Secret Mind relayed Ralph's music to her, giving her a sound track to go with the view outside her window.

Sally's Secret Mind had a nice grasp of the big picture. It was seven years old; Sally herself was fourteen. She had started growing it that time Ted and Marc had made two women have sex with them when those women would rather have died than done so.

So Ted convinced them to kill themselves. That's when Sally began to smell her own death coming.

But she couldn't let The Three know it. And that was hard, because they could find out what *anyone* was thinking, all of the ordinary people who lived in the ordinary world around them. The Three played with people, manipulated them. No one could stand against them, no policeman, judge, lawyer; no scientist or doctor, no government or army. The Three did exactly what they wanted; and they were so good at it, people hardly even noticed that anything was being done.

The highway patrolman had already forgotten them. And they didn't have to *make* him forget. His own concerns had let his mind drift elsewhere. That was how it worked. That was why people with television sets, computer internets, and a space program didn't know that The Three lived among them.

Sally gazed out her window at the desert, thinking of the people who lived beyond it, the civilization that didn't know her and couldn't help her. She had to rely on her own ingenuity. She always had.

The Three had complete access to every neuron in Sally's neural network. But that was where they made their mistake. They didn't know that Sally could build a secret mind *outside* that neural net.

Right at this very moment, if Ted, Marc, or Susanna decided to surprise Sally with a mind-search they would find nothing but the roadrunner and things they had seen before. Even if they followed her every neural pathway to its conclusion they would never find that *other*—the one who spoke to Sally the same way she spoke to the minds of other people. It wasn't physically connected to any part of her main neural network, though it passed through the same centers and structures. It had its own pathways.

So they never looked for it. And why should they? Who had ever had two minds living (unconnected) in one head before?

That other net was very sophisticated now. It watched Sally's mind to make sure it stayed obedient and pliable to The Three. It watched Susanna, Ted, and Marc, to see what they were planning, what they were doing, that they were happy with what they saw in the children's minds, that they were fooled.

They were!

Sally smiled a guileless smile and leaned against her pillow, blocking the scene outside her window, looking instead at the occupants of the bus; especially at the back of Marc's handsome head. She adored him, utterly. He was kind to them when he wasn't linked with Susanna and Ted; he made sure they were fed; he drove their bus while the other two drove separately (but never really separate) in their Volvo.

I love you, Marc, she almost told his mind, almost disturbing his concentration, almost embarrassing herself beyond redemption; but even *thinking* about sending the message gave her a thrill. *Someday I'll be your lover.*

Sally's Secret Mind would never have let her send the message. It was so disciplined now, it could even prevent the other children from accidently revealing things. That wasn't easy, fooling five talented minds into seeming less than they were. Six, actually, when you counted Sally.

Thrall, warned the Secret Mind as it felt the brush of the Mastermind, that creature The Three became when they were working together. A moment later, the Thrall descended, blotting out most coherent thought, dulling Ralph's opera performance to a faint shadow of itself. Poor Ralph hated to lose his music; but The Three hardly bothered to humor him about it anymore.

Sally's Secret Mind peeked at the Mastermind. There it was, a spider thing with six eyes. Ted's eyes were the biggest, and sat on top. All of the eyes were looking at the children.

Our Kronos Kids are getting out of hand, said the Mastermind. It glared into every corner of their minds with an odd mixture of suspicion and contempt. It found nothing to warn it of danger or betrayal, but that only made it more suspicious. It tucked the children beneath its spider legs, as if they were young who needed to hatch. Their eyes blinked sleepily from its belly.

Sally's Secret Mind rode piggyback over the Mastermind, an unsuspected parasite. *Kronos,* it remembered, *who ate his children.* Every time Sally heard that name, she saw the illustration by Goya that went with it. Her Secret Mind saw the Mastermind perching on the child-eater's head, its six eyes glazed with a hunger that more than matched his.

The Three knew perfectly well what role they played in the painting. One would have thought it would shame them.

Instead, it pleased them.

Now, commanded the Mastermind, *where is Olympus?*

The children looked down the road. They couldn't see Olympus, they could only feel it. Sally's Secret Mind saw more: It saw the Wall, for one thing. The Wall didn't just go up and down, side to side; it went over and under, around. In fact, the wall sometimes seemed to occupy *all* space. But Olympus was somehow on the other side of the wall.

Cunt. Ted spoke directly to Sally. He had never bothered to use her name. It wasn't even anything personal; he thought of all females below the age of puberty as *brat.* Every female over eleven was *cunt,* except for Susanna.

Cunt, he called her, and he accompanied the name with thoughts about her vulva and vagina, images of her spread-eagled and open to him—and everyone else. *Where's the hole in the wall?* he demanded, and didn't even catch the foolish pun, he was so intent on her answer.

We need to travel down this road for another hour, was all Sally's mind could tell him.

Then what?

I won't know until we get there.

Ted replied with images of himself touching her genitalia. He didn't stop with just the images; he prompted changes in her brain, reactions to his advances that she wouldn't normally have. Sally wasn't surprised by the attack. She had seen it coming ever since her breasts had started to grow. She did her best to endure it, for the time being.

Now, Ted, Susanna chided, her mental voice as clipped and British as her speaking voice. *You're going to upset her, and we need her to do this job for us.*

Ted ignored her.

Leave her alone, Ted, said Marc, and Sally could feel his outrage and pity. But she could also feel his absolute unwillingness to deny Ted anything he wanted.

Sally's Secret Mind let an appropriate amount of time pass. It let the anguish, shame, and desire build in her and then began to impair the Olympus signal. Olympus flickered before the Mastermind, then faded into nothingness.

TED! screamed the Mastermind. He abruptly stopped what he had been doing to Sally.

Don't touch the girls again! ordered the Mastermind, even though Ted was still part of it. *We've got to get the signal back!*

Sally's Secret Mind let Susanna try to make clumsy repairs in her psyche. It marveled that it now thought of Susanna's work as *clumsy.* Yet it was, compared to what the Secret Mind could do. It discreetly boosted and corrected Susanna, never revealing itself, until Sally's mind was back to the way it had been before.

The Olympus signal became strong again. It beckoned The Three. And in the meantime, the pain of

Ted's assault was completely wiped from Sally's memory.

Not from my *memory,* the Secret Mind told itself. It filed the incident away with a thousand others, and settled in to wait.

Rest, it told Sally. *I'm here.*

ally rested. She fell asleep, right there on the bus,
leaning against her pillow, which was propped
against the window. She had slept that way many
times. It wasn't hard to do. Sometimes, it was even
fun.

Like now. Now there was music; but not Ralph's
music. At first Sally had thought it was part of the
rattle and clank of the bus. But then it got closer and
louder, and she realized it was voices. People chanting.

Sally opened her dream eyes. She saw dozens of
people grouped around a fire, in a huge cave. They
were naked. They were the chanters—all of them except for one fellow who stood in their midst, facing
Sally. She felt as if she were about ten feet away from
him. She could feel a ghostly heat from the fire, and
was even aware of the hard dirt of the cave floor
under her feet.

Sally gazed at the one who was standing, and he
gazed right back. His body was large and heavily mus-
cled. His features were heavy, especially his brows.

Cavemen, she thought to herself.

Neanderthals, said her Secret Mind.

The fellow who was standing looked right into her
eyes. His jaw lacked a definite chin, but he looked no
less determined for it. He was young, and in his own
way he was handsome. His eyes were larger, rounder
than the eyes of *Homo sapiens* and looked like the

eyes of an eagle above his huge nose. They were intelligent; but there was something in them that Sally didn't understand.

"Who are you?" she asked him.

"King Monkey," said the young Neanderthal.

He said it with such pride and self-confidence, Sally couldn't help but be impressed.

"What are you doing?" Sally asked.

King Monkey cocked his head and listened to the chanting of his people. His eyes continued to look into Sally's, as if he were asking her to understand what he was hearing. She reached for his mind, reflexively; but she didn't quite get where she thought she would. Instead of *reading* him, she seemed instead to *intercept* him in some midground place, almost as if he were another . . .

Sally gasped. "Are you like—"

"I am King Monkey!" he cried, and now Sally understood what the chanting was for. It was for *him*. It would send him into battle.

Now she could see him through his own eyes. It was as if *he* were the one who was dreaming, and Sally had accidently stepped into the picture. King Monkey was the star of that picture. He was a strong man, the most brave and intelligent of them all. He was the youngest man ever to have become a hunter, certainly the youngest to become king; the hair had only just finished growing under his arms and in his groin.

He stood with his receding chin up, his protruding brows knotted together in a fierce scowl.

A shaman stood behind him, watching him feverishly. "King Monkey!" cried the shaman, his voice rising above the chanting of the other men. "You fight! We pray! You fight!"

King Monkey listened to the chanting of his people, and showed them his brave face. But Sally could feel what was behind that face.

"You don't feel brave at all," she said. "You're afraid."

King Monkey was shocked. He gazed at Sally from across the big chamber, with the fire behind him, the chanters all around him; but he might as well have been alone. His eyes looked deep inside her and found himself reflected there.

"You are not one of my goddesses," he said. He was frightened by the thought. He didn't know what to think about her. Sally felt his doubts almost as if they were her own; but she could not quite grasp them. This was something different from what she knew, a way of thinking that was tantalizingly familiar, yet unfamiliar at the same time.

King Monkey sometimes heard voices that spoke to him out of the air, just above his right ear—the voices of his gods and of spirits. But Sally could not remember ever having heard voices that way. Her Secret Mind didn't *sound* like that. The Three didn't *sound* like that, and neither did any of the people or animals whose minds she sometimes *read*.

She knew that King Monkey was even more confused by her *voice*. She did not speak to him the way his people did. They could not express ideas this way. She spoke to him much like the Enemy did. Yet she also spoke gently, like a mother would.

"I'm not the Enemy," said Sally, hoping this would reassure him.

After a time he nodded, and his eyes lost their dread of her. "I am afraid," King Monkey admitted. "The Enemy acts like a spirit, but he is not a spirit. He is like me. Only he is better."

"How is he better?"

King Monkey concentrated. Sally knew he was no longer afraid of her, but he wondered about her. Could she be the Enemy, addressing him with a false tone of friendship? But in the past, the Enemy had shrieked at him. It had shouted things about him that were private, that only King Monkey could know. This was how he had learned that the Enemy was like him: a man who could hear thoughts and move things with his will.

"Me too!" said Sally. "I can do those things too!"

"Who are you?" he finally asked.

Not anyone you know, yet. Sally's Secret Mind answered, before she could say anything. Sally bowed to the wisdom of her Secret Mind, as always. *I'm just curious,* it said.

Yet, thought King Monkey, thinking that Sally must be from the Yet To Be (which was perfectly correct). Sometimes King Monkey caught little glimpses of that, in his dreams.

"You are a voice from the future," he said, pleased that he could confront her with the truth.

You understand that there is a future?

"I understand," said King Monkey, with pride— though he hoped she would not ask him to explain. He understood with his gut more than he could express with his new skill of words. Yet King Monkey was courageous, he was worthy to be king of his people; he used as many words as he could, because he knew this was the only way he would master them.

"Listen to my story," he said, "and tell it to your children. Of all my people, only I have this thing inside my head that makes me King Monkey. Of all of *his* people, only the Enemy is lord. His thing is like my thing. But his thing is also better."

You mean his talent. How is his talent better than yours?

"I don't know," said King Monkey, and he showed his teeth. For a moment, Sally thought he looked like the monkey he was named for. The thought shamed her. The other people had named him that, the ones whose lord was the Enemy. The Newcomers. They had done it with contempt.

The Newcomers traveled from place to place. They had faces that were thinner, bodies that were taller, minds that were *different.* They had more words; they had taught him to speak as they did. They had named him King Monkey as an insult, but soon they had learned to say the name in respect. So he had kept it.

Who is the Enemy? asked Sally's Secret Mind. *What does he look like?*

"I don't know!" raged King Monkey. "He does not live among his people as I do. He does not help them. He has never shown his true face to me. He has kept his distance and watched me."

Then how do you know he's one of those *people?*

"Because ... he is clever. He is clever in ways I do not understand. And so are they. They have more things-for-doing. They have dreamed them, they have seen how they are used, and then they have made them."

Tools? You must be talking about tools. They might be more clever than your people, now. But you could learn from them.

"I have thought this was so. But I have dreamed of the future. His people are there. Mine are not."

"Uh-oh," said Sally. This was true. In her time, people would be arguing about what had happened to the Neanderthals. *Homo sapiens sapiens* would be arguing, and no one would be sure whether *Neanderthals* lurked in their genetic history.

King Monkey shed a tear. Sally realized that she was the first person to whom he could tell the misfortune he had seen in the future. He couldn't tell his people; they would be afraid. He couldn't tell the Newcomers; they might see it as a sign from their gods. A sign that they should kill King Monkey's people.

King Monkey's gods already knew. Three of them had come to him and advised him, already. Sally wondered what these gods were like; but his mind was already elsewhere. He was thinking about his great enemy.

The Enemy. He knew about the future too. He had taunted King Monkey with the knowledge, many times. He had threatened to tell the other Newcomers. But what he had done the night before was the worst thing of all.

"He has stolen my son!" cried King Monkey, overwhelmed anew by grief and outrage. He had been so proud that he had been able to quicken his wife with a son when he was barely a man himself. His gods had told him that it was because his will was strong. But his joy was ashes, now.

"My son, who is almost like me! He took him and said, 'Now you see how you are helpless!' He mocks me at every turn!"

The King Monkey pounded his chest in rage. Sally was impressed by the depth of his feelings. The chanters, seeing his display, were filled with joy. They had been frightened since the Newcomers had entered their lives. They had worried when they saw their king worrying. They picked up the pace, working themselves into a controlled frenzy. King Monkey felt his heart pound in time to their voices.

"It was a challenge," he said. "I must face it."

Sally felt her own mind begin to respond to the pattern of the chant. It was mesmerizing—she loved it! The chanting voices changed direction and pace constantly, weaving back and forth in a confusing manner. But who were the chanters trying to confuse?

"Spirits," said King Monkey, reading her as easily as she read him.

"They can only move in a straight line," he continued, and then laughed bitterly at the idea. "But the

Enemy can move in many directions at once. *We* are the ones who can only move in one direction."

I love stories, said Sally's Secret Mind. *I've heard stories from all over the world, and from all times. But this is the oldest story I've ever heard. What are you going to do, King Monkey?*

The chanting filled King Monkey's brain, evoking emotions much deeper than the ones Sally was feeling. It mixed with his rage and the anxiety until it was a storm. Sally rode over the storm, observing it with wonder; and then light suddenly poured into his mind and hers, together.

"I will change," said King Monkey, his voice filled with awe. "I will move in several directions at once, like the Enemy. And when I find my son, I will change him too. And then I will change my people."

Sally wondered what he meant by *change.* Did he mean it literally or figuratively? But King Monkey did not grasp the differences between those two concepts.

Not *yet.*

"King Monkey," cried the shaman who led the chanters, "son of a god!"

"No," King Monkey whispered, so that only Sally would hear him. "My father was a monkey.... I am the one who shall be a god."

Sally felt an awe that was all her own, not just the leaking of King Monkey's feelings into her mental space. *What do you mean?* she wanted to ask him, but that would have led right back into that confusion about the difference between metaphor and the concrete. He didn't know what she meant when she asked that question.

"Why doesn't he know?" she asked her Secret Mind.

He is still evolving, it answered.

Sally tried to look at King Monkey again, but it was hard to focus on him. She could still hear the chanting, though. If anything, it was louder. It seemed to be eclipsing her visual grasp of the dream.

"Is he really a Neanderthal?" she asked her Secret Mind.

He appears to be.

"Do you think they really died out without mixing with our other ancestors?"

They might have.

"But he was so . . . *human!*"

I have a theory, offered the Secret Mind. *I believe that some Neanderthals mixed with other prehumans, and others didn't.*

Sally listened as the chanting began to fade and turn into the rattle and clank of the bus. She was sorry to lose her picture of King Monkey. She had liked him.

"Who did and who didn't?" she asked her Secret Mind.

The ones who were cut off from other prehumans by the fluxes of the Ice Ages couldn't *mix with other prehumans. They would have become very inbred because of their prolonged isolation. They would have become more Neanderthal-like, more like what is now known as classically Neanderthal; and finally they might not have been able to interbreed with other prehumans, once the waning of the Ice Ages allowed them to visit their neighbors again.*

"That's a good theory," Sally agreed, trying to picture King Monkey's eagle eyes in her mind. She didn't quite succeed. She could still hear the chanting, just barely; but her imagination was beginning to change it into something more modern. She was losing it. It was like losing something precious, but she was helpless to hold on to it.

"And the ones who *did* mix, they must have been less what we've come to think of as Neanderthal-like," said Sally.

They might have been pre-Neanderthals. The fossil

evidence does seem to suggest that. At least, it does to me. But even if the Neanderthals never mixed their genes with our ancestors, they contributed something else.

What?

A challenge. A puzzle. Ways that were different from the ways of so-called Homo sapiens. There was a sort of intellectual explosion some forty-five thousand years ago, when suddenly both groups began to make more complex tools. I think their interaction may have caused it.

The sound of the chanting was completely drowned out by a change in the sound of the bus. Sally opened her eyes, and noticed that they were pulling into a motel parking lot. She was glad at the sight; but sad too. Food and rest would be gotten here. But people would be manipulated into giving it to them for free. If they were strong-minded people, that could become an ugly process. Sally would have her work cut out for her, trying to prevent anything really dreadful from happening.

Ted and Susanna had already parked the Volvo. They were already going into the office, getting ready to do a little pushing.

Sally sighed, holding the remnants of the King Monkey dream to her for one last moment. He had been so brave and self-assured. People always used the word *Neanderthal* like it was an insult. But anyone who was descended from King Monkey—if there *was* anyone—could be proud of their ancestor.

Sally's Secret Mind watched what Ted was doing in the office. Ted certainly was no King Monkey.

In fact, in many ways, Ted was barely human.

What makes you think you are worthy of Olympus? Sally's Secret Mind wondered as it regarded The Three, who were now resting in their respective motel rooms. *You are not gods; you are monsters, like the Titans. You are Kronos, who ate his children.*

They had checked into the motel at 5:00 P.M., easily nudging the owner into accepting no payment; and then they had done the same to the people who ran the coffee shop, and the children had been fed. Sally had enjoyed her favorite meal, a double-decker hamburger with french fries and a strawberry shake. Now Sally was in the room she shared with Caitlin. She had put the other girl to sleep so she could concentrate more easily on The Three and what they were doing. But they weren't doing much.

Ted was busy taking apart the motel owner's refrigerator. He loved to take things apart. That was what he spent most of his time doing when he wasn't using the Mastermind to build things or mentally molesting people. Ted had left a trail of disassembled clocks, computers, appliances, and machinery behind him that led through thirty-three states and seventeen countries. It was the most harmless thing he did to people.

Susanna and Marc were making love. They hadn't done that in a long time. Sally's Secret Mind thought that they were probably about to enter a new phase of their relationship, one that was far closer than anything they had ever achieved before. But Sally was hurt seeing them together that way, so she left them alone and set up an early warning system so she could get her own work done in peace.

Now was the best time, perhaps the last chance she would have before they got where they were going.

Sally's Secret Mind activated the Mastermind it had been building secretly for the past seven years, the one that excluded The Three.

Everyone fell comfortably into place, even Caitlin, who was about ten times more antisocial than Ted was. She was also about ten times more powerful, but Sally had gone to great lengths to conceal that fact from Ted over the years. If he had suspected, he would have killed Caitlin.

Just like he killed Marty and Lydia.

It's better this way, Susanna had told the children to comfort them. *Now there are six of you. Six is such a lovely, symmetrical number. Marty and Lydia were outsiders, they wanted to leave us; now we're a perfect family.*

The others, in their fear and grief, had eagerly embraced Susanna's comfort. Sally had just gone along with it. Unlike the others, she remembered five other children who had died for similar reasons. She knew perfectly well that she had barely managed to dodge several bullets, so far.

Marty's and Lydia's death had taught her something important:

The best way to shield from Ted was to let him in. The best way to deceive him was to leave your precious secrets out in the open, while you shielded other, less important secrets. These others would draw his attention, give him the satisfaction of invasion, and give him a completely false impression of what was going on in the minds of his Kronos Kids.

Sally didn't know it yet, but she was more of a Master than Ted could even imagine.

Let's have a good look at the Wall, she said. Everyone obliged—sort of. They weren't really awake or even conscious of Sally or her Secret Mind. Every time she made her own Mastermind, she had to create temporary Secret Minds in its members. It was the only way. Most of them would never have cooperated, otherwise.

So, there was the Wall. It was an indescribable thing, but a very palpable one. Sally could look and look at it, but it only became more baffling. Right now the Wall wasn't really the thing that caught her attention, though. The thing that immediately began to pull at her, evoking vast tremors of terror and wonder, was the Gate.

The Olympus Gate. Now it was in the center of her universe. It really was a door. It had a massive frame with carvings that changed into different things as you looked at them. It didn't have a doorknob, because you couldn't open it with your hand. You could only open it with a Mastermind.

And on the other side? Olympus was there. But what was Olympus?

Sally remembered how excited Ted had been when he first started to dream of Olympus. They had been in Tibet, building another one of his improbable temple/fortress/citadels. The Mastermind had caught a glimpse of something on a distant mountain peak. A week later, Ted had the fit.

He had gone mad for a while. *THIS IS SHIT! THIS IS WORTHLESS! THIS IS NONSENSE!* he had raved, and pulled the Mastermind together to vent his rage on the ordinary world. Even Marc and Susanna had been afraid as Ted forced the Mastermind to destroy every building they had ever created together.

Nothing remained but dust after he had finished. Dust and the shattered bones of servants.

"Now, Ted," Susanna chided when Ted finally lay panting and foaming on the floor. "Those were perfectly good buildings."

Ted shook his head. "No," he said. "Not when you compare them to the real thing."

Sally's Mastermind regarded the Gate. Ted's dream was on the other side, the perfect place that was worthy of his perfect self. After he got the Gate open, he would dispose of the children. He didn't want rival gods in his paradise.

It was the truth she had been trying very hard not to think about, so as not to tip her hand to The Three. She knew that she and the others were going to be murdered, soon.

How are you going to do it? Sally's Mastermind wondered. It slipped into the minds of The Three. What it found hurt its feelings.

Their bus was falling off a cliff. *Right into the Grand Canyon.*

Isn't that a bit melodramatic? wondered Sally's Secret Mind. *You could simply use Sally's power to spread our atoms all over the universe. Or Caitlin could burn us to cinders, or Joey could stop our hearts.*

But no. It was Marc, actually, who wouldn't hear of that. He was the one who had taken care of the children for the past fourteen years, and he was the one who had the right to kill them.

Because he loved them. And because it would be such a thrill.

Enough of that, Sally's Secret Mind said as Sally's grief overflowed. *Survive first. Cry later.*

Sally obeyed.

Locate the Gate.

Sally's Mastermind looked. The Gate was close, only about two and a half hours away. You could even find a road that led to it. That couldn't have been an accident. The Gate was in a building.

The Indian School, said the mind of the waitress in the coffee shop. She had been a student there, twenty years before. She hated the place. *I'm glad they closed it down,* she added passionately, then wondered why she was tormenting herself with unhappy memories.

Sally dissolved the Mastermind, link by link, and its members drifted into real sleep. Caitlin was the last. Sally was about to let her go when Caitlin's Secret Mind suddenly reared up like a cobra. It was awake, aware, and seething with hatred.

You think you know everything! it spat. *But you don't know* anything!

Sally dissolved Caitlin's Secret Mind. It raged at her as it went, fighting oblivion.

Sally opened her eyes and gaped at Caitlin's sleeping form. The girl was sound asleep, her fiery hair spread out on the pillow. Sally could feel Caitlin's personality surging and pounding like an ocean in a storm. But that was normal for Caitlin.

Sally realized she was shaking. It took her several minutes to calm down.

"Mungy Bungy?" she whispered.

A cat came out from under the bed. It was a white cat with odd, striped patches on it. It gazed at her with clever yellow eyes and then jumped up on the bed and curled against her side, purring. It continued to look at her, as if asking a question.

"Do you love me, Mungy Bungy?" whispered Sally.

Mungy Bungy kneaded Sally's side with his front paws and purred louder. His eyes were wide and humorous, pleased to have her in their sight.

Sally knew the cat loved her. His body language told her so: his perky tail, his ears cocked forward, his lips relaxed in that ancient cat smile. He was her secret friend. He was magic; he always came out of nowhere, from under beds, inside cupboards or drawers, closets or suitcases. No matter where she traveled, all she had to do was call him and out he came. He was always the same, never sick or hungry, never angry or scared. He had arrived in Sally's life after she had begun to dream of the Olympus Gate, seven years before. That was years before Ted had had his own vision of Olympus, never dreaming that Sally was its source.

Sometimes Sally liked to imagine that Mungy was a messenger from Olympus, that the gods had sent him as a symbol that she was loved, that someone was looking after her, from afar.

But Sally wasn't counting on that. It was just a daydream.

By the time she fell asleep, she knew what she was going to do when the bus went over the side of the Grand Canyon. Her Secret Mind mapped the plan out to her, step by step.

But she fell asleep worrying about the Olympus Gate. They couldn't avoid it. Her Secret Mind agreed. The Three would accept no other possibility; they had to open the Gate.

And when they did, all hell would break loose.

Susanna appeared to be about forty, but only because it suited her purposes, made her seem more "motherly" to the children. She was trim and elegant, and her upper-class British accent had most Americans fawning with delight the moment they heard it. Even if she hadn't been an empath, she could have played most Americans like fiddles.

But she *was* an empath, so she played them to distraction.

"Your kids are so well behaved," the motel owner gushed, intercepting them in the lobby just as they were about to go into the coffee shop. "How do you do it?" she asked Susanna.

Susanna stopped and lit a cigarette. The owner didn't bat an eyelash, despite the NO SMOKING signs that were posted in five different spots (because the owner had an allergy to smoke). Joey and Jim were smoking too, two fourteen-year-old boys flagrantly breaking the law. The motel would lose its tobacco license if an agent were to see what was going on. The owner could serve time in jail and pay a stiff fine. Yet she never even glanced at the boys.

"We emphasize education," Susanna said. "Of course, the children are all highly intelligent, and it's so much easier to reason with intelligent children."

The owner had been about to tell Susanna about her own children and how proud she was of them; but she thought better of it. Susanna had managed to make her feel less certain of her own brood, simply through the tone of her voice.

"Enjoy your breakfast," she said, twitching under Susanna's gracious smile.

Sally watched the whole scene as objectively as she could. She was hungry—it was easy to concentrate on that. She followed Susanna into the coffee shop, but didn't feel inclined to sit with her after the way she had treated the motel owner. Instead, Sally sat in a large booth with the two underage smokers—in the nonsmoking section—and ordered apple pie.

Caitlin sat with Susanna. She was unconsciously imitating Susanna's feminine airs. Sally couldn't help but admire those airs herself. How she had adored Susanna! Her perfumes and powder puffs, her trim figure and high heels. Sally had vivid memories of special times spent with Susanna, just the two of them at Fergussen's Cafeteria, sipping fruit drink and eating pie.

Caitlin had identical memories. They were planted. Susanna never wasted time building real relationships when she could generate false ones.

When the bus had driven through Phoenix the day

before, they had passed a Fergussen's Cafeteria on Indian School Road, right near the freeway. Sally had held her breath, hoping that they would stop and go inside, that somehow the memories of happy times with Susanna were the *real* memories; and the horrors that had been seen mostly out of the corners of her eyes for the past fourteen years were just nightmares.

But they hadn't stopped.

Joey pulled another cigarette out of his pack and glared at it. Twin heat rays came out of his eyes and converged on the tip, which glowed red. It was one of the few fire tricks that Joey could perform, and he loved it. But his main skill lay in his power over the human body.

He put the cigarette in his mouth and sucked it down to the filter in two seconds, exhaled with a big smile, then lit another one and did it again.

"Help me do it too," Jim said. Joey obliged. Doing the heat-ray-vision trick made him feel like Superman. Joey even had hair like Superman, glossy black with a curl that fell down his forehead. His skin was a lot darker, but that was an improvement, as far as he was concerned.

He couldn't fly like Superman, though. And that was too bad. Sally would need someone who could fly, or someone who could catch the bus while it was falling and make *it* fly. It was a big problem. She wondered if she could do it herself. She wondered if she could do it with the help of her secret Mastermind. She had never had the chance to find out, not with The Three watching so closely.

Sally finished her pie. She knew she had better do it soon, or she wouldn't be hungry anymore. Joey was seeing to that. He had forgotten his cigarette. All of the toxins in the smoke and in the food they were eating must have finally reached some critical mass and made him react automatically. Now he was sitting and staring straight ahead, the half-burned cigarette dangling from his limp fingers.

He wasn't just fixing his own body. He was fixing *all* of their bodies, making sure the cigarette smoke did no lasting damage. He cleaned the cholesterol out of their veins and burned the excess calories from the (already eaten) pies. He supplemented the vitamins and minerals that were missing from their diets, stealing from other foods in the diner; even stealing from other *people* in the diner when he had to. He did all of this without the slightest flicker of effort to trouble the smooth surface of his coffee-and-cream skin.

"I don't see how you kids can be so healthy, the way you eat," the waitress said as she came over to refill their Cokes. She cast a withering look over her shoulder at Susanna who was blithely unaware of her disapproval.

The Three never seemed to wonder or care what people thought of them. The Three had the same opinion of people that they did of animals.

But Sally liked the waitress. She was an "Indian." Sally had already traced the woman's genealogy—it was one of her favorite hobbies—back several thousand years, to people from Asia, Russia, Japan, and Europe.

The woman looked at Sally measuringly for a moment before asking the question people inevitably asked when they saw the kids, with their black and white and brown skins. The woman decided Sally was mature enough to answer—and Sally wasn't even manipulating her! It made her feel proud to be liked just for herself.

"Are you orphans?"

"Yes," Sally answered, with complete honesty.

"Where are you all traveling to?"

Sally had to think for a second before she could answer. "A new school."

The waitress nodded sympathetically. She was the one who had been to the Christian Indian School and hated it so much. She assumed Sally and the others were going to a Christian school too, and she felt sorry for them.

"My name is Marie," she said, touching the name pin on her breast pocket. "Call me if you're still hungry."

Marie, Sally thought. The pin with the name had been right there in front of her nose; but because Marie hadn't been *thinking* her own name, Sally hadn't picked up on it. It was funny.

As the waitress left, Ralph and Timothy came in. Timothy was guiding Ralph as if he were blind. Ralph was busy with Philip Glass's opera *Akhnaten.* It was about an Egyptian pharaoh—an understandable choice, considering that very soon the children would be trying to open the Olympus Gate, that place where the gods dwelt. Sally wondered . . . when The Three went through, would it be Anubis waiting for them on the other side, instead of Zeus? Would he weigh their souls against a feather and judge them worthy?

Timothy helped Ralph into the booth right next to Sally's. Ralph moved mechanically—quite soon he would be eating that way too. Marie went over to take their orders, from Timothy, of course.

"I want strawberry pancakes," he said, his voice grave and much lower than one would expect. "My brother wants a hot fudge sundae."

Marie brought Timothy his pancakes and Ralph his sundae. She came back to refill Sally's Coke glass and asked, "Is your friend autistic?" meaning Ralph.

"No," Sally replied. "He's just busy."

"What is he doing?"

"He's a composer," Sally said.

This wasn't strictly true. Ralph could reproduce performances; he could even stage mental productions with his favorite orchestras, soloists, and conductors performing music they had never actually played in their lives. That's how well he knew music and musicians. But he hadn't *composed* anything yet. Sally was sure The Three were holding him back. Once he was no longer under their influence . . .

If anyone was autistic it was Ted. Just now he was out behind the hotel with the owner's husband, taking apart the man's brand-new Cadillac. The man was helping him, having convinced himself that he *wanted* to help, that Ted was somehow doing him a favor; just as the owner had convinced herself that her current guests needn't pay their bill because she was so delighted to have such well-behaved children on her premises.

Because neither of them really wanted to know how afraid they were.

They were growing ulcers trying to convince themselves that they liked what was being done to them, that they didn't mind, that it was their choice. They were fighting the growing sense of humiliation with stomach juices that were burning holes in their tender places. Sally had seen it so many times before. She was almost glad it was all about to come to an end, one way or another, because when she thought about the things that had happened over the years—

"Maybe I'll hear some music by your friend someday," Marie was saying.

"You will!" Sally said, with more hope than confidence.

"What's his name?"

"Ralph," Sally said, pronouncing the name *Rafe,* just like the name of her favorite composer, Ralph Vaughan Williams. Like the famous composer, Ralph was always annoyed when people pronounced his first name with the "l" in it.

"What's his *last* name?"

Sally faltered. The Three had never bothered to give them a family name. "Smith, for now," she said.

"I know what you mean," said Marie. "For a long time they made me say my name was Jones, because we weren't allowed to use our Indian names. But now I'm Marie Little Bird."

"Little Bird is a heck of a lot prettier than *Jones*," agreed Sally.

Marc chose that moment to come into the coffee shop. Sally took one look at his handsome, deceptively young face and remembered what he was planning to do to them. Grief rushed over her in a huge, black wave, almost overwhelming Joey's attempts to regulate her bodily systems. She was surprised by the intensity of the feeling; and horrified too, because Marc noticed it. Susanna noticed too and looked at Sally. This is probably what saved Sally's life.

A mental image of the two of them making love popped into her head. Sally blushed and deliberately shielded herself.

Susanna turned away with a little smile. A moment later, Marc passed by and ruffled Sally's hair. "You know you're my special girl?" he whispered. Sally nodded.

Marc sat down next to Timothy and Ralph. He didn't want to sit next to the smokers; he disapproved of the children smoking. He worried about their health.

It would be a shame if they developed lung cancer before they went over the cliff.

Sally tuned in to Ralph's music, letting every other thought slide out of her mind. By the time she was conscious of anything again, she noticed how Jim was stealing glances at her. His empathic talent was almost as strong as Susanna's, and he had probably "heard" Susanna and Marc making love last night too.

He knew perfectly well that Sally loved Marc, and

he was curious to see how heartbroken she would be this morning. Sally tried not to look at him. He bore an uncomfortable resemblance to Marc, and just now he was wearing the expression that Marc might soon be wearing when he pushed them into the Grand Canyon.

Jim wanted to see how hurt her feelings were. She let him see that. She just didn't let him see *why*.

After a little while, Jim grew bored of Sally's feelings and settled into waiting mode. They were all doing that, even Marc and Susanna. They were hardly even thinking anything (except for Ralph and Timothy, who were nearing the finale of Glass's opera).

And what were they all waiting for? Even Marie had begun to wonder. Everyone had finished their breakfast; now they were all just sitting around.

Waiting for him, someone was thinking, rage beginning to build in her blood. *Day after day, year after year, waiting for* him *to say what* he *wants!*

It was Caitlin, of course. Sally didn't need to glance over at the redheaded girl to see the knitted brows, the mouth set in a tight line, the fire glowing in those green eyes. Caitlin had always been bad tempered, but never in a way that Susanna couldn't smooth out.

At least not until puberty had set in. Since then, Caitlin's rages had grown astonishingly in proportion and intensity. Susanna didn't know that; if she had known, she would have had to tell Ted about it. Sally had been acting as a filter, hiding the true extent of Caitlin's feelings from The Three for three years. And that was no easy task.

Just the thought of Ted out back, taking that stupid car apart while everyone else had to wait, was enough to put Caitlin in a killing mood. She was imagining him with his blood heating to a critical level, his inner organs bursting, his face swelling up bigger and bigger, redder and redder, blood leaking out of his ears, nose mouth, even out of his fingertips. Out of his penis and anus, out of the pours in his skin . . .

And when he was dead and his body was destroyed beyond recognition, there were the hotel owner and her husband, her children, Marie and her family too. She would happily kill them all, and then maybe she would be satisfied with that.

And maybe she wouldn't . . .

Sally kept Caitlin's rage from leaking into Marc and Susanna's range of perception; but calming the girl down was another matter altogether. It was a tricky process. The moment Caitlin suspected Sally was even thinking of interfering, all of the rage and force that she was building up against Ted would be instantly hurled at Sally, instead. Sally could have forced calm on the other girl, but that would have instantly attracted the attention of The Three; so Sally always had to play it sneaky, play it sideways. She had to fool Caitlin, and that was getting harder and harder to do.

But just now she had a rare opportunity. Joey was in touch with Caitlin just as he was with everyone else in the group, doing his customary body regulation. Caitlin always allowed him into her bodily systems because she was horrified at the slightest hint of fat or unattractiveness. Joey kept her beautiful, as far as she was concerned.

Sally's Secret Mind rode piggyback on Joey's connection. It altered the chemicals in Caitlin's bloodstream, slowly calmed her. It heightened her awareness of the boys in the room, distracted her until she was busily constructing fantasies of herself as the object of their worshipful attention.

Sally's Secret Mind didn't have to touch Caitlin's thoughts at all to inspire *that* scenario.

In the meantime, Ted had grown bored with the car. He left it half undone, walking away from the owner's husband when the man had been speaking to him, cutting him off in the middle of a sentence. Rage bloomed in the man's mind then, but Ted didn't care. Ted was the most accomplished telepath among them, yet he never seemed aware of anyone's emotions unless he was directly focused on them. And he never deigned to stay focused on anyone for long.

Maybe Ted really was autistic. An intelligent autistic who never knew or cared what people were feeling. That would explain some of his obsessive behaviors, his lack of emotional connection to anyone. If he hadn't been a telepath, he might *never* know what anyone was feeling.

Sally was glad he didn't always know. If he did, he would see that sick horror she always felt at his approach. He would know *everything*. He would turn around and punish the owner's husband for hating him, for daring to realize that he had been screwed. But he just walked away, leaving the man to sit down in shocked amazement in the litter of his prized toy.

Ted strutted into the coffee shop. He neither knew nor cared that anyone had been inconvenienced by his "hobby." His eyes passed over Marie and discarded her as a nonentity, leaving her with a little shiver. His eyes looked for Sally and stayed with her.

Sally braced herself for invasion. But something odd happened. He didn't call her *cunt*, for one thing. He had finally realized what a crucial link she was to the Olympus Gate. He merely looked at her to see if she was functioning properly.

Sally's Secret Mind watched him. It pondered what had almost happened, earlier. It had come close to letting Caitlin attack Ted. Caitlin was almost strong enough to do what she dreamed of doing. She couldn't do it alone, of course; she would have had to have formed her own Mastermind and directed all of the telekinetics at Ted's bodily systems.

The Secret Mind had measured Caitlin. She could

have grabbed the others, but she couldn't have kept them; and in the ensuing chaos, most of the children would have been killed. So Sally's Secret Mind let Sally do what she was accustomed to doing with Caitlin, and it didn't tell her what had almost happened.

Ted gloated at Sally. He chased Caitlin away from Susanna's booth. When Caitlin wasn't angry, she was as afraid of Ted as everyone else was. She didn't know herself how powerful she was. Sally worked very hard to make sure Caitlin remained in the dark about that, for now.

Ted sat next to Susanna, where he had an unobstructed view of his little guide to Olympus.

The signal? he demanded.

Strong, Sally answered, letting him see how frightened she was by him and by the looming Gate. This pleased him, made him certain he was on the right track.

Ted ordered steak and eggs, gobbled them up like a starving animal. Marie served him with skill, never once attracting his attention. She was thinking of him as a "type," one she had encountered before. Marie had learned her life lessons well, or so she thought, and her instincts were telling her that Ted should not know she was in the room. For a nontelepath, she was admirably perceptive.

Of course, it helped that Sally was doing her best to keep Ted occupied. She was letting glimpses of the Gate leak through her shields, giving him the impression that the door was phasing in and out of his universe, calling to him. Before long, he was consumed with desire for it.

We'll be gods, he was telling himself. *After all these years of rolling around in this* filth, *this* dirt . . .

He meant the real world, of course. The ground he had to walk on, the air he had to breath, the animals, the bugs, the *people* who weren't much better than the animals. The shoddy buildings, the machines that were hardly worth taking apart anymore. The Three were too good for all that. The Three were meant to ascend, and now their tools were going to make that possible.

It's why we made you, he told Sally. *It's what you were meant to do.* She braced herself, waiting for him to complete the thought, to let her see what he intended to do with his *tools* once they were no longer of use. But the thought never even crossed his mind. He wasn't hiding anything; he simply didn't care. They had no meaning for him beyond what they were to do for him. His thoughts were on his own future, not theirs.

Ted got up and walked out of the coffee shop. It was the signal for everyone to follow him. Now that he was ready to go, no one could delay, no one could go back to a room for something that had been forgotten. No one could ask for one last trip to the bathroom or a drink of water. It was time to go *now*.

Sally caught Marie's eye on the way out. "Goodbye Mrs. Little Bird," she said, subtly touching Marie's mind. Marie glanced at Ted, sensing that she was being warned, then smiled at Sally; and Sally read the concern in the woman, the sympathy for someone who was about to go through what Marie had been through herself, years before.

"You can get through it," Marie said. "Then pick the name you want for yourself."

"I will," Sally promised, etching every detail of Marie's face in her memory. The waitress was the sort of person Sally liked best, the kind who reminded you that love and compassion weren't just things that could be cynically planted in your head by people who wanted to manipulate you.

And now if they could just get on their way without an incident. Sally was monitoring all of the kids; they were eager to be on their way, blithely unaware of what was really ahead of them. Marc was warming up the bus's engine; Susanna had pulled the Volvo out and was waiting while Ted loaded the suitcases in the trunk.

The owner's husband was still out back, stewing and fretting over his car. The owner was in her office with her calculator, trying to convince herself that she could absorb the cost of free service extended to orphans.

Marie was busing tables in the diner, hoping Sally and the others would be all right. Her instincts were warning her that there was far more wrong with Ted than she dared imagine.

And now Ted was ready to get into the Volvo. Sally was the last person to climb on the bus. Marc was closing the door behind her, giving her a warm look as she passed him on her way back to her seat, letting her know she was his "special" girl. She accepted the compliment, knowing she would need the strength it would lend her when the final pain came. When the truth would finally come out into the open and she would be fighting for their lives.

Almost out of here. Just one more minute.

And then Marie's adolescent daughter came out of the room she shared with her little sister.

The girl had budding breasts, long silky hair, large, dark eyes like her mother's. She had been curious about the boys on the bus—they were all so handsome, and she hadn't even had a chance to talk to them. She wanted to have a last look at them before they left, before Papa spotted her and told her to get back inside. Papa was rewiring an outlet in one of the rooms on the other side of the court, so she had a few moments to peek to her heart's content. She arched her back, swept her hair behind her shoulder, and tried to see through the reflected sunlight on the bus windows.

Ted glanced over and saw her.

Cunt, he called.

Sally gritted her teeth. She hadn't been fast enough to push the girl back into hiding. Now it was too late. Ted was inside the girl's mind faster than lightning, spreading her open like he had done to Sally the day before, like he had done to a million other girls before that. The girl's face went red, then dead white. Her body snapped rigidly upright, as if she were a puppet whose strings had been yanked.

Ted sat looking utterly calm and relaxed in the car. But this was an illusion. Endorphins were being released in his system at an astonishing rate; his mental pleasure was a thousand times what a man could normally expect to feel having real, physical sex with someone. He wallowed in the girl, ferreting out her secret fantasies and expanding, perverting, exaggerating them, making her believe she was being exposed for all the world to see: her mother and father, the boys on the bus, the hotel owners and their children, her sister . . .

Everyone, everyone . . .

Ted was in rare form. Sally had never seen him go at someone with such a vengeance before. The mental images were almost unbearable to witness. He didn't stop with the spreading of the vulva, he just kept spreading and exposing, probing through her vagina for more tender organs, pulling each quivering, maddened, overstimulated bit of the girl out into the open, then thrusting it aside, probing yet deeper, until she was like some dreadful butterfly.

With each orgasm, the girl's shame and terror increased. Within the first minute, she had at least a thousand of them.

Within the second minute, her mind started to go numb. Sally was glad for that.

Ted, in the meantime, was reaching new, undreamed-of heights. He had been lazy in the past, he realized that now. He had gone for quick satisfaction without really exploring the limits, without ever pushing the envelope. He had cheated himself. Now he wallowed in new sensations, prolonged them to the last possible moment.

His face began to show what was going on inside him. If the girl's papa had come out just then and seen the look on Ted's face, he would have tried to strangle Ted with his bare hands.

After the third minute, the girl began to vomit. She stood there with the bile spurting from her mouth in odd spasms, unable to bend over and do the job properly. Ted's face pulled into a dreadful rictus as he began to reach climax; then smoothed, turned benign, almost sleepy.

He sighed, and released the girl. She fell on her face in the gravel, retching in earnest now, her stomach working like a pump.

Ted waved his hand, and Susanna started the Volvo's engine. He leaned back in his seat, looking at nothing, riding the smooth waves of the afterglow. Now that he had had his virgin sacrifice he was calmed, gentled, ready for the challenge ahead of him.

The Kronos Kids gazed at the girl through their windows. She pulled herself painfully to her knees, staggered upright, and hurled herself at the door to her room. Sally watched her claw the door open and fall inside.

Marc pulled the bus out after the Volvo, heading for the highway.

The girl's sister was saying, "What's wrong, Perla? What's wrong, Perla?"

Sally stared at the back of Marc's head. He hadn't liked what Ted had done, but he had been otherwise indifferent throughout the whole ordeal. His favorite kind of women were older, and he usually didn't have to force himself on them. He didn't usually have to do more than a little mental nudge. He was never cruel unless Ted was doing it with him. Ted hadn't wanted to do it that way for years. Ted didn't really like to physically touch people.

"Perla, stop crying like that! You're scaring me!"

The kids had been mostly indifferent too. Ralph had turned up the volume of his music, until it was like the trumpeting of the gods on Judgment Day. Timothy was tuned completely in to Ralph; Sally could almost believe that they had been unaware of the incident.

But if they had, why the volume?

"I'm going to get Mama! Please, Perla, stop!"

The bus was up to sixty miles an hour now. It was rapidly taking them out of Ted's mental range. He wasn't paying attention to anyone but himself at the moment, basking in his pleasure. The second they had driven past his limit, Sally reached out for Perla.

She borrowed what she had learned from Joey to soothe the girl's stomach first. She filled Perla's bloodstream with calming chemicals and lulled her into a presleep state. Then, as gently as she could, she entered the girl's mind. She began to undo the chemical bonds of the new, painful memories Ted had given her. This wasn't easy. The memories were practically burned into Perla's neurons.

But Sally was patient. She was delicate. She was meticulous. She pursued every possible connection, every possible association. She invented a new reason for the girl's trauma, one that could be lived with.

Perla had gone out to steal a peek at the boys on the bus, but she hadn't known she had stomach flu. While she was standing there, trying to look attractive and interesting, vomit had suddenly shot up her throat and out her mouth. Like that gross movie, *The Exorcist*! It was so embarrassing, Perla just wanted to die.

Everyone had seen her! Everyone was probably laughing at her!

Sally gave Perla a mild stomach flu, so she would be sick for the rest of the day. Marie would fuss over her, soothe her, make her feel like it wasn't the end of the world.

Just as an extra touch, Sally projected the image of Jim's face in the bus window, creased in sympathy and concern. Jim was the handsomest boy in their whole group. Perla would remember that image once she was feeling a little better.

Sally withdrew.

She sailed through her own mindscape, back toward the bus. At times like this she almost felt like she could do more, could sail through space and even time. She liked the feeling; but it was scary too. She could see the Gate, far ahead of the bus. It was never clearer to her than when she was out of herself. She tried not to focus on it. She had to get back before Ted suspected she had meddled in his affairs.

Sally flew back to herself—and crashed right into someone.

It didn't hurt, but it startled her; the person had meant to be offensive, cause her pain, frighten her.

It was Caitlin, of course.

What do you think you're doing? demanded Caitlin.

That's my private business, said Sally, flustered and still unhinged by the surprise.

You went back and fixed *her, didn't you?*

Yes.

Why?

Caitlin was radiating contempt. Sally knew she wouldn't be able to make her understand—at least not within the next century. So she simply said, *Why not?*

They're just stupid people! *They're not important! Why should you care how they feel?*

They're not stupid!

They're like animals compared to us! We can do whatever we want to them! That's why we have our powers!

Sally had always known that Caitlin held that attitude, so she didn't bother arguing with her. Once she had them safely away from the influence of The Three, all of the Kronos Kids would become real people. They could afford to have feelings then; they could do anything they needed to do without hurting *anyone.*

That's what you think, Caitlin sneered. Sally hadn't tried to screen her thoughts, and Caitlin had picked them up without effort. Sally felt a twinge of fear. Would Caitlin tell Ted what she had done? (She was wise enough to screen *that* thought from Caitlin, at least.)

You think you're *going to be the boss of things after they're gone, don't you?* Caitlin demanded.

What do you mean, after they're gone?

Caitlin was taken aback for a moment. *You know what I mean.*

Yes, Sally admitted. *You mean after they've gone through the Gate. And what do you think they intend to do to us once they don't need us anymore?*

Caitlin didn't answer. But she knew; Sally was sure of it.

They'll treat us just like you want to treat ordinary *people,* Sally said.

I'm not ordinary! Caitlin roared, her mental self burning like a white-hot sun. *You just try me and see how ordinary I am!*

Sally was astonished. She had inadvertently tricked Caitlin into revealing the true scope of herself, a scope that even Sally, with all of her subtle maneuvering and shielding of Caitlin and the others over the years, hadn't grasped. Sally had been so good at fooling Caitlin, she hadn't suspected that she could be fooled herself.

THRALL, warned Sally's Secret Mind.

Oh, shit, Sally cried. *Ted's coming!*

Caitlin was instantly gone. Sally rushed back, trying to appear as normal as possible. She had no sooner centered herself when she became aware of eyes on her, and the force of the three minds behind them.

The Thrall descended on her, making her feel as crushed as if a hundred gravities were weighing her down. The eyes of the Mastermind pierced her, seeing her fear, her panic, her guilt.

What do you think you're doing? it demanded, taking her heart in its grasp and threatening to squeeze it dead if she didn't answer truthfully.

Nothing! Sally pleaded, but she knew it was useless. The jig was up. She was dead.

Sally's earliest memory was of being hungry. She was lying in her crib. Her brain was new; many faculties had yet to develop, both normal and supernormal. Only one thing made her different from other babies back then: She knew not to cry. Ted hated crying.

Sally was always hungry back then. Joey was lying in another crib, his powers of healing and dietary supplementism nothing more than a potential in his genes. Sally didn't even know Joey existed then. She only knew about herself, about someone who came to feed her sometimes, and about an angry, deadly someone whom she could sense nearby, the same way a mouse can sometimes sense a cat.

Don't move and he won't see you. No one had told her that. She didn't understand language yet. But she felt the warning in the way she was held when she was fed. She felt the tense muscles, heard the terrified silence.

Sally was hungry, but already she had learned patience. She thought about food. She hoped someone would bring it to her.

Eventually, someone came and leaned over the walls of the crib. He touched her with warm, strong hands, enjoying the feel of her baby skin. He picked her up and held her. She was able to see his face clearly.

He was Marc. She might have fallen in love with him right then.

Marc gave Sally a bottle. He cuddled and kissed her. She could feel that he liked her, that he was concerned about her. She hoped she could stay in his arms forever.

But eventually he handed her to a woman. Sally recognized the woman—she was the usual feeder. She didn't want to go with the woman, but she didn't cry about it. As soon as the woman had touched her, Sally had sensed something. The woman was afraid of Marc.

Sally couldn't imagine why this would be so; but back then Sally couldn't imagine a lot of things. She simply relied on the one thing she understood for sure in those early days: caution.

Sally grew a little older. She became aware of the other kids gradually, and they became aware of her. She was pleased to have their company—except that she didn't like Caitlin very much. Caitlin had a bad temper and liked to pinch.

"What's my name?" she asked Marc, when she was two. He thought for a moment and said, "Sally." He was feeding her and taking care of her more than the women by then. She adored him, and the time they spent together made her happy. It seemed to make him happy too. He took pleasure in her smiles, in her hugs and kisses. He would have been enough for her if there had been no one else in the world.

And then one day he came into the room with a lady. Sally knew instantly that the lady wasn't like the other women. For one thing, she wasn't afraid of Marc.

"My name is Susanna," said the lady, pronouncing the words in a way Sally had never heard before. Susanna slipped elegant gloves off of her hands and stood regarding them all, perfectly balanced on her high heels.

At the time, Sally believed that Susanna had only just come into her life. She didn't know that Susanna had been living with Marc and Ted all along; that she just simply hadn't bothered with the kids yet. Susanna didn't like babies.

Sally was about three when Susanna decided to make her first appearance. Once again, Sally fell in love. Susanna was so ladylike, so perfumey and silk stockingish. She sat the girls down for tea parties, and even Caitlin behaved herself as Susanna taught them how to serve and sip tea, how to hold their forks. How to dress up in pretty hats.

Back then, there had been five girls sitting around the table, instead of two.

Sally couldn't remember exactly what had happened to the first two—or to the three boys who had been killed before she was five. But she remembered every detail of what had happened to Lydia—and then to Marty, because Marty had known what Lydia was going to do, and he hadn't warned Ted.

Funny that Sally couldn't think of Lydia without thinking of something else too: a ray of light that she had once glimpsed on a distant mountaintop.

They had all been about six by then. It was a strange time. Sally's brain development had progressed to the stage of hallucinations, nightmares, and imaginary friends. Her sense of time was sometimes distorted, and she was beginning to develop some of her telekinetic powers.

Sally couldn't even remember if they lived in one house during that time, or if there had been a succession of houses. But she could remember Lydia standing in a hallway somewhere, looking at her.

The hallway was dark; there were no windows. Sally couldn't have glanced outside and seen the mountain, seen that wonderful light; but somehow the two images went together. Lydia had transformed the hallway. And that light, which couldn't have come from any earthly source that Sally could think of, had transformed the mountaintop.

But Sally could never remember where the mountain was. It had not been just outside the house. She had not found it in any of their travels, years later. But she had seen it again many times, in her dreams.

She had seen Lydia too. Lydia had been so lovely, so quiet. Sally had been a little jealous of her. Sally had plain brown hair; Lydia's was midnight black. Sally's skin sunburned easily; Lydia's turned golden brown. Sally's eyes were an undetermined blue; Lydia's were gray-green, the sort of color that commanded your attention from across a crowded room. Lydia's hands were slender, her legs already long and willowy.

Lydia wanted to be a ballet dancer—Sally remembered that. Sally, Lydia, and sometimes even Caitlin had staged mock recitals for Marc and Susanna.

Sally hadn't dreamed that Lydia wanted to kill Ted. In fact, she hadn't known very much about the girl at all. Looking back many years later, she had to admire that a six-year-old girl had been able to hide so much, to plan so carefully, to gather her courage and strike at a man whom everyone had feared but no one had yet dared to acknowledge. Who knows what Lydia would have become if she had lived?

But, of course, she hadn't.

Lydia's lips were moving. She was standing in that hallway, trying to tell Sally something. But Sally couldn't hear her. She tried to read the other girl's lips. Years later, she tried to read her mind. But the dream-Lydia had no mind. She was all light.

"I can't hear you!" Sally would say. "You're not making any sound, Lydia!"

The light shone on the mountaintop. It wasn't a peaceful place; Sally could see eagles and other birds of prey circling the peaks. But they were such noble birds. The had no malice in their hearts, even as they killed.

Sally looked for Lydia there. She liked to think of the girl in paradise. But not the Christian paradise. Valhalla was a better place for Lydia: the place where the brave go after they've died in battle. Sally looked for those immortal halls in the rocks at the summit. The golden light shone there. Someone must be there. But who was it? It wasn't Lydia.

Sally woke up to the sound of roaring. The mountain was gone. Now there was a monster in her head. Sally had seen monsters before, dreamed or hallucinated them many times; but this monster was different. This monster was *real*.

It had six eyes. Two of those pairs belonged to Marc and Susanna. The other pair, the biggest pair, belonged to Ted. Sally knew them, even though she had made it a point never to look directly at Ted.

Sally saw Lydia too. She was standing in what Sally would later learn to think of as the Puppet Position, the same position Perla would later be in when Ted mentally raped her. But Lydia wasn't being raped.

There was a gun lying on the carpet at Lydia's feet. She had waited for Ted to fall asleep, and then she had tiptoed into his room, gun in hand. She had planned to shoot him in the head.

It was a simple plan, an elegant one. Ted couldn't be attacked any other way; he would have sensed any sort of telepathic or telekinetic aggression. But once a bullet had had a chance to destroy a significant part of his brain, not even Ted could have saved himself.

No one had the slightest idea where Lydia had gotten the gun. Marc was pretty sure she hadn't made it herself. It had a Smith & Wesson label on it, and he thought she probably wouldn't have bothered to add that detail.

Lydia had carefully blanked her mind and aimed

the gun at Ted. But she had stumbled into one of Ted's machines on the floor, making an awful racket. Once he was awake, she had found that she couldn't even think, let alone move.

Five little girls, sitting around a table, drinking tea with their pinkies extended.

The Mastermind had exposed every thought in Lydia's mind.

You want to see what happens to people who cross me? It had shrieked. *You think you can kill me? Me, who made you! I'm gonna unmake you!*

And then the Mastermind had reached up through Lydia's vagina and pulled her inside out. Not mentally, the way it had done Perla. Not symbolically. *Physically.* It slowly pulled her inside out, keeping her alive and conscious throughout the whole agonizing process, keeping every one of her nerves active and functioning so that she felt *everything.* Every moment, every nuance, every snap of bone, every tear of tendon and muscle.

How the Kronos Kids had screamed. They had screamed and screamed, they had begged. They had tried to block the image of Lydia's torment out of their minds, but they were not allowed. Her punishment was their's too.

She didn't so much die as fade away, like the Doppler shriek of a train bearing prisoners to some far away death camp.

The Mastermind crouched over the bloody ruin that had been Lydia. *You're shit!* it told the children. *You're fucking garbage! Dirt! You're fucking little stinking animals!*

Now, Ted, Susanna had warned, pulling slightly away from the Mastermind. *We've gone to a lot of trouble to make them. Let's not forget that.*

I'm going to kill every single one of the ungrateful

little bastards! I knew they'd come after us once they got a taste of power!

Let's take a look, soothed Susanna. *Let's see who else is plotting.*

I didn't mean to! poor Marty had cried from under his bed. *I didn't mean to!*

So, of course, he had been caught sooner instead of later. He hadn't plotted, but he had loved Lydia, and she had tried to talk him into helping her. He had been afraid to help, but he had hoped she would succeed. And then he and Lydia could go away together. . . .

Don't hurt me like Lydia! he had begged.

Marc broke his neck, instantly, before Ted could pull another inside-out trick. Marty slipped away into oblivion, safe, beyond pain and grief, beyond Ted's vengeance.

And for one terrible moment, Sally had thought Ted would kill Marc for that. But Marc was the mental hands of the Mastermind. He was not a helpless opponent, like Lydia had been.

We can't afford to drive them out of their minds right now, Marc had said. *They'll be basket cases, and then what good will they be?*

They'll be fucking satisfying kills is what they'll be! Ted insisted.

Think, Ted, Susanna had said. *The plan! Think of the heaven we're going to build with their help!*

It's no good! They'll each try to kill us as they get stronger!

Why should they kill us? Marc had asked him. *They love us.*

They love you.

Ted! Susanna had snapped. *This is our last chance! Philip made them, and we can't make another Philip! He's gone forever. And once they're gone, it's back to the same scrabbling we've done all our lives.*

Ted was silent.

Fifty years, Susanna said. *We've struggled for fifty years to rise out of the dirt. This is it, Ted.*

I can't trust them, he insisted.

Then let's look at what they've got in store for us. Let's look, together.

And so the Kronos Kids had each cringed and suffered under the mind-search. Their thoughts, desires, dreams had been hauled out and inspected by the raging, paranoid monster with the six eyes. It had looked twice, three times, unwilling to believe (for instance) that Sally's greatest desire was to go to tea parties with Susanna, to dance ballet with the other girls, to someday become a princess and live in a palace with a handsome prince who bore a suspicious resemblance to Marc.

Such simple dreams, compared to what Lydia had plotted, what Lydia had understood.

The rest of you are the runts of the litter, Ted had told them, and then let them go.

Susanna had carefully soothed the images of Lydia's and Marty's death from everyone's memories. The children had been grateful to let go of the horror. But there had been a disagreement about how *thoroughly* the memory should be wiped.

"Let it serve as a warning," Ted insisted, hating to think that what he had done would be rendered impotent with forgetfulness.

"We can't let them keep the memory," Marc said. "It'll ruin our chances to ever make a useful bond with them."

The two men could not agree. At the time, Sally hadn't known how extraordinary that was. Later she would wonder what sort of man Marc would have become if he had disagreed with Ted more often.

But in the end, it didn't matter. In the end, Susanna

had left a nameless dread that was triggered whenever thoughts of rebellion or escape surfaced.

Six is such a lovely, symmetrical number.

They wanted to leave us. . . .

Sally was the only one who ever thought about Lydia and Marty anymore. Sally's Secret Mind had followed the dread to its source and retrieved the truth.

Sally's Secret Mind filed it away, along with all the other horrors and wonders.

Lydia's lips were moving. Sally could never hear what she was saying. No Valkyries had come to fetch Lydia when she died, despite her courage, despite her pain. Someone else was on the mountainside.

"I can't hear you!" Sally would say. "Lydia, you're not making any sound!"

But Sally's Secret Mind knew what Lydia was saying.

Susanna had given it the clue: *Philip made them. He's gone forever.*

What Lydia was saying didn't make complete sense, yet. But Sally's Secret Mind listened, attentively.

Philip says hello, Lydia was saying. *Philip says hello.*

The two women had been lesbians.

They had been young lovers. They were attractive in a suntanned, athletic, self-confident sort of way. Their careers were successful and compatible. They had been together five years, long enough for the first bloom of love to wither or to mellow into the compassionate love of longtime companions.

They still loved each other. They would have spent their entire lives together.

But the Kronos Kids had begun their journey.

The bus and the Volvo were on the road. The house or houses that the children had lived in had been abandoned, and the women who had tended the children were gone. Sally didn't know if they were dead or if they had simply been sent away. She didn't even know if one of those women had been her mother.

Now The Three were searching for the perfect place, the place where they would build their citadel/temple/fortress, the place from which they would ascend to heaven.

Had their plans always been so nebulous, so half-baked?

The children never questioned whether they had or not. They obeyed. They were blooming, and their skills were mercilessly appropriated and manipulated. They were just seven years old. Ralph had begun to play music in his head.

Sally was already able to tell what everyone else was doing and thinking. It was not always comfortable for her to be constantly encountering new people. She would have been happier to live in a house and have tea parties.

But no one had asked what her preference was, and she didn't offer it.

The two women had been on vacation. They were bicycling through Oregon when The Three and their Kronos Kids encountered them in a motel parking lot. Sally couldn't even remember what town it had been.

The children had been cheerfully unloading the bus, looking forward to burgers and shakes in the motel coffee shop. Susanna had gone to lie down in her room. Ted had been looking at the pop machine, wondering if it was worth taking apart.

Marc had noticed the women first, when they were walking their bikes to their motel room. He had made sure they noticed him too. But they had barely glanced his way, and he had been puzzled that their reactions had been so neutral; so he went over to talk to them.

Sally was hurt that he had noticed them.

He's a grown-up, she reminded herself. *When I'm a grown-up, he'll notice me too.*

But when Sally looked in the mirror, a plain person always looked back at her. Caitlin was beautiful. Lydia had been so beautiful. (*Don't think about that!*) Why did Sally have to be so ordinary? She wasn't even smart, or funny. Marc would never have any reason to notice her.

Marc was attracted to both of the women; but they were trying to think up ways to put him off without revealing that they were lesbians. People sometimes acted crazy when they found that out.

But Marc already knew. He was intrigued by the fact. He nudged them. They still weren't interested in him; handsome Marc, who was used to having women want to do anything for him. That intrigued him even more.

Ted wandered over too. He had been attracted by the mountain bikes first, but he had been distracted by the trouble Marc was having with the women.

Marc felt challenged by them. He wondered if even lesbians could be seduced if a man nudged them in the right places. He kept trying.

They still weren't interested, so he nudged harder.

Sally was starting to feel nervous. Why didn't the women want Marc? Even if you were only interested in other women—Marc was *special.*

Even if you were in love with someone else.

Ted picked one and put his hands on her breasts. She reacted with a wave of fear so primitive it made Sally's stomach heave. He squeezed her breasts, hard; and now she felt rage, and her lover was afraid for her; but neither of them could move to defend themselves. Sally cringed, feeling her own muscles doing what theirs could not.

Marc pulled the other woman close and kissed her, tenderly. The woman watched him with a dazed horror. The touch of his lips on hers made her sick.

Sally closed her eyes, feeling Marc's lips as if they were on her own. It made her heart pound to feel him kissing the woman that way.

But the woman hated it. And the woman was thinking about what dreadful Ted was doing to her lover, things that were even worse.

But suddenly she was getting excited.

But Ted was hurting her lover. He was enjoying the pain he was causing, he was enjoying seeing them suffer at the sight of each other's shame, he was . . .

He was *in their heads!*

Stop it! Sally wanted to yell at Ted and Marc. *Can't you see they don't want you?!*

From the outside, the women *looked* like they

wanted it, like they were enjoying it; but Sally knew they weren't. Ted and Marc were making them smile, making them do lascivious things with their hands.

"Do it to me," Ted made the woman say.

Sally ran into the bathroom she shared with Caitlin. She crawled into the bathtub, as if the porcelain could insulate her from what was happening. Of course, it couldn't.

Ted and Marc took the women into their motel room. They made the women give them blow jobs, then raped them both, repeatedly. In between times, Ted beat them black and blue. Marc gave them intense, multiple orgasms, and prolonged both his and Ted's sexual stamina for almost two hours. He could have kept it up indefinitely, but Ted got bored and went outside to take the bikes apart.

Sally lay in a fetal position in the bathtub. She had jammed her fingers in her ears and shut her eyes as tight as she could. But she saw, heard, felt everything. She knew how much it hurt the women to see each other treated that way. Their fear for each other was worse than their outrage and panic. They couldn't even take refuge in madness for very long, because concern for each other kept dragging them back, kept making them *look,* see what was happening. Sally felt so much pity for them she was almost choking on it.

She also envied them as Marc kissed them, as he lingered over their bodies. Sally wished it was she with Marc, she who had the grown-up body that he wanted.

She also wished he would stop. But she couldn't help enjoying him. The conflict was rapidly driving her as mad as the women.

Sherri! someone was thinking, trying to call her lover's name, trying to say, *It's all right,* with a paralyzed throat.

Sally couldn't tell which one she was. Both women were being pushed to the edge. Sally was already there. They were going to topple over soon, and no one cared to stop them.

Susanna didn't care. She knew what was happening, but she didn't give it a moment's thought.

The other children didn't *want* to care. They were playing on the motel playground, hoping they wouldn't have to wait much longer for supper.

Marc didn't care. Except for his pleasure in their bodies, he was blank. He felt *nothing*. It was like when Lydia was being ...

Don't. Don't. Don't.

And Ted. It was Marc who had made him feel like he wanted to touch the women. And he, in turn, had given Marc pleasure in the beatings. Now they were separate again. Marc was getting hungry, ready to call it a night.

He let the women go.

Sally breathed a sigh of relief. It was over, over. She could step back from the edge, rest. She let her hands drop, her eyes open a crack. She looked at the white, smooth porcelain and envied its blankness.

The women lay on their bed. They couldn't move. They couldn't look at or touch each other. They were in shock, but they were both thinking about something in particular.

How much it hurt. How much they wanted to die.

How they had brought a gun with them, for protection. How useless it had been against Ted and Marc,

Don't feel bad, Sally wanted to tell them. *It's over now. They'll forget you. You can get over it. I got over—I got over Lyd—*

Lydia ...

Marc closed the door to their room, locking it behind him. He headed for the coffee shop.

Ted glanced up at him. He thought briefly of the women, and touched their minds, almost reflexively.

He saw the gun. He saw what they wanted to do

with it. They wouldn't actually do it; they just needed to think about it until it shocked them into picking up the pieces.

Ted nudged them. Then he went back to his work.

Sally lay limp in her bathtub. She saw the juggernaut coming. It was like watching someone fall in front of a train. *She's going to die!* you think, and you clutch your face and scream, and the train just keeps coming.

Ted didn't react to the sound of the gunshots.

Sally lost consciousness.

Some time later, Sally felt someone touching her face tenderly. She opened her eyes. She looked up and saw Marc leaning over her. He picked her up. He had showered; he smelled like shampoo and deodorant, masculine perfume. She breathed deeply, wrapped her arms around him and gazed into his eyes.

Inside her was an empty, echoing place. You could drop a penny in there and it would fall forever without making a sound.

"Aren't you hungry, sweetheart?" he asked.

Sally shook her head.

"I'll bet I can get you to eat something."

"Not hungry," Sally croaked. She didn't think about why. No images came into her head at all.

Marc carried her into the motel room. Caitlin was asleep. Sally wondered, vaguely, how late it was.

Marc sat down at the desk and pulled Sally into his lap. He had brought a burger and french fries in a doggy bag. He had cut the burger into four sections. He coaxed her into eating one of them.

"That's my good girl," he said. He fed her a french fry. His lap was hard, all muscle and bone. His chest felt that way too. He had a smell of his own, underneath the soap and deodorant, a man smell. It made the taste buds at the back of Sally's tongue tingle pleasantly.

He wasn't thinking about the women. Sally remembered them; she knew he remembered them too. But she couldn't bear to let her mind wander in that direction.

She loved him so much. When he held her like this, she could believe that he loved her too. He might not love her like he could love a woman—

Don't. Just eat the fries.

She had felt what it would be like to be stroked by him. What it was like to have him inside. . . .

"It had nothing to do with you, baby," Marc said, somehow both referring to and *not* referring to the women. It was the first and last time he ever bothered to explain his behavior to Sally.

"Ted is mean," Sally said. And it was the first and last time she ever spoke that way about Ted to Marc.

"Shhh," he said.

Sally ate the fries. She even sort of enjoyed them. Then Marc carried her to bed. He tucked her in. He kissed her on the cheek and told her to sleep tight.

He went away.

Sally lay awake.

In another motel room, the bodies of the two women were still cooling and stiffening.

Once again, Sally felt herself close to the edge the lovers had gone over. She peered down into the gulf. She remembered the *nothing* that Marc had felt after Ted had separated from him and he had been left with the women. The *nothing* that had been where remorse should have been. Or even pity.

The *nothing* that was where the memories of seven dead children should be.

The *nothing* that would be where Sally had once been.

Sally looked over. She looked down. She was frightened of the fall.

Something bloomed in the darkness.

Sally peered at it. It had a face, but she didn't recognize it. *Who are you?* she called to it.

Sally's Secret Mind peered back. It was new, and it was just beginning to learn. But there was a great deal it already understood.

You, it called back.

*W*hat are you doing? demanded the Mastermind.

Sally cringed. She had been caught using her talent without permission, and now The Three wanted to know why. They were about to find out that she had interfered, that she had helped Perla. She couldn't even take a moment to think up an excuse, because her thoughts weren't private.

She couldn't even be frightened for her life, because that would reveal that she knew it was in danger.

An image flickered behind her eyes. She grasped for it like a drowning girl after a straw.

"The Gate!" she said.

The Mastermind had seen it too. It gobbled her up, seized her mind and rifled through it, looking for its heart's desire, discarding everything else as useless. Sally acted instinctively and showed it the Olympus Gate as she had last seen it.

It saw the Wall that was more than a wall. The door that was made of will, not wood or stone.

The Mastermind was stilled. It was awed.

It had never seen the Gate this way before. It had only seen nebulous glimpses. Now Sally was finally forced to show it what the Gate really looked like to *her*. She did it to save her life.

She succeeded. For the moment. But something odd happened when the Mastermind focused on the Gate. The Gate got bigger, more tangible; its features became clearer. There were veins in the door, along which flowed pulses of energy like the kind that leaped from synapse to synapse in a human brain. The symbols that writhed and curled around the massive frame were glyphs, almost like Egyptian or Mayan symbols, but not really like either of them.

They were aware of the Mastermind.

They beckoned. *You can understand us if you really want to,* they seemed to be saying. *And when you do, you can come in. You can be what you dream. Just understand us. Just understand. . . .*

Where are you? demanded the Mastermind. *Show us the path!*

Sally didn't delay. There was no avoiding what was at the end of their road. It was close now. It was no more than a couple of hours away. And now it had seen *them.*

It helped her show the way. It created a map in her mind, with lines that led from itself to Sally. In Sally's imagination, the lines were red.

The Mastermind gazed greedily.

The bus and the Volvo turned off the highway onto a road that hadn't been used in two decades. Not since the Christian Indian School had been shut down.

We're coming! promised the Mastermind. And it *squeezed.* It squeezed the children for every drop of power they had: Poor Ralph's music dwindled into dreadful silence; Timothy became a mindless lens; Caitlin reared and froze like a preying mantis who sees the crushing boot overhead.

And even they were not enough for the Mastermind. It drew on sources *outside* the children, on ordinary people, on animals, on the plants and the rocks, on the world. Sally had never felt such power, had never dreamed The Three would approach it. The Gate was facilitating matters in some way, she could sense it. But why? What did the Gate want with them?

Was somebody waiting for them on the other side? What would that someone do, once the door was open?

The Thrall became unbearable. It pushed and gripped until Sally could barely think at all. Sally's Secret Mind was all that was spared from it. It rode high over The Three, like an eagle scouting the way. It observed them, their single-minded passion.

This is unwise, it thought to itself. *You should never be so eager to eat the apple that's dangled in front of you.*

But when had The Three ever denied themselves anything they wanted? When had they ever done anything but pursue every desire, every whim? When had they ever suffered anguish, guilt, remorse, grief, regret when those desires had proven disastrous?

Never.

But Sally felt all of those things. Just now she was having considerable misgivings concerning the Gate.

She tried to keep her mind on the road that blurred outside her window, on the mountains and the hawks riding the thermals above them; but she really wanted to contemplate the glyphs, to follow those pulses of energy. That's what The Three were doing, and they were utterly seduced. There was no trace of doubt or skepticism in any of their minds.

Marc's and Susanna's driving had become utterly mindless, a reflex.

Sally wished a truck would come along and end their ambitions. But the road was abandoned, and they were quickly closing the distance to the Gate.

Sally could sense the forces building behind it. She didn't know what they were, not remotely; but she knew that The Three would be surprised by what they found. She had learned that surprises were usually nasty.

She and the other children might be able to get out

of the way. They might escape in the confusion. Sally tried to assess the other children's current capabilities without alerting the Mastermind. She needn't have been so stealthy; it was completely enthralled by its vision. But old habits died hard.

Old habits for the Kronos Kids too. They were almost mindless under the Thrall.

It's up to me, Sally knew. *This is the big one.*

The hawks over the mountains turned to electrical pulses, jumping from synapse to synapse. Sally tore her eyes away and fixed them on something else. The back of Marc's neck.

He might be the "hands" that opened the Gate. It was he who might be the first to meet what was on the other side.

Tears rolled down Sally's cheeks.

Perhaps he would only go away, forever, when he passed through the Gate. But even that was painful to contemplate. She had never allowed herself to think about final outcomes. Other concerns had always come first, like self-preservation.

Just now, her instinct for self-preservation was stronger than ever. It was as if they were about to expose themselves to some sort of deadly radiation. Her danger signals were jangling so loud she was amazed that no one else could hear them.

But they heard nothing.

And now the Gate was closer.

And it was fabulous. If it wasn't the door to Olympus, it was certainly something beyond the ordinary world, beyond everyday limitations. It was eternal, of the mind and spirit. None of the great religions of history did more than remotely approach it, aspire to it. It was beautiful, it was terrible.

It was waiting for *them.*

Sally blinked. Marc's solid image began to slip, to

blur. She was impossibly tired. One would think she hadn't had a good night's sleep.

She felt like she had never slept in her life.

She couldn't help closing her eyes. The Gate waited for her, there. *Peace,* she wanted to tell it. *I don't want you. You're not for me.* But she couldn't lose it, couldn't stop wanting to gaze at it until she had unraveled its secrets.

Such incredible secrets.

Wouldn't it be wonderful if it really was the Gate to Olympus? Wouldn't it be wonderful if they could all ascend, do more than glimpse that perfect, golden ray on a distant mountain peak? Some tiny part of Sally wanted to believe it. It wanted to believe that The Three knew what they were doing.

Sally sent a jolt down her own nerves, stunning her body with pain. It did the trick. She lost her wistfulness, became aware of The Three again.

That gave her another bracing jolt. She could smell their overconfidence, their absolute certainty that they could tangle with anything "out there" and win, simply because they had never encountered true rivals. They were blind to the danger. How surprised they would be if they knew what Sally knew.

Warn them! she thought to herself, for one stupid, fleeting second. How good it would feel to reveal to them just how powerful and clever she really was. If they knew, wouldn't they recognize her as an equal and welcome her into their circle? She could convince them of their error in wanting to kill the Kronos Kids; she could show them what sort of Mastermind they could all achieve together. Then perhaps they could all ascend to Olympus.

And Marc might see her as a woman, at last. Someone he could love.

Sally cherished that thought for one glorious moment. Then she let go of it. She imagined it going over a cliff like the one that The Three had planned for her and the other children. She imagined how The Three would laugh.

Let them laugh. Sally was as ready as she was ever going to be. If she could only get some rest, stop worrying about it for a little while ...

Sally's Secret Mind dumped soothing chemicals into Sally's bloodstream, lulled her into a restful state. Sally would only torment herself until the time came to act. Sally's Secret Mind would take as much of the burden from her as it could. They were two hours from their destination. She must rest.

Sally drifted into numb sleep. The Three were still using her, using the others too; but Sally didn't need to be conscious for them to do it.

Sally's Secret Mind was in the driver's seat now. It monitored the situation. It had special talents. It could see into the past. It could see into the future.

It knew what was on the other side of the Olympus Gate.

Too soon, was its conclusion. It was too soon to open the Gate. But there was no way to wrest control away from The Three at this time. The children were too young, too inexperienced. Sally's Secret Mind could have rallied an effective attack against The Three; it would still do so if forced. That was one of the possibilities that loomed in the future.

It could have combined the talents of the Kronos Kids to mount a physical attack on The Three. It could have used Joey to direct that attack through healing channels he had already established, which he had maintained for so long that The Three were no longer aware of them. Caitlin and Jim could have ferreted out the mental weaknesses of their enemies and assaulted them on that front; and Timothy could have fine-tuned their combined efforts to laser efficiency.

And then there was Ralph. Poor Ralph, who was

sitting there without his beloved music, without the comfort of the brother who loved him. He was a musical genius, to be sure; but Ralph had other talents, unsuspected even by himself, talents on the quantum level that were going to come in handy very soon.

Yes, Sally's Secret Mind could have killed The Three then and there. It could have resorted, if necessary, to Caitlin's embryonic pyrokinetic abilities. Caitlin could harness the power of the sun itself, if she had the proper help.

But that would be like lighting a cigarette with a flame thrower. That would certainly be a "final solution," one the planet would not recover from anytime soon. No—Sally's Secret Mind preferred to bide its time, to pull its trump card of Ralph's unsuspected abilities at the last possible moment.

To buy time. That was the only chance for the Kronos Kids. After that, their own weaknesses and strengths would decide their fates.

Sally's Secret Mind could see those futures too. But for the time being, it kept them to itself.

Sally, in the meantime, was occupied with a dream.

It wasn't like any dream she had ever experienced before. It wasn't even like the King Monkey dream, which had seemed so real. That might have been because of the Thrall; but Sally didn't think so. This was something different, something new.

Sally was on a boat, drifting down a man-made canal. The boat was narrow and pointy like a fat canoe, but rode higher in the water like a small barge; and the canal was elevated, making it look almost like a Roman aqueduct.

But the city that passed on either side of her might not have been Roman. It was hard to say exactly what sort of architecture she was looking at. Greek? Roman? Etruscan? All she could be sure of was that it was marvelous, alluring, and deadly in the way of all cities ever built by men and women.

Egyptian? Sumerian? Babylonian?

There was a woman in the boat with Sally. She sat on a seat in the center, sideways, her left profile presented to Sally. She wore clothing that could have been ancient or futuristic, depending on context. She was small—Sally could tell that even though they were both sitting. She wore a veil that was combined with the scarf that bound her hair. She turned to look at Sally with gray, tilted eyes.

Do you know me? she asked Sally.

No, Sally answered after searching her memory.

In time, you might, the woman told her. *And what do you think of the city? Is it worthy of the gods?*

Sally looked once again at the city, its architecture which, like the woman's clothes, could have been ancient or futuristic, despite a lack of obvious technology. It was a fabulous city; even Sally's untrained eye could grasp its genius, its perfect blending of function and beauty. Was the architecture Aztec? Mayan? Toltec? Incan?

This city would have moved The Three. They had never achieved its like. But was it worthy of the gods? Perhaps not. There was something inherently human about it, something mortal.

It's not worthy of the gods, said Sally. *But superior men and women would live here.*

The woman regarded Sally without blinking her gray eyes. *And what defines superiority in men and women?* she asked.

Sally thought of several qualities; but they were qualities that she had seen in many people she had encountered in her journeys. Yet no one she knew, no one she had ever met, could have designed a city like this one.

Mesopotamian? Nubian? Minoan? Mycenaean?

I don't know, Sally admitted. *But the people who designed this city must be superior. I don't know why I know, but I can see that it's beyond anything mortal men have ever done.*

Perhaps not so far beyond, said the woman. *If you look, you can find elements of ancient designs here. This is a city of the future* and *the past.*

Indian? Siamese? Chinese?

Is it a city in our *future?* asked Sally hopefully.

It is possible, said the woman, her eyes boring into Sally like the eyes of The Three could never have done. Yet, somehow, Sally did not feel invaded.

Is this what we'll find after we pass through the Olympus Gate? she asked the woman.

Gray eyes regarded Sally silently, making her wonder if she had committed some presumption, some error. But she couldn't think what she had said wrong. She was too ignorant.

Now, said the woman, *now you are ignorant. There is so much to learn, Sally. So much to feel. And you yourself have said this city is not worthy of the Gods, and no one you know could have designed it. Yet the Gods lie beyond the Olympus Gate, don't they?*

Do they?

I don't know, admitted the woman. *But if they do, and they are as you imagine them, how will they regard you? And how will they regard The Three, who are not even fit to clean your shoes?*

Sally was mildly shocked to hear someone criticizing The Three so openly. Yet this woman could get away with it. She was safe from them. She was stronger than them.

I am, said the woman. *But I am in your future. I don't know you yet; and you don't know me. I can't help you now. You must help yourself.*

If you don't know me, then how come we're talking now? Sally demanded. She had been feeling so safe, so honored sitting in the boat with this powerful woman who said things to her that she wished someone had been saying all along. To find out that there was no help. . . .

You have some talent as an oracle. It has sought me out. But you won't develop it unless you pursue your present course. Alone, Sally. Alone, for now.

Sally felt a sinking in her heart. But it hardened into resolve. Of course she was alone. She had always been. Except for Mungy Bungy; but he was just her little friend. He had no powers, except to appear when she was lonely.

Right on cue, Mungy climbed out from beneath her seat. He leaped onto her knees and curled in her lap, looking up at her with his intelligent eyes. *Of course I'm your friend,* he seemed to say. *You're my special person.*

Sally looked up, to see if the woman could see Mungy Bungy too. No one else had ever done so. But the woman wasn't looking at her anymore. She was looking at the city. She seemed lost in thought. Sally petted Mungy, wondering if she should intrude on the woman's reverie. Then she caught a glimpse of someone who was standing in the bow of the boat.

A man. He was standing with his back to her. He wasn't touching any controls; his hands were resting on his hips. He stood ramrod straight, most of his attention on some task: guiding the boat, Sally suspected. But he was also listening to her, aware of her. He had heard everything Sally and the woman had said.

Whoever he was, he must be handsome. Trim, well-muscled without being bulky. He was wearing a kilt and a shirt that, like the woman's clothes, had elements of both the ancient past and the distant future in them.

Sally looked down at herself. She was wearing jeans and a cotton shirt.

I'm from the blue-jeans generation, she thought to herself, with a touch of humor. *No escaping it. But they . . .*

They were from an older time.

The man had short, black hair, just like Marc. Sally admired the back of his neck, just as she had admired Marc's neck through all of the years she had watched him from her seat on the bus. It was so masculine, so beautifully made. She loved the way it flowed into the architecture of his wide shoulders. Sally looked at the man in the front of the boat and felt stirrings that made all of her previous sexual feelings for Marc seem embryonic in comparison. Their intensity surprised her.

You're becoming a woman. The gray-eyed woman was looking at her again. *These feelings will grow stronger.*

I like them, said Sally, feeling bold.

Good, said the woman.

Sally looked at the man again.

He was gone.

Mungy was gone. The city was gone.

Sally was back on the bus. The Three were holding her and the others in Thrall. She could barely breathe. The woman turned to look at her from the seat that was just in front of hers, the seat that was normally empty.

None of the other children ever sought Sally out for companionship. They had accepted her as one of them, nothing less, nothing more.

You are alone, said the woman. *Now you must act, as you have planned. Your judgment is sound.*

Thank you, said Sally, too crushed by the Thrall to feel more than a shadow of gratitude.

You can't hold me any longer, said the woman. *A*

word before I go. That wonderful city you saw—if it is ever built, you will help to build it.

If it's ever built . . . Sally said, and then the woman was gone.

You will help build it. . . .

Sally was disappointed. Now she was sure she had just been dreaming. For years, she and the other children had tried to build the marvelous structures Ted had wanted. But they had failed.

The bus droned on. The Three crushed her as they sped toward the Gate, down the red lines in Sally's imagination. She could not stay awake in their grip. She drifted back to sleep. She hoped she would go back to the aqueduct, the boat, the wonderful conversation and the view of the handsome man who might turn at any moment and show her his face. But she didn't dream about that.

Instead, she dreamed about the bus. It was so much like it was now, like it had always been, that for a long time she wasn't aware that she was dreaming again. She thought she was merely dozing. There was Marc, the back of his neck as she had seen it for so many years. That unchanging, youthful skin, those strong shoulders.

Was it you, in the boat? she wanted to ask him. *Is that some future you, what you could become if you weren't part of The Three anymore? Will you be my lover, after all?*

But the woman had been there too. Her eyes had been beautiful, mysterious. She might be Marc's lover too. Or instead.

My girl, he had said. *I'll bet I can get you to eat.*

The smell of his shampoo, the man's deodorant.

It had nothing to do with you. . . .

It was night now, and they were still driving. That couldn't be right. It had been morning, with the Gate only a couple of hours away. So this must be a dream too.

Yes—when Sally thought about it, she remembered where they were going. California. They were about to pass through Blythe, right near the California border. It was early, almost two A.M., yet it was hot outside the bus, perhaps a hundred degrees. Inside it was the same temperature it always was, the temperature that Marc found the most comfortable. Sally shouldn't have been aware of the heat outside; but she was. She could feel it pressing on their little microcosm, trying to get in.

Sally was tired. She just wanted to stop at a motel and slip between cool sheets, sleep a whole day, maybe. But they wouldn't be stopping. They would be driving straight through until Ted found that illusive somewhere that would satisfy his criteria. Then they might stop a night; but the next day the work would begin. The work that the children could barely grasp, that they didn't dare do wrong.

They were ten, now. They were getting better at it. But they still weren't good enough. Sally was beginning to suspect they never would be.

So tired. Her mind was wandering.

The other children were asleep or in a stupor, like Sally. They offered no companionship or comfort. Probably they didn't know how. Each of them had something to comfort himself and that was hard enough to keep.

Sally tried to look out the window. Reflections of light warped by the imperfect glass confused her. Beyond was a relentless darkness.

Mustn't fall asleep, Sally warned herself. *Remember, this was when it almost happened. When someone almost—*

What had she been thinking? About the other kids? And why they didn't need her. Caitlin had her fantasies of admirers. Ralph and Timothy had their shared music. Jim had ... What *did* Jim have, anyway? She didn't know. She should have found it out, but she hated to intrude. Intruding was what The Three did so thoughtlessly.

So hot outside. Wish I could sleep.

The bus roared on into the night. Sally bounced along with every bump and pothole in the road. She never quite went to sleep, never was quite awake either. Consciousness came and went.

They don't think they need me. But they do.

"Look at that! A whole busload of meat. You know what we could do with that?"

Sally started awake. The bus wasn't moving anymore. They were at a filling station. It was closed, but that never stopped Marc. He was filling the huge tanks. He was alert, not a bit tired. But his mind was far, far away. He didn't know that three men were watching them from the darkness.

"Girls and boys. You have a preference?"

"Not if I can do what I want."

"You can do what you want. All weekend."

"All *week*. Two days ain't enough. I want to take my time."

"You always say that, and then you get all worked up and blow your whole wad at once."

One was creeping up behind Marc. Sally studied him for a moment, mesmerized by what she saw in his mind, what he had planned for her and the other children.

Torture. Rape. Sodomy. Slow murder. The three of them had been doing it for five years now, as a team. First this one would stab Marc in the kidneys. Then he and the others would get on the bus, tie up the children. Then they would drive out to a special place they liked to go.

Then ...

Marc. Sally touched his mind, gave him everything she knew about the men in one fraction of a second.

Marc turned casually. The man froze, five feet away from him. He uncurled from his semi-crouch, waiting for the least sign of aggression from Marc.

Marc just kept pumping gas.

"Evenin'," said the man. He got a good look at Marc's handsome, trim form, at Marc's utter self-confidence, and he hated him.

His two friends walked out in the open, ready to join him. Obviously it was going to be a little more work than they had thought. But they weren't worried yet.

"Not very friendly, are you?" the man said to Marc. He watched carefully for signs of fear, apprehension. Marc wasn't showing any, so something was up. The man waited to see what it was.

"No one else around," said one of his friends. "Guess he's just too stupid to know when he's in bad company."

Sally watched the three men, unworried. She had been awake to warn Marc. That was all that was necessary.

Marc turned his back on the men. The tanks were full now. He turned off the pumps and closed the valves. The first man began to move again, his knife in attack position.

He disappeared in a flash of light.

Sally raised her eyebrows. *Disintegrated.* That was something she had never seen before. She memorized the process, filing it away for future need.

The other two men barely had time to realize that their friend had disappeared when they were disintegrated too. All neat and tidy. Swatted like flies.

Sally was a little surprised that Marc hadn't been more brutal; and she was more than a little relieved. But she was hurt too. After all, those men had planned to do terrible things to her and the other kids. Didn't Marc care about that?

And then he turned and smiled at her.

You're my special girl, he told her, with such warmth and admiration that Sally melted under the sunshine of his regard. Sally had warned him. She had been alert and saved the day. She was smart.

She was special.

You are, he assured her. *You're the one who sees the Gate.*

Sally looked down the road. The Gate was waiting up ahead. She was amazed; for a short time she had managed to forget it.

Sally blinked. Someone was walking down the road toward them, a silhouette against the light of the Gate. Sally stuck her head out the window to get a better look.

It was Lydia who was walking down the road.

Lydia was still six years old. She was slim and willowy and lovely. Her lips were moving. Sally strained to hear what she was saying.

"Where's Marty?" Sally called to Lydia. "Didn't he go to heaven with you?" That was what Marty would have wanted. But Marty belonged in the Christian heaven, the one with fatherly Jesus who would pat Marty's head. Valhalla was not for sweet lambs like Marty.

But Lydia didn't mention Marty at all.

"Philip—" said Lydia.

And then Sally woke up. She blinked in the blinding light.

The bus had stopped. Marc had shut everything off. He had stopped regulating the temperature in the bus, and it was rapidly becoming hot and stuffy inside. It was getting hard to breathe in there.

He was moving mechanically, with a shadow of his usual grace. He opened the door.

"Time to go, kids," he said, his tone so cheerful it made Sally shudder. She got up with the other children. She got in line behind Timothy and Ralph. Jim and Joey brought up the rear. The Kronos Kids shuffled down the aisle, down the steps, and out the door, into the blazing furnace of an Arizona summer.

Sally looked across the asphalt, through ripples of heat-distorted air, and saw the Christian Indian School.

It was boarded up, chained, and locked. Ted and Susanna were standing near its front door, waiting for the children.

Come on, snapped Ted. *You're going first.*

So. Ted was not oblivious to the danger, after all. He knew that what was inside might kill, and he wanted to make sure he wasn't first in line.

Sally knew that. The other Kids knew it too. Fear began to creep into their minds, even under the weight of the Thrall.

They took a step forward, like robots moving in unison.

They took another step.

S ally was in the process of taking a third step when the other children, The Three, the school, and the heat faded away into nothingness. Only the light remained. It shone over endless fields of snow.

Huh? Sally thought to herself.

Another dream, said her Secret Mind.

Right now? I'm kind of busy!

We can't help it, said her Secret Mind. *It must be an important dream.*

Hope blossomed in Sally. Maybe she would learn something from this dream that would help her inside the school, something that would give her a clue about how to survive. She waited patiently. She could feel the cold, a little, but not enough to bother her. She could see something moving on the horizon, coming toward her. It came closer, and she realized it was a man.

She waited until she could see his face. She didn't recognize him. But her Secret Mind did.

King Monkey? it called to him.

What? Sally wondered. This man didn't look like King Monkey. King Monkey was a Neanderthal. This guy looked like a modern man, although he did have a rugged quality one didn't see very often in modern times, sort of an intrepid look.

He heard Sally's Secret Mind. He stopped and listened. He looked across the frozen steppes, but there was nothing, no one.

"Can't you see me?" asked Sally.

"No," he said, and looked closer. His eyes passed over Sally, giving her a tingle. He squinted in her general direction, but it was obvious he couldn't see her this time.

King Monkey, it's me! said Sally's Secret Mind.

Sally felt herself falling into that state she had known in the first dream, the one in which she almost felt as if *he* were the one who was dreaming *her*. She knew, suddenly, what he knew.

It had been millennia since anyone had called King Monkey by that name. She had stirred old, old memories for him.

He no longer had any name at all, save "Hunter" or "Scout." He no longer even resembled his former self, and neither did any of his people. He had changed them, just as he had promised he would. He had changed everyone of his race that he had ever encountered in all of his long years. No one could have known him as his former self; no one who was still living.

Except for his great Enemy. But this was not he.

No, it's me, your friend from the future.

"You!" he said. "I thought I would never hear your voice again!"

Many centuries have passed for you, haven't they?

The idea of the century had not been invented yet; but he recognized it from his dreams. He could feel the passage of time even when he couldn't see the position of the sun. "More than fifty centuries," he said, proud that he could now grasp those numbers.

"You've been alive for five thousand years?" Sally asked incredulously.

"I have," he said. "I shall always be alive."

Sally was stunned by the idea. Could she live that

long too? Was that what Marc was really doing when
he made himself look young? Was that what Joey
could do when he cleaned the toxins out of their
bodies?

The Ice Ages seem to be in full swing, said Sally's
Secret Mind, as if it weren't surprised by the idea at
all. *How did your people fare?*

"They survived," he said grimly. "When I changed
them, I used my Enemy's people as my models. And
then the Endless Winter came, pushing us all from
our homes after our prey animals. They ran through
the frozen world, away from the comfort of the old
caves. We had to follow them, or die."

Did you make your people smarter?

"I . . . changed them. I do not know yet if they—if
I am smarter."

Not even after five thousand years?

Sally watched him rub his doeskin clothing. She
heard the rustling of the long grasses that he had used
to line it, to insulate himself from the cold; but she
realized this was a formality. He could have gone
naked in the snow and not suffered. He did not age,
he did not grow sick. He could feed himself on air
and ice if he desired. He knew himself, and others, on
the smallest, most basic levels possible.

Like Joey, thought Sally.

But King Monkey wasn't exactly like Joey, or like
Sally either. Sally could still feel a difference in him,
one that wasn't apparent from the outside. It was his
mind that was still different. He still knew things with
his *gut* more than his mind. He still could not quite
grasp the concept of his own mental space.

But he *did* know that there was something he didn't
know. Something important.

"After five thousand years," he said grimly, "I have
learned many things. But I cannot become better than
the best there is. I cannot dream anything greater."

I know just how you feel, said Sally's Secret Mind, surprising her.

"Do you?" said King Monkey.

I have the same problem. It's hard to improve when you can't imagine what form the improvement should take. But you have time, don't you? You can wait and see how things develop.

"I have always waited," he said, then began to walk. Sally became aware of a band of hunters far behind him. He was their scout; they would wonder what was wrong if they saw him standing still, talking to the wind.

Sally wanted to look at them, to see what men had been like in that long-ago time. But King Monkey was too strong an image; he eclipsed everything else. She found that she was caught up in his story again.

He was no longer a king. He did not want to be.

Are you very lonely? asked Sally's Secret Mind.

"Sometimes," he admitted. "My mother and father are long dead. My brothers and sisters too, and all who knew me as their kin. My wife could not . . ."

What? What happened to your wife?

"She wanted to be with our son, in Paradise."

Oh. Then your son— I'm sorry.

He gritted his teeth. Steam came from between them and drifted on the breeze. Tears rolled down his cheeks. He wiped them before they could freeze.

"I found him next to me when I awoke, the morning after I first heard your voice. Every one of his bones was broken, every one of his organs was torn open. His tiny face was twisted with suffering. My Enemy spoke to me then. He said, 'I will kill every child you make. Do not make more!'"

Sally cringed. It was too much like what Kronos had done. It was too much like what The Three were planning to do to her and the others. Was this the way it always was with Kronos Kids? Did they always inspire such jealousy from their Enemies?

What would happen to Sally's children, if she ever had them?

King Monkey had fallen silent. He was remembering the horror, the rage that had followed the discovery of his murdered child. He had screamed his grief, he had torn at his body and hair. He had cried an ocean of tears.

Only his wife had been able to make him stop. She had been so silent, her spirit crushed. She had touched the body tenderly; she had kissed it before she placed it in its grave and put flowers inside to keep it company.

Then she had simply sat in the shadows, staring.

So he had stopped his rages. He had tended to his wife as well as he could for the rest of her life. She had lived long; she had outlived everyone who knew them. And that was long, for King Monkey had loved his kin. But they had all longed for Paradise, in the end.

She had longed for it too. So he had sent her there.

How do you know there's a Paradise? asked Sally's Secret Mind.

"I don't," he said. "But she did."

And you haven't had any more children?

"I will not," he swore, "until he is finally dead."

Have you come any closer to killing him in all this time?

Sally held her breath. That question upset him. But she was glad her Secret Mind had asked it, because she was wondering the same thing herself and she would not have had the courage to ask.

King Monkey kept plodding forward. He was great among men; Sally could have seen that even if she hadn't been able to see so deeply into his heart. He had known it so long, he no longer cared if others knew it.

Yet she could see that he had never seen his Enemy face-to-face, he had never fought him as a man should.

The Enemy was always one step ahead of him, always just out of sight. He never struck directly, never came face-to-face.

"But I'm getting closer," he said. "Once, I almost grasped his hand. I brushed his fingertips before he could snatch them away. One day, I will grasp that hand in mine, and we will end our long war. This is why I still live."

Sally's Secret Mind was silent for a long time. Sally could think of nothing to say herself. She admired King Monkey's struggle to become better than he was. She thought about his Enemy, and was frightened. His Enemy must be as terrible as hers were. If only he could give her a clue about how to triumph over them! But he didn't know how. He was just as helpless as she was.

He knew she was still with him; he could feel her presence. He thought of her as a companion, as someone who understood. Sally wished she could offer him more than that.

Suddenly he stopped. He was looking at something behind Sally. She turned and saw an old woman squatting in the snow. But this was no ordinary woman. Sally saw her through King Monkey's eyes. She was one of his goddesses, and she could see Sally.

Mother Goddess, King Monkey was thinking.

Mother Goddess grinned with the same snaggle-teeth she had always possessed; but her face was thinner than it had been. Sally could see an older image of her in King Monkey's vaguest memories. The goddess no longer had the receding chin and protruding brows of his origins. Even she had changed to look like the Newcomers; though *he* had not changed her. She had changed *with* him.

"Ask the voice if she is female," said Mother Goddess.

I am, said Sally's Secret Mind.

"Ask her if she is a woman."

Not yet. I'm still a girl.

"Ask her if she loves you," said Mother Goddess, grinning wider.

Sally was astonished, then embarrassed. King Monkey sensed her feelings, and smiled. He was pleased. He thought she was reacting just like a young girl should.

I do, admitted Sally's Secret Mind. Sally felt wonder at the revelation. Did she love him? Her Secret Mind was wiser than her. It must have felt that he was more worthy of love than Marc.

Sally peered at King Monkey as if she were seeing him for the first time. Shyness began to creep into their link with each other.

He kept walking, right past Mother Goddess, who reached out and grabbed his leg before he could leave her behind. He stopped, a little frightened by the expression on her wizened face.

"What is it, Mother?" he asked respectfully.

"Ask her when you shall be together with her," she said.

In about thirty thousand years, said Sally's Secret Mind.

Mother Goddess laughed silently. When she could catch her breath again, she said, "Now you have something else to live for."

And then she disappeared.

Sally gaped at the place she had been.

"What does she mean?" King Monkey was asking her.

"I don't know!" Sally said. "Was she really a goddess? How come she knew so much about us?"

But he didn't answer her. He couldn't hear her anymore. He was looking for her, questing with his senses. As far as he knew, she had disappeared along with the goddess.

"Where are you?" he was crying.

Sally could still feel him, a little; just enough to know that he missed her. Almost as much as he still missed his wife. He had been with other women since her death, but he would not give them children. A man could not make a marriage unless he could make children.

Sally wanted to blush when she realized what else he was thinking. He thought that when they met in the future, they could have children together.

"I will kill the Enemy first!" he promised. "Thirty thousand years should be long enough to do that!"

"Ha ha haaa!" Sally heard Mother Goddess screaming from nowhere. "When you kill him, you might as well kill yourself too!"

King Monkey spun around, but he couldn't find her. Not her or Sally.

"What do you mean?" he shrieked, not caring if the other hunters heard him; after all, their own gods spoke to them in the same manner. "What do you mean by that?"

He stopped and listened for her answer. He was looking across the frozen steppes, right through Sally.

But there was nothing. No one.

"I'm here!" Sally cried.

We're waking up, said her Secret Mind.

"But I didn't learn anything. I'm still not ready to go through the Gate."

We have to face it. We have to do our best.

"But why did we dream about King Monkey?"

We won't understand until later, admitted her Secret Mind.

"Later is too late! I need to know now!" Sally could feel her legs moving. King Monkey was getting smaller, turning into a black dot in the distance. The cold was gone; heat was beating against her body. She was taking a step.

"I need to know now!" she said, but he couldn't hear.

She took another step.

Sally had finished taking the third step when she woke up and bumped into Caitlin. For once, the red-haired girl didn't react. She was too enthralled, too frightened.

They were standing in front of the door to the Indian School.

It was heavily barred and chained; but that was nothing significant. Sally wished the chains could have had magical powers to keep them out. She wished they could have been made out of the same substance as the Gate itself, something that The Three would take seriously.

But they were ordinary metal. The chains fell away, and the door swung wide.

For a moment, Sally pictured that scene in *The Wizard of Oz,* when Judy Garland and her companions had walked down the Great Hall to their audience with the Wizard. That hall had been grand and spooky.

This hall was dismal. It was a humble thing with worn floors and peeling paint. Yet it was a thousand times more dreadful than that Great Hall of Oz had been.

The children stepped inside, Sally and Caitlin leading the way. It wasn't that the girls were any braver than the boys; it was just that they were more powerful, and Ted wanted his heavy hitters up front. Their heels clicked on the tiles and echoed off the walls on either side of them. Sally could hear other sounds too, whispers.

The sounds of miserable ghosts.

The Indian students had been unhappy most of the time at this school. There were traces here and there of joy, of unexpected pleasure in things learned, in the sight of the face of a special teacher or friend; but most of it was bad. Sally tried to sort Marie Little Bird out from the crowd; but there had been so many Marie Little Birds. Girls who knew that if they were going to keep happiness, they would have to keep it secret, let it grow privately until they could escape from enemies who would crush it if it didn't reflect the values of the Master Race.

Why is the Gate here?

Because this was hell, that's why. This was the Underworld.

Then why is the door to Olympus here? Sally wondered, her thoughts like molasses under the weight of the Thrall. *Where are we really going?*

And then another thought: *Where is the* Wall?

The Wall had been so pervasive before. It had seemed to be everywhere at once. But now Sally wasn't getting any sense of the Wall at all, as if it had ceased to exist, as if the Gate were some black hole that warped space far out of its shape. What had been solid was now empty, canceled, unreliable—irrelevant.

They walked down the corridor, occasionally peeking in through doors that swung open under Marc's power. They would peer inside, fearfully, at dusty desks, books, and chalkboards, then move on.

Where is it? the Mastermind kept asking Sally.

In here somewhere, was all she could say.

The Mastermind tried to goad and prod her; but she was oblivious to threats now. Something was pulsing at the edge of her consciousness, something so great and terrible that it withered other considerations.

The hall came to an end and turned left. They turned with it. At the far end they could see a battered bulletin board. An old poster for *Godspell* was still tacked to it. Sally couldn't take her eyes off it.

She was the one in the lead now. Even Caitlin had dropped back.

It's there, said Sally's Secret Mind.

Where?

At the end of the hall and to the right.

Sally moved; and as she moved, she passed through layers of time and memory.

Students were punished if they spoke any language but English.

Students were beaten if they were suspected to have been following their own traditional beliefs.

Students knew better than to say aloud that they were proud to be Indians.

Students fell in love with each other. They married and had children. They promised each other that they wouldn't make their children go to the Indian School. Over the years, the flow of students trickled to nothing, then died.

The end came in the seventies. Only five students attended the viewing of *Godspell*. They liked the movie very much.

Sally stopped at the end of the hall and turned her head to the right. She looked at the door to the girl's bathroom.

In there? demanded the Mastermind.

Yes, said Sally.

Go!

Sally put her hand on the door. It felt hot under her skin. She shoved it inward. It went without a sound.

Inside: old, rusty plumbing, a row of stalls, the faint smell of ammonia, and the sound of a slow drip.

Sally turned her body and stepped through the door. She felt the others behind her, like a crowd of frightened children in a haunted house, hiding behind the brave soul up front. But Sally wasn't brave. It was her doom that compelled her—her *weird,* that Norse word that meant so much more than *fate.* It was hers; it was waiting.

It was *there,* just around the corner in one of the stalls.

Sally walked past a long row of sinks. The rust stains in them looked like old blood.

The next-to-the-last stall had light leaking around it. Sally didn't even take a deep breath as she pushed it open. She didn't have the room in her chest. The door swung open, then disappeared into the raging maw beyond it.

The Gate flowed out of the stall. It devoured the other stalls, the bathroom, the school, until Sally wondered if the school had ever existed at all or if the Gate had invented it, built it like a shell around itself. It hummed inside her skull, it tingled against her skin. The glyphs around its edges danced for a moment as they always had, then accelerated and blurred.

For another moment, the electrical matter on the door leaped and snapped; then it was gone. The Gate opened. Sally tried to peer through it. On the other side a vast gulf was waiting. Sally couldn't see anything in it at all, no features, no landscapes. It just looked like nothing.

You first, said the Mastermind, and it gave Sally a push. She tottered at the threshold, then fell through.

She landed on her feet, on the other side. A bright light was in her eyes, and something hard was under her feet. She touched her body, expecting to find burns or some other sign of her passage through the Gate; but there was nothing wrong with her at all. She had felt nothing when she passed through.

She took a few stumbling steps and blinked until her eyes adjusted.

The stuff under her feet was asphalt. She raised her eyes and found the bus, with the Volvo parked nearby.

Uh-oh, she thought. But then she raised her eyes further, and saw the rest of the world.

Mountains raised impossible peaks on all sides of her. The sky was azure, and the majestic clouds that sailed across it were touched with golden light. Sally's heart expanded at the sight of them and her eyes filled with tears.

This is not our world, said Sally's Secret Mind. And then it did something odd. It put Sally under a Thrall. She went, willingly, because she could sense what was coming behind her.

The other children were coming through the Gate, The Three right behind them. Sally went dumb, letting herself turn into the automaton they expected her to be.

The children stumbled through, their faces blank and docile, like animals who had been stunned by an electrical charge. Marc was next, his expression not much different from theirs; and then Susanna. Ted was the last one through the Gate, which promptly disappeared afterward. He didn't even notice it had gone. He was looking around him, his eyes glazed. He nodded, once.

Yes, this place should be Olympus, said the Mastermind, its voice uncharacteristically subdued with awe and joy.

Right, Sally's Secret Mind warned her. *Now comes the hard part.*

It was time to be murdered.

Sally sat in her customary place on the bus. They had been driving for many hours, though it didn't feel like it had been that long. In fact, it only felt like minutes, when Sally really thought about it.

But it must have been hours, because they had started in that parking lot and driven down a road that looked brand-new, through the heart of those impossible mountains. Now they had almost reached the first summit; the clouds were floating by underneath them.

They had seen no one in all that time. The bus and the Volvo appeared to be alone.

Who built the road, then? Sally wondered vaguely, then worried that Marc might be listening to her thoughts. But he wasn't listening.

His mind was in Olympus.

Sally tried hard not to laugh. She wouldn't have been laughing at *him*, despite the trick she was planning to play. It would have been a nervous laugh. They were coming close to the place where they would be pushed over the edge, and Sally was waiting to activate the secret Mastermind. She was ready, but she couldn't help being nervous.

Nervous. Excited. Grieved and betrayed. Terrified.

Stop counting them up like a market list, she warned herself, and steadied her nerves. Soon she could go on automatic, and she wouldn't be so damned conscious of everything that had happened.

Not to mention everything that was *supposed* to have happened.

She remembered all the details. The sounds of their footfalls in the empty Indian School. The feeling of doom, as if some hungry beast were waiting for them in the girls' rest room. She remembered putting her hand on the door.

She remembered the stall where the Gate was waiting. How the light had crept around the edges.

And then?

The Gate had been there. She was sure of that. But

now its details were fading in her memory, and that was odd. It had been anticlimactic somehow. It hadn't been the big deal that it certainly should have been. And no one had been waiting for them on the other side. No challenge had been issued, no struggle had ensued. And now they were driving the bus and that silly Volvo again, through mountains that certainly seemed wondrous, certainly deserved to be explored. But were they the mountains of Olympus?

The Three thought so. Sally's Secret Mind was working hard to make sure of that. It had painted a picture of different events for The Three as they had passed through the Gate; it had tinted the whole event with wonder and triumph. They were still glowing with it. It had enthralled The Three with that wonderful memory that was so close to what they had hoped for. They were going deeper into it with every moment that they contemplated it and basked in it.

They thought they had succeeded, and now their wonderful future stretched out before them. But they had one little detail to take care of first. It was what they had always planned to do, as soon as the Gate was open.

They had to dispose of the children.

They had thought they would do it from the heights of Olympus, with godlike remote control. They had thought they could send the children over the edge of the Grand Canyon. But there wasn't any Grand Canyon here, though there were plenty of other, higher precipices to choose from.

And they weren't quite gods yet. Apparently that was going to take some work. No matter; they could already feel the atmosphere of the place working on them, building their powers to even greater heights. They would settle for driving these old vehicles one last time. This might even be better; they could savor one more act of murder while they were still human.

Surely when they became gods they would be above all that.

The bus was climbing. Sally's body enjoyed the feeling, as if she were on some sort of carnival ride. It was like the part of the roller coaster just before the drop. Sally had always liked the *up* part better than the *down* part.

As they were going around one of the curves, Sally caught a glimpse of the Volvo behind them. She saw Ted and Susanna in the front seat. Their faces were bland, quite normal in appearance, but she knew they were as enthralled as Marc.

Where are we, really? she allowed herself to wonder. She had thought they would encounter something. Some*one*. Why had she thought so? And why did she *still* think so?

The road, maybe. But the road seemed a little too convenient, like it had appeared simply because they needed it.

The bus lurched to a stop.

Sally grabbed the armrest, her heart pounding. *So soon? It's going to happen* now?

Be ready, warned her Secret Mind.

Sally forced herself back in her seat. Marc was putting the engine in idle and setting the brake. He got up. She waited for him to turn and look at her. But he didn't even pause. He didn't look at *any* of the Kids as he climbed off the bus. He left the door open.

He didn't even say good-bye.

Sally took the deep breaths she would be needing for the next step. Or they were supposed to be deep breaths. They sounded more like sobs. Tears streamed down her face and mingled with the sweat of her terror.

She wouldn't be able to start until after they had gone over the cliff. There would be a moment of free fall.

Sally took a brief inventory of the Kids. They were dazed, but no longer under the Thrall. The Three didn't know that, and Sally didn't want to blow it at the last moment. She would have to work fast, once the fall started. She would have to be steady and sure.

Ted and Susanna climbed out of their Volvo. Marc went to stand beside them at the edge of the cliff. They all wanted to get a good view. The ground was far below, and obscured by clouds; but Marc could enhance their sight with his powers. Seeing every moment of the show wouldn't be a problem at all.

Sally looked into their minds. She saw what they expected to happen. She carefully recorded every image, every nuance of feeling.

Ready? asked her Secret Mind. *Here he goes ...*

The brake came undone with a clunk. Sally watched the gear shift into drive. The bus rolled slightly, but Marc had to give the gas pedal a mental shove before it would really go over.

She felt his anguish.

With a flourish, he sent the bus over the cliff.

"At least they won't smoke anymore," he told Ted and Susanna.

Sally felt a moment of weightlessness, and then gravity gripped the bus in its merciless hands. Terror blossomed in the minds of the Kronos Kids. Sally allowed the emotion to be conveyed back to The Three, who observed it with satisfaction. Then Sally activated her Mastermind. She triggered an illusion and sent it back along the link.

The bus punched through the clouds. They were already halfway to the ground.

Now!

Sally activated her telekinetic talents, used Timothy to fine-tune the effort. The descent of the bus slowed, finally leveled out into a swoop. And then ...

We're flying! Sally thought with delight. But the

feeling was a shadow of what it should be; she was still too busy with the illusion that was playing itself out in real time.

The Three were seeing what they fully expected to see, a busload of children screaming down to the ground, smashing, bodies being torn and broken, minds instantly being snuffed out.

A moment of silence. And then the explosion.

Sally would have thought The Three would walk away at that point; after all, they had places to go, gods to become. But they stayed and watched the bodies burn.

Sally ruthlessly smothered her own pain as she saw the pleasure/pain Marc took in her death, the fascination he felt at watching the fire consume the Kids. He had loved them. He was wallowing in the grief. Why? She had never understood it. Soon it would reach some critical point, and he would extinguish all emotion—there. He had done it. Now there was *nothing*.

The *nothing* he had felt for Lydia. The *nothing* he now felt for Sally.

We're not your kids anymore, Sally thought with sadness and relief.

The Three turned and got into the Volvo. Marc sat up front with Susanna, who was already looking younger. The two of them held hands as Marc drove back down the canyon.

The bus continued to burn. The Three hadn't noticed that the fire wasn't dying down, wasn't running out of fuel. They had become bored, once the bodies had been reduced to ashes, and so they had left.

The illusion of the burning bus was so powerful and so well constructed that anyone who passed the site would continue to see it for another week. Sally wasn't concerned about that yet. After all, who was there to see? She just wanted to get away from The Three, finally and forever.

But she couldn't resist one more peek into Marc's mind. He was basking in the warmth of the Mastermind, which had finally achieved Olympus.

A tiny voice inside his head asked him, *When did you achieve that? Where is Olympus? Is this really it?*

He tried to pursue the question, only to find himself tangled in the convolutions of his own desires, skillfully enhanced by Sally's Secret Mind, who knew him better than he could ever dream of knowing himself. He found himself back at the certainty that the task had been done, the journey completed.

He would be convinced of this for many more days.

Sally felt the miles stretching between them.

The bus was invisible to human eyes now. It was flying into the deep places between the mountains. Sally was looking for a cave that would be big enough to hide the bus, a cave they could all live in for a while.

We're free, she kept telling herself. But she kept a mental eye on The Three, watching them go farther and farther away.

Sally looked at the spectacular view through her window. It was even more beautiful when you looked at it through a Mastermind. The Three didn't know what real grandeur was.

There was a cavern up ahead. It had been closed for millennia by rockfalls and erosion. Sally used her own abilities to vaporize the rocks that blocked the entrance, then weaved an illusion around it to make it look like it had before. No one would see the cavern unless they walked right into it, which wasn't very likely.

Unless they're drunk, Sally thought, and laughed feebly. She felt a little drunk herself. No, tired. Wrung out.

The Three were farther away now.

Sally wouldn't feel safe until they were out of range.

And even then, she would worry about when they might come back. But for now, she had time. She could work on this new Mastermind, build the skills of the Kronos Kids until they could face The Three on equal ground. In time, they would have a fighting chance.

The bus flew toward the mouth of the cavern. Sally watched with fascination as they appeared to fly through solid rock.

Inside was a place that human eyes had never seen. Golden light spilled through the entrance. The illusion didn't extend to the inside.

Sally set the bus down in the most level place she could find. She sat for a long moment in the silence, waiting. The Three were about to pass out of range. She watched them dwindle.

Going, going . . . gone.

Gone. And now Sally was alone with the other Kids.

They were still dazed. She let them stay that way. She wasn't ready to answer questions yet. She wasn't ready to make suggestions about the future.

She wasn't ready to fight with Caitlin about who was going to be the boss.

So Sally put the other Kids to sleep. They went, without protest. Even Caitlin slipped under like a lamb. She was as exhausted as Sally was. She was the only other Kid who had admitted the truth to herself.

At least, the truth about The Three. Whether or not Caitlin understood other truths was something that remained to be seen.

You should sleep too, said her Secret Mind. Sally agreed. She let the soothing chemicals creep into her bloodstream. She let it happen slowly, so she could savor the feeling.

Her Secret Mind could become one with her now. There was no reason to be separate and secret anymore. Sally was going to be more than she had been before, by the time she woke up. She sighed, and let her eyes droop shut.

Someone was coming down the aisle of the bus.

Sally heard the soft footfalls. *Caitlin?* she thought to herself, and reached out for the other girl.

Caitlin was asleep. It wasn't her.

Sally tried to pry her eyes open, but she couldn't. The soft footfalls came slowly down the aisle and stopped at Sally's seat. Sally could feel someone looking at her.

Someone touched her hand. The fingers felt small, delicate—like a child's hand.

"Lydia?" whispered Sally.

Sleep, someone answered.

And Sally did.

The sleep was peaceful; the waking, sudden but gentle. One moment Sally was drifting, and then she was opening her eyes to a golden light.

Something was odd. She took a moment to pinpoint it, then breathed a deep sigh of relief as she realized what it was.

For the first time in her life, she wasn't afraid.

Nervous, yes. Excited, happy, anxious, worried, curious—you name it. But not afraid. The Three were no longer in charge of her fate, her life. She was! Whatever happened from this moment on, it would be Sally who determined what she would do, what she would think, what she would be. For that reason alone, her plans had succeeded.

Outside the bus, the light shone on the rocks of the cavern, glittering in some places, pooling or glowing in others. There were stalactites, stalagmites, fabulous columns and formations. Sally looked out at them with pleasure, savoring her moment before the other children woke. There would be challenges ahead; but in the meantime, this place was a fairyland for her alone.

She felt a soft touch on her shoulder. She knew it was Joey before she turned to look at him. He had touched her through his link with her before he had touched her with his hand. He rested his chin on top of his arms, on the seat behind her, and gazed at her with great seriousness.

"You did it," he whispered.

Sally gazed back at him. His eyes were brown with hidden streaks of green. She had known that about him, but she had never had reason to look at him face-to-face this way before, not with this sort of concentration. Such an exchange would have been noted by The Three and deemed suspicious.

"Did you know?" she asked him.

"Did I know they were planning to kill us?"

"Yes."

He considered his answer for a long moment. Sally could have gone into his mind and traveled with him through the process of decision, but she didn't. It was *his* process. And she liked this exchange they were having, this intimate conversation between equals. She liked that he knew that she could pry, but that she wouldn't.

"In a way, I knew," he said. "I mean, they've always wanted to kill us, haven't they? We've all been keeping our heads down for a long time. Ever since . . ."

He might have said *ever since they killed Lydia and Marty,* but he didn't. Perhaps he couldn't speak their names without invoking Susanna's planted imperative.

"Do you remember our fall?" Sally asked.

"Over the cliff? Hell, yes. I was the one who was keeping everyone calm, remember?"

Now that he mentioned it, Sally did remember. The feelings she had been broadcasting to The Three had been an illusion after a certain point. She had used Joey's abilities to keep everyone on an even keel; and he had been the one to put everyone to sleep.

"I wouldn't have slept if I hadn't wanted to, you know," he said.

Sally didn't answer that. He was wrong, but she didn't want to sound like a bully. Besides, she liked Joey. He had hidden depths. Now she was going to get the chance to really get to know him, to find out what he really thought about things. She had a feeling that would be rewarding.

But for now, there were still scars to deal with, behaviors that had to be unlearned. Slow and careful going; unless she wanted to act like The Three and force it.

She could force it. She could seize the day and strike right at that very moment, changing every one of them to reflect her thoughts, her values, her goals; even Caitlin, who would struggle like an enraged dragon. Even she would be swept away if Sally struck *right now,* right when the iron was hot.

She looked into Joey's brown-green eyes and saw a trace of fear in their depths—fear of *her.*

"I'm not like *them,*" she said. "Your mind belongs to you."

He didn't answer. She couldn't tell if he believed her or not. He wasn't broadcasting any feelings at all through his link with her. He was being neutral, cautious.

Just as she would have been, in his place.

"Do you want to take a look outside?" she asked him.

He glanced out the window, at the mouth of their cavern. He seemed intrigued by the idea. Sally got up and tiptoed down the aisle, and he followed.

The others were still asleep. Sally hoped they would stay that way for a while.

Marc had left the door open. Sally felt a stab of dismay, which she quickly stifled. It was silly to grieve that he hadn't cared enough about their safety to close the door when he had then gone and pushed them off a cliff. In fact, it was almost funny.

She went down the steps of the van. She was about to put her foot on the floor of the cavern when she had a sudden thought: No human being had ever set foot on this ground before. It might as well have been the surface of the moon. Sally's footprints would be the first. She set one foot down, felt the soft dust moving under her shoe.

"That's one small step for a girl . . ." she said.

"One giant leap for girl-kind," said Joey, and giggled.

Sally shushed him and took another step.

"Don't be such a scaredy-cat," Joey whispered. "I want to make footprints too."

So Sally got out of his way and walked across the cavern to its mouth. She stepped into the light that was pooled there. It felt good. For once, she wasn't scared that it would burn her. Joey came to stand beside her, and his brown skin seemed to drink the light up until he was glowing with it.

"No UV," he said.

"Huh?"

"No UV rays. Ultraviolet radiation, causes cancer and premature aging. I usually have to filter them out for everybody, but there aren't any in this light."

"Why wouldn't there be any UV?"

He shrugged.

"Isn't it the same sun we've always had?"

"Beats me. This is Olympus, remember?"

Sally let herself really feel the sunlight now, feel it with her talent instead of just her skin. It seemed to be doing everything that normal sunlight did. She stepped out under the naked sky to look at the sun. Joey looked too, automatically protecting their eyes from the intense light.

Sally magnified the sun in her mind's eye, studying the surface. What she saw was awe-inspiring, the workings of a titanic nuclear furnace. She could have gazed at it for hours, completely enthralled; but that wouldn't have done any good. She couldn't figure out why no UV rays were reaching them. She didn't know enough about suns.

She turned away. Joey looked for a moment longer, his irises replaced by twin balls of fire. Then he looked away too.

"It feels good, anyway," he said.

The two of them surveyed their new world. The Three had dumped them off a mountain range that stood at the edge of a wide plain. In the distance, they could see many other mountain ranges. The plain itself was grassy and full of wildflowers.

"Nice," said Sally.

"Where are the roads?" asked Joey.

Sally hadn't remembered seeing any roads down on the plain the day before; but then, she had been plummeting straight toward the ground at the time—certainly too preoccupied to notice.

She got an idea.

"Are you willing to try something new?" she asked Joey.

"What?" he said cautiously.

"Remember how I flew the bus yesterday?"

"Yes."

"Will you fly up with me to have a look at the place we were dropped off?"

He thought about it. He didn't seem scared by the idea. He looked intrigued.

"Sure," he said. "Let's go."

"I won't drop you," promised Sally.

"I know that. Come on!"

So Sally lifted them up, just as she had lifted the bus. She had a moment of nervousness at the beginning, as if she were flexing new muscles; but then it just seemed to come together, and off they went. As they flew up, their view got better and better. Sally couldn't decide whether to look at the rock formations on the mountain behind them or at the enormous plain with its wealth of flowers.

It took a while to get all the way up.

"Jeez, did we fall all this way?" Joey asked.

"Yes," said Sally. They went up through the clouds to where the air should have been thinner. But it wasn't. Joey told her so. Another interesting thing to file away for future examination.

Finally they were as high as the highest peak. "Do you see the road anywhere?" asked Sally.

"No."

"Didn't it wind through all these peaks?"

"Maybe it was over *there*," he guessed. So Sally flew them in that direction. No roads were to be found, even when they found the cliff from which they were both sure they had been thrown. And they had good reason to be sure. Because they found the fire.

"Down there," Joey said, though Sally had already spotted it. They descended again, and hovered a respectable distance from the scene of their own imaginary deaths.

The fire was exactly as it had been the day before when The Three had tired of looking at it and had driven away. The simulacrums of their burned bodies were still inside, still suspended in the moment before they would have disintegrated into piles of bone and ashes.

"If The Three see this . . ." Joey said.

Sally knew what he was getting at, but she was too awed by the sight to do anything just yet. The illusion was completely convincing. Only the knowledge of the passage of time would cause suspicion in anyone who saw it.

She thought about it for a long moment, then made some changes. In less than a second, the fire died and a cold ruin was left in its place. Sally let the simulacrums inside fall into their piles, let the wind blow the ashes about.

"Maybe we should find a better place to hide," said Joey. "Far, far away."

"If we don't know where they are, we might run right into them," said Sally. The ashes flew into her face and she blinked to keep them out of her eyes.

"You don't know where they are?" Joey asked doubtfully.

"I only know that they aren't *here*," said Sally. "I don't want to probe for them, because I don't want them to feel me doing it. We're dead, remember?"

"You think they really believe that?"

"They did when they left. I'm sure of that."

He frowned and hovered closer to the imaginary wreck. He seemed to be trying to convince himself that it would fool The Three.

"I think we'll be farthest away from them if we stay right here," said Sally. "They're going to be roaming the world in search of their ... happiness, I guess."

"And when they don't find it, maybe they'll wonder why," said Joey grimly. "Maybe they'll start to suspect they were tricked."

"You're right," Sally admitted. "I guess we'll have to be ready to be attacked. But on the other hand, maybe they *will* find their happiness."

"And live happily ever after. . . ." Joey snorted.

"It's a slim hope." Sally wondered if she should even bother with the illusion of the ruin. If The Three suspected something was up, it might not buy the kids more than a few moments of time.

But maybe those few moments would be crucial.

"And in the meantime," said Joey, "where are the roads? Did The Three get rid of them?"

"I don't know," said Sally. She pictured the Volvo driving away, the road rolling up behind it. That was a strange notion, but why not? The Three wouldn't need the roads when they were gods.

We don't need the roads either, she thought to herself. She could fly, and she could tell that Joey was learning the trick from her. Soon he wouldn't need her help at all.

Suddenly he gasped. "They're waking up," he said, meaning the other children.

"We'd better hurry," said Sally, and the two of them flew through the air as fast as birds. The false ruin was quickly left behind. Sally decided to leave it there, for the time being.

Sally glanced at Joey when they were almost back at the cave and saw a look of pure joy on his face. He had always wanted to be like Superman, and now he was flying. She was glad that something good had happened for him already, just one day after gaining freedom.

They landed softly outside the cavern. It still appeared to be blocked by solid rock from the outside. A moment later, Ralph and Timothy passed right through the barrier, startling Sally—even though she knew there was really nothing there.

Ralph was even paler-skinned than Sally, if that was possible, but he looked like a hungry flower drinking up the sunshine. By contrast Timothy looked like a living shadow.

Caitlin came out a moment later, adding fire to the scene.

"Where's Jim?" asked Joey, a note of anxiety in his voice.

"Still sleeping," said Caitlin groggily.

Joey hurried in to wake his brother. He had ridden across the aisle from Jim for most of their lives; he wanted him here now. Sally wondered about his urgency, then saw the look on Caitlin's face as she blinked in the sunlight.

The confrontation was coming, and Joey knew it.

Don't let her shake you, she told herself, thoroughly shielding her thoughts. Caitlin was heavily shielded too, which was part of what warned Sally that Caitlin was up to something.

"I'm hungry," said Ralph.

Sally almost jumped out of her shoes at the sound of his voice. She couldn't remember ever having heard him speak before.

"Are you all right?" she asked him shyly. She had never spoken to him directly. He had always been too absorbed in his music and she . . .

She had been too busy trying to keep them all from being murdered.

"I'm all right," he said. "Just hungry."

"We'll figure something out," she promised. "For now, we'll probably just have to ask Joey to supplement for us."

"I don't want Joey to supplement for me," said Caitlin. "I want something real to eat."

Her tone had been perfectly normal, but there was a subtle underside to it, an implication that Sally's idea had been stupid and inadequate.

"By all means," said Sally. "Get something real to eat."

Caitlin didn't reply. She acted as if Sally hadn't even spoken. She surveyed the new world like a general plotting a battle.

"Is this Olympus?" Timothy asked. His voice sounded deeper than usual, almost as deep as a man's; but he looked like a bewildered child. He was staying close to Ralph, as usual, the two of them trying to support each other.

We're frightening them, Sally thought sadly. *Caitlin and I. At least with The Three they knew what to expect.*

"It's a pathetic copy of Olympus," Caitlin said before Sally could answer him.

"I don't think it's pathetic," Ralph offered. "It reminds me of . . ."

A Vaughan Williams symphony began to play in his head. Number Three, the Pastoral Symphony, second movement. Tears came to Sally's eyes. The music captured the place perfectly.

Joey came outside with Jim. Sally tried to catch Joey's eye, but he was unwilling to meet her gaze. Jim looked calm and unflappable; in fact he was just a little *too* unconcerned about his surroundings and the events that had brought him there.

"Don't be afraid of me," Sally said suddenly.

"I'm not afraid of you," said Caitlin, with chilling nonchalance.

"I'm not talking to you," said Sally. She turned back to the others and gently but firmly demanded their attention. "I'm not like *them*," she said, then projected an image of The Three to them all, including Caitlin, imbuing it with her own sense of horror and evil. For a moment, they were all as they had been before, helpless prisoners. Then she let them see the present again, let them feel their freedom.

"This is the way things are *now*," she said. "Compared to the way things used to be, our problems are a lot smaller now. We don't really have to worry about food, shelter, or water—we can get those things with our own talents, without *making* anyone else do it for us. Heck—in time, we may not even need the same things we used to! We can take the time to find out what we can really do, what we can really be! Without worrying that we'll be killed for it."

They were excited by that idea. Even Caitlin was. They were looking at the world around them and thinking that maybe it was an adventure. Maybe it was heaven.

Maybe it really was Olympus, where the gods dwell.

"What about The Three?" asked Caitlin.

"They could come back," admitted Sally. "They might try to kill us."

"What would stop them?" demanded Caitlin.

"We're not helpless anymore. We're not the same people we were before they let us go."

"Really?" Caitlin said skeptically. "How are we different?"

"Joey can fly now," said Sally. "Joey, show them!"

He didn't need to be prompted twice. He lifted himself up into the air and stayed there, enjoying himself despite his anxieties.

Caitlin didn't even look at him. "So?" she said.

"The Three can't do that."

"It wouldn't take them more than a second to figure it out."

"But they *haven't* figured it out," Sally said. "That's the point. They haven't even imagined it! They're so arrogant, so sure that they know the exact dimensions of reality, they can't believe that there are any avenues they haven't explored. But we *know* there are plenty we haven't explored yet. We can let ourselves find out what's possible."

"In that case," Ralph's quiet voice broke in, "there isn't *anything* we couldn't do. The possibilities are endless. We're only limited by time and space, if that." He was excited about the idea, but he wasn't thinking about battling The Three. He was thinking about his music.

Caitlin was the one who was thinking about battle. "They're older than us," she said. "They have more experience."

"Yes," admitted Sally.

Caitlin glared at her. The pretense of unruffled calm was dropped, and her true personality revealed itself. "Why didn't you kill them when you had the chance?" she asked.

"I couldn't," said Sally, surprised by the question.

"Liar!"

"I'm not! If I had tried to kill them, they would have killed some of us instead!"

"You could have done it," said Caitlin, mercilessly driving the dagger home. "You might have had to sacrifice a few of us, but you could have done it, and then the rest of us would have been *really* free. We would have had a chance! But no, you had to be the big bleeding heart, you had to save your *boyfriend* because you're hoping one day he won't care what a plain-Jane you are and he'll fall in love with you."

Sally went cold inside. The others were listening to Caitlin now. Apparently, Sally's crush on Marc hadn't been so secret after all. But she stuck to her guns.

"I didn't want any of you to die," she said. "I knew we could get stronger if we could get away from them for at least a little while. That was the best plan."

Caitlin snorted. "And now you're going to use your big bad powers to save us all."

"I hope so," said Sally, feeling ridiculous as she said it. But she knew that Caitlin was on the rag now, and she wasn't going to stop until she had vented her spleen. She was going to stand there in the fresh air and the golden sunlight, with lovely wildflowers waving on all sides of them and titanic mountains looking down on them, and claim that none of this was good enough for her.

"If you weren't so *stupid*," snarled Caitlin, "you would have figured out a way to keep us from being shoved off a cliff in the first place. But *no,* you had to be the *boss.* You had to do things the *hard* way. If you had bothered to *ask* anyone's opinion, we wouldn't be here, we would be—"

"WE WOULD BE DEAD!" Sally used her abilities to both amplify her voice well beyond any range Caitlin could hope to reach and to project an instant, brutal jab of certainty in everyone's mind of the power and cruelty of The Three. "I AM THE ONLY ONE

WHO WAS ABLE TO BREAK OUT OF THE
THRALL. YOU COULDN'T DO IT! SO DON'T
WASTE ANY MORE OF MY TIME WITH YOUR
BULLSHIT BITCHING, BECAUSE I'M NOT
GOING TO TAKE IT FROM YOU! YOU AREN'T
THE FUCKING THREE, CAITLIN!"

"No," Caitlin said, utterly calm and innocent again.
"That's your job."

Sally was stunned. The others had moved back, out
of the painful range of Sally's punishing voice. Joey
was perched on some nearby rocks, like a bird ready
to take flight. He was ready for the two girls to fight,
to hurt everyone else in the process. And worse; now
he was leaning toward Caitlin's side of the argument,
because Sally had lost control.

Damn! she thought. *I hate politics!*

"I am *not* going to force my will on you," Sally
insisted, "I'm *not*. I may yell when I get mad, but I'm
not going to hurt you. I promise!"

"You just lost your temper," Jim said, looking directly at Sally for the first time. "She goaded you. I
saw what she was trying to do."

Caitlin spun on him, but she was speechless. She
was too surprised and hurt to attack him in turn. He
had managed to sting her only Achilles' heel: her delusion that the boys all worshiped her because she was
so beautiful and desirable. He had punctured her bal-
loon in a way that Sally never could have managed.
Sally marveled at his perceptiveness, even as she worried how it would ultimately be used against *her*.

Don't be so paranoid, she warned herself. *You'll
turn into a Ted.*

"Let's make a bargain," she said. "Let's spend some
time to find out what sorts of things we can do and
worry about who's to blame for what later."

Caitlin didn't answer, but she didn't argue either.
Sally had a feeling the other girl would lick her

wounds in private and pretend that she wasn't hurt at all. She had apparently recovered from Jim's betrayal in record time, and now she looked perfectly calm and controlled.

Don't you believe it, Sally told herself. *You haven't seen the last of Caitlin's accusations.*

"I'd like to work on breakfast first," suggested Ralph, then looked disappointed as he realized he wasn't hungry anymore. "Oh. Never mind."

Now it was Joey's turn to be embarrassed. "Sorry. I already took care of it. I'm used to doing it."

Sally pressed her hand on her own belly. It was flat; she had never had an extra ounce of fat on it in her life, thanks to Joey. She wondered if it was just a little flatter now, perhaps even leaning toward the concave. She hadn't eaten real food since the day before, and now the day before seemed like years ago.

Yet she wasn't hungry at all.

"How do you do it?" she asked Joey. "Did you just tell our brains we weren't hungry anymore?"

"Of course not!" he said, looking a little offended by the idea. "I borrowed from the territory."

"You *borrowed*? What was there to borrow from?"

"The ground, the rocks, the plants, the sun ..."

Sally looked around her. The sun seemed no less bright; the flowers hadn't faded.

"Will you show me how?" she asked Joey.

He went a little blank at that. She was intruding into his territory. But then he said, "You taught me how to fly, so I'll teach you how to borrow."

"Teach us all," said Sally.

Now it was the other children who looked blank. Even Caitlin seemed skeptical that she could learn Joey's skill. "We all have different talents," she said. "We would already know how to do it if we could."

"Joey couldn't fly before," said Sally. She went to

Joey and took his hands in hers. "Okay," she said. "Show me how."

At first he just looked at her without expression. She realized that he never really thought about what he did. He just did it. Now he had to think about the process.

"Feel the stuff around you," he said.

She assumed he meant with her talent, the same one that told her what a roadrunner's genetic structure was. She reached out with that sense and was flooded with information.

"You don't need to know that much," said Joey. "Just look for nutrients. Just look for stuff you can use."

Sally tried. Now the picture was different. It was as if she had been looking at a multicolored scene and then all of the red and yellow had been taken out.

"This would be easier if you were hungry," said Joey, "but try to see what you need. Try some Vitamin C, that never hurts."

Some of the flowers were rich in Vitamin C. Sally touched them, but nothing happened.

"Gently," said Joey. "You don't want to kill the plant. If we're not careful, we'll blight the whole place, and then there won't be anything left to use."

Sally ate the Vitamin C. She was extremely careful about it, horrified by the notion of hurting their beautiful new home. Before she could withdraw, she felt someone else take some Vitamin C. It was Timothy.

After him, Ralph tried some.

Caitlin and Jim stayed off to one side, observing but not taking part.

Sally let go of Joey's hands. He looked pleased. She suspected that he was just as pleased that she wasn't his equal at borrowing as he was that he had successfully taught her the skill.

"Thank you," she said.

"You'll get better every time you do it," said Joey.

"You were right!" said Timothy, and Sally was startled by the passion in his voice. "Ralph! We really can do *anything*. Anything!" He turned to Sally and demanded, "Show me how to fly!"

Sally was perfectly willing to do so, but she was a little taken aback. Like Ralph, Timothy had always been preoccupied; in fact, he had been preoccupied *with* Ralph. Now he was a stranger. A handsome stranger who was almost a man.

"Sure," said Sally. She reached for him tentatively, but he was not so shy. He seized her in a mental grip that brought a blush right up her neck and into her cheeks. "Like this," she said, and rose into the air.

He copied her instantly. Nearby, she heard Joey gasp. Timothy had done in a second what it had taken him several minutes to learn.

"Like this, Ralph!" cried Timothy. "Time and space! Time and space!"

"Time and space," said Ralph softly, and he rose too. Vaughan Williams's Third Symphony began to play in his mind again, this time starting from the very beginning. It seemed to lift him with it.

And this time Jim and Caitlin did not sit out. They rose too. The six children drifted up, becoming one with the violins and oboes in Ralph's symphony, the musical sounds of wind and rustling grasses on the plain. They flew up and up, almost to the clouds. No one spoke. They let the music speak for them. They went where the currents blew them. And if Sally had a thought at all, it was to wonder that they could all be so close without being in the Mastermind. This was a wonderful thing that Ralph could do; a marvelous thing.

It was Caitlin who finally broke the spell.

"Why isn't it cold up here?" she asked.

Everyone paused in mid-swoop. Sally looked down.

They were miles above the surface now, with mountains and plains looking like checkers and dots. She surveyed the world from end to end; it curved out of sight. She saw no roads, no cities, no lights or any other sign of Human habitation. And the colors! So vivid, so unspoiled by smog or blight.

Like a wonderful dream. And why wasn't it cold? It felt warm, just like it had when their feet had been on the ground.

"Maybe we're compensating for the changes automatically," suggested Timothy.

"No," said Joey. "I know when I'm doing that, and I'm definitely not doing it now. It's not cold up here, and we can breathe normally. The air isn't any thinner. There should be almost no oxygen up here."

"This is Olympus," said Caitlin. "Remember? We could go to the moon if we wanted. We could go into outer space. Come on!"

She shot straight up at an alarming rate.

"Caitlin, stop!" cried Sally, and zoomed after her. "We can't be sure we'll be able to breathe up there! We have to be more careful! Take it slowly!"

But Caitlin ignored her, and pretty soon it looked like the girls were in a race to see who could break out of the upper atmosphere first—Caitlin because she wanted to beat Sally, Sally because she wanted to be there in case Caitlin needed help. The others followed close on their heels, and Sally could have screamed with frustration. *This is ridiculous! We're all rushing to our deaths because we're too stubborn to give up the argument! How The Three would laugh if they could see us now!*

But she needn't have worried about dying. It wasn't too long before the children all realized that they weren't going to break out of the upper atmosphere. Sally stopped, only to find that Caitlin had already stopped too (wanting to be first in that, as well).

Sally looked down. "Does it look any smaller to you down there?" she asked the others.

"Maybe a little," said Ralph. "Just the tiniest bit. But I have a feeling we could shoot straight up as long as we wanted and still not get much farther way."

"But why?" demanded Joey. "Is this place all in our heads?"

"We'll never fly out of here," said Jim. "Not any more than we could ever get out of our own skulls."

Sally looked at him. He sounded almost smug. But his expression was bemused.

"We *can* get out of our own skulls," Sally said. "We do it all the time."

"Do we? I'm not so sure."

The children formed a loose circle, facing each other.

"I'm real," Sally told them. "I'm sure of it. And I think *you're* real too. I can feel you, just like I felt you before we went through the gate."

"Only better," said Timothy. "We do everything better here."

"So what does it mean?" Joey seemed to be asking Sally, not anyone else. In fact, they all looked to her now. "You're the one who found the Olympus Gate. What was it, really?"

Sally tried to picture the Gate in her mind. What she ended up with was a pale imitation. It was almost as if it had never existed outside her imagination at all.

"You're thinking that it might have been an illusion?" she asked, "based on Ted's delusions? And now we're all inside some sort of . . . simulacrum of Olympus?"

"Why not?" said Jim, but Joey was shaking his head.

"The stuff here isn't fake," he said. "I can feel it. If we fell from this height, we would be smashed on the real ground."

"Do you think they could see us up here?" Caitlin asked suddenly, real dread behind her question. "The Three? Are they watching us from a distance?"

Everyone looked around. Sally and Joey quested with their talents as well. They found no other humans within their range of perception.

Sally noticed something else missing too; but she decided to keep it to herself for the moment. "Let's go back down," she said. "We've been through a lot today."

No one argued with her. They drifted back down to the ground. Sally looked at the world on the way down. It was no less wonderful than it had been before. In fact, in some ways it felt even *more* wonderful.

What's going on? she wondered, and for the first time since she had awakened, she missed her Secret Mind. Maybe they had melded too soon. She would have liked to confer with it, to ask its opinion. But her Secret Mind had been *her;* she should have all of its knowledge now. And since she *didn't* know the answers now, it couldn't have known them either.

Still it would have been nice to have someone to talk to, someone who was always on her side.

"What are we going to do with that old bus?" Timothy asked when their feet were on the ground again.

Sally shrugged. The question hadn't even occurred to her. "What would *you* like to do with it?" she asked him.

"Let's turn it into something comfortable. I don't want to sleep on seats anymore, and I sure as heck don't want to find out how comfortable the ground is, not even if I can make myself like it. I'd like to change the bus before I change *me,* if you know what I mean."

"Sure," said Sally. "I don't mind. Anyone else?"

"So now you're the president," said Caitlin, but she wandered back inside without making anything more of the argument. Timothy followed her, ready to begin his work. Ralph was close behind, still not ready to be on his own yet.

Jim gave Sally a lingering look that she couldn't interpret. Then he went inside too, leaving Joey outside with Sally.

"You felt it too?" asked Joey.

"You mean I *didn't* feel it," she said.

The two of them walked toward the plain, with its waving flowers and grass. But they didn't go far. They looked out at the beautiful, but *empty,* world.

"There are no animals here," said Joey. "No insects or birds."

"I thought I saw some birds earlier," said Sally.

"Me too, but I can't feel them now."

"They were flying over the distant peaks, and they must have been really big. Like giant eagles."

"So what do giant eagles eat?"

Sally frowned, trying to picture the distant birds in her mind once again. Now she couldn't remember if she had seen them today or the day before. The more she thought about it, the more the half-remembered birds seemed to evoke another memory, one that was even more nebulous.

They are such noble birds. They have no malice in their hearts, even as they kill. . . .

"Something about Lydia," said Sally.

"*What?*" Joey said, almost fearfully. The sound of Lydia's name distressed him.

"I know it's painful to remember her," said Sally. "But there's something important I've forgotten, and it's all tied up with her."

"She was murdered," said Joey, his voice shaking.

"I know," soothed Sally.

"I remember what they did to her. I just pretended to forget. Do you suppose they'll do it to us, once they found out we've fooled them?"

"No," said Sally, her voice hardening. "We're not helpless little children anymore. They'll get a nasty surprise if they try that on us now."

Joey swallowed several times, as if there were a lump he couldn't get rid of. Sally didn't try to probe him for his feelings, but she did tell him one last thing.

"You could kill them through your link with them, Joey."

"I don't have it anymore," he said.

"No, but you could make it again, in an instant. You know you could."

He nodded hesitantly.

"Wherever we are, it's better than where we used to be. Don't you agree?"

"Yes," said Joey. "But better than hell isn't necessarily heaven."

"No." Sally gazed at the beautiful plain, its waving grasses. "But maybe it could be."

"Be cautious," said Joey. "Don't hope for too much."

He could have elaborated on those remarks, but instead he turned and went inside to help the others. Sally resisted the urge to sneak into his thoughts and see what he really thought of her now. She had made that decision from the moment she had opened her eyes that morning. No more prying, no more forcing. Not if she really wanted heaven.

She was about to follow Joey inside when she noticed movement among the grasses, just a few feet away from her. It wasn't the movement of the wind. This was something that only a living thing could cause, the movement from the passage of a small body. Sally squatted down for a closer look.

A field mouse emerged and froze as it spotted her. For a few moments the only part of it that moved was its twitching nose, which was busily smelling the air.

It hadn't been there a moment before, Sally was

sure of it. She looked inside it, examined its cellular structure. It really was a field mouse, just like a hundred other field mice she had examined over the years. Its little heart was beating frantically at the sight of her. Her own heart was in a similar state.

She calmed the little creature. It stood up on its hind legs, now merely curious about her.

"Where did you come from?" she asked it. But its brain did not comprehend her. It was a mouse, living in its natural habitat. But alone? How would it survive?

And then Sally heard the sound. It was familiar, yet utterly surprising. It was the sound of a songbird. A moment later, another species of bird chimed in, making its own claim on the territory.

And of course, the insects must be on the way. And the predators.

Sally looked toward the distant peaks. The giant eagles were there again, gliding on the thermals.

Sally felt a blossom of joy beginning in her heart. But it was tempered by something else, something disturbing.

This filth, this dirt . . .

The air he had to breathe, the animals, the bugs . . .

Ted wouldn't like the changes that were occurring in his Olympus. He would notice them, and he would wonder why they were there, and then . . . *We'd damn well better be ready,* thought Sally. *We'd just damn well better be.*

She turned and went back into the cavern, where modifications of the bus were already under way.

In a short time, the cavern was as close to homey as it was going to get. They did what they could to make it more comfortable; for instance, they could regulate the air temperature with very little effort. That was Marc's old trick; he had done it inside the bus for years. Sally had learned it without even thinking about it, and it was easy to teach. Even Jim, who had shown no prior evidence of telekinetic powers, learned to do this as easily as he breathed.

Once Sally had scouted out the best places to do so, she made a few windows, angling them so the rain wouldn't come in. She was rather surprised to find out how easy it was for her to instantly disintegrate tons of rock.

Some people would have said that was a godlike power. It was certainly tempting to think along those lines. But then Sally would remember years of living like slaves under The Three, years of not having even the most rudimentary control over her own life.

"Remember, Kronos ate his children," Ralph said to her, making her realize that she still had an open link with him from her days of listening to his music. She hadn't realized that the link went both ways. She was also surprised that he would bring up such a gruesome subject; gentle Ralph, who cared only about music. But bring it up he did, and went on to make a point that she hadn't considered. "It must have been dreadful to be eaten," he said. "But clever Zeus out-smarted Kronos, and he freed his brothers and sisters; and then they all went to Mount Olympus to be gods, and Kronos was exiled to the fields of Elysium."

"Is that where we should exile The Three?" joked Sally. But Ralph took her seriously.

"Either that or kill them," he said. "Whatever we do with them, it will be very difficult."

The children explored their cavern. It was smaller than it appeared, its main chamber going back only a hundred feet or so. It had passages that led to other, smaller chambers, including one that had a phosphorus pool at the very bottom of it—one thousand feet down. There were passages that were too tiny and too clogged to explore physically. Sally's talent told her that some of them linked with tunnels that went all the way through the near mountain range. She made a note of them, thinking that someday it might be useful to clear them out and use them, much like the goblins had done in Tolkien's story about the Hobbits.

"That would be fun!" Timothy said. His enthusiasm had been growing by leaps and bounds ever since their adventure with flight. "We could build giant feasting halls just like the dwarves! And make *mithril* armor, and magic rings!"

Sally didn't try to bring him back down to earth, especially since he might have been right. She didn't want to say there was anything they *couldn't* do, not until they found out what they *could*. And anyway, it was fun to work on their new home, to dream about what could be done with it, even if those dreams seemed outrageous. Ralph had traded Vaughan Williams for Gustav Holst ever since they had gone back into the caverns, and was indulging them all in various performances of *The Planets,* especially the more mystical movements, which seemed to go perfectly with the fantastical mineral formations that glittered and sparkled on all sides of them.

Everyone had scouted out a particular place that they could call their own, and pieces of the bus were cannibalized and reshaped to make furnishings and partitions. The seats had been transformed into beds. They weren't terribly comfortable, as beds went; but then, the children had slept on them for years, anyway, so at least they were familiar.

One of Sally's first acts was to remove every speck of dust from the cavern floor. It had been fun to make footprints in it; but everyone got sick of that pretty fast. Joey didn't waste his talent stifling sneezes, especially when the matter could be taken care of by other means. After that, as it started to get dark outside, the conversation turned to supper. *Real* supper.

"Could we make food out of the stuff around here?" Ralph asked. "You know, cooked food that we could actually eat and taste?"

"We ought to be able to," said Joey. "It's just a matter of . . . learning how."

"Where are we going to find cows?" demanded Caitlin. "And fruit trees? I didn't see anything like that outside."

Sally hadn't seen them either, but she had a feeling the story might be different by the next morning. She had poked her head outside of the cavern a couple of times since she had seen the mouse, and it was getting noisier out there by the minute. Right now she couldn't sense any fruit or dairy animals, but she did find something useful.

"How about some kind of bread?" she asked.

"With butter and honey!" said Ralph.

"I'll try," said Sally, knowing perfectly well that she wouldn't be doing a very good job this first time. But with Joey's help, she did locate some wheat. She brought it to the cavern, where it hung in midair, awaiting its fate. "What else goes into bread?" she wondered.

"Sugar," said Joey. "Yeast. And salt—*that's* easy enough. And oil—oh, boy. That one is tougher."

They searched and searched for various ingredients, substituting whatever they could find for whatever they couldn't, guessing at the proportions. The floating glob got bulkier as the new ingredients arrived, but it never looked much more appetizing. *Maybe after it's cooked,* Sally hoped.

"Okay," she said bravely, "now we've got to blend them together and expose them to heat."

"You should be able to just make it instantly!" Caitlin said, irritated and disgusted by their incompetence. Sally didn't point out that Caitlin didn't seem able to make bread instantly herself.

"This is our first time," she said. "We'll get better at it."

"I sure hope so!"

And finally Sally and Joey produced something that vaguely resembled bread. It even tasted a little like bread, though it had an odd sweetness to it.

"No butter or honey?" asked Ralph sadly.

"The bees are still making the honey," said Sally. The bees had only just arrived on the scene, and they were busily making themselves at home. Joey shared a long look with her—he had become aware of what was happening outside almost as soon as she had.

"Now if only some apple trees would grow," he said. "We could have apple pie." That was Joey's favorite. Ralph, of course, preferred hot fudge sundaes, and that was probably going to take some time to figure out.

Sally was just glad they didn't have to do it the old-fashioned way. They wouldn't have lasted long under those circumstances. She couldn't imagine how human beings got along without talents. She was awed by their ingenuity.

Sally wondered how The Three were doing things. As long as she had known them, they had made other people do all of the practical things. Now they had no one but themselves to rely on.

Don't think about what they're doing, she warned herself. *You'll have nightmares tonight.*

Joey made up for the nutrients they were missing from the bread, and then Sally tried an experiment of her own. She concentrated on her hair and skin, on separating the oil, dirt, and bacteria from them. She had to learn to do it without stripping too much natural oil and moisture; but it turned out to be easy. It was even easier than controlling the air temperature.

She showed everyone else how to do it.

"Not as much fun as getting naked and lathering up," Jim said, looking Sally right in the eyes, "but it'll do for now."

He kept right on looking at Sally that way until she blushed, wondering why he would do so. She wasn't pretty, like Caitlin was. He had no reason to pay attention to her that way. Unless she was misunderstanding him. She could have probed him to find out if that was the case, but she was actually afraid to know the answer. If he was attracted to her, she was too shy, tenderhearted, and inexperienced to figure out what to do about it. And if he wasn't—well, that shouldn't be such a bad thing, but why did he have to look so much like Marc?

"Who's going to take the first watch?" asked Timothy. His earlier excitement had crystallized into a restless anxiety.

"I've set up a warning system," said Sally.

"What do you mean, *a warning system*? What's it made of?"

"Water molecules. It will detect any of The Three

if they physically pass through it. I know their brain patterns by heart." Sally was proud of this new system, which was only vaguely like the ones she used to set up when The Three had ruled their lives. Those early models were only designed to warn her if The Three came questing her way with their minds. This new system would tell her anything she wanted to know about *anything* that passed through it. Yet it was also the perfect camouflage. It looked and felt simply like water molecules. The Three wouldn't think twice about it.

"And what if they probe us?" demanded Timothy.

"We'll know that as soon as it happens," said Sally.

Timothy frowned. "I'd still feel better if someone was awake at all times."

"Okay. You want to take first watch?"

He nodded. "Ralph, you want to go second?"

Ralph didn't answer. He and Joey were standing partway out the door, looking at something. "Hey, Sally," Joey called. "Is this your warning system?"

She went to join them. The world outside was dark now, except for a glowing shroud of mist.

"That's it," said Sally, pleased to see her work manifested so plainly and beautifully. She had only thought up the trick a few hours before. Now she could feel every living thing moving in the mist for miles around them.

There seemed to be more living things out there every minute. But so far, no animals with the brain patterns of The Three had shown up.

Timothy peered out into the fog. "How close do they have to come before you can feel them?"

Sally estimated. "Thirty miles."

"And you'll wake up instantly?"

"Yes."

A muscle jumped in his jaw. "And we'll form a Mastermind, like the one we made yesterday?"

"Yes," said Sally, though she wondered what form this new Mastermind would take. The one she had made before was made with temporary Secret Minds in other children's brains. They had evidently been more aware of them than Sally had known, but that didn't mean they would form a new Mastermind as easily as they did the old one.

"Maybe we should form one right now, just to practice," said Sally.

"No!" said Caitlin emphatically. Everyone turned to look at her. She returned their stares measure for measure, her green eyes flashing dangerously.

"Why not?" asked Sally.

"No one is ever going to do that to me again," said Caitlin, her every word like iron. "I will *not* do it, not unless our lives are in danger."

"But our lives *are* in danger."

"I agree with Caitlin," Jim said suddenly. "I don't want to do it. It's like being forced."

Sally felt a cold hand closing around her heart. She hadn't anticipated this kind of resistance. She could force them, of course; but that was exactly what she was trying to avoid. The Three fell into their Mastermind instantly, without hesitation. Combined, they would be more than a match for any of the individual children.

Give it a rest, Joey sent to her—the first time since the crash that he had communicated that way. *They're not ready yet. Give them a little more space.*

I have no choice, she sent back.

None of this argument was soothing Timothy's nerves. "I won't be able to sleep tonight, anyway," he said. "I might as well stay awake."

"Do you want help getting sleepy?" asked Sally.

"No."

She let him alone. Things weren't going to be as easy as she had hoped they would. She couldn't have known how the other children would react to their new situation; she realized that now. She hadn't known them the way she thought she had. Perhaps she hadn't known them at all.

Sally turned away from the mist and went to her own "room." As she passed Jim, he said, "Sleep tight," in a tone about two octaves lower than his usual. Sally almost blushed again, but this time she controlled the reaction. She also had to resist the urge to turn around and look at him again when she felt his eyes on her back.

He's teasing me, she thought uneasily.

Caitlin was already in her own bed. She had closed herself off from the others completely. That, at least, was what Sally had expected. Sally lay down on her new bed and gave herself a little nudge into the sleepy zone.

Good night, Joey sent.

Good night, Sally sent back.

Ralph was getting into bed too. He felt safe knowing that Timothy was on guard. He knew that he would be aware of danger just as quickly as his brother would. He was playing quieter music to himself now, some of Rachmaninoff's suites for two pianos. Sally let herself drift away with the music.

The last thing she felt, before falling asleep, was Timothy, just outside the cavern with the mist pressing close to him, watching. Watching without his eyes.

Sally dreamed what felt like a true dream; at least, it did at first. She felt cool stones under her feet, saw beautiful designs in them. She smelled incense and scented oils. A cool breeze was coming in through an open terrace. She walked a few steps forward, trying to get a sense of where she was. Something clung to her legs and she looked down to see what it was. She gasped.

The something she had felt was fine linen. She was wearing a transparent Egyptian dress. She was naked underneath. But instead of the little buds she really had, there were fully developed breasts under her bodice, pushing her nipples tight against the material. She touched them wonderingly. They felt real.

They're nice, said someone just behind her. She felt his breath on her neck, but she couldn't make herself turn to see who he was. *Your hair is nice too.* She felt a tug on her hair. A hand came around from behind her, holding a strand of it. The hand was large and masculine; the hair he was holding was long and curly, with gold highlights in it. Not Sally's plain, mousy brown.

Isn't it pretty? said the voice. Someone pressed himself against her back and put his arm around her. From the way he felt, he must have been at least a head taller, and his arm was muscular. He was wearing armbands. He tickled her cheek with the strand of hair.

This is how you could look if you wanted to, he said. He licked her ear. Sally's body responded instantly. Her nipples hardened and she felt heat in her groin. But that wasn't what excited her the most. What excited her was that she realized he was right. She could change her body any way she wanted. She didn't have to be plain. She didn't even have to be a woman if she didn't want to!

The voice laughed. *Don't be hasty. I like you as a woman.* He stroked her nipples and kissed her neck. *Do you know what we're going to do?* he asked her.

Sally knew. She felt his erection pressing against the small of her back.

Let me see you, she begged.

He laughed again. He held her tight, so she couldn't turn. He lifted her and pulled her toward a low couch.

Sally wanted him. She enjoyed being handled that

way. She loved the kisses, the way his hands felt. She let him push her onto the couch, but when he tore her skirt away from behind, she struggled.

Not that way, she insisted.

I like it this way, he said, trying to pin her. But she kept struggling.

Not this way! I don't bend over for anyone! Not unless I want to!

The struggling only got him more excited. *This is fun,* he said. *I knew you'd be fun. . . .*

They were both sweating now, becoming slippery. Sally squirmed in his grasp until she was facing him. But she couldn't see him; her eyes must be closed. She opened them.

And he was gone. She was sprawled on the couch, alone.

Sally got up, breathing hard. *Where are you?* she demanded.

Maybe I'm in your own head, laughed the voice. *Maybe I'm your animus.*

But she felt his moist breath on her ear. She began to suspect who he was.

It doesn't have to be like this, she said. *Face me. Kiss me on the mouth, if you're such a great lover.*

I'm the best you'll ever have, he said. *I know more about the fine art of fucking than anyone in history.*

I'm sure you do, said Sally.

I'll make you sure. I'll have you the way I want you, you can bet on that. And you'll love it.

Then please me now. Kiss me on the mouth. Let me see your face.

There was no answer. Sally turned around, slowly. No one was there.

Why does it have to be this way? she asked him. But he was gone. She could feel his absence, even if only in the freedom of her own movements.

He was probably hoping she would be devastated

now that he was gone. Or at least frustrated. But Sally was still too happy about what he had revealed to her about her own capabilities. She could change herself any way she wanted. She had memorized the genetic patterns of millions of creatures over the years, just to amuse herself. She knew life inside out. She could shape herself any way she wanted. Or she could just look into her own biological clock and advance it a few years.

Or take it back. That was what Susanna and Marc had been doing for themselves all these years.

Sally went out on the terrace, into the night. As she expected, it was beautiful out there. It was like a Hollywood set of the Nile River, with Egyptian architecture all around, and barges and crocodiles. That should have tipped her off immediately. It was *too* Hollywood. Jim had a vivid imagination. Sally laughed aloud.

"Who's there?" said a man's voice, quite different from the one Jim had affected. Sally jumped at the sound of it.

Someone else was on the terrace. He was tall and thin; he had only an amber-colored cloth wrapped around his body, and his head was shaved. He looked like a priest. He came forward into the dim light, searching Sally's face intently. Suddenly he froze.

"You," he gasped. "It's you."

"Me?" said Sally, wondering if he recognized the real her or just the body she was in.

"My voice from the future," said the priest, his eyes shining with unshed tears.

Sally felt as if she had been struck by lightning. She looked at him; his face was not familiar. But she said, "King Monkey?"

He nodded. "Yes. I have changed. So many millennia have passed since you spoke to me last. How I have missed your voice."

"I'm sorry," Sally said. "I didn't know. For me it's been only a few days. . . ."

He came closer, yet seemed afraid to touch her. "How beautiful you are," he said.

Sally was ashamed to tell him it wasn't her. The tears were flowing freely down his face now.

"Are you really here?" he asked. "Has our time together begun?"

"No," said Sally, wishing she could tell him what he wanted to hear. "I'm dreaming again. I think we still have a few thousand years to go."

She felt his suffering at that revelation. Yet his face did not crumble, as Sally's certainly would have. He accepted the truth, stood up under it. He reached out to her with one hand and touched her shoulder. They both gasped when his hand did not go through her. She felt his touch. He felt her skin.

He came closer, put both of his hands on her shoulders.

"I can touch you," he said.

Sally was afraid to move. She was afraid she would spoil it. She kept perfectly still as he moved closer, leaned down. He was going to try to kiss her. She wanted that kiss more than anything, more than she had wanted Jim's kiss.

She studied his face as it came closer to hers, watching every nuance of expression. It was a strong face, softened with tenderness. It was the face of a genius, a general, a lover. His lips, when they touched hers, would be firm.

Sally kept her eyes open. She felt his mouth pressing against hers. She dared to press back. She felt like a bandit, cheating time and history.

When he was done kissing her, he didn't pull away. He pressed his forehead against hers. "I don't want to let you go," he said.

"My name is Sally." She raised a hand to his cheek. "What are you called now?"

"Osiris," he said.

"Osiris! Watch out for your brother, Set. He's up to no good!"

He laughed, and pulled her closer. "I know," he said. "I'm the one who invented that fable."

Suddenly she couldn't feel his hands anymore. She tried to get a better grip on him, but he was slipping away. He was still laughing. She could feel his breath on her face.

"I'll be back," she told him. "Never doubt it. I want to see you again!"

But he didn't hear. He was laughing, he was like a strip of movie footage, still playing out, no longer acting with *her*.

And then he was gone.

Sally was in her hard, makeshift bed again. She kept her eyes closed, hoping to recapture the dream. If she could be with Osiris every night, the rest of this would all seem worthwhile. She could face anything during the day if she could be with him at night.

But he was really gone. And Sally knew she wasn't going to be seeing him every night. Whatever force that was drawing them together was a whimsical one. She might never see him again.

Osiris. When she had last seen him, he had been a scout for a hunting party. He had not seemed to want to be king anymore. But eventually he had gone on to Egypt and become a god.

And how much time had passed between those intervals? Ten thousand years? Twenty thousand?

A *god*. Someone had already done what The Three wanted so desperately to do. But if he had succeeded, where was he now? Was he in Olympus, or in some Egyptian heaven? If he was still alive, surely he would have contacted her long before now. No, he must be dead. Long dead.

Sally sat up. She couldn't get Osiris back, but she could have a talk with Jim. She wasn't going to be a pawn in a game he was playing to amuse himself, that was for sure.

But when she felt for him, he was outside with Timothy. They were talking with each other about the things they wanted to do, now that they were free.

Ralph is going to start writing symphonies, Timothy was saying. *He's already started preliminary work on the first one. He's going to be the greatest composer the world has ever seen, and I want to help him any way I can.*

You could write your own symphonies now, Jim was saying. *You know enough about music.*

Sally could feel Timothy's smile. *I'd rather write sonatas. As soon as I can figure out how to make a piano, I'm going to—*

Sally stopped listening. They were talking with each other, not her. She lay back down and tried to remember what had happened in that first dream.

Maybe I'm in your own head. Maybe I'm your animus.

That was a disturbing thought. She could have sworn the man was Jim. That last thing she needed right now was to be ravished by her own imagination. Of course, if it really *was* Jim, that was equally disturbing. She could tell that he and Timothy had been conversing for a long time, probably during her dream. If he could slip into her mind and interact with someone else at the same time, he was far more sophisticated than she had realized. Sophisticated and manipulative.

You think you know everything! Caitlin's secret mind had spat at her once. *But you don't know anything!*

Maybe I don't, thought Sally. *But I'm learning.*

She rolled onto her side and went right back to sleep.

Seven hours later, Sally opened her eyes. Golden light was pouring into their cavern.

This is our second morning.

She had not dreamed that this time of the day would be so beautiful, or that she would love it so much. Had she ever noticed mornings before? Not that she could remember.

Sally sat up and stretched. Others were already stirring. They weren't under any kind of thrall now, so they would all obey their own circadian rhythms. Sally cleaned her face and teeth using the technique she had taught everyone the night before. It was actually quite refreshing; soon she wouldn't miss the old-fashioned way anymore. It had only been a matter of habit, that was all.

She walked through the doorway of her "room" and started out across the main chamber. Out of the corner of her eye, she saw someone moving in an intercept course. She glanced over and froze.

Marc was coming across the room.

Sally stopped herself before she could kill him. She held herself in a grip as tight as a vice. Something about him wasn't right. He froze as he sensed her impending attack, but he didn't lash out at her as he ought to have done.

He was too young. He couldn't be more than sixteen. And he was a little more muscular than the last time she had seen him.

"Jim?" choked Sally.

"Who do you think?" he said. He was trying to soothe her emotions just as Susanna would have done. Sally let him. She could have done it herself, but it gave her an opportunity to observe him through his link with her.

"What have you done to yourself?" she asked him, still not daring to move.

"I aged myself a little bit," he said. "Joey showed me how."

He came closer, moving very cautiously. Now that she had had time to observe him, she could see that he didn't look exactly like Marc. He was still himself. He had always been a little different around his mouth and jaw. But his eyes sure looked like Marc's. Sally was finding it a little difficult to meet them.

"About last night . . ." Sally said.

"Hmmn?" He was still soothing her. Other than that, he didn't react at all, as if he had no idea what she was talking about.

"The dream we had," Sally said boldly. But he still wasn't reacting. He wasn't hiding anything; he would have had an elevated pulse if he had been doing that. Or he ought to, anyway.

Sally scanned him.

"What are you looking for?" he said, with apparent innocence.

"I dreamed about you last night," said Sally. "Did you talk to me in my sleep?"

"No," he said, and meant it. But he could have meant that he had used another process to pull the trick off, and she simply hadn't described it properly. Yet he didn't seem to be hiding anything. He didn't seem to be lying.

"Why did you age yourself?" she asked him.

"Why not? If we looked the way we are inside, we would look seventy-five. So why not skip all that preadolescent crap and get where we want to be anyway?"

Sally had to admit he had a point. "Who else has done it?" she said.

"Just Joey. Caitlin doesn't need it"—his gaze briefly flickered down to Sally's budding breasts, subtly implying that she *did*—"and Timothy and Ralph don't care. Timothy looks sixteen anyway. In another year, I bet he'll be a head taller."

That's what Jim was now. He must have been over six feet tall. And he had put on weight. Sally wondered how many nutrients the two boys had had to borrow in order to make the change. And how long it had taken.

"A couple of hours," said Jim. "There's a lot more stuff here now, so it was easy to borrow. Want me to show you how to do it?"

Sally realized she wasn't all that eager to do it. It was nice to know that it could be done, sometime later. But right now it seemed ... unnecessary.

"Not yet," said Sally. "I'd like to accomplish some other things first."

"Like what?"

Sally felt a lump growing in her throat. She was going to cry in another moment, if she didn't do something about it. Where did that come from? Was it seeing Jim that way, looking so handsome, looking so much like Marc?

Or was he manipulating her?

"I'm all right now." Sally gently disentangled herself from his ministrations. "Thank you."

"You would have killed me if I hadn't stopped you," he said with utter confidence.

Sally didn't let him know that she would have killed him if she hadn't stopped *herself*. There would have been nothing he could have done about it. "You startled me. You look a lot like Marc, did you know that?"

"Sure, but I'm not his twin. And I still look like a teenager."

"Has everyone else seen you yet?"

"No."

"Better warn the ones who haven't. Especially Caitlin."

He gave her a winning smile. It easily equaled anything Susanna could have done. In fact, he surpassed her.

"Your mist is gone," he said. "The morning sun burned it off."

"I know. I think we need to rely on our other senses during the day. We shouldn't get overconfident and take things for granted."

"Spoken like a general. You and Caitlin will keep us puny men jumping."

So now he was calling himself a man. And he certainly looked the part. He towered over her now. He looked strong, and his face and body were very pleasing. He smelled good too. Sally had to clamp down on her own body's reaction to his pheromones.

"So what were you planning for today?" he said. Somehow he seemed to be standing much closer than he had a moment before.

"First I'd like to try our skill at breakfast, see if we can do a better job than we did last night. Then I'd like to explore some more."

"Yeah, that sounds like a good idea," Jim said, and he walked away from her. Suddenly he seemed not to care whether she was there or not. Sally felt an unhappy twinge, but swatted it away.

Idiot, she told herself. *He's playing you like a fiddle. Just like Susanna did to people.*

She followed him outside, into the warm light. Caitlin and Joey were already there. Sally hardly recognized Joey; his growth spurt had hardened all of his soft edges. He was showing Caitlin the trick of looking into the sun. She turned when she heard Sally and Jim approaching. For a moment, her eyes were twin suns, just as Joey's had been. In Joey, the effect had been interesting. In Caitlin it was terrifying.

"I hope you can do breakfast better than you did supper last night," snapped Caitlin, her eyes still burning.

"I hope so too," said Sally.

Caitlin's eyes turned green again, but to Sally they still looked like they were on fire.

"There are a lot of animals today!" Joey called. He flew up to his favorite rock and surveyed the countryside. Sally flew up there to stand next to him. She felt as shy of him as she did of Jim. He had become a handsome young man.

The fields and the mountains looked different. They were just as beautiful, maybe even more so; but now they were full of living things. There were nut and fruit trees, several different kinds of wild beans, herbs, and spices growing everywhere. There were fish swimming in brooks and lakes, and lots of fat game birds. The giant eagles, who still could be observed riding up and down the thermals, seemed more exuberant than they had the day before.

"Any milk cows?" Sally asked hopefully.

"Yes," said Joey. "But no chocolate beans, so we can't make a hot fudge sundae for Ralph yet."

Sally found the milk cows grazing in a meadow about ten miles from their position. The animals had water nearby, and seemed quite content.

"Find any tobacco yet?" asked Jim.

Joey laughed. "No. I can show you how to give yourself a cig jolt if you really want one. We can even make some fake ones to hold while we're doing it."

But Jim shook his head. "Where's the sin in that? It just wouldn't be the same."

Sally wished he hadn't mentioned the word *sin*. She was so easily embarrassed these days; and he had to go and be such a ... *male*.

"Shall we start with some cold milk?" she asked, hoping to get the conversation back to a more neutral subject.

"Milk?" Ralph emerged from the cavern, his hair rumpled and his eyes still puffy with sleep. "Can we make a sundae yet?"

"We're learning." Sally concentrated. She separated the milk from the cows and held it in midair, where the others could see it. *Today I'm going to do better,* she promised herself.

She pasteurized the milk, then chilled it. She borrowed a little honey from a nearby hive, to sweeten it. *Now all I need is to make a cone,* she thought. She concentrated on the shape she wanted, and put the frozen milk there as if it had been scooped. She was wondering what ice cream cones were made of when something struck her.

With just a little more effort, she could make the invisible cone graspable. She did so, then presented Ralph with the result. He held it wonderingly.

"What is it sitting in?" he asked, gazing with wonder at the blob of pseudo ice cream that appeared to be magically suspended above his grasping fingers.

"A . . . force cone!" said Sally.

"I can feel it!" he said. "It feels like a real ice-cream cone, only stronger!"

Caitlin snorted. "Why not just make a real ice-cream cone?"

"Because I haven't figured it out yet," said Sally, presenting everyone else with their own force cones, then making one for herself. "Besides, this way we don't have to trouble with plates and glasses yet."

Sally tasted her own concoction. It wasn't really like ice cream, but it was good. *Very* good. She smiled happily, ignoring Caitlin's scowl. She noted that the other girl gobbled up the result anyway, regardless of its shortcomings.

Sally and Joey sat down on the rock together to finish their cones. Sally felt very aware of the new body sitting next to her. Joey had lost his feeling of sexual neutrality. Perhaps that was why he had done it. Maybe *neutral* was the last thing a boy wanted to be.

A man, she corrected herself. She wouldn't be able to think of them as children anymore.

"What about fruit?" demanded Caitlin. Sally had been about to say *You can find it yourself,* when Caitlin did just that. She brought herself an apple and an orange.

"I want to try making apple pie tonight," said Joey. Sally looked at him sideways. He was smiling. A curl was falling down his forehead, making him look more like Superman than ever. "Is there sugarcane?" she asked him.

"Haven't found any yet," he said. "It's amazing what you miss when you leave civilization. Stuff you never even thought about."

As if Joey had cued him, Ralph began to play *Variations on a Theme of Thomas Tallis* by Vaughan Williams.

At least that's one thing we don't have to miss out on, thought Sally.

Ralph's music went perfectly with the morning. Sally watched the sun climb higher over the mountains and the flight of the eagles over the distant peaks. Everyone fetched fruit for themselves, just as Caitlin had done; and for once, Joey didn't have to supplement very much to make up for what they were lacking.

"Sally, I've been thinking about your force cone," Ralph said suddenly, without even interrupting his own music. "With a few modifications, I think it would make an effective personal shield."

He demonstrated what he meant by creating a shield around their group.

"We're going to suffocate in here!" snapped Caitlin.

"No, we won't," said Ralph. "See? The shield would *react* to force. The more force directed against it, the stronger it gets. Right now, air is flowing in and out of it normally. But if something were to come running at us, it would bounce off."

"That won't be any good against The Three," said Caitlin. "They won't attack us with their bodies."

"But maybe we *could* adapt it to work against The Three," Ralph said. "It all depends on what telepathy really is. After all, when you place a thought in someone else's mind, aren't you really just causing neurons to fire in a particular way? It isn't even telepathy, really. It's telekinesis."

Sally nodded. Ralph was on to something. But the idea worried her too. If she made a shield, couldn't Marc just dismantle it? No matter how powerful it was? On the other hand, it might take him *time* to dismantle it, and that would take away his element of surprise. . . .

Ralph and I will work on it today, sent Timothy. He was still lying in bed, but he had been listening to the conversation. He was eating an ice-cream/force cone he had made for himself. Sally didn't doubt that he and Ralph would have some interesting answers by evening.

"I'm going to explore today," said Joey. He looked at Sally and said, "Alone, this time. If you don't mind."

"Me too," said Caitlin. "I need to get away."

Sally realized that she felt the same way herself. She wanted to go out alone. She had never been alone before, except in her inner journeys; and even then, her Secret Mind had been with her. She would have thought that the concept of solitude would frighten her, but it didn't at all. In fact, now that she could have it, she was excited about it.

Sally gazed toward the distant mountains, the ones those giant eagles seemed to favor so much. That's where *she* wanted to go.

"Do you want to meet back here at lunchtime?" she said.

"I'll come back when I feel like it," said Caitlin.

"If you run into The Three . . ." Sally began. Everyone looked at her, waiting for her to suggest what they could do under those circumstances; but she really had no idea. She took a deep breath. "Don't try to fight them. Run and call for help. We'll have to form a Mastermind, I'm sure of it."

No one agreed with her outright. But no one said no, either.

"Have a good day," Sally told them, meaning it; and she flew away like a bird, toward her mountains.

The first thing she wanted to do was get a close look at those eagles. If they were large enough to be seen from such a distance, they must be very large indeed. Sally kept Ralph's version of the force shield around her, just in case they turned out to be *really* big.

By the time she had been flying for a hour and still hadn't reached the mountains, she had decided the eagles must be as big as pterodactyls. They were growing steadily larger in her sight, along with the mountains, which were proving to be downright monumental. It would take her at least another hour to reach them.

She wondered if she should try to find one of the eagle nests, or if that would be asking for trouble.

This was all reminding her of something. These mountains were like the mountains that had inspired the dream of Olympus in the first place. And those eagles were Lydia's eagles. They were tied together with Lydia in Sally's memory.

Are you here? she called, hoping and dreading that Lydia would answer her. *Is this where you went after you were killed? Did the Valkyries take you to Valhalla after all?*

Lydia didn't answer her. Instead, something crashed into her force shield so hard it knocked Sally right out of the sky.

She tumbled wildly. She couldn't get a fix on where she was and what direction she was going, let alone on what had hit her. Every move she made seemed to make things worse, so Sally stopped moving altogether. She concentrated on slowing her descent. When that happened, the tumbling slowed too, and she was able to stop it.

Sally was now suspended motionless about ten feet above the ground. Nothing moved for miles around her. Even the eagles seemed to have disappeared. She hadn't quite reached the foothills of the mountain range; she was still over the plain. The grasses were drooping in the dead air.

Sally was breathing hard. She quested with her talent, trying to find what had attacked her. She sensed her brothers and sister, far away, seemingly safe. But she couldn't find anything else except for small animals.

None of those animals were moving within a square mile around her. Everything was keeping perfectly still.

"Who's there?" called Sally; but her throat was so constricted it came out as a squeak. She remembered her advice to the others about what to do in an emergency and wondered if she should take it herself.

"Who's there?" she called again, forcing her throat into a normal condition.

No one answered. But someone heard, she was sure of it.

"Why don't you—" she began, but then her shield was struck again, harder than the first time. This time Sally was shot off sideways, parallel to the ground. But she stopped the movement immediately.

And she got a glimpse of her attacker. He was running away from her at an incredible rate, faster than a car could go. He was naked, and his skin was an odd gray-black color, almost like metal.

Sally gaped at him. In an instant, he was gone. She didn't know what to do. Would he attack again? Which direction would he be coming from? And who the hell was he, anyway?

Sally decided that she wouldn't try to look in all directions at once. She would stand firm and concentrate on keeping herself in the same position. The shield should make him bounce off, and she could get another look at him.

Sure enough, in another minute he was running *toward* her. He was coming in from her right, so Sally watched him from the corner of her eye. She tried to get a good look at his face, but it was blurred by his speed. It took every speck of willpower she had to let him crash into her.

This time she didn't move; the force of the crash was even harder than it had been the last time. He bounced off and flew backward. In the instant before he got to his feet and ran off again, Sally got a better look at him.

His features were half formed and he had no apparent genitalia. He zoomed away before Sally could speak to him. She wondered just what she was supposed to do next.

She decided to see if she could outrun him. She waited until he was in sight again, this time coming in from her left. She noted his trajectory, and then flew off at top speed.

The shield kept the wind from buffeting her. It solidified against the force until Sally could see light prisms breaking away from its curved surface. Behind her, the creature was gaining. Sally increased her speed.

It did too.

Sally increased again.

It came even faster.

How fast can I go really? Sally wondered. *The speed of light? Beyond? Will it catch up to me anyway?*

And in another second it did. It smashed into her with a sound like exploding dynamite. It was so loud, Sally had to repair the nerve cilia in her ears.

The crash sent her forward at blurring speed. She assumed they must both be supersonic by now. The boom of their collision probably had been heard for miles around, probably by her brothers and sister, possibly by The Three as well.

Can't keep this up, Sally decided, and let herself sink back down to earth.

She came to rest on a mountain peak. She couldn't see the attacker, but she knew he would be back any second. And he would strike her shield again, making another loud boom. She tried to think what could possibly be the reason for this approach, whether it could be some elaborate trick from The Three. But she could barely think. She was so scared now, she was close to panic.

It was coming back. This time it was heading straight toward her from the front. It was coming faster this time; it would certainly hit harder.

The harder I resist, the stronger it gets, she thought, frantically. *Like an inside-out version of Ralph's shield.*

Something clicked in her mind. Sally turned her

shield off. But the attacker didn't slow. He was going to hit her full force.

He'll kill me, Sally thought. But she held herself still.

Closer, closer, he was a hundred feet away, and in one tenth of a second he was one foot away.

And then he stopped dead.

Sally let out her breath in a rush and sucked it back in again. He still didn't move. She kept her shields down.

If he had had eyes, he would have been staring right into hers. He was intimately aware of her on some level, aware of her exact energy output. Sally tried to keep that output at a natural level, just enough to maintain her bodily functions.

"What are you?" she asked.

It wasn't alive, not like she was. And it wasn't one of The Three. Beyond that, it was a complete mystery. It barely even looked real. Light bent around it in odd ways, as if it didn't even belong in the her universe, as if it were from someplace where light had different properties, different physics.

Sally made herself relax, almost to the point of unconsciousness. "Who are you?" she asked.

A place opened in the attacker's face where a mouth would normally have been. "The world is far stranger than you can dream you imagine," it said, in a voice than was neither male nor female, loud nor soft.

And then it sped away, as fast as it had come.

Sally gazed after it, swaying on her feet. It had just taught her something that had catastrophic implications. Ralph's shield was a marvelous idea; but it wouldn't work against The Three. It could be turned inside out, until the protected one became her own attacker. You would be kept so busy against such an attack, you wouldn't have time to defind yourself on any other level. Your attackers could simply set up a sort of loop, one that would intensify the attack in response to the intensity of your defense. The two forces would feed on each other indefinitely, and in the meantime ...

The Three would be free to do whatever they wanted to do to you.

"You figured that out quickly," said a man's voice behind her.

Sally didn't recognize the voice. She hadn't felt the man until she had heard him. She turned slowly, too afraid to pretend braveness. She fully expected to see Marc or Ted standing there.

But it wasn't either of them. Sally didn't recognize this man. He didn't look like any human being she had ever seen, yet he was undisputably human.

His skin was brown, a little lighter than Joey's. His eyes were black, and so was his hair, which was close-cropped. He had a nice build, slender like Marc's. He might have been thirty, but his face showed no sign of the onset of middle age. He had a sort of timeless look. He was wearing a short kilt, of the Egyptian variety, and a simple shirt that might have been linen.

"Ted?" said Sally. He could have been Ted. For years Sally had watched him reach into people's minds, changing what they thought they saw.

"I'm not Ted," he said.

Sally rather liked the sound of his voice. It fell into the masculine midrange, like Marc's did. But she didn't think he was Marc. Why would Marc mask everything about himself but his voice?

"Who are you, then?" she asked.

"Well," said the man, "since this is Olympus, then I must be Apollo."

He didn't seem to be joking or mocking her. "Is this really Olympus?" Sally asked.

The man who had named himself Apollo simply looked at her; or rather, he looked *into* her. He did this in a way that Sally had never felt before. This was not the invasion of The Three, nor was it the communication she shared with the others, not even with Ralph. It was as if she were a window, and he was merely seeing what was in front of his eyes.

She threw all caution to the winds and flew over to perch right in front of him. He didn't seem concerned by the move.

"I'm not going to let you kill me," warned Sally.

He didn't answer, but his eyes seemed to be challenging her. *I see you,* they said. *Now open your eyes and you will see me.*

Sally opened her eyes. She let herself see into him as he saw into her. She expected to encounter a shield or a maze of deceptive thoughts. But he let her in without any resistance at all, and that was what defeated her.

Good trick, she thought as she fell.

His mind was deeper and older than any mind she had ever touched. It was the sort of mind she might have expected to find on the other side of the Gate. She rushed backward down his time line, dizzy with the scope of the journey, zooming at the speed of light, until she could no longer tell where she was or where she was going. She felt herself disappearing.

Then, mercifully, she came to the end of her journey and the end of her strength.

When Sally awakened, she was in Apollo's house. He was sitting patiently by the bed. He didn't move when she woke. Sally didn't sit up yet. She tentatively felt the place out.

The house and everything in it had been shaped. It took her some time to determine this, and she was awed by what she found. Everything had been shaped by the mind of a master, if not by a Mastermind. She was only able to determine this by searching for the telltale signs of hand and machine crafting: grooves made by blades and that sort of thing. They were completely absent. Apollo was not bumbling around the way Sally and the others were. He must have had centuries of practice in making what he needed.

She watched him. He didn't make a threatening move. She sat up, then got up; still no action was taken against her. She walked across the room and looked out the window.

Apollo's house was a remote place, an eagle's eyrie shaped out of the solid rock of one of those mountain peaks that had drawn Sally's curiosity. The view took her breath away.

She made herself turn away from it and face him. "Who are you, really?" she demanded. "You can't be as old as you felt."

There was the shadow of a smile on his lips. "I don't feel old at all," he said. "Do I look old?"

She wondered if he was offended by the word. But no, it seemed more like he was trying to get her to examine her own logic.

"You don't look any older than Marc," she said.

"How old is Marc?"

"At least fifty, but he looks twenty-five."

"Fifty, twenty-five. Those are small numbers."

Sally remembered what it had felt like to fall into his mind. She looked at his features, which no longer existed on the faces of any living race. "So you're forty thousand years old. That's what you felt like, forty thousands years, give or take a few millennia. That's impossible. So who are you?"

Then he smiled openly. It wasn't one of Jim's seductive smiles; it was real, it even crinkled the skin around his eyes.

"Apollo," he said.

"You are not."

"How do you know?"

"He was Greek."

"His worshipers were Greek. Perhaps he was not."

"Was he or wasn't he? You're the one who's supposed to be old enough to know."

"He might have been Greek. But then, who am I?"

"You look sort of like an Indian."

"I am not from India. Though I visited there at the birth of its current civilization."

"Oh, so I suppose they thought you were Krishna."

"They didn't. But I knew Kali when I was there. She was much like your Caitlin."

"If you're Apollo, then where's your sun chariot?"

"I had to give it up after it was proved that the earth orbits the sun. I was sorry to let it go; it was the best set of wheels I ever had."

Sally shuddered. But it was a good feeling. This man was like no one she had ever met before. She could almost believe he was an Olympian.

"You're like me," she said. "You're a Kronos Kid."

"I *was* a Kronos Kid. But now I am a man."

"You're a lot more than just a man . . . Apollo."

"I could be much less."

"You could be like The Three. I know what you mean."

"Yes, you do. You know better than any of the others." He rose and went to the door. "Come with me. You look hungry."

Sally was starving. She followed him from the room and into a kitchen. It had large windows in two of its walls, revealing mountain peaks and gliding eagles. It had a huge fireplace in the corner between the windowed walls, sills that were large working counters, cupboards on the other two walls, and one large door that led into a courtyard. The door was open, and a cool breeze was coming through it.

A large wooden table stood at the center of the room. It had been shaped as one piece. Two chairs were tucked under it. Sally wondered if one had been made for her, or if someone else customarily sat there.

"Sit," invited Apollo.

Sally pulled up a chair and sat in it. It was made of hard wood, but it was comfortable. There was a bowl of fruit in the middle of the table, full of bananas, strawberries, grapes, apples, and pears. Sally nibbled on them and studied the kitchen while Apollo worked, memorizing its details. She noticed it didn't have a sink or a faucet, yet the water he gave her was pure and cool.

He wasn't apparently using any special powers to prepare the food; but Sally could *smell* that something was happening. He was doing something far beyond what she and the others had managed. He was like Jesus, making one small fish feed a village. She resisted the urge to ask him if he had ever been called by that name.

"Eat," Apollo said. He had prepared a stew with meat and vegetables in it. The meat looked like beef; the vegetables were carrots, potatoes, celery, and onions. He produced a spoon. Sally studied it for a moment; it had the design of a sphinx on its handle.

"Did you make this?" she asked.

"I made everything here."

"You didn't make *me*."

He smiled again. Sally spooned up some of the stew and tentatively tasted it. It was marvelous.

Apollo ate too. This only reinforced her assumption that he was like her, a human being with talent. Sally decided he was handsome, though not in the Greek fashion. His hair was thick, black, and very short. His skin was brown, but had a touch of olive in it. His black eyes, when they looked at her, would have seemed inscrutable if his mind were not so open to her.

She especially liked the back of his neck, which was smooth, strong, and very masculine. She liked the way it . . .

. . . flowed into the architecture of his wide shoulders . . .

"You saved your own life," said Apollo. "And the lives of the other children. It's rare for a girl with your abilities to have such compassion."

Sally shrugged. "Susanna made me that way. She made sure I was softhearted so I would have weaknesses."

"I understand."

Sally felt such longing and pain suddenly, she almost felt like she could burst with it. She wanted to ask, *Do you really understand? Are you the Olympian who sent me my magic cat? Will you love me now that I've proved myself worthy?* But she shielded those thoughts from him. Or she hoped she did.

"I can prove it to you, if you want," he said.

"Prove what?"

"Anything you might desire. I can let you into my mind again. But you fainted last time. You should finish your lunch first."

Sally gobbled her food. She wanted to go in again, but her cautious nature was warning her to wait. After she had finished lunch, she said, "Can I come and visit again? Maybe then we can ... do it again?"

"Yes," said Apollo. "Whenever you're ready."

"Is your name really Apollo?"

"If you like. Or Osiris, or Krishna."

"Can't you just tell me your real name?"

"Certainly. My real name is King Monkey."

Sally heard a ringing in her ears. It was caused by a combination of the constricted veins in her body and the dead silence in the room.

"I didn't ... recognize you," she said. "I'm sorry."

"I don't look the same. You don't look the same way you did when last we met either."

Sally blushed. "I'm sorry. That wasn't me, that was just a fantasy. I'm still growing up."

"I can see that."

In her dream, when he had called himself Osiris, he had wept. He didn't look like he would do so now. He seemed calm, in control of himself.

Sally got up and went to the door, carried by an inexplicable wave of embarrassment and confusion. She would have just gone out with a mumbled goodbye, but she had to turn and ask him something before she could leave.

"Are you disappointed with me?" she asked. "Now that you've really met me?"

He didn't smile. "No," he said. "Not at all."

"Then I'll come back another time and we can talk again."

"I wish you would, Sally."

"Good-bye, then." And she rushed from the room.

*   *   *

Outside, in the courtyard, part of Sally wanted very much to linger and explore. She wanted to look at the mosaic in the cobbled pathway, at the little statues placed here and there with such aesthetic skill. She wanted to sniff the flowers and gaze over the cliffs at the matchless view.

But he was still aware of her, though his eyes were no longer on her. Sally didn't want to ruin her exit. Besides, she had a lot to think about now. Too much to think about.

So she lifted herself into the air, over his mountains. She was astonished to realize how far away from her cavern they were. *Going to have to fly fast to get home before supper. . . .*

In order to do so, she would have to generate a version of Ralph's shield again. But she picked its intensity level herself, instead of making it reactionary. She didn't want to provoke another attacker.

She wondered just what else was waiting to be triggered in Olympus. . . .

But Sally's trip home was uneventful. She probed ahead for her brothers and sister; they were home and waiting for her long before she got there herself. But when she reached their hidden cavern, Ralph was the only one who was outside to greet her. He seemed very preoccupied, possibly even a little sad.

He was sitting atop a small hill, under a willow tree, looking at the waving grasses in the meadow. Sally went to sit next to him without speaking. He was listening to Vaughan Williams's Ninth Symphony. Sally was fond of that one, but Ralph didn't listen to it very often.

"Who's conducting this one?" she asked.

"Sir Adrian Boult," said Ralph. "This was the performance he recorded the day after Ralph Vaughan Williams died."

Ah, thought Sally.

"If I had been alive then," Ralph said, "I wouldn't have let him die. I would have mended him and returned his body to a younger age. Then he could have continued to write. He might have even saved classical music."

Sally leaned back on her elbows. The Ninth Symphony was an interesting one. It was hard to grasp when you heard it the first few times, but it grew on you. It contained some very moving sections, places that lingered in the listener's memory long after the music was over. "His friends would have wondered how he got young again," she mused. "And you would have had to fix his wife too. He would have been lonely without her. And his best friend, Gustav Holst—"

"If we live," said Ralph, "sooner or later people will know about us."

Sally hadn't thought about that. She had assumed that they would stay secret. But why should they, really? Assuming they ever got home again. Why should they hide themselves? But it was all too complicated, too huge. People would be frightened, or envious, or suspicious. . . .

"So much to do." Ralph sighed. "If only we had the time to do it right."

"Your shield—" began Sally.

"I know. We heard the boom. And I felt what was happening through our link. I'm so glad you figured out what was wrong. That could have been such a disaster."

"It started out as a good idea."

He shrugged. "So did the atomic bomb."

Sally listened to the music for a time, without comment. She looked at Ralph out of the corner of her eyes. It was interesting that the Kronos Kids all shared the same genetic origins. At the moment Ralph looked very much like one of the British composers he admired so much; but his genes were African, Irish, Slavic, Native American, and Semitic. He should have resembled Timothy, who should have resembled Sally, and so on. Yet none of them resembled each other. The only one in their whole group who looked like anyone else was Jim, who looked like Marc; and that was probably just a coincidence.

Each of them was a different color, from very dark to very light. It was as if they had been designed as a spectrum. . . .

"If it hadn't been for the wars—" Ralph started to say.

"The world wars?" Sally asked, when he had drifted off again.

"George Butterworth was killed in World War I. He could have been another Vaughan Williams. The two wars came along just when the world was moving into the golden age of music. So many talented composers were killed, so many people with promise. They died in the trenches, or they starved in the cities, or they were exterminated in the death camps."

He sighed, his eyes focused on something far away and long ago.

"And then," he said, "after the Second World War, the popular music industry came in and did the rest of the damage. They wanted two minutes of music to prop up the commercials. People don't even know how to listen to classical music anymore. They branded it as *high brow* and dumped it in the trash."

Sally was amazed, because she was just beginning to realize that for Ralph, The Three were a secondary problem, an obstacle that was keeping him from the *real* issues of classical music. And what was even more amazing, she was beginning to see what he meant.

"Philip Glass is doing okay, isn't he?" she asked.

"Thank God for him," Ralph agreed. "But he took

his music in a postmodern direction. There wasn't anyone to pick up the reins after the post-Romantics died. Except for Aaron Copland. But he was modern, and people think of him in connection with film score composers these days. Those composers were wonderful—I like their music very much; but listen to this."

The Ninth Symphony had ended, and now Ralph was playing Butterworth's *The Banks Of Green Willow*.

"That's what we lost. That's what was killed in that war," said Ralph.

Tears came to Sally's eyes. She didn't stifle them. Ralph didn't mind. He was crying a few of his own.

"Vaughan Williams served in World War I, did you know that?" asked Ralph.

"No," said Sally. "Wasn't he in his forties by then?"

"Yes, but they let him join. He drove a munitions wagon. All through the war, he organized musicians among the soldiers. They performed every chance they got."

"That must have cheered the troops up."

"I think it reminded them of what was worth preserving in the world. And it also gave the upper-class fellows a chance to see that the working-class guys had talent.

"And everyone respected Vaughan Williams, looked up to him, because he was older. He was sort of a father figure to some. Once, when he and another fellow were driving the wagon—the wagons were pulled by horses, back then—the fellow turned to him and said, 'Do horses have dreams, Mr. Williams?' He was worried that the war was giving the horses nightmares."

Sally suspected that the man had been right. But she didn't say so.

"That's what I'm going to name my first symphony," said Ralph. "*Do Horses Have Dreams, Mr.*

Williams? It's not that I disapprove of the new composers; it's just that there should be so much more variety. Styles of music shouldn't cancel each other out, they should coexist! But if that's going to happen, I'm going to have to try to pick up the reins myself."

"You and Timothy."

"Yes, we're like Vaughan Williams and Gustav Holst. We inspire each other."

"You inspire me too," said Sally.

He looked at his hands and blushed. Now she had come to the heart of his problem.

"Ralph," she said, "I know you need to compose. It's what I wanted for you."

"But if I'm preoccupied, and The Three come—"

"I'll call you for the Mastermind. But until then, I understand that you have to do your own work. Besides, that may be our best defense, to develop our talents to the fullest."

"I don't think we're going to do The Three in with a symphony."

Sally laughed. "Don't be so sure," she said, and then for some reason she thought of Apollo. He had spent centuries developing his talents. He would be more than a match for The Three if they ever attacked him.

Ralph hadn't mentioned him yet. Didn't he know Sally had met someone else in their world, someone besides The Three?

He didn't. Apollo didn't appear in his thoughts at all. He was thinking about Vaughan Williams and Holst, about Respighi, Rachmaninoff, Prokofiev, Stravinsky, Bax . . .

If he had known about Apollo, he would be asking her questions about him, about what his appearance meant. And surely the others would be curious.

But they weren't either. No one knew about Apollo but Sally.

Did I imagine him? Is he the animus who teased me in my dream?

If he was, Sally certainly didn't want the others to know about him. She had enough to worry about without being embarrassed too. Caitlin would use the knowledge to undermine her; Jim would use it to manipulate her.

She was already thinking of them as enemies. Maybe The Three wouldn't have to do anything to them, after all. They could do it to each other.

"Compose your music, Ralph. If you have any ideas for our defense that you'd like to share, I'm always ready to hear them. But I'm not going to pressure you away from your life's work. I want to see classical music saved too. I think that's the noblest thing I've ever heard."

Those words might have sounded corny to someone else. But Ralph let out a long sigh, as if the weight of the world had just been lifted from his chest.

"Okay," he said. "Please tell the others not to feel hurt if I'm not . . . available for a while."

"I understand," said Sally.

And then she got up and left him alone. He was already back at work on his own music. Nothing would be able to shake him loose from it now. Nothing except an all-out attack from The Three.

Sally didn't really know if it was wise or not for Ralph to be diverted away from matters of defense just then. But she didn't have the heart to chide him about what he really wanted to do. Maybe it was weak of her. The Three never would have shown such compassion.

She was glad that she had thought of that. It made her feel like she had given the right advice after all.

She entered the cavern. Everyone was in his or her room, but they all knew she was there. Sally had intended to go straight to her own room to think for a while, but instead she found her feet going toward Timothy's. He was waiting for her.

He didn't look up when she came in. He was closed, very hard to read. Sally wondered if she should just ask him what was wrong or if she should wait for him to tell her.

"The shield was a bust," he said.

"Yeah," said Sally. That wasn't what was on his mind, though.

"Ralph took it hard."

"It was a good lesson. We learned something from it."

The muscle in his jaw was jumping again.

Sally looked more closely at him. He was taller than he had been that morning. He was more muscular too. He looked at her suddenly, and she almost jumped.

"I was going to try to get him away," said Timothy.

"Ralph?" she asked. "You mean . . . today?"

"No!" he snapped, as if she hadn't been listening properly. "Before. Away from The Three. If they attacked, I was going to get between him and them, and I was going to move him far away while they were busy killing me. But when the time came, I just sat there like a dumb sheep."

Sally didn't know what to say. He was angry with her, she was sure of it. But she wasn't sure exactly why.

"The Three controlled us all our lives," she said. "Besides, what happened was another good lesson, because we know that we might freeze up if—"

"Shut up about your goddamned good lessons," he snarled. "Who the hell do you think you are? My mother? My teacher? Sometimes it makes me sick the way you fuss over us."

He really meant it. Sally would have been crushed if she hadn't been so surprised. After seeing Timothy attending to Ralph so devotedly for all those years, she would have thought that he would understand her need to *fuss*.

"Ralph is the only one I care about, get that straight," said Timothy. "And Caitlin is about a million times better-looking than you, so if I want a girl, I'll call on her. As for you—just don't get in my way and we'll get along fine."

He glared at her then, dismissing her. But Sally stood her ground.

"I can't believe it," she said. "You're jealous."

He sneered at her, but he was putting on a show. She had hit the nail right on the head.

"Ralph asked me if he could get on with his work, and I told him I thought he should."

"No one needs your permission," said Timothy.

"No, he didn't ask my permission. He asked my *opinion*. That's what's burning you up." Sally was just guessing now; it was all coming to her as if in a revelation. Ralph had asked her opinion because he respected her. That made her feel wonderful, and she wasn't going to let Timothy ruin it.

Timothy looked away from her eyes. His skin was developing a purple tinge from the neck up.

"You should grow your feelings up to match your body," Sally said gently, and then left him alone.

He didn't send any angry thoughts after her. Sally walked away from his room with a straight back, amazed at her own resilience. His comments should have hurt a lot more than they had; but she was learning a lot about relationships. They didn't operate too differently from Ralph's force shield.

She wondered if the others had eavesdropped. She didn't really care if they had. They were probably in their beds now, trying to grow their bodies some more. She hoped they wouldn't all be eight feet tall by morning.

No one had even asked her to fix supper. That was

okay; she wasn't hungry. Let the others worry about how to make this and that for a change. Maybe Joey had made progress with his apple pie.

Sally lay down in her own bed. She had just wanted to think for a while, to muse about Apollo and ... things. It was only early afternoon, and she hadn't thought she was tired. But slowly, inexorably, her thoughts became more jumbled, until sleep crept up on her and carried her away in bits and pieces, like ants carrying crumbs away from a picnic.

Beware, came the thought. Sally was still too disintegrated to pay it much heed, but it fluttered about and made a pest of itself until it started to make sense.

Look out. You're asleep, and sleep isn't safe from them.

From whom? she wondered. *From The Three?*

From anyone who can come in.

At the moment, Sally couldn't even remember who everyone was. She couldn't even remember who *she* was. But she remembered who Apollo was. She wondered what he was doing.

Could he come into my dreams?

He should be able to do so. In fact, she wanted him to. She wanted him to come to her like Jim had. She bet that he could make love well enough to melt her knees, to make her wish she didn't have to wake up, ever. Where was he? What did he look like, again? Come to think of it, what did *she* look like?

She tried to visualize her body. But it wouldn't hold the shape she wanted. She couldn't even grow bumpy little breasts like the ones she really had. That hardly seemed fair. If she could just concentrate, integrate ...

But instead, her self drifted farther apart. She became like the mist that she had sent out to guard the perimeter the night before. She drifted here and there, feeling mildly curious from time to time about the things or the people she encountered. The only thought she was able to form was, *I really should wake up. I really should. Come on, wake up . . . wake up . . .*

And then she saw herself. But wait, wasn't she a girl? No, that's right, she was a man. She was Osiris.

All right! Osiris is Apollo! Isn't he? Wasn't he? I can touch him, I can . . .

Touch *herself.* Touch *himself.* But no, he was too weary for that. Too lonely. And the Enemy would laugh, later; would confront him with his perversion.

Not that he thought touching himself was perverse. It was what one did when one was lonely. But tonight, all he wanted was sleep, just uninterrupted sleep. He was tired of the dreams, the torment of the Enemy, his ancient Enemy who would poke and prod him in his weakest moments. If only he could just once grasp his tormentor in his hands, tear him, strike him, strangle the life out of him. But he always slipped away, just out of grasp.

Tonight, I swear it, if he comes I will seize him. Tonight he won't get away.

But he didn't really want a confrontation tonight. He didn't have the heart for it. He was hoping that nothing would happen at all, nothing until he was stronger. He lay down on his pallet and let his body relax.

His body is so sexy. I wish I could crawl on top of him and . . .

If only he weren't so sleepy, he would enjoy making love. Yes, he could almost imagine the girl he would like tonight. Her name was Sally.

If I could just concentrate and grow some boobs. Dammit!

What strange thoughts he was having. What strange dreams. He almost felt . . .

He almost felt he wasn't alone.

His heart constricted, but his body still lay para-

lyzed. His Enemy would have him now, while he was
helpless. But no, he had no such human limitations.
He would move, when the time came. He would lie
there like a dead man, and at the last moment he
would spring.

He flooded his system with oxygen. But he let himself be very still. Someone was moving closer. He felt
the brush of fingers on his hand.

. . . the fingers felt small, delicate . . .

. . . sleep now, Sally . . .

No, the fingers belonged to a man, the hand of a
warrior. In another moment, he would grasp that hand
in his own and confront the ancient Enemy, the man
who had haunted him for thirty-five thousand years.
He had never come so close before, and now, now—

He seized the other hand in his. It grasped him in
return, with the same ferocity; but this only brought
a fierce joy to his heart. He had him! He had the
Enemy in his grasp, the man who had killed his son,
who had shouted private things, shameful things about
him, who had doubted and tormented him. He had
him! And now he would open his eyes and stare into
the face that belonged to the hand.

He squeezed hard, and felt something odd. When
he gripped his Enemy's hand, *he* was the one who felt
the pain. He squeezed again, hard enough to break
bone. Agony raced up his nerves and into his brain.
His eyes flew open, and he looked into the face of
the Enemy.

It was his own face that grinned back at him.

"Now," himself laughed, "at last you have met your
greatest Enemy, the murderer of your son."

And then he saw himself, his Neanderthal self,
doing the deed.

"No," he said, and, "No," again; but it was true.
He had done it. He had killed the child who would
one day become a monster, who would one day be

like Ted and Marc and Susanna, like Caitlin, like Kali, he had seen into its heart, its future, he had seen and he had acted.

It was him! It was him! It was himself!

I'm sorry. I'm sorry. . . .

"I'm sorry," said Sally. She sat straight up in bed. The words came out as a croak; but they tore her throat just as badly as a scream would have; and she had to gasp for breath for many minutes afterward.

She didn't understand the dream at all. Had she dreamed about King Monkey? Had she dreamed that *she* was King Monkey? But it hadn't felt like a true dream anyway, it had felt like a regular dream, disjointed and arbitrary. It had felt like her tired brain was simply throwing images and sensations at her, amusing itself.

But that business of the hand! And when he had opened his eyes, he had seen his own face. And then when he realized he had killed his own son. . . ! It was as if he had had a Secret Mind all those years; yet it wasn't. A Secret Mind would have been able to talk to him directly, tell him the truth. The Enemy didn't do that. Wouldn't do that.

Couldn't do that?

It scared her to think about it. Why had she dreamed about it? She breathed deeply and tried to sort it all out. Then she became aware of another sensation: She had to urinate.

That's why you had the nightmare! You just have to pee, that's all. That had happened to Sally many times. Her brain had wanted her to wake up and take care of the discomfort, so it had thrown disturbing images at her until she woke up. What a relief!

Sally got up and went to the hole she had carved in the rock to serve as a toilet. She sat on it and disintegrated the urine just as quickly as it left her body. Afterward, she felt almost normal again.

Normal! Normal is the way Marie Little Bird lives. This will never be normal.

Sally! Jim called.

Here! she ran out of her room and into the main chamber to meet him. He had sounded urgent, even a little frightened. He was sweating and out of breath.

"I found a house," he said.

Sally gave a guilty start. He must have found Apollo's house, and now she would have to explain why she hadn't told them all about it sooner. "It's in those mountains to the west of us," Jim was saying. "Come on, I'll show you."

In the west? But Apollo's house was in the mountains to the north of them. Jim had found *another* house? Sally's heart started to pound.

"Was anyone inside the house?" she asked as he pulled her outside. The wind was blowing now, and a storm was coming. Rain sprinkled her. She pulled her hair out of her face and looked in the direction Jim was pointing.

"I didn't go near it," he said. "I saw it from a distance. It's right on that third peak there."

Sally enhanced her vision until she could see what he was talking about. The house was nestled into the mountainside, sitting on a bump just below the top. It didn't look anything like Apollo's house.

Timothy had come out after them to find Ralph, who was still composing under his tree, oblivious to the storm. He led Ralph back inside the cavern. Ralph was almost as preoccupied as he had been before they had come through the Gate, but as he passed Sally and Jim he did manage to say one word.

The word was: "Trouble."

Timothy threw Sally a look over his shoulder as he escorted Ralph back inside. Whatever she planned to do about this new development, Timothy was going to look after Ralph, first and foremost.

"I think we'd better go take a look at it," she told Jim. "Warn the others, let them know that they need to be alert."

"You think they're trying to draw us out?" he asked grimly.

"Maybe," she said. She wondered if she should tell him about Apollo; but that seemed rather complicated at the moment. She needed Jim's cooperation. "On the other hand, trees and animals and things have been appearing because we needed them, so maybe—"

"Maybe we need a house now?" He frowned. "That's weird. Is that what Olympus is, then? A place where you get what you need?"

"Sounds more like heaven, doesn't it?"

"Heaven wouldn't be so bad. But if we're in heaven, how come The Three aren't in hell?"

Lightning struck the mountains about a mile away from them. A moment later, they heard the thunder.

Great Zeus, thought Sally, *don't zap us with your lightning.*

"We'd better go now," she said, "before it gets too wild."

I'm setting up your early warning system, Joey called. *But I can't get it to stretch all the way to that house. Close, though.*

We'll warn you the instant something happens, Sally told him. Then she took a brief inventory of everyone in the cave. Timothy, Ralph, and Joey were all apprehensive, alert. But from Caitlin she couldn't feel anything at all. Caitlin had taken the last couple of days to build herself an absolutely flawless shield, one that would take serious work and effort to penetrate.

What's she up to? Sally wondered. But she didn't have time to puzzle it out.

"Let's go see what's up," she said to Jim, and the two of them took off into the air.

Flying in storm conditions wasn't easy until they realized that they shouldn't be trying to act like birds. They couldn't let themselves be bothered with wind conditions; after all, they weren't flying through the usual lift, drag, and thrust methods. Once that was understood, they moved easily through the air, and they were no longer potential targets for lightning.

God, we're dumb, said Jim. *We're still thinking like we used to.*

It's hard to improve yourself when you can't imagine what form the improvement should take, said Sally.

But we should be able to imagine! We're smarter than other people.

Sally didn't think so. She had touched the minds of people who thought in dimensions she couldn't even imagine. Having talent didn't make the Kids mentally superior, not at all.

I think we're about to get the chance to find out just how smart we are, said Sally, because now they were closing on the house in the mountainside. *I just hope we don't blow it.*

They slowed their approach when they were within two hundred feet of the place. Sally wished she had thought to weave an illusion of invisibility around the two of them, but now it was too late. If The Three were inside, the jig was up.

"That doesn't look like Ted's kind of place," said Jim.

It really didn't. It was more of a cottage than a house. Ted went in for Olympian architecture, with pillars and columns and things.

"It looks English," said Sally, anxiety stabbing her heart. It looked like some of the cottages they had seen in England when they had visited there. Ted hadn't liked England; he had thought the castles and churches were boring and unimaginative. But Sally had loved all of the *little* places they had seen, the cottages, barns, pubs, shops, and tiny churches. She had thought them charming. And perhaps that was why this house was here now, because *she* had liked it.

But how had Susanna felt about England? And of course she would have known how much Sally had liked it. . . .

"We might as well go in," said Jim.

Sally agreed, and not just because the rain was starting to come down so heavily—they were shielded against the wet. She wanted to go in and get it over with.

So they put their feet on the ground and walked up the meandering path that led to the front door. "Like Hansel and Gretel," snorted Jim.

Sally wished he hadn't said that.

"That's peat moss growing on the roof," Jim said, when they had reached the front door. "Just like some of the country places we saw in England."

Sally put her hand on the front door handle, which was shaped like a lion's head. "This is more French," she said. "Like the kind of thing you might find in Provence."

They crept in the front door. Sally drew her breath in; the place was completely furnished, beautifully so in antiques, except for a few notable exceptions like a big comfortable couch and some modern appliances. The two of them tiptoed across the wooden floor, which creaked under their weight until Sally thought to compensate for it.

No one seemed to be home. Sally and Jim stopped in the center of the front room. Sally was no expert in antiques, but it seemed to her that the furnishings were eclectic, picked to suit someone's particular taste rather than to represent a period or a theme.

The furnishings suited her *own* taste very well. She especially liked the clawfoot legs: lion paws on the legs of tables and bookshelves, goose feet on little stands, horse hooves on the couch. Sally had always liked furniture that almost looked like it could walk somewhere by itself.

Did I make this place myself? Unconsciously?

"What do you think of it?" she asked Jim.

He shrugged. "Nice. I could live here."

"Would you design it differently, if it were up to you?"

He looked at her sideways, but he answered her question. "Yes. I like Egyptian stuff."

Sally stifled a blush as his remark brought back an uncomfortable memory.

"Let's look and see if we can find any signs of habitation," she said. He nodded and started off. Sally followed him, not wanting to be alone when The Three suddenly popped out of a closet.

They looked in the kitchen first. It also had modern appliances mixed in with other antiques. Sally opened the cupboards and found dishes, glasses, cookware; but more interestingly, she found packaged foods.

There were teas, cookies, spices, crackers, all sorts of things. Some were American items, and some were from other countries. She found Greek and Russian lettering on some of the boxes, names and directions in French, Spanish, Japanese, and Danish.

"There's a quart of milk in the fridge," said Jim. "And orange juice, and wine, and soda pop—cheese— butter . . ."

Sally looked under the sink. There were no cleaning supplies and no pipes. But when she turned on the faucet, cool water came out of the tap and went down the drain. She put her lips to the faucet and tasted the water. It was as good as spring water.

"What do you think?" said Jim.

She looked at him. She knew her expression must be just like his: scared, curious, worried. "Look how tidy it is in here," she said. "No crumbs, nothing out of place."

"That's easy to manage," he said.

"I know, but it's a little ... *obsessive*. Like something Ted would do."

Jim nodded. "Let's look at the bedrooms," he said.

There were four of those, which was a strange number. The Three would need one less, and the Kids would need two more. So maybe the house wasn't made for any of them. Maybe it was a real place out of someone's memory.

Just before they entered the largest bedroom, Sally got a premonition.

"Someone's in here," she said.

Jim stopped dead. He reached out with his own talent. "No," he said, "it's empty."

Sally chewed her lip. Her talent told her the same thing, but her gut told her otherwise. Jim opened the door, and they peeked in.

No one seemed to be there.

"Come on," he said. He went in and looked around, then turned to Sally, who was still standing in the door. He smiled at her. "Come in and look. It's nice."

She went in. The room had a wardrobe, but no closet for anyone to hide in.

"Look at the bed," said Jim. "Big enough for two."

Two. Like Marc and Susanna, thought Sally.

She went slowly around the room, looking at quaint little paintings of fairies and animals. The wardrobe was empty, so she went to inspect a vanity with a three-way mirror.

Jim didn't help her look. He just watched her.

"Sally?" he said.

"Huh?" She opened the drawers in the vanity, which were also empty.

"You have a beautiful ass. Did you know that?"

Sally's heart started to pound. She couldn't think of what to answer. She continued to look through empty drawers.

"You *didn't* know it. Of course, you've never seen it." He laughed. "But I see it. In fact, lately I've been seeing it in my dreams."

Sally blushed before she could think to stop it.

"You were bent over a bed like this one, naked. That gorgeous, round ass of yours was right in my face. It was incredible. You should see yourself the way I see you, Sally."

"We're not safe here," she said, and was pleased that her voice was perfectly controlled.

"Yes, we are. Can't you feel it? They're not here. This is *your* place, Sally. It pleases you, that's obvious."

He moved across the space that divided them, so easily, so casually. She almost cringed when he came that close. He was intimidating with his new size and bulk.

"I'm not going to hurt you," he said, in an utterly believable tone of voice. "Here, turn around. I want to show you something."

He made her turn, and then he moved one wing of the three-way mirror so she could see her back.

"Look," he said.

Sally looked. And she was surprised to realize that he was right. Her bottom was beautifully rounded and firm. She had always been so concerned about her breasts, she hadn't thought she might be blossoming anywhere else.

"In my dream you had on a garter belt and some stockings," he breathed into her ear. "And nothing else." He leaned over her and cupped her bottom, pulling her close. "You want to know what happened next?" he whispered.

Sally wanted to say, *Yes*. She also wanted to say, *Not now, we've got work to do!* In the end, she didn't say anything at all.

He kissed her earlobe. He looked like Marc, even felt like Marc if she just used her imagination a little bit. He took her hand and pressed it against himself. He had an erection. Sally closed her eyes, then opened them again.

Something moved in one corner of the mirror.

Sally moved the mirror slightly, until she found what was moving.

Susanna. Looking at them.

"Jim!" screamed Sally.

He jumped like a cat, hearing the terror and panic in her voice. He whirled on Susanna, who was standing near the door, as if she had just come in. He gasped as if he had been struck. Susanna looked just like she always had, only younger. She was wearing a tailored skirt and sweater, high heels and perfume; and of course, she was perfectly made up.

For a moment, the three of them just stood there, staring at each other. Then Susanna tried to run.

Sally found herself moving faster than she had ever believed she could. She had to stop Susanna! She couldn't let her warn the other two! She seized the woman and threw her across the room so forcefully, the window rattled when Susanna struck the wall. Susanna collapsed on the floor, breathing hard.

Sally flew at her on a wave of rage. How wonderful! She wasn't scared at all, she was just *angry*! So *angry*! Then she was slapping Susanna's face, over and over, unable to help herself, she hated Susanna so much, after all of those years of oppression, all of those years of fighting for her life!

She had pulled her hand back to deliver yet another blow to Susanna's terrified, pain-ridden face, when suddenly Jim leaned down and kissed the woman on the cheek.

Sally was flabbergasted. She was shocked out of her attack.

"What are you doing?" she demanded.

Jim flushed, but his face was stubborn as he said, "I love her."

"You *love* her?"

"Yes! Just like you love Marc! And it's none of your business!"

His seductiveness had completely drained out of him. Sally clamped down on his voice box and gave him a tightly shielded message: *She's an empath, you idiot! She's manipulating us!*

Jim sent her his return message in a passionate rush, a message clogged by images and feelings that Sally could barely believe.

There was Susanna, whom Jim privately thought of as *Mother. Mother* was masturbating him, holding his libido firmly in her soft hands, guiding his masturbation with intense images of sex between mothers and sons. There she was when he was three, tickling him in his most sensitive places; there she was when he was eight, kissing him over every inch of his body; there she was when he was twelve, congratulating him the first time he ejaculated, sending him images of herself passionately licking up the result. . . .

I like it, Jim insisted. *It's better than anything anyone else could ever give me, better than* you, *Sally! I only went after you because I thought I would never see* her *again! What she does to me feels good, and I'm not going to give it up just because you don't approve of it!*

You'll have to give it up when she kills you! Sally replied urgently.

She might kill you, *but she's not going to kill* me! *She wouldn't!*

Sally sent him an image of their bus going over the

cliff, of Susanna's laughing face as she watched them fall. But he refused to acknowledge it.

Sally looked at Susanna. The woman was terrified, all the way to her core. Every cell in her brain was resonating with the emotion; she was the perfect picture of helplessness.

But Sally knew better. She could have kicked herself for the ease with which she had fallen under Susanna's spell again. She had been in the woman's control for fourteen years; she should have known better. She should have known that Jim and she would be no match for Susanna's emotional powers. Not in a fight.

"Thank God you didn't do to us girls what you did to the boys," said Sally. And then she stopped Susanna's heart.

"What are you doing?" screamed Jim. "Stop! Stop it!" And he tried to counteract Sally's will with his own; but he wasn't strong enough, he didn't know enough. When that failed, he attacked her physically, pounding on her with his fists. But Sally put a shield around herself so that his blows felt like the blows of a child. Nothing would deter her from what she needed to do. Nothing and no one.

As she watched, Susanna's face relaxed out of its terrified state into the calm, cool face Sally knew so well. Susanna hadn't even had a chance to put up a struggle. She was dead before she could send a mental cry for help, before she could even be afraid. There had been only one genuine emotion in the woman at the moment of her death.

Surprise.

Sally stood there and methodically ruptured Susanna's organs and brain cells until she felt completely safe in assuming that she was really dead.

"Don't worry," Jim said numbly, "she's dead." He

had given up his attack and now stood with his arms limply at his side. "I wish I was dead too," he added.

Sally's hands were shaking. She tried to take hold of Jim's hands, but it was like handling something dead. They were utterly limp and cold in hers. She sent him a mental message of her deep regret, of her shame, even. Because she *was* ashamed. She felt sick.

Jim just shrugged.

"She could do what you're trying to do now," he said. "A hell of a lot better than you ever will."

"Jim," said Sally, her eyes aching with tears, "you *know* she tried to kill you. You know it!"

"Yeah, I know it." He pulled his hands free and turned away from her, away from beautiful Susanna who lay cold and still on the floor. "I don't want to live in this house now."

Sally felt the numbness creeping from his mind to hers, like a tide that wanted to drag her away. She wanted to just stand there with him and stare at nothing, feel nothing while Susanna's body cooled and stiffened on the floor. But she couldn't; they had to get away as fast as they could.

"We've got to bury her," said Jim. "I won't leave her like this."

So Sally and Jim carried Susanna outside into the rain. Once Jim had the dead body in his hands, he treated it almost casually. But Sally knew how much he was suffering. He didn't need to weep to tell her that.

They flew Susanna far away, to the foothills of Apollo's mountains. Sally didn't know why she had wanted to go there to do it. Maybe it was just a need to put space between herself and Susanna's house.

And Ted. And Marc.

"They must be furious," said Jim. "They must want to kill us."

"They always did," said Sally, and that was the last

word she spoke in her own defense. It would have been better if she had said more then. She should have explained, comforted. But she was occupied with too many dreadful feelings of her own—including grief, which had sneaked in like a thief and surprised her. Grief for all of the false memories she had of joyful times with Susanna. The Susanna who never was.

Sally moved tons of rock with her talent and placed Susanna in the resulting hole. Then she covered Susanna up again.

"Good-bye," said Jim.

Sally wanted to say something too; but she couldn't think of anything. *Sorry* might have been appropriate. *I'm sorry it was so easy to kill you. But at least it hurt me to do it. At least I didn't laugh as you went over the cliff.*

Someday she might even convince herself that killing was all right. It had been self-defense, after all.

Sally raised her eyes and saw Apollo standing on a nearby hill, looking at her. Her shame burned her then, and she had to lower her eyes.

The killing had poisoned her. She was no longer worthy of Apollo's friendship. She wouldn't visit him again. She looked away, hoping he wouldn't know that she had seen him.

Jim's grief washed over her in one last wave, threatening to drown her with him. Sally was stunned by it, awed. She wondered if she should make him go to sleep.

And then he shrugged it off, like a man taking off a coat. In another moment, he felt perfectly fine. He was even a little cheerful.

"Come on," he said. "We'd better get home. Ted and Marc could show up any moment." He raised himself into the air and flitted toward home with an unburdened heart.

Sally gazed at him with horror.

What have I done? she asked herself. And then she flew after him. Whatever she had done, the results would become plain to her soon.

Very soon.

The sun was going down by the time they got home again. It turned the storm clouds spectacular colors, but no one seemed inclined to enjoy the show.

The others were waiting for Sally and Jim outside the cavern. They stood in the rain, under their force shields. Sally cringed when she saw their expressions. The boys seemed to be torn between grief, fear, and joy—except for Ralph, who looked completely blank.

"Ralph?" Sally asked him.

"Leave him alone," said Timothy. "He doesn't know how to feel yet."

"He doesn't have to feel anything at all if he doesn't want to," said Jim, who was regarding the others with an air of mild impatience. Sally looked sideways at him.

On the way home, he had reversed everything he had said in the cottage about loving Susanna, about how she would never have killed him and how he had wanted to be with her.

"She was at me almost every night," he had snarled. "Sick old broad."

So now he was saying he had hated her. But if that were the case, then why did he resent Sally so much for killing her?

The only one who didn't look upset was Caitlin. In fact she seemed to have found a new calm and self-confidence in herself. Sally would have been happy if this were really the case; but she didn't think it was. She couldn't sense anything at all from Caitlin, and she found it hard to believe that the firestorm that had always raged inside the girl was now cool.

"Now the other two will come after us," Caitlin was saying.

"But there's one less of them." Sally felt another jab of shame for what she had done, but she felt compelled to point out the advantage they had gained. "Now their Mastermind will be weaker."

"Not by much," Caitlin said. "Susanna was the weakest of The Three. Marc and Ted have the talents that matter. The ones that can really hurt us."

That was true. In fact, when Sally looked beyond her own grief and shame, she had to admit that she was terrified about what Marc and Ted might do next. In her wildest dreams, she had never planned to attack The Three; she had planned to *escape* them. But now *she* was the aggressor. She was the one who had made the first hostile move. That was how it looked, anyway.

"You're stronger than Marc," Caitlin said calmly. "You'll have to be the one to fight him."

Sally nodded. "And you're the best match for Ted. Do you think you could face up to him?"

Caitlin didn't react at all to the suggestion, except to pause slightly before answering. Sally wondered if she had frightened her. "I don't know," Caitlin admitted.

"He has more experience," Sally said. "And he has confidence. But you have . . ." she groped for a diplomatic term, then gave up. "You have a bigger ego. And you have more fire than he does."

"Youthful exuberance," snorted Caitlin, looking almost like her old self for a moment. But then the curtain was drawn again. "I'll defend myself when the time comes. I'm never going to be meek again. You can count on that."

Sally certainly did count on that. If on nothing else.

Ralph was so pale, Sally wondered if he was going to pass out. She took a step toward him, then thought better of it as Timothy put his arm around Ralph and started to guide him inside again.

"Is he all right?" Sally asked Timothy. "Does he need Joey?"

"I'm taking care of him," said Timothy.

Sally watched helplessly as Timothy took Ralph back inside. Caitlin followed. Jim looked around for a moment, as if enjoying the storm. He smiled cheerfully at Sally and said, "I'm glad I'm not you." And then he went in too.

Only Joey remained.

Sally gazed at him, too frightened of being rejected by him to say anything. He looked miserable and apprehensive. Even his considerable healing powers couldn't keep the signs of pain from his face.

"They think I'm on your side," he said.

Sally had to swallow hard before she could bring herself to ask. "Are you?"

"Yes. I was always on your side. Ralph was too, but he's . . ."

He lost his focus on her for a moment, and Sally realized that he was trying to reach Ralph. Then he looked at her again and said, "Timothy is blocking me. He says he wants to do everything for Ralph now, so he can compose. But there's something weird about it. Have you noticed Ralph is going back to the way he was before we came through the Gate?"

"He looks worse than that now," said Sally. "How come he's not playing his music?"

"He is," said Joey. "Only Timothy can hear it now. He's shut that door to everyone else."

Sally dared to move closer to Joey. He didn't flinch or back away, which was a relief. "Why?" she asked.

"I don't know. He never used to be jealous like this. But maybe he didn't have a reason to be. He was too busy trying to protect Ralph from The Three to worry about anyone else back then."

"I'm not trying to come between them," said Sally.

"You don't have to try. Ralph likes you. That's enough."

Sally had never suspected that Timothy would behave this way. She had been so blind.

"One other thing," said Joey. "I don't know how important it is, but I saw Timothy and Caitlin kissing last night."

That was astonishing. "I hadn't thought Caitlin would allow anyone to get that close to her," said Sally. "Let alone touch her."

"She has a big advantage over you. She doesn't give a damn about anyone but herself. She's not that different from Ted."

"She has one difference," Sally was surprised to hear herself say. "She knows how other people feel. Ted doesn't."

"All that means is that she knows where to stick in the knife."

Sally let out a long sigh, overwhelmed with it all, with the horror, the guilt, the suspicion, the apprehension, emotions that blended together to form one monstrous, unbearable burden. "Why does it have to be so hard?" she asked no one in particular. "Why can't there be just one moment of respite?"

Joey didn't have an answer. He only had another question. "Why does it hurt so much to know that Susanna is dead?"

It wasn't a rhetorical question. Sally stopped and thought about it for a moment. "We loved them," she said. "They made sure of it."

"We *needed* to love them," said Joey. "But they didn't love *us*, and we knew they didn't. From the beginning, there were big holes in their deception. None of us forgot what happened to Lydia, not even for a moment. We just let them think we did so they would leave us alone. And you know what, Sally? If they hadn't been so damned lazy, they would have seen right through our deception. If they had taken just a little extra time and really looked."

Sally wished she could think of something comforting to say. All she could come up with was, "We're more human than they are, Joey. That's why we needed love, fake or otherwise."

"Are we?" he asked. "Is Caitlin? I'm almost as scared of her as I am of them. Maybe I should be a lot *more* scared of her."

"I understand," said Sally. "But she's not our biggest threat. Not right now, anyway."

He shrugged, and Sally couldn't tell whether he agreed or not. He looked to the north, at black rain clouds that promised much heavier rain than what was trickling down on them at the moment.

"You know what?" he asked again.

"What?" said Sally.

"I know how I feel. I feel sorry that Susanna is dead. But if she had attacked me, I hope I could have done the same thing you did, Sally. Because I *know* she wanted to kill us. I saw her try to do it. No one is going to make me forget that."

Rain began to pour on them. Joey suddenly turned off his shield and let the rain soak him. He raised his face and closed his eyes. Sally gazed at him for a moment, then did the same.

It felt good. It was cool and sweet. It was making the plants grow, giving the world a refreshing bath, and filling the streams that would lead to the rivers, to the oceans. Distant thunder rumbled. It sounded as beautiful as Ralph's music.

"It's worth it, Joey," said Sally. "This moment."

"I know," he agreed.

After a little while, they went in, together. The cavern was dim. Everyone else had gone to his or her room. Joey stood a little apart from Sally, not looking at her. There was something almost shy in his manner. But she wasn't sure exactly what he was feeling. She hadn't been nearly as aware of the thoughts and feelings of her brothers and sister as she had been before they went through the Gate.

Now why was that? Shouldn't it have been the other way around?

"Why can't they let us go, Sally?" Joey asked, meaning The Three.

"They made us," she said. "So they thought we belonged to them."

"But they could have let us go," he insisted. "If they didn't want us."

Sally shook her head. "No, it's just like fathers who murder their families. They can't bear to think that everyone would go off and have a life without them."

"No," he said. "It's not that simple. I'll bet you." And then he walked off toward his own bedroom.

Good night, he sent to Sally. She was glad to hear it. Glad to know that not everyone hated her now.

Sally was alone. *Really* alone. She didn't feel anything from anyone. That had never been true before, never in her life.

If you forced it, you could break down all of their shields and know everything you wanted to know, she told herself, and knew it was true. But she couldn't bear to do that. Not after what she had already done.

She didn't want to hurt them. Not her brothers and sister. She would never hurt them, even if they threatened her.

She went off to bed herself, believing that.

She woke briefly in the night and tried to turn over. It took her several moments to remember why she couldn't.

They had tied her to her bunk. Well, that was not so bad; at least they hadn't killed her, like they had originally planned to do. She had charmed them quite well. Given time, they would be eating out of her hand.

She flexed all of her muscles, the closest she could come to a stretch under the circumstances, and then she went back to sleep.

Sally turned onto her side. Why had she thought she couldn't turn over? That must have been a dream. Something about being tied up. But that wouldn't be a problem for Sally; she could disintegrate any rope or chain. How silly to be scared of something like that.

She sighed and went back to sleep.

She felt a hand on her face. When she opened her eyes she saw one of the Germans leaning over her. She hid her surprise. She had forgotten and thought she was back with the English soldiers again.

Are you thirsty? he asked her in German, much more concern in his voice than he had shown her the day before.

Yes, she replied, also in German.

Languages had always come easily for her. It had been easy for her to get a job in the British Secret Service once the war had started. It had also been easy to get a job in the German SS, the French Underground, and then the Russian Secret Service. . . .

All of them thought she worked for them. But really, Susanna worked for herself, only herself now, all of her patriotic feelings burned out of her in North Africa where they had had no bloody right to send her. She had done things for her country that no one had any right to ask a woman to do.

Now she just survived. In fact, now she did more than survive. Now she worked to get herself on the top of the heap. Of *any* heap, English, German, American, whoever ended up with the best heap of all.

He helped her drink. He put his hands under her and lifted her, held her. He was very careful with the water, trying not to spill it on her. He was burned by the sun, but he was still so fresh and young and pink—so young she almost pitied him as she looked into his eyes and saw him falling in love with her. He was a charming young man, and she loved charming young men, their innocence, their eagerness to please. Back home, she had had so many boyfriends. . . .

It's hot, yes? he asked.

Yes, Susanna agreed, in between sips.

Back home, she had owned so many nice things. Silk stockings, perfume. She had been given her first pair of stockings when she was twelve. Mother hadn't liked that. Mother had taken a good deal of charming to get over that. Older people were always harder to charm.

Like the German captain. He had been almost too smart for it. He had taken great subtlety; but then, Susanna had learned all about subtlety in her new job. She wasn't the same person she had been when she left Winchester. She was only twenty, but there was very little that the German captain could have taught her in the way of new tricks.

She heard him outside, barking orders. He was coming toward the tent.

Get ready, she told herself. *It's time to go to work.*

And then everything just seemed to blow apart.

It started with a shout, that staccato German bark that was so distinctive, so unforgettable when you were on the receiving end of it. The young man who was helping Susanna stiffened, then dropped her as the gunfire began. He ran out of the tent.

"Don't leave me!" she cried in English.

People were screaming, a thousand guns seemed to

be shooting. Susanna struggled to get loose from her bounds, but an expert had tied her. Why did Germans have to be such damned experts at everything?

Someone had started an engine, something was on fire, explosions, more gunfire, the captain shouting orders, someone shouting back. . . .

And then just the engine. Susanna listened, hoping it wasn't coming her way, hoping it wasn't a tank headed straight at the tent with a dead driver at the controls. Because he *was* dead, all of them were dead, she could feel it. It was like her gift for charm; she knew how people felt, sometimes even what they thought. It was just so obvious to her, she had often wondered why no one else seemed to know it. You had to tell other people everything, just everything, how dim could you get!

The tank went away. She heard a dull thud as it drove into something and the engine died.

Susanna took an hour and a half to struggle out of her bonds. Her skin was broken and bleeding by the time she was out, but that would look good to whoever had killed the Germans. It would evoke sympathy, at the very least.

She peeked through the tent flap. Nothing was moving out there.

That was scary. Susanna had sensed someone out there, fighting the Germans. In fact, it should have been several someones. Now she couldn't feel *anyone* out there. Where had they gone?

She stepped out. The sun was high and blazing. Bodies were strewn in the sand. The young man had only gotten a few paces before he had been gunned down. Now he lay dead with all of the other young men, all the young men who died in wars. . . .

George Butterworth was killed in World War I. He could have been another Vaughan Williams. So many talented composers were killed, so many people with promise. . . .

The Germans had camped at the mouth of a valley. It was the Valley of Kings. Susanna hadn't thought they were that far into Egypt. She had gotten completely turned around weeks ago, had stumbled from place to place, side to side.

Someone was in the valley. Susanna began to walk. She had no definite plan, but she couldn't stay with the dead Germans. She didn't know how to drive a tank.

Yea, though I may walk in the shadow of the Valley of Death, she thought to herself, but didn't add the part about fearing no evil. She feared plenty of evil. She had seen so much of it lately.

Someone was up ahead. He was just standing with his back turned to her, as if he were looking at something fascinating. But there was nothing to see. All of the tombs were hidden. She walked within ten paces of him, then stopped herself.

From behind, he looked so ordinary. He was wearing a linen suit, which was characteristically rumpled. The skin on the back of his neck was sunburned, but not terribly wrinkled. He might be thirty.

Suddenly he turned and looked at her. He was as ordinary from the front as he was from the back. At least, he *looked* ordinary.

He stared at Susanna briefly, then he was inside her mind, probing and fingering at private places.

Not bloody likely! Susanna told him, and shrugged him off.

He was astonished. He tried again, this time without the nasty stuff. But Susanna shrugged him off again.

He laughed. "You're like me!" he said, with an American accent. "Amazing! I've never met another one."

"Me neither," said Susanna.

He grinned at her, then gestured at the Valley. "This all has to be preserved," he said.

"Preserved?"

"Saved. We have to keep them from destroying it."

Susanna didn't particularly want to see Egyptian relics destroyed either; after all, they were rather pretty. But she wondered why he cared so much.

"It's the art of the gods," he said. "It will show us the way to ascend. We have to study it."

"And precisely to whence shall we ... ascend?" asked Susanna, interested despite herself.

"That's what we need to find out," said Ted. "Someplace that's worthy of us. Someplace that's better than this. You want to be at the top of the heap? The top is a lot farther up than you might imagine."

He had picked that out of her mind in just the few seconds he had touched it. And he had given her his name.

"Ted is a funny name for a god," said Susanna gently.

He shrugged. Her attempt to stroke his emotions had fallen a little flat. He didn't feel much. He hadn't felt anything when he tricked the Germans into killing themselves except for a mild fascination with the bloodletting and the machinery, an almost childish fascination.

"I can always change my name," he said.

"Why not?" she said. "But in the meantime, what are you going to do?"

"My slaves have food and drink," said Ted. "They'll keep us comfortable. And we can keep protecting this place, until the stupid war is over."

"Why this place, and not Greece? Or Turkey?"

He frowned. "I would protect them too, if I could. I had to pick one."

"Well then, why don't you just make them end the war? Like you made the Germans kill each other?"

"Why don't *you*?"

He was right, of course. The war was a juggernaut. Changing a few minds wouldn't stop it. Changing a *million* minds wouldn't stop it. Change Hitler, and another Hitler would step into his place.

"I tried it already," admitted Ted. "I've got no more time to waste."

He walked briskly past her. Susanna followed, thinking that he must be leading her to the slaves, to the food and water. But he led her back to the tank. He poked around inside it until he found some tools. Then slowly, methodically, he began to take it apart.

Susanna watched helplessly.

"Go lie down for a while," said Ted. "This could take days."

"But—" said Susanna.

"The slaves are coming. They'll bring food."

Susanna turned away from him. She walked back to the tent, through the bodies. The sand was absorbing the blood. Soon it would absorb the corpses too.

Cheer up, she told the body of the young man. *You're resting with kings. Maybe when Ted and I reach heaven, we'll see you there. And then what fun we'll have!*

She laughed and went into the tent. She lay down and closed her eyes.

She fell asleep, again.

Sally woke with a start.

She had to stop and make sure she really *was* Sally. She replayed her memories of the last few days; she even looked down at her own body. She was definitely Sally. But for what had seemed like hours, she had been someone else.

She had been *Susanna.* She had shared Susanna's ambitions and fears.

I've got to go look in that grave. I have to make sure she's really dead.

But she didn't move. What good would it do? If she had been fooled then, she was still being fooled now. She remembered very clearly what it had been like to kill Susanna, what it had *felt* like. If The Three could pull off that kind of deception, Sally had underestimated them badly.

You pulled it off yourself. You made them think you were dead. You made a fake bus and fake bodies, and now they're ashes, waiting to fool anyone who goes to look at them. Turnabout is fair play.

So if that was the way it was going to be, she shouldn't be surprised.

But how interesting it had been to be Susanna. Susanna was a *spy* during World War II! And that was when she had met Ted. Maybe. It might all be a story, but Sally had to admit she was curious. If it was all true, the two of them must have met first, and then Marc . . .

Marc . . .

SALLY! came Jim's hysterical cry.

Sally jumped up and ran to the main cavern. But a lot happened before she could get there, in just those few seconds before she could see what she already knew.

Marc was home.

Jim and Joey were the first ones to spot him. They were both terrified and happy to see him. He was his same smiling old self, human and not godlike at all, and maybe they could talk him into joining them, maybe . . .

Marc! Sally thought to herself, not daring to send him a message yet, not daring to hope but still unable to keep *wanting* to hope. In another moment she would see him, talk to him, make him understand.

Marc looked around the cavern, wonder clearly

written on his face. Then he saw Jim. He took a moment to observe the changes the young man had made in himself. He smiled.

He attacked.

He tried to explode every cell in Jim's body, just as he had done to the would-be killers at the gas station. Sally saw it coming, she knew what the process felt like, and she clamped down on it immediately.

Marc took one second to realize she was there, and she felt a surge of pride in him as he saw her vastly improved ability. Then, while still trying to explode Jim's cells, he tried to do the same to Sally. She stopped that too; and the struggle began in earnest.

Yet still she couldn't bring herself to attack him.

Stop, she begged.

He didn't answer.

Listen to me! It doesn't have to be this way!

He stabbed out at Ralph.

Sally reacted reflexively. She blocked his attack and returned it, making sharp, random stabs at his inner organs. She set up an automatic system, so that even *she* didn't know where she'd be attacking next; so he couldn't anticipate her if he happened to slip through her shield.

Good girl, he said, completely surprised; betrayed and hurt, as well. These reactions were genuine and horrible for Sally to observe. They undermined her efforts, made it twice as hard for her to do her work.

Please, Marc, can't you be part of our Mastermind now?

He grimaced as one of her attacks ruptured something and he had to repair it.

Remember the hamburger and fries you used to feed me? Sally pleaded. *Remember how we used to dance for you? Caitlin and me and Lyd—Lydia—*

He was sweating now.

Please, stop! We'll talk, we can work out an

agreement! We'll put the past behind us and figure out a way—

No, sweetheart.

Why not? We're your children! You love us; I know you love us!

You're not in our league, Sally. And you killed Susie.

I'm sorry I killed Susie! I'm sorry!

He responded by doubling his efforts to kill her. She was feeling the pain now, feeling her body trying to fly into a billion fragments. Almost, she wanted to give in to it, because seeing him this way, feeling him killing her, was unbearable, it was agony, it was like the grief she had felt after Susanna died magnified a thousand times, a million times; and there he was, her handsome love, her Marc, and he wanted her dead, and it just couldn't go on.

It just couldn't.

So she ruptured his heart; and when he tried to fix it, she wouldn't let him.

He was astonished for one moment. He struggled, unable to believe that she could pull it off. He struggled, and he failed; and then he knew.

I'm sorry, baby, he sent to her as he died. *I'm the one who's not in* your *league.*

Sally watched his body fall. *Don't go!* she cried after him. *I didn't mean for you to go!*

But he was dead. He was *really* dead, because Sally was half dead herself. Her injuries weren't imagined, they weren't illusion. She was bleeding from every pore; and Jim was lying not far from her, howling in his own pain.

Sally gazed at Marc, wanting to go put her arms around his body, wanting to howl herself. But she couldn't. She couldn't move or speak; she could barely breathe. Her heart felt like it was turning to stone and being squeezed right out of her chest.

Marc . . .

No answer. He was an empty shell. Whatever patterns had sparked in his brain to make him the man she had adored, they were dry and dead. They were ashes.

"Stop carrying on!" Joey shouted at Jim. "You're distracting me!"

He was healing Jim's wounds. He was pumping calming chemicals into the other boy at the same time. Sally wished he would do the same for her. But maybe she was beyond healing.

No, she was healing herself. She hadn't realized it; she was doing it automatically. In fact, she wasn't even sitting up anymore, staring at the body of her love. She was almost unconscious, she was sprawled in a heap, and no one was coming to help her.

Alone. You'll have to do it alone. . . .

Jim can't do it for himself, sent Joey, sounding both annoyed and sympathetic. *You can. You're as good as I am. I'll come help you when I've got him squared away.*

Squared away. Sally would never be squared away. Her mind kept going back to the moment of Marc's death, probing the sore place inside her. Every time she relived it, it felt worse. She couldn't even cry, because the grief felt like it was clogged in her throat, jammed there by its sheer volume and growing larger every moment, choking her. She wanted to reach out and touch his body, feel it while it was still warm. She wanted him to get up and hold her, love her, tell her it wasn't her fault.

She had talked so calmly of killing The Three after they had first come through the Gate. But she hadn't really understood what that would mean, how that would feel. And now she knew it wasn't worth it. She wished she had let him kill her instead.

The back of his neck. All those years. I didn't get to

*plant even one kiss there. Just one kiss, and to breathe
in his smell and feel his arms around me.*

You'd better get a grip. Joey's thought seemed to
come from a million miles away, oddly calm and hol-
low. *Your feelings are getting in the way of the healing.
Put them away for a while.*

Sally knew how. Why not? If she kept on with the
pain, it would drive her to extinction. She had fought
too long, too hard to just let go like this. Time was
supposed to heal all wounds, wasn't it?

Wasn't it?

She changed the chemical balance in her brain very
slowly. The grief ebbed away like the morning tide,
going farther and farther from her shore until she
could stare calmly at it from a great distance.

She made the major repairs first. Then she stood
back and surveyed the rest of the damage. There was
quite a lot of it, but it was mostly cosmetic. Her skin
was a mess, her hair had all fallen out. Her body was
rapidly replacing ruptured cells with new ones, and
she was excreting the ruined stuff from every orifice
and pore. She cleaned up the mess, but otherwise did
not interfere with the priorities that her body had set
for its healing. It was interesting, diverting, she hardly
felt any emotion at all besides curiosity as she observed it. That was a relief.

She confronted Marc's death again. How long ago
had it happened? A few hours. She supposed they had
removed his body by now.

*Oh, well. He was dangerous. Life is going to be safer
without him.*

Sally wondered if she shouldn't try to move herself
from the floor of the cavern. She didn't want to be
lying there for days, like a piece of furniture that everyone had to walk around. She tried to move her
head, open her eyes to ascertain her position.

She *thought* she opened them. But she was disoriented by what she found. Darkness and straight angles. A carpet under her. A musty smell that was familiar.

The hallway. Behind her should be the window, and out the window she would see the wonderful mountains. Sally moved her head, painfully, slowly, through sheer will alone, because her muscles didn't want to work. She found the window. But there were no mountains out there.

Instead, she saw their cavern. The others were all clustered around someone on the floor. As Sally watched, the person on the floor levitated. There was Joey; he was moving the person away.

Marc's body? Haven't they buried him yet?

But this person dripped fresh blood. This person was Sally.

Are they going to bury me too? But no, they were moving her into her room. Joey was placing her on her bed.

Sally! he called.

Here.

Jim is okay. You were hurt a lot worse than him.

I see you...! She almost felt like giggling, but wasn't quite amused enough.

I'm going to keep monitoring you, but you're doing a good job.

I'm not even there. I'm in the hallway again. I'll bet Lydia is here, somewhere.

He got a funny look on his face. He looked around the room.

You're dreaming, he said.

No, I'm not. I bet she'll talk to me any minute.

Quit trying to scare me. You're not going to die.

Sally wondered about that. Her body was healing well, but things didn't feel quite right, still. Something big and bad was wrong. Big and bad.

We'll see, she said.

Don't leave me, Sally. Please. I can't face them alone.
I'm working on it, she promised. *I'm always working on it.*

He sat down on the floor next to her bed. She felt vaguely sorry for him. He seemed worried. He should try what she was doing, just toy with those brain chemicals a little bit and your worries are all gone, they're history.

Sally turned her head again. She had to drag it along the floor to get it back into a comfortable position. She felt the old carpet under her cheek, smelled that familiar musty smell. A little light was leaking into the hallway now from the window. As Sally watched, the light turned golden, and someone at the end of the hall was illuminated. Someone walking toward her prone body.

She was torn between the desire to turn her head and look out the window again—because surely the mountains were out there now, those symbols of her hopes and dreams—and the desire to see who was coming. Her protesting muscles decided for her. She kept looking down the hall.

And damned if it wasn't Lydia, after all.

"Hello," Sally tried to call, but only managed to croak. *Hello, Lydia. Are you going to say something coherent this time?*

Lydia's lips were moving. Sally could read them, a little. She could see them shaping the word *Philip*.

"Philip—" Lydia plainly said.

"Yes," croaked Sally. "Philip?"

"Philip says . . ." said Lydia.

"Who's Philip?"

But Lydia was gone. Someone else was coming down the hall now. Someone tall and trim, someone handsome.

"Ask Lydia what she meant," said Sally. "Who's

Philip? Is she talking about Philip Glass? What does Philip Glass say? 'Keep up the good work, Ralph'?"

The person stopped. He looked down at her. He was Marc. He looked puzzled. "What have you done?" he asked Sally.

Sally felt a pang in her chest.

"I—" she said, but couldn't speak the words.

I have killed you. I have done what you did so ruthlessly before me. But I have grieved for you.

"Have you?" he said. "Are you?"

Yes. I loved you.

"I loved you too. And what did I feel when you were dead?"

Nothing! You felt nothing! You turned it off.

"You've learned my trick well, Sally. I never expected that of you. Not my special girl."

Yes, this was how Marc had felt about killing *her.* This was how he had done it all those years, killed without regret; this was how he could kill the people he loved. He clamped down on the feeling of remorse and grief at their source, in his brain. That way he could have the best of both worlds, enjoying the love and the compassion and then being ruthless and expedient when he wanted to.

"But you were always different," he said. "No one could love like you did, Sally. No one."

He was sad that she had changed. That was the greatest puzzle of all. Sally could see how it had gone. She could see herself going there too.

No. That's not what I've worked so hard for. Defeating The Three just so I could become them. No.

"Sally, where am I?" asked Marc. He looked frightened now.

You're with Lydia. You're with Philip.

That shocked him. "No," he said. "I can't be. They're dead."

So are you, Marc, she said, and felt all of the tears flowing back to her.

"No, I'm not," he said, but he was scared that she was telling the truth.

Please don't be afraid. Find Lydia. She'll help you.

He shook his head. "No," he whispered.

I love you, Marc. I'm sorry. I wish I could go back and change everything.

"Change everything," he said. "That's what you would have to do, all right."

And then he was gone. The hallway was gone too. Sally was back in her room, on the hard bed, with Joey crouched nearby. She started to cry. Once she started, the sobs racked her whole body.

"That's too much," Joey told her. "Calm down!"

But Sally wouldn't, not even when he tried to make her. *It has to be like this,* she told him. *This is how I have to feel if I still want to be me!*

And she did. Even though Joey couldn't comfort her, didn't know *how* to comfort her, because when had any of them learned such a thing? There was no one. But that was the way it had to be.

I don't understand you, said Joey, but to his credit, he stayed anyway.

⚜

"What's taking her so long?" Sally heard Caitlin ask Joey.

"She's got a broken heart."

"What a waste of time! Who does she think she is? We all loved him, and now we're all over it. He wanted to kill us, for chrissakes!"

"She loved him more than we did."

"She still doesn't get it." *Sally! Our biggest danger is past now! You killed the only one who could have killed us!*

Sally didn't answer Caitlin. She wanted the girl to go away and leave her alone.

Can't you figure it out? Don't you understand why Marc came by himself? Ted is afraid of us, Sally! He's terrified! He's always been worried that we would turn on him, the big coward. That's why he killed Lydia. And now we have *turned on him! He's going to hide in the darkest hole he can find and stay there!*

That's nice, said Sally, not really caring.

There was a long pause, during which minutes or days may have passed. Sally steeped in her misery. But she continued her healing process, carefully avoiding the temptation to tamper with her brain chemicals again. Occasionally she could feel Joey trying to help.

"You're making me sick," he said. He had to withdraw from her every time her grief got to be too much for him. But he kept coming back.

Eventually Sally found herself thinking less about Marc and more about what Caitlin had said. *Why did he attack us alone?* she wondered. *And why did Susanna?*

Why hadn't they formed their Mastermind? They always did that; Sally had never known them to face a threat any other way. Of course, the Kids hadn't done it either; but they had been too startled, too inexperienced. The Three should have fallen right into it.

What if Caitlin was right? What if Ted really was afraid?

She thought back to the time of Lydia's death.

It's no good! he had said. *They'll each try to kill us as they get stronger!*

She tried to remember what his feelings had been, but that was pretty useless. She had been a child, and she hadn't comprehended him very well. But it was tempting to think that he had been afraid. Especially after he had figured out that they weren't really dead.

When had he done that? When had The Three realized they weren't really in Olympus? Was it when the animals and the bugs had shown up? Maybe Ted had tried to make them go away again, and he hadn't been able. But why should he have cared? He should have ascended to godhood by then, whatever the hell that was.

Yes, whatever that was. What form could he have taken? Maybe that was the problem: He had waited to sprout wings, and it hadn't happened.

This was all speculation, of course. Just as it was speculation to wonder if Susanna and Marc were really dead or just casting an illusion like the one Sally had cast. Sally could keep an open mind and try not to assume *anything* about what she was seeing and hearing and feeling. That might be the best course.

Or it might drive her right out of her mind.

"One day at a time," said Marc.

She heard him, clearly. For a dead man, he sounded quite lively.

He sounded like he was standing right next to her. Sally tried to open her eyes. At first she couldn't do it, but in another moment she could see everything.

There was Marc, and he really was alive. But things weren't quite what they seemed. For one thing, she wasn't in Olympus anymore, and neither was he.

For another thing, she was Susanna again.

She knew it instantly; but this time she didn't lose herself in the other woman. This time she was able to sit back and quietly observe, almost as if she were watching a movie through Susanna's eyes.

She could also smell through Susanna's nose, taste with her mouth, and so on; so it wasn't quite like a movie. Not quite.

For instance, there was the way Marc was looking at her. And the way he reacted when she tried to manipulate his feelings.

"That's interesting, what you're doing," he said with a half grin. "But you don't need to pull my strings to make me like you, baby." He looked her up and down, making her feel thrilled and worried at the same time. This one was not like Ted. He understood his emotions perfectly well.

And he was *powerful*.

He was powerful in a way that Susanna had never experienced before. Ted was into thoughts, and she could move emotions. But this man could move *things*.

"I take things one day at a time," said Marc, moving another huge boulder into place by just glancing at it. He wasn't making anything in particular, just a sort of Stonehenge to occupy his attention and hone his talents. "I used to only be able to move small things," he said. "But every time I use it, I get stronger."

Susanna watched him speculatively. She had encountered him by accident, felt him working his talents from a distance when she and Ted had been driving through the Arizona desert. Ted was obsessed with Arizona for some reason, had always said that he felt the gods calling him there. Susanna could feel them calling herself, now that she was looking at Marc.

He lived in Tucson. He didn't do much of anything except entertain himself, though he had said that once he had been in the Marines.

"It was too easy," he said. "Everything is too easy. I didn't even have to kill anyone when I was in Korea. But I killed someone when I got back. Some asshole who tried to hurt my mom."

His mom was dead now. He still grieved for her. Susanna wanted to slide herself around the emotion, move him with it. But he changed his feelings back as soon as she touched them. He looked at her with that grin and he grabbed her with his hands, pulled her close.

"That's right, baby," he said. "You just change a few chemicals and they're eating out of your hands, right? Like this."

And he was inside her body, heating it up, making her want him. She didn't fight it, but she went cautiously. Susanna was thirty-five now. She had been with Ted for fifteen years. She liked Marc a lot better; he could be moved with sex. Ted only wanted mental sex with helpless victims, and Susanna would never play that role with him.

Marc, though . . .

"You're beautiful," he said, and kissed her.

Sally enjoyed it more than Susanna did. Sally reveled in it. She knew it wasn't for her, and she knew it was from the past, but it was all she had. She wished she could make Susanna's body do what *she* wanted it to do, make it say what she wanted to say. *Marc, I love you! Don't become one of The Three, don't let them turn you into Kronos!* But of course if he listened to her, she would never exist. She and the other kids would never be made. Made by . . .

"Right here," said Marc, and he pulled Susanna down to the soft grass and kissed her, kissed her, touched her with his wonderful hands.

"You don't have to be satisfied with building giant blocks," said Susanna. "Like a child, playing. You could build something better."

"Like what?" he murmured, intrigued despite himself.

"We can find out, love. We can find out."

And now he was pulling their clothing apart just enough so that he could slide himself inside of her and stroke her with a wonderful, hot, slow rhythm. And more, he was making it last and last and last. . . .

"Let me do it," he urged. "I'm in the driver's seat. I've got you, baby."

And how he did. She loved it, how she adored young men with their strong bodies and their hot rush of feelings. And she was still beautiful, Susanna, only thirty-five now and extremely well-preserved. She still turned heads.

"I can keep you young," said Marc. "I can keep you looking this way forever. I could fuck you every night if you want."

"I want," said Susanna. "I believe I do." She and Sally reveled in the moment, letting go, letting him do what he wanted, which just happened to be so delightful. He really *could* keep Susanna young, that was a nice thing to have discovered. He might even be able to teach her how to do it herself. He hadn't been able to do it for his mother, though; he hadn't been able to save her from dying. He hadn't had the skill back then. That made him very sad.

But right now he wasn't sad. Right now he was outrageously, marvelously horny. Right now he was using every naughty trick he had ever learned to please her and himself.

Sally would have wept if she could. But maybe it was good that she couldn't.

Ted had been frightened when he had seen that Marc could move objects with his mind. But he had been intrigued too; and over the years he had learned to accept what Susanna could accomplish with her talent, just as she had learned to believe in his dream. They really *could* ascend, they really *could* become gods. And now Marc would help them, and Susanna would be very, very grateful, oh so grateful, so delightfully, completely . . .

She moaned, letting him see how much she loved it. He grinned that maddening grin. "It's only the beginning," he promised.

Yes, only the beginning, because he was coming with them. He was one of them. Soon he would learn about the Mastermind; and then nothing would be impossible for them.

Good work, Ted sent.

I know, said Susanna, and she smiled back at Marc, seeing the love in his eyes, love that she hadn't had to manipulate.

Sally, said Joey.

"Wait," she moaned. Susanna was headed for her first climax, and Sally wanted to feel it too.

What are you doing?

"Wait . . ."

Yes. Yes, it was coming, it was surging over her and it was so good. "I knew you could be like this," she told Marc, and felt real tears coming out of her eyes. But they weren't Susanna's eyes, they were hers, and now she could see Joey looking down at her with a bemused look on his face. The last spasms were passing through her, leaving her relieved, satisfied; still sad, but somehow past the worst of it.

Susanna and Marc were gone, back in the past where they belonged.

"You must be feeling better," said Joey.

"Yeah," said Sally, still crying.

"Are you ever going to stop doing that?" he asked, meaning the tears, not the spasms.

"I don't know," she admitted. "But I feel better. I think I can sit up."

And she did. Sitting up made her a little dizzy, and once she was there, she couldn't think of anything much she wanted to do. But it was progress.

Joey was alone. She realized that he had been alone for most of the time he had been watching over her. He looked a little haggard, which surprised her. There was no reason he should look that way, not with his healing abilities. Yet he had been strained to his limit, that was the problem. He had suffered by watching her suffer.

"I'm sorry," she said.

He shrugged. "My choice."

Sally felt her skin, which was whole again. She rubbed her new hair. "How are—what are the others doing?"

"I saw Ralph crying after it happened. Timothy too, but he wouldn't let me get near the two of them. Jim just shrugged it off, and Caitlin's been flying around the countryside like a queen bee. She's been a little . . . scary."

Sally took a deep breath. She tried to perk up, to do what Joey had taught her about supplementing. Her body had been doing it for her automatically, which might have explained Joey's state. She might have been borrowing from *him*. That would explain why he had to keep leaving, to recover.

He had been there for her. She hadn't expected that.

"Thank you," she said.

He shrugged again. She couldn't sense very much emotion from him. He must have been too worn out.

"Do they blame me for Marc's death?" asked Sally.

"*I* don't. I saw what he tried to do. You aren't the only one who figured out what was going on over the years."

"Really, Joey?"

He nodded, keeping his brown eyes squarely on hers. He sent her a thought image. Sally recognized some of the stuff that Susanna had been doing to Jim.

I wonder why Marc wasn't enough for her, she thought, remembering the passion she had felt from Marc and Susanna. *They must have changed so much over the years....*

"She did it to all of us," Joey said. "She made the other guys love her. But I never did."

"How did you avoid it?"

"Sort of like you did with Ted, but not as good as you. Mainly I killed my sex drive."

"So ... when she sent those images to you, you didn't feel anything."

"I felt annoyed. That was all. And she didn't like that. Sometimes she got mad at me and I would try to damp the annoyance so I didn't feel anything at all; but that just hurt her pride."

"Didn't she get suspicious when she didn't get the feelings she wanted from you?"

"No. Mostly she felt bored. But she kept trying anyway, and that's how I learned how she was doing it. I used to think she sent and received emotions just like Ted did with thoughts. But she was really more like Marc. She changed people's brain chemicals, just like you were doing to yourself after you killed Marc."

Sally winced at the sound of it.

"And now I'm thinking maybe Ralph was right when he said telepathy is telekinesis. The Three all had the same talent, it just came out different in all of them, like it did in us. And if you take long enough to learn, you can do anything anyone else can do."

He said it in such a wooden way, Sally almost stopped listening to what he was saying, almost didn't catch what was happening underneath it all. Or what *wasn't* happening. What was wrong with him?

"You're stifling your emotions just like I did," she said.

"Yes."

She sighed. How could she convince him not to? He had seen what she had gone through.

"Why did you stop it, Sally? Why did you let the bad feelings come back?"

Sally wished he could feel what she had just felt between Marc and Susanna. She wished he could have seen Susanna when she had first met Ted. They hadn't been perfect back then, but they hadn't been the sort of people who could kill children either.

"Stopping the bad feelings is what Marc used to do, Joey. That's what he did after he thought he had killed us."

"You're afraid we're going to be like them?"

"Yes."

Joey shook his head, as if she were a stubborn child and he the adult. "We *are* like them, Sally. What's so bad about that?"

She couldn't answer, not with a million words, not if he didn't already know. Or did he? She reached tentatively toward him with a scan. He didn't resist it, so she went deep. She found out that he wasn't actively stifling his emotions, it was more a matter of habit. He had reversed that habit after they had gone through the Gate, but now he was back to it again, coping with grief in his old fashion. If he kept it up, before long he wouldn't be able to feel grief or compassion at all; but his ability to reach into other people's bodies would still be horribly intact.

"Let me change you back, Joey."

"Why?"

"You know why."

His heart rate began to accelerate. He *did* know why, and what's more, he trusted her. He respected her. But he was afraid to feel what she had felt.

"Ted is still out there," he said.

"But his Mastermind is gone."

"He still has us."

Sally started. "What do you mean? We aren't his thralls anymore!"

"You and I aren't," said Joey.

Sally's heart began to pound in time with his. She hadn't asked him too much about the others yet. She was almost afraid to.

"You've been trying to respect everyone's privacy," said Joey. "I know why you want to do that. But these people, our brothers and sister—I don't believe they all respect *respect*. You know what I mean."

"Yes," said Sally.

"So. You still want to change my feelings back to normal?"

"Yes."

"And I'll feel bad. Like you were feeling bad."

"Maybe. Probably."

Joey looked at her in his direct way, probing only with his eyes. She didn't even feel a feather brush from his mind. But he seemed satisfied with what he saw. "Go ahead," he said.

When it was done, Joey was sad. Angry too. But his feelings weren't as intense as Sally's had been.

Years of damping them had made his emotional connections with The Three weaker than hers.

"You did the right thing," Joey said, but he walked away before Sally could ask him if he was talking about what she had done to him or what she had done to Marc.

Sally didn't pursue him. She needed time alone herself. She rather hoped the others wouldn't want to talk to her when she came out. But she needn't have worried about that. When she went into the main cavern, no one came out to greet her. Jim and Caitlin were outside somewhere, heavily shielded so that she couldn't even pinpoint their exact location unless she really pushed it.

She assumed Ralph was in his room working; but that was a guess, because Timothy was the only one she could find. It was as if Timothy had completely surrounded Ralph with himself. Sally had no access to Ralph at all unless she probed straight through his brother, something he probably wouldn't let her do without a fight. Timothy was acutely aware of her. He had seen what she had done to Marc, and now he was waiting for her to attack him too. But Sally would never do that.

I'm not like The Three, she told him. He didn't answer, and he didn't relax his guard.

Sally went outside. The world was still there, still beautiful. The mountains to the north were calling her. Apollo's mountains. Looking at them brought back an old feeling, one she had forgotten in the last several days.

Hope.

I won't try to find Apollo. I'll just fly around for a while, get familiar with the place. Caitlin is right. We aren't in as much danger now that Marc and Susanna are dead.

If they're really dead. . . .

But if they weren't, it wouldn't do any good to mope around the cavern waiting for the others to appreciate her, to realize that she was trying to do the right thing. There was still so much to learn out there, out in Olympus. And Apollo ...

Probably won't even talk to me, now that I'm a murderer.

So? If he wouldn't talk, that was his business. If she could face herself, she could certainly face him. And she wanted to do something, to fly, to stop feeling miserable!

With that last thought, she felt herself rising in the air, rushing toward the mountains. She sent a brief message to Joey, to let him know where she was going.

Okay, he said, keeping the barest trickle of a link open with her so they could warn each other if Ted attacked.

I know what I'll do, she thought to herself. *I'll go find the mountains from my visions of Lydia. Maybe they really do exist! If they do, they'll give me some real hope, and if they don't ...*

If they didn't, she would just have to keep looking for them anyway.

She didn't bother with a shield this time. In fact, looking back on it, it was funny that she hadn't tried to use any sort of shield against Marc when he had attacked her either. She had countered each of his blows as they had come. She hadn't had time to think, to decide which defense would work the best. So had she won by skill, talent, or both? Or had it all been dumb chance?

Whatever the reason, she didn't feel the need to shield herself now. The world was either safer than it had been before or more dangerous than she could possibly imagine; either way, a shield was not appropriate.

She saw the eagles. She made herself as innocuous as possible and followed them. They were hunting. Those that had found prey were eating it and flying back to their nests to regurgitate it for their young.

Sally followed them and perched a short distance away on the face of a cliff, masking herself from their sight—even going so far as to mask sound and smell too, since a quick scan told her that they could detect her on those levels as well. They were especially vigilant now that they had chicks to care for.

Sally forgot her troubles as she watched them. She almost forgot *herself*. It was very easy not to think, to just *be*. She wondered what it was like to be one of them, wondered if she could do it without forgetting that she was a human being. After all, once the brain had altered to that extent, wouldn't she cease to exist as Sally? But what if you could modify the design so that the brain was still intelligent and you could keep your memory patterns intact? It would be incredibly complicated, but it ought to be possible. Theoretically.

"Yes, it's possible," said Apollo, softly, right in her ear—yet without startling her, almost as if he had been one of her own thoughts.

She turned her head and found him perched right next to her. Like her, he was in an awkward, impossible position, maintained by sheer will alone; yet he looked graceful doing it, as if such impossible physical feats were well within his unaugmented abilities.

"You can keep your own mind, but you may lose your desire to be human again. And thusly, you may lose your humanity. But is it worth keeping? That's the question you must ask yourself."

"Did you ask yourself that question, once?" said Sally.

"Yes."

"And what was your answer?"

"What form do you see before you?" he said.

"I might have a different answer, though."

"You might."

It was tempting. She could leave her troubles behind, just fly away and live an animal life among creatures who wouldn't know she was anything more than what she appeared to be, who wouldn't try to sneak into her mind and kill her. And Timothy would be glad to see her go. Jim and Caitlin too.

But Ralph and Joey would be alone then. And Sally was pretty sure they needed her.

Apollo watched her silently. She had forgotten how handsome he was, how much his presence startled and disturbed her. He was human; and her memory of Susanna and Marc's first meeting was not so dim in her memory that she had forgotten certain other feelings either.

"You were going to come to lunch," said Apollo.

"I've been too busy murdering people."

He didn't frown, but she almost wished he would. He looked directly into her eyes and said, "You don't believe you're a murderer, so why should I?"

"I *do* believe it."

But she was being stubborn. He knew perfectly well that she didn't, because she was as much an open book to him as he was to her. No shield was between them at all, not even the unconscious one that all human beings had; there was no barrier to hide thoughts or motives. Sally didn't know whether she was more embarrassed or intrigued. How could *he* stand it? But he was Apollo; his thoughts were pure.

He laughed. "Not pure. But they are yours for the reading if that's what you want. And what will you do once you know them? Kill me? Love me? Laugh at me? I'm not afraid."

Sally blushed. She didn't try to stop the physiological reaction, since he was aware of the emotion that was causing it. It was the word *love* that had seized her. Marc had said it himself: *No one could love like you did, Sally. No one. . . .*

"You know what I did," she said. "You probably saw it while it was happening. You tell *me.* Am I a murderer?" She held her breath as she waited for his answer, dreading it, but wanting to know it just the same.

"If I call you a murderer because you have killed, then I must call myself the same," said Apollo. "And I am not inclined to do so. Ah—you're surprised by my answer. You were thinking that I was above such human weaknesses. But I am not a god, I am a man, and I like to think I'm good, not evil. So I justify my actions. And I will be happy to justify yours as well, if you wish."

Below them, the eaglets were crying for their supper. Their parents regurgitated prey for them, and they ate it happily, hungrily, perfectly content with the world and their place in it. They felt no guilt over the death of other animals. Once again, Sally longed for their simplicity.

"Guilt is the fruit of the Tree of Knowledge," said Apollo. "If eagles could think like men, what lies would they tell themselves when they killed? Perhaps they would be even greater liars than we."

"Perhaps they wouldn't," said Sally.

He didn't smile, but he was pleased with her. "Kronos Kids have always been dangerous. I don't have to tell you why, Sally. While you were growing up, you were in danger every minute of your life. It's that kind of experience that makes some of us more than men and some of us *less.*"

When he said that, Sally couldn't help thinking of Marc again, how he had looked when he smiled, how his hands had felt. A tear rolled down her cheek before she could stop it.

"Come for lunch," said Apollo. "Someone is waiting to meet you."

"Not Kali, I hope," said Sally, remembering their first conversation. "Caitlin is bad enough."

"Kali is long dead," said Apollo; but he didn't mention whether or not he had had anything to do with her death, and Sally didn't ask.

"Will you come?" he asked.

"Yes," said Sally.

And in the next moment, they were in Apollo's courtyard. Sally blinked, unable, for a moment, to believe her own eyes. She searched her memory for the flight that should have brought them there and found nothing.

"How did you do that?" she demanded. "I thought it was amazing enough just to fly!"

"We did fly," said Apollo, and he gave her a smile that made all other smiles look like crass impostors. "We just didn't fly through the *air*."

He turned and walked into the house, fully expecting her to follow him; and she did.

Someone was waiting for them in the kitchen, a Greek woman. Sally recognized her as such immediately, thanks to her hobby of tracing genealogy. This woman was quite a surprise, genetically. Her line was so pure, Sally could trace her back to a time before Greeks were called by that name; to a time when faces like this woman's were the models for stone Kouris. Her clothing was a little more modern than that, though: loose slacks, an embroidered cotton blouse, and sandals.

"Hello, Sally," said the woman. "I am Aphrodite."

Since this was Olympus, Sally had to assume the obvious. "The Goddess of Love?" she asked.

"The very one."

Sally just nodded. Aphrodite didn't look like Sally's idea of a love goddess. She should have been blond, tall, long-legged, and large breasted. But instead she was entirely earthly. She was very short, not even five feet tall; and her body was compactly built, not outrageously curvy. She was probably beautiful, in the ancient-world sense of things; but . . .

"I'm no sex symbol," said Aphrodite, without smiling.

Sally flushed. "Well, neither am I."

"Child," said Aphrodite, as if she were going to chide Sally; but nothing followed that solitary word, perhaps because it was enough. She came closer, looking at Sally with gray, tilted eyes.

Gray, tilted eyes, and a veil that covered her head and the lower part of her face. And they were going down that river, and the woman was asking, "Is this the city of the gods?"

But that had been a dream. She had dreamed of Apollo too, when he had been Osiris; and before that, scout and King Monkey. Yet he didn't speak of it, and Sally didn't see it in his open mind. She didn't see the river in Aphrodite's, whose mind was almost as open as Apollo's. Almost, but not nearly as much, because Aphrodite was younger. Sally could feel it. Aphrodite was—

"Eight thousand years old," said Aphrodite. "I haven't seen one like you in centuries."

"You haven't really been looking," said Apollo.

Aphrodite nodded.

"Show me the Olympus Gate," she commanded.

Sally stared at her dumbly. For several moments she literally couldn't decide what the woman was talking about. The Gate? They had gone through it, it was history, why should she care about it? Sally wasn't even sure you could look at the Gate from this side of Olympus; and to top it off, she couldn't quite remember what it looked like.

"Haven't you seen it for yourself?" she finally asked.

"No," said Aphrodite, stone-faced. Sally glanced past her at Apollo, who had positioned himself so Sally couldn't get through the door without going through him first. And now she wondered if his mind was so open to her after all, because she hadn't seen before that moment that he expected her to run.

He shook his head. "We're not going to force you."

"Why would you want to? And why do you need to see the Gate? Are you hoping to get back to earth and become gods again?"

"We don't have to become gods," said Aphrodite. "And we are part of earth, just as you are."

"You're Kronos Kids," said Sally. "Just like we are, but you were born thousands of years ago. You must be our ancestors. And you're more knowledgeable than me, more powerful than me, so you should be able to look at the Gate anytime you want."

"We won't," said Aphrodite.

"Why not?"

"Because it's *your* Gate, Sally."

"What do you mean, *my* Gate?"

"You made it, didn't you?"

Sally was beginning to feel very frustrated. If she had had any ideas about what Aphrodite and Apollo were, what they knew, what they could tell her, they were now exploded. She almost said, *Why do you think I made the Gate?* but that would just be another question to be answered by a question, generating more questions. So she considered her next remarks very carefully.

"I don't remember making the Olympus Gate or any other Gate," she said. "I thought I *found* the Gate. I thought it was a natural phenomenon that already existed." *So there. Deal with that.*

But they didn't seem disturbed by her answer, only

intrigued. And she only knew they were intrigued because of the feelings they were sharing with her; their faces were completely cool, calm, and unruffled.

I wish I could do that, thought Sally.

"What did you expect to find on the other side of it?" asked Aphrodite.

"I didn't. *Ted* did. Ted thought Olympus was on the other side. We were just his tools to get there."

Sally noticed that Apollo had moved away from the door. He joined Aphrodite, and the two of them presented a united front to her. "Think back to the time before you went through the Gate," he said. "Concentrate. Go there, if you must, and remember if there wasn't *something* you expected, even if it was just a vague feeling."

"What do you mean *go* there?"

"Like Ralph does when he studies his composers and his musicians," said Aphrodite. "Look down the time line."

"I didn't know you could ... look down the *time line.*"

Apollo didn't sigh, but something in his demeanor suggested the gesture. "Let's have lunch," he said. "Let's relax. We are only going in circles now, and I wanted this to be an exchange of ideas, not a cross-examination."

Sally was relieved to hear him say that. She was only growing more frustrated with each question. Look down the time line? She didn't know Ralph was doing that. He had never tried to hide anything from her; she just hadn't realized that was what he was doing.

Aphrodite seated herself at the table (which now had three chairs), so Sally did the same. She tried to watch Apollo out of the corner of her eye. That was a little embarrassing, because Aphrodite was watching her too. She was watching with those cool, gray eyes that seemed to see everything. Sally thought she looked a lot more like the Goddess of Wisdom than the Goddess of Love.

Apollo took things out of cupboards—plates and glasses and utensils—and the food simply appeared on them. Sally tried to follow the process that went into the making; it was just what she and Joey had been trying to do. The difference was that Apollo knew exactly what he was doing. It was like the difference between a child taking piano lessons and a concert pianist in his prime.

Sally ate with them. She didn't feel relaxed, exactly; but when she really stopped to think about it, she was glad to be there. They were like the beings that Ted had hoped he would become. Sally found herself wondering if the meal they were eating was anything like the ancient dishes Apollo and Aphrodite had eaten, back in the "Dawn of Man." Wondering about that made her wonder about whether or not they had known any other "gods."

And then she remembered something.

"Intelligence," she said.

They stopped eating. "Yes?" said Apollo.

"Intelligence on the other side of the Gate. Something that was aware of me."

"One intelligence, or several?" asked Aphrodite.

"I'm not sure. I was never sure."

Sally could almost see the Gate again. She could see it the way it had looked that time after she had met King Monkey. She had seen into his Neanderthal life, and then she had looked at the Gate through her secret Mastermind. . . .

And there it was, with those weird glyphs dancing around its frame, calling to her. . . .

King Monkey. She had seen King Monkey, forty thousand years ago. She *had* looked down the time line. Or rather, her Secret Mind had. But it was part of her now, she should be able to do what it did!

She came to herself, suddenly. She was sitting there with her mouth open, like a stunned cow. She snapped it shut and tried to regain her composure. Apollo and Aphrodite were staring at her intently.

"This intelligence . . ." said Aphrodite, "was it hostile, or friendly?"

"Neither," said Sally.

They didn't react to that. Sally wished they would. She wished they would say, "What do you mean by that?" or "Isn't that interesting." But they just looked at her. She almost got mad then, almost said, *I'm not going to do all the work around here! How about some input from you guys?* But something told her to be quiet. Something told her to listen instead of shooting her mouth off.

"When you arrived here," said Aphrodite, "did you sense anyone else was already here?"

"No," said Sally. "Were you aware of us when we arrived?"

Aphrodite paused. Then she said, "Yes." But Sally wondered about the pause. There was something Aphrodite wasn't saying, something she was unsure about.

"Who else is here, besides us?" Sally dared to ask.

"I don't know," said Aphrodite.

That was a little shocking. That was definitely most ungodlike. Or at least it wasn't what one expected of an *omniscient* god. But on the other hand, the Greek gods hadn't been omniscient.

"*We* certainly aren't," said Aphrodite. "Mentally, we have the same limits as any human beings. We can't learn any faster, we have no better grasp of mathematics or psychology. There is still so much I must learn about this world before I can answer your questions. There is so much to know, I wonder if I will ever finish learning it."

"You're pretty cerebral for a love goddess," said Sally.

Aphrodite laughed then, unexpectedly and whole-heartedly. She took Sally's breath away, and for an instant she was who she was supposed to be: Aphrodite, Nefertiri, Erzulie, essentially female and beautiful.

"Sex begins in the brain," said Aphrodite, when she had recovered enough to speak again. "So I am justified in my cerebral pursuits, don't you think?"

"Sure," said Sally, blushing. She had blurted out her thoughts without ... thinking. Aphrodite wasn't laughing at her, though; she was pleased with her. That made Sally feel good. Susanna had never spoken to her this way.

"I understand why you don't trust what you see down the time line," Aphrodite continued. "I was an oracle in my earliest days. I spoke for the gods. They showed me the present and the future. It was thus for six thousand years, until a terrible thing happened."

"What?" asked Sally, picturing conquering armies, erupting volcanos, political assassinations and executions.

"All of the above," said Aphrodite. "Yet, by themselves, these events did not cause the great change in my life. It was their combined effect that drove people together who had never been together before. A funny thing happens when people are faced with so many challenges, so many new ideas and customs. They begin to *think* in ways they never thought before. They begin to adjust, whether they know it or not."

"That's what's happening to me and my brothers and sister," Sally said, trying to talk around a mouthful of curried something or other.

Apollo and Aphrodite didn't exchange looks then,

but something passed between them. Sally was sure of it.

"Men were changing," Aphrodite said. "I changed with them. And then one day I glimpsed the truth, and I was shattered."

She didn't look shattered, sitting there with her trim, compact body and her rock-steady gaze; but Sally believed her. "What was the truth?" she gasped.

"It was not the gods who were speaking. It was I. *I* looked down the time line. *I* told what I saw. I then tried to interpret the facts for men with my limited knowledge.

"Yes! Even after six millennia I was limited by the parameters of the human brain, just as your Jim said. My own skull was my prison. When I was a believer, I put my faith in the gods that even when things didn't turn out as I hoped, as they *should,* the gods had their own reasons and designs. But when I realized that I was the source of the messages, I had no one but myself to blame when things went wrong."

Bummer, thought Sally, but didn't trust herself to come up with anything more intelligent than that. She couldn't imagine being thousands of years old, and she certainly couldn't imagine being *sacred,* believing herself an instrument of the gods and then having that all snatched away from her.

"I prophesied for King Theseus," Aphrodite said. "I saw that he was going to have a stroke. At that time, I didn't have the talents I have now; I couldn't heal him. So what good would it do to warn him?"

Sally tried to imagine what she would have done in Aphrodite's place. And then something occurred to her. "You saw into the future?"

"Yes."

"You can do that? You can tell people what's going to happen?"

Aphrodite shook her head. "The future isn't often that concrete."

"So you can't tell what might happen to *us*?"

"You might die," said Aphrodite. "Or you might live, and we might all *wish* you had died."

"Why would you wish that?"

But Aphrodite wouldn't answer. She looked away, focusing on something far away and long ago. It was Apollo who answered.

"Kali."

"Yes?" said Sally; and when he didn't respond immediately, she said, "The Goddess of Destruction, right? I've read books." *Or at least I've read* people *who've read books.*

He knew what she was thinking. He knew she didn't understand. His handsome face was stern and uncompromising as he read this weakness in her. She could barely stand to return his gaze when he looked at her this way; yet she couldn't look away. She wanted the truth, so he told her. "Before she was Kali, she was Durga, who fought demons. And before she was Durga, she was Devi; or sometimes she was Parvati. Each time she was confronted with adversity, she became more powerful, more fearless, more bloodthirsty and monstrous; because how else to fight monsters than to become them?"

Sally was beginning to understand what he was getting at. "Did you know Kali?" she asked.

"Yes," he said. He didn't look at Aphrodite, but Sally could tell that he meant she had known Kali too.

"Did you want her dead?" asked Sally, finding that she had to ask the question around a lump in her throat.

"Yes," he said, making Sally cringe. She wasn't even sure why she was reacting that way, except that maybe it was too much like what The Three had wanted for their Kronos Kids. Even what King Monkey had wanted for his son, perhaps what every Kronos Kid wanted for their children, ultimately. And if Apollo wanted Kali dead . . . how did he feel about Sally?

And he must know what she was thinking; in fact, she knew he did, because she knew his mind too. Yet he didn't deny or confirm it, didn't try to warn or comfort her.

Big surprise, Sally thought bitterly. *Like anyone ever has or anyone ever will.*

The next several moments were spent in a silent struggle to contain tears, to control the emotions that were provoking them without stifling her ability to have them in the first place. Apollo and Aphrodite didn't speak to her then, allowing her a chance to fight this inner battle without interference.

Sally could hear the birds outside, could see the eagles flying in and out of their thermals. She could smell the flowers and other plants in Apollo's garden; she could even smell a trace of rain on the wind. From a great distance, a voice seemed to say to her, *Patience, patience. . . . There is always hope. Just think of those mountains, the ones from your dreams. Lydia's mountains. You still live, you still love, you still care.*

And when it was all under control again, Aphrodite took her hand and said, "Sally, come look at something for a moment."

Sally let the older woman pull her to her feet; she knew instinctively not to resist. Aphrodite led her into another room. Apollo stayed where he was, returning Sally's backward gaze until he was out of sight.

The room was feminine in design and had a lovely dressing table with a big mirror. Sally felt a stab of jealousy as she wondered whether Aphrodite stayed in this room when she was visiting Apollo.

"How long before I earn my own room here?" she asked, regretting the question as soon as it was out. But Aphrodite didn't answer anyway. Instead, she gently pushed Sally in front of the mirror. When Sally looked at her own reflection, she was unpleasantly shocked.

She hadn't really looked at her face in a long time. She had been a child the last time she had given her own image a thorough inspection. She had expected that great changes had occurred since then; but her image failed to live up to her expectations. It failed to reflect her *inner* self, the Sally who was mature, intelligent, sexy.

"So I'm ugly," she said. "So what else is new?"

"You're not looking," said Aphrodite. "Look at me, then at yourself."

That was even more depressing. Aphrodite might not be Sally's idea of what a love goddess should look like, but that didn't mean she wasn't beautiful. That didn't mean she didn't make Sally look like a total nerd in comparison. Sally was embarrassed that Apollo had seen the two of them in the same room together. She would never get anywhere with him now.

Sally looked at herself again. Except for her height and her sprouting breasts, she might as well be ten years old. It wasn't even her lack of frontal equipment that bothered her the most; it was her soft, chubby face.

A child. She looked like a child. She glanced at Aphrodite, who raised her eyebrows, as if to say, *Exactly.*

Sally said, "I'm a kid, and I look like one. But I'm not really like a regular kid, not *inside.*"

"You could always change your face," said Aphrodite.

"I haven't really ever thought about that," said Sally.

In fact, she hadn't really ever thought about her face at all. She hardly ever looked at it, because she didn't like it. She only ever saw people's *reactions* to her face, which were usually either negative or neutral. No one had ever looked at her face and said, *Well! Va-va VOOOOM!* Except maybe Jim, but he had been playing with her.

"If you think it's such a great idea to change faces, why haven't you ever changed yours?" asked Sally, feeling a little annoyed by the whole subject.

"I did," Aphrodite replied, unruffled by Sally's tone.

Sally looked at the other woman critically. "Well," she asked, not peevishly but out of genuine curiosity, "why didn't you *update* it?"

"Beauty is always beautiful," said Aphrodite, with enviable dignity and confidence. "Through the ages."

"You mean that *your* opinion of beauty hasn't changed."

"That's a good guess," said Aphrodite. "And a true one. But I have found that men who view my face are pleased with it, and I am pleased with it. It is the face of the Goddess of Love, so it is *I* who define beauty. And I have."

Sally tried to look critically at herself again. "Maybe I will change my face," she said. "Do you think I'm . . . ugly?"

"No," said Aphrodite. "Ugliness and beauty are extremes. Your face is the face of a child."

"But what can I do to improve it?"

Aphrodite studied her. Finally she said, "I find that subtle changes are the best. Let us start with your eye color. Perhaps green would be better."

Sally shivered. "Caitlin's eyes are green."

"I was thinking of a different sort of green, one that would seem almost gray or brown at first glance. But let me think for a moment."

Sally gazed at herself, beginning to get interested, despite herself. Green would be nice, but she didn't want to be like Caitlin. And Sally had a feeling her sister would react negatively to the imitation. So what other colors could they try? Plain gray might look too washed out.

"Try violet," said Aphrodite.

Violet! Like Elizabeth Taylor's eyes. That sounded a little improbable, but Sally tried it anyway. She thought she had an idea how to do it. She concentrated, and in another moment it was done.

And it looked *good.*

"I like it!" she said. "It really looks good!"

"It does," said Aphrodite. "And your skin is just the right color for it. Now, your hair—"

"Should I darken it? Make it black, like Elizabeth Taylor's?"

"No. Let's make your original color richer, bring out some highlights and get rid of the dinge."

Dinge was what Sally had, all right. Her hair looked dingy even when it was clean. She had always envied the other girls' hair. Especially Lydia's.

"Will you let me do it for you?" asked Aphrodite.

"Yes," said Sally, pleased for the offer, because she didn't have a clue what to do herself. She could manage the process of touching up the color, but not the sensibilities behind the *choice* of color.

"Like so," said Aphrodite. "And so. Do you see what I'm doing? Your hair will grow like this now, but you may need to evaluate it from time to time and see if it's presenting the effect you want it to have."

Sally nodded. She had watched carefully to see what Aphrodite was doing, and she thought she understood. Her hair was pretty now. It was actually pretty! It had hints of auburn now, and the browns were richer. It no longer looked dull and colorless, and it made Sally's skin glow.

"I'll give you a hint, for the future," said Aphrodite. "I have only done what your body could have done itself. I have followed the pattern your own genes have set; I have only enhanced them here and there."

"I think I know what you mean," said Sally. She was so pleased, she could hardly believe it. She had almost forgotten her troubles, the problems she would face when she went back to the cavern, her grief. . . .

"And now," said Aphrodite, "your breasts."

Sally blushed. "They're funny-looking."

"Breasts often are when they're first growing. But it isn't the size that troubles you. It's the shape. Perhaps a little filling out around the edges."

"I don't want to be big. They'll laugh at me if I come home big."

"I agree that big isn't appropriate for you now," said Aphrodite firmly. "Again, subtlety is the key. Take off your blouse."

Sally did, with some trepidation. She took off her training bra too. And there they were, those silly knobs. They looked like cartoon breasts, like someone's idea of a joke. But Aphrodite didn't laugh, and Sally didn't mind that she was looking at them. Aphrodite had suffered through puberty herself, and she had watched generations of girls suffer after her. They must have prayed to her about it. Well, now Sally was praying, in a way.

"Ready?" said Aphrodite.

Sally nodded, and the change began. It was slow, and it wasn't terribly extensive. But it was significant. What had been knobs became gentle, conical curves. Sally gazed at the result, amazed.

"They will grow larger as you mature," said Aphrodite. "But for now, they're quite attractive, don't you think?"

"Thank you," was all Sally could say. How she had dreaded ever revealing those breasts to a man. Now she wouldn't be ashamed. Now she could be proud of what she had.

"And the others won't notice," Aphrodite was saying. "You won't be going home 'big.' "

"Thanks," Sally said again, unable to really tell the woman how grateful she was. But she didn't have to. Aphrodite knew. She looked pleased with the results of the changes in Sally.

"The others don't really have the benefit of mature advice when they make their changes," she said. "But you do, and I think you'll be glad, in the long run."

"Me too," said Sally. And then something occurred to her. Soon they would go back to see Apollo again. What would he think of the changes?

Aphrodite read her thought. "Apollo used to be shorter than me, you know."

Sally couldn't picture him that way. "When did he get tall?" she asked. "After he met you, I suppose."

"No. I didn't care about his height. It was after he met *you*."

Sally watched herself blush in the mirror. It looked interesting. In fact, now that her hair and eyes had been enhanced, it looked downright charming. She laughed.

Aphrodite smiled at her. "Good," she said. "You show promise."

"Do I?" wondered Sally. "Could I change myself until I'm like you and Apollo? Could I change my brain?"

"Conceivably. And you could change the others too."

"I already did Joey."

"With his consent."

"But I can't force the others."

"*Now* you don't want to," said Aphrodite. "You haven't seen Caitlin become a Kali yet. You haven't seen her enslave thousands of men and make them do murder in her name. You haven't seen her eat human flesh, or laugh with glee as her sacrifices are burned alive."

Something had been bothering Sally ever since Apollo had brought Kali up in the first place. Suddenly she knew what is was. "But Kali was not an evil goddess. She *destroyed* evil."

"There is a price to pay for that sort of escalation," said Aphrodite, unmoved. "If you must become Kali to destroy The Three, you will not find your way back again. And Caitlin is already halfway there."

Sally wanted to say something in Caitlin's defense, but she couldn't think of a thing. "Okay," she said, "then why *not* change people if they're monsters? Why not unmonsterize them? And why didn't I think of doing that to Marc?"

"Perhaps because it couldn't be done."

"Says you! I bet I could do it."

"And *how* would you do it? What processes would you attack first? What genes, what memories, what autonomic functions, and what glands? What is the essence of monsterism? What is the real and complete cause?"

Sally opened her mouth, closed it again.

"I'm not saying it can't be done," said Aphrodite. "I'm not saying it *shouldn't.* I'm just asking: How? And if you make a mistake, what will be the consequences? And in the last analysis, is any human being really fit to pass judgment on any other? Judgment on every single aspect of the other's life, on all of those subtle personality traits that add up to a whole—or in some, less than a whole? Are you that judge, Sally?"

"I don't know," said Sally. "But maybe you had the right idea when you were talking about my hair and my eyes. Subtlety. Maybe the key is subtlety, little changes."

"And maybe those little changes will deceive you," said Aphrodite. She turned away from Sally and looked around the room, as if wondering if it should be redecorated. She was done arguing, that was for sure. Sally knew that the argument would have to continue at some later time, perhaps sometime when she had a better idea what Aphrodite was talking about.

She let it go. Enough had happened that day already. She was content.

"Let's join Apollo again," said Aphrodite. "Are you ready?"

Sally nodded. She was ready to see what kind of reaction she would get. She was looking forward to it.

As they returned down the hall together, a question occurred to Sally.

"You said you were an oracle first, Aphrodite. When did you become the Goddess of Love?"

The other woman didn't pause before she answered. "When I was needed."

"Oh," said Sally, not really understanding, but hoping (perhaps as Aphrodite had once hoped when she had still believed in the gods) that someday it would become clear to her. Someday she would understand.

Back in the kitchen, Apollo was waiting. He stood when they reentered, and gazed at Sally. His expression was pleasing. It said, *Well! Va-va VOOM!*

"Do you really like me this way?" Sally asked, too happy to be shy.

"Yes," he said, and her heart expanded with joy, because he couldn't deceive her. He really meant it.

They sat again and finished their meal, which had stayed warm and fresh for them. Sally ate with much more appetite this time. Her frustration was gone, her mind clearer.

"I really needed this conversation right now, didn't I?" she asked them.

"Yes," said Aphrodite. "You really did."

Sally didn't try to think back on everything that had brought her to that moment, her struggle to survive, to save the others . . . the deaths of Susanna and Marc. She didn't have to think of them; they were part of her.

"Thank you for making things a little clearer," she told Aphrodite.

"We need you to help us understand this world as much as you need us," said Aphrodite.

Sally almost dropped her spoon. She gazed at the woman, then at Apollo, who didn't deny what had been said. "That's really scary," said Sally.

Aphrodite smiled. "Now you know how I felt two thousand years ago when the gods went away," she said.

Apollo put his hand over Sally's, steadying her. His hand was warm, and she rather hoped he wouldn't take it away again for a while.

"One last thing before you go," he said.

Sally was almost afraid to ask what it was.

"A gift," said Aphrodite.

And suddenly Sally was somewhere else. The house was gone, Aphrodite and Apollo were gone. Sally could still feel the warmth of Apollo's hand. It faded as she stood there in the open air; but she didn't mind so much, because she knew where she was instantly. The angle of her view was different, because usually she was looking *at* these mountains, not standing on them. But still she knew them. They were the mountains of her dreams.

Lydia's mountains. And among them was that particular mountaintop upon which Valhalla would be, and Sally was there now. And there were her eagles, and the golden light slanted down and touched Sally's face.

They were real. And they were not too far from where Apollo lived. If Sally had looked, she would have found them herself. But she was glad she hadn't had to. She was glad that they had done this for her, because this was an act of love, undeniable love.

She fell to her knees. "Thank you," she said, through her tears. "Bless you."

They had surely been blessed thousands of times in their long lives, but Sally didn't care about that. She only wondered if Apollo would mind when she built her house so close to his. But if he had minded, he wouldn't have done this for her, this wonderful thing.

Sally wept for a long time. But these weren't the sort of tears she had wept for Marc. These were different. These were good. They meant something wonderful.

Because now she knew. There was reason to hope, after all.

Sally didn't go back to the cavern until sunset. Joey was waiting outside for her. Before she could speak, he grabbed her elbow and lifted the two of them into the air. They were well away from the cavern before Joey finally whispered, "Let's get some distance before we talk."

Sally didn't argue, though physical distance wouldn't keep them that much safer. Joey's heavy mental shielding would be what made the difference; in fact, it was so effective that Sally wouldn't have even known how paranoid he was feeling if it hadn't been for their slender safety link, which was still firmly in place.

The link. He must have guessed something of what had happened to her today because of it.

"I was going to tell you tonight," she began, but he shushed her.

He wasn't willing to speak again until they had reached the false ruins of the bus. He set them both down gently and walked over to the simulacrum.

We'd better talk this way, he sent to her on what she was beginning to think of as a "tight beam." With their shields working together, no one would overhear them.

I was going to tell you what happened to me today, she said.

Something wonderful. He kicked a skull to see if it

would make the noise it ought to when it tumbled along the ground. It did. *I felt a little of it through our link.*

Sally wondered where to begin, decided to take it slowly. *I found something I've been looking for. Something I used to dream about.*

He waited patiently for her to tell him what it was. Sally wondered fleetingly if there wasn't something *Joey* had been looking for, something he wanted badly. If there was, he was keeping it a close secret.

A place, said Sally. *Some mountains.*

I caught a glimpse of them through the link, he said. *They looked—they seemed like—*

Like they belong to another world, Sally suggested. *I think Ted must have glimpsed them in my dreams, over the years. I think they must have seemed like Olympus to him. Remember the time when he went crazy, when he wrecked everything we had built?*

I could never forget. I thought it was the end for us too.

Those mountains are real. But they're mine, not his. I was there all afternoon. I was thinking about building a house there, but I don't think I'm quite ready yet. Quite ready to . . . build it right.

He didn't say anything for a while; he just looked at her. His shield tightened around him until Sally couldn't read his feelings at all. Even his anxiety seemed to have disappeared. But the illusion didn't lend him an air of confidence; it only made him seem more vulnerable. It was a stark contrast to the way it was with Apollo and Aphrodite, who were so open yet so *in*vulnerable.

I've met two other people here, Sally told him at last, deciding he had a right to know. Everyone did, actually, but she didn't mind telling Joey first.

He didn't look entirely surprised. *I thought our link*

*was getting kind of . . . distorted or . . . complicated. I
don't know. I thought I felt . . .*

*Someone else? You probably felt them. They don't
shield themselves. They aren't afraid of anything or
anyone. They weren't even afraid of The Three.*

Why not? demanded Joey.

They're very powerful.

*How come I haven't seen them yet? And how come
they didn't interfere when Marc tried to kill you?*

Sally didn't know the answer to those questions. In
fact, she hadn't asked herself the same things, even
though they begged answers.

I don't know, she admitted. *I think maybe I was
supposed to—to prove myself to them, I guess.*

You guess.

*Guessing is all I can do. What do you think, Joey?
What would you do if some people you didn't know
were having a battle to the death? Would you interfere?*

He shrugged. *Okay. So what are their names?*

Sally took a deep breath. This was where things
were going to get really difficult. *Apollo and Aphrodite,* she said.

His mouth quirked, and Sally had to fight down an
urge to laugh herself, from sheer embarrassment.

The gods? he asked, full of doubt and cynicism.

Sally rallied her self-confidence and gave him a message containing more than just words. She tried to
show him what Apollo and Aphrodite were really like:
how they sounded, what they looked like, smelled like,
felt like. *I don't know exactly what they are,* she said.
*Except that I'm fairly sure they're Kronos Kids, like
we are. I think they have lived for thousands of years,
like we could, Joey, if we figure out how. They taught
me some things today.*

You changed your eyes and your hair, he said, reminding her of what she had already forgotten.

Aphrodite showed me how, she said, and blushed.

Advice from the Goddess of Love about how to improve your looks—some people would pay a fortune for that.

Sally swallowed and said, *Do you think they're improved? Really?*

Yes, he said without hesitation. *I always thought you could be better-looking with just a little help, Sally. I was thinking makeup and stuff, but who needs that when you can use talent to change your features?*

Right, said Sally, wondering if he knew what else she had changed and hoping that he didn't. Joey was as good-looking as Jim was, in his own way; he was tall and muscular now, and it made her feel shy to be discussing good looks (and whether or not she had them) with him.

Why did Apollo and Aphrodite come to you first? asked Joey.

Sally had suspected that it was because she was special, because she was more powerful than the others. But she couldn't help being a little skeptical of that notion, now that she had brought it out in the open to look at. Why indeed? Could there be another, less flattering reason?

Could you have dreamed them up? Joey wondered. He was thinking about the house that had mysteriously appeared. Jim had wondered the same, and even Sally wasn't sure whether it had been created by herself or by Susanna. She hadn't had time to think much about it since . . .

Since she had killed them. . . .

Caitlin has been talking about you, Joey confided. *For days, now. She's been trying to put doubt in everyone's minds about you and about this place.*

That shouldn't have surprised Sally. But it frightened her. It frightened her because she was wondering about many things herself, and she was afraid of what might happen if Caitlin got the answers before she did.

. . . *"You haven't seen her eat human flesh, or laugh
with glee as her sacrifices are burned alive . . ."*

What? said Joey. *Who? Caitlin?*

No, Sally said. *That's what Aphrodite said about
Kali. The Goddess of Destruction.*

The Hindu goddess.

Right.

Aren't we kind of mixing our metaphors here?

Sally shrugged. Human history was one big mixed
metaphor, as far as she was concerned. And anyway,
wasn't it mixing metaphors that had led to the revolu-
tion in human thought Aphrodite had mentioned?

Joey dropped his mask, revealing the true depths of
his paranoia. *She might just as well have been talking
about Caitlin! She's dangerous. I'm afraid of her, Sally.
I think she's just as likely to try to kill us as Ted was.*

Sally shivered. She had shared rooms with Caitlin
for as long as she could remember, and she knew the
potential for murder was there. All these years she
had told herself it was Ted's fault. Maybe it was Ted's
fault, but that didn't change anything.

She's cut my healing link with her, Joey was saying.
If she attacked me, I wouldn't have any warning.

Why would she attack you? It's me *she hates.*

*Because I'm not siding with her. You know she
thinks all of us guys should worship her. If I won't,
that's an insult. And if she thinks I'm working with you
against her—*

Are you?

*Yes! I'm not going to be her prisoner! We didn't
free ourselves from The Three just so we could find
another master!*

Sally wanted to comfort him, but that wasn't what
he wanted. He could comfort himself ten times better
than she could do it. She sighed and sat down on what
was left of one of the bus seats. It felt as real as the
one back at the cavern.

Has she drawn the others into a Mastermind? she asked.

Not yet. Not that I can tell.

I used to do it without anyone knowing, warned Sally.

I don't think she's as strong as you. Or as subtle. Joey squatted next to another set of false bones. He picked up the skull and examined it as if he were trying to tell who it had belonged to.

Have the other guys gone over to her side? Sally asked.

Timothy has. And he's controlling Ralph completely now. Jim is always looking out for number one—he'll go whichever way the wind is blowing.

Sally nodded. She was wondering if she and Joey should leave and build a house on her mountain. But wouldn't that just delay the inevitable confrontation?

I won't leave the other guys, Joey said. *I know they don't deserve it—except for Ralph—but I care about what happens to them.*

Sally nodded again, mostly reflex this time. She was trying to plan, to decide what the best course of action was; she had been doing the same thing for years, secretly, under The Three, and she had done it well. So why couldn't she think of a plan now?

Well, that wasn't true. There was one thing. She could kill Caitlin.

This is your skull, Joey said, holding up the simulacrum.

Sally looked at it, startled. *I didn't know—I didn't think . . .*

That the simulacrums had been that detailed? I knew everyone inside out, Sally. And you used me to make them. He put the skull down, gently, and stood over her. He was being strong now, being male. Being stern.

More than anything else, he said, *that's why I side with you.*

Sally made herself look at him and listen to what he was really saying. She opened herself for him as if he were Apollo, let him see how she really felt. He looked.

It's not because I love you, Sally, he said. *I don't think I know how to love yet. It's because I recognize what's in you, what you can do.*

My talent, said Sally, wondering whether to be hurt or flattered.

He shook his head. *No. What you can* do *with your talent. Caitlin is retarded, Sally. She's like Ted. She's a monster.*

Sally was ready to ask him *What do you suggest we do about it?* but she never got the chance. The simulacrum of the wrecked bus suddenly vanished, sending her sprawling. Joey reached for her, horrified, and the two of them ended up in a heap.

They gazed at each other, their hearts pounding.

Did you do that? Joey asked, hopefully.

No, Sally said.

They got slowly to their feet and looked around them. No one was in sight. Sally made a mental sweep of the area, using a much more powerful probe than she had been inclined to do since they had gone through the Gate. She didn't find anything but animals.

Maybe no one *had to make the fake bus disappear,* she told Joey. *Maybe it was just out of juice. I haven't been consciously maintaining it, and now that Susanna and Mark are dead . . .*

Maybe, said Joey, dusting himself off, *but it would be just like Caitlin to pull a mean trick like that, just to try and scare us.*

No, it wouldn't. It would be just like Caitlin to make our heads explode, and to hell with scaring us.

Joey laughed at that. After a moment, Sally was

laughing too, It felt good to laugh. It felt good to feel *good,* and that had been a rare thing, lately.

If we can just take enough time to learn what we need to know, she told Joey, *we can face anyone.*

She won't give us that time if she can help it, he warned.

She's our sister. Whatever she's going to do, we just have to face up to her. She's not going to go away.

I wish Lydia had been the one to survive, not Caitlin. Sally nodded sadly. *Me too.*

They grasped hands and ascended into the air.

Can I tell you something that might make you mad? asked Joey, as they flew home again.

You might as well. You're the only one on my side these days, anyway.

Jim still wants you.

Sally's heart started to flutter again. *Okay. But he's the one who would get mad at you for telling me that.*

If you play up to him a little, he might switch sides.

Oh. I see what you mean. She didn't add that she had very little idea how to "play up" to someone. She also didn't add how much it hurt that Jim looked like Marc, and that he had rejected her for Susanna.

Once he sees your new eyes and your new hair—they look really good, Sally. Just look at him a little more. Let him know you care what he thinks of you.

Sally blinked as if the wind were in her eyes, but they were wet for other reasons too. *I'll try,* she finally promised.

And I won't be sleeping for the next several days.

She looked at him with dismay. He didn't look tired, but she hated to think of the strain he would be putting himself through. He gave her a grim smile. *I can do it. I have the capabilities. I could do it for months, if I had to.*

I hope you won't.

Me too.

She couldn't help staring at him throughout the remainder of their flight. She was amazed at how strong he looked, how determined. He should have reminded her of Superman again as he flew through the clouds, his hair blown by the wind. But Superman was part of Joey's childhood, and he was a child no longer.

We're home, he said, as their feet touched the ground.

No one greeted them outside. But Sally could feel everyone *in*side, waiting. She gave Joey's hand a last squeeze.

Let's go fix supper, she said.

Caitlin didn't show herself for supper. Sally tried not to be nervous about that; Caitlin had never been terribly sociable to begin with, so there needn't have been a sinister reason for her absence.

Timothy insisted on taking Ralph's supper in to him.

"Is he all right?" Sally asked, letting the worry show in her voice.

Timothy gave her a curt nod. "Of course he is. Why wouldn't he be?"

"He just ... never seems to come up for air anymore," said Sally, meaning, *You never let him!*

"Mind your own damn business," said Timothy, and left with Ralph's food.

Jim was the only one who seemed to want company. He had looked twice at Sally when she had come in. She had made herself hold his gaze, let him see her (genuine) shyness. He seemed to like it, though he was still rather cool with her.

"You guys are getting better at this," he said, digging into the pizza they had made. And he was right, they had done quite a respectable job of it. They had been able to find all of the ingredients, including milk for cheese, and put them together in the proper combinations. It was a vegetarian pizza, though; Sally still didn't know how to get meat without causing dreadful pain to an animal in the process. She would figure it out eventually, of course, maybe starting with fish if she could find out how to prepare it.

I'll have to ask Apollo's advice, she thought to herself, trying not to feel self-conscious when Jim stole glances at her.

He stayed after the meal was over and even chatted with Joey and Sally in a friendly manner for a while. Sally did her best to encourage him without looking too eager. He was stealing glances at her chest by the end of the evening, and Sally could tell he was wondering what other changes she had made.

"Nice start," Jim said to Sally when he finally got up to go to his own room.

Sally waited until he was gone and then looked at Joey. He didn't need telepathy to tell her what he thought then. He just gave her the thumbs-up.

"Good night," he said. *I'll be awake and ready.*

Are you sure you want to do that? Sally said. *I mean, I could share the watch with you.*

He shook his head. *You're not as good at controlling your own body as I am, yet. And you need your rest. You're the heavy hitter.*

Okay. Sally almost gave him a kiss on the cheek before leaving, but settled for a mental pat instead—a wordless message of comfort and support. He accepted it gracefully.

Just as Sally was entering her room, she thought she felt Caitlin behind her. She turned, but no one was there, and the feeling had gone.

Her shield slipped, just for a moment, Sally thought, sure of it. *She still doesn't have perfect control.*

That confirmed it. Caitlin was watching her, waiting. Joey was probably one hundred percent right about her. In a way, it was a comfort to know that, to know what to expect.

But in another, bigger way, it was anything but.

D espite her worries, Sally went right to sleep. In fact, she was surprisingly comfortable about doing so. She felt safe, warm, snuggly. Maybe it was because she knew Joey was watching over her. Whatever the reason, she drifted off as if she had been drugged, reveling in the sense of relaxation and safety.

It would have been simply perfect if it hadn't been for the obnoxious noise:

THUMP THUMP THUMP THUMP THUMP THUMP THUMP THUMP . . .

Like an enormous clock ticking with a giant heart, or like a robot knocking on a wooden door with mechanical precision, so rhythmic, so mindless:

THUMP THUMP THUMP THUMP THUMP THUMP THUMP THUMP THUMP THUMP THUMP THUMP THUMP THUMP THUMP . . .

"Cut it out," said Sally irritably. "I'm trying to sleep."

THUMP THUMP THUMP THUMP THUMP THUMP . . .

"Nobody's home! Go away!"

THUMP THUMP THUMP THUMP THUMP THUMP . . .

"Goddammit!" someone screamed from the other room, some man, sounding so crazy and angry and dangerous that Sally bolted upright in bed. And the man was yelling, "Stop that, you fucking little bastard, or I'm going to rip your lousy little head off! Stop it! STOP IT!"

THUMP THUMP THUMP THUMP THUMP THUMP . . .

Sally wasn't in her own bed, she was in someone else's. There were dirty stuffed animals everywhere, and it smelled like pee. The sheets felt gritty against her skin, and it was very cold in the room.

She wasn't alone in the bed. Something behind her was going THUMP THUMP THUMP. She turned her head with agonizing slowness, but what she found was more weird than scary: a boy of about eight or nine, ramming his head rhythmically and single-mindedly against the headboard.

THUMP THUMP THUMP THUMP THUMP . . .

The door to the bedroom slammed open, and Sally almost had a heart attack right on the spot. A big man was standing in the doorway. He was wearing one of those old-fashioned sleeveless T-shirts with the string straps and some pants that were loosely held up by suspenders. He had a big mustache, stubble on his sweaty chin, and stank to high heaven of alcohol.

He had the face of a maniac.

THUMP THUMP THUMP THUMP THUMP went the boy, like he wasn't even aware of the crazy man.

The man took two steps into the room and bent over almost double. "STOOOOOOOOOOOOOOOOO OOOOP IIIIIIIIIIIIIIIIIIIIIIT!" he bellowed, like a foghorn.

THUMP THUMP THUMP THUMP THUMP went the boy, completely oblivious.

The man took two more steps and bellowed again, "STOOOOOOP IIIIIIIIT!" Then two more steps, and again, and again, until he was moving like a freight train, right straight for the kid, who never seemed to see or hear him.

Sally cringed, but the man ignored her and grabbed

the kid. He pulled him off the bed and onto the floor. "Stop it, you dumb little bastard!" he howled. "You stupid retard!"

The boy didn't react at all, except to start hitting the back of his head against the wooden floor: THUMP THUMP THUMP . . .

"Yeah!" the man punched the boy in the face. "Yeah, hit your head, hit your hid! Yeah!"

Sally tried to grab his arm, but she bounced off him like a fly, like a moth, as he hit the boy again and again. And when she tried to reach out with her talent, that was shrugged aside too, as if she were just an ordinary girl. "Stop it!" she was screaming. "You're going to kill him!"

The boy's face was covered with blood. The man paused for a moment, to catch his breath.

Breaking the rhythm.

"Wrong," said the boy.

The man froze. "What?" he demanded. "What did you say?"

"You're wrong," said the boy, without inflection or tone, like someone in a trance.

The man gaped at him. He couldn't seem to believe that the boy was actually speaking. He wouldn't have looked more surprised if the kid had suddenly flown out the window.

"I'm not retarded," said the boy, astonishing the man even further.

"Well," he panted, "then you shouldn't—you should stop that infernal . . ."

He wiped his face. Now that adrenaline wasn't being dumped into his system anymore, he looked like he was getting ready to pass out.

"Papa," said the boy.

The man just grunted.

"I hate you."

The man snorted. He took a swipe at the boy, but

his coordination was shot. "Shouldn't talk that way to your old man," he muttered. "Show some respect."

"No," said the boy.

The man pushed himself away from the boy and landed flat on his butt. He blinked rapidly, looked around the room to focus his eyes.

"What time is it?" he asked, as if he had forgotten why he had come into the room in the first place.

"Time to die," said the boy. "Time to die."

Sally wanted to hide under the sheets. Something was very wrong; something was making the hair on the back of her neck stand up. She had been afraid of the man first, and she had pitied the boy. But now the tide was turning. Now it was the boy who scared her, far worse than his father had.

"My friends want to meet you," said the boy, in that awful, toneless way.

"You ain't got no friends, you miserable fuck," said the man, then laughed at his own wit. "Who the hell would be friends with you?"

"Lions and tigers and bears," said the boy.

Sally began to shake.

"Wolves and sharks and gorillas," said the boy.

A low growl filled the room. The man looked up, blinked. Shadows were slinking around the walls, creeping out of the corners.

"Who's there?" asked the man.

"Eagles and crows and snakes," said the boy. "My friends."

The stuffed animals were moving. They were changing, growing fangs and claws, filling with blood and bone and muscle. Their button eyes glistened moistly. Their noses sniffed the air, and their lips pulled back in snarls and growls. Their pacing became stalking.

"Don't," said Sally. "Why don't you just send him away? You have the power. Why don't you just tell him to go away and never come back?"

"Time to die," the boy said tonelessly.

The animals fell upon the man. Sally wanted to look away, but she couldn't help seeing most of it anyway. It was amazing just how many of them could get at him, just how much damage could be done to him while he still lived, just how much of him there was to shred. He screamed and pleaded throughout most of it, until he had nothing left to scream with. And then he was very, very quiet.

"Well," said the boy. "That's the end of that."

Sally made herself look at him. He was looking at her, seeing her. And his tone had changed; he was speaking normally now.

The man was lying next to him, whole and un-scathed—but utterly dead. The stuffed animals were just what they had always been, and there was no blood except for a thin trickle coming from the man's nose.

"It was an illusion," said the boy. "He believed he was being torn to pieces, so he died."

Sally didn't ask him why he had done it. His face was swollen from the beating he had taken and still caked with blood.

"He beat me for years," said the boy. "He didn't understand me. He didn't know I was really a genius."

"Did you know it yourself?" asked Sally. "That you were a genius?"

"No," admitted the boy. "I just wanted to bump my head. I liked the perfect rhythm. And I liked to take things apart. But I was like an animal. And then one night it just all seemed to come together for me."

"Your father broke the rhythm," said Sally.

"Yes. And so I killed him."

"And then what did you do?"

The boy shrugged. "I still had a lot of things to figure out. But eventually I knew enough to make my way in the world. I found out how to make people think what I wanted them to think."

Sally stared at him. He was only nine years old, and his face was too swollen and bloody to give her a good look at his features. But her gut told her.

"Ted?" she asked, her voice shaking.

He just smiled.

Sally got out of the bed. She edged away from him. He kept grinning a grin so horrible that Sally's skin wanted to crawl right off her body at the sight of it. She backed away from him, out the door, and then she turned to run.

But it was one of those dreams where you want to run but you can only move like molasses. She was afraid to look behind her, afraid to see the boy following with that terrible smile. She forced her feet down the hallway.

If Ralph were here, he'd be playing music from Bernard Herrmann's Psycho suite now. That part in the movie where the lady is about to find the dead mother propped up in the basement . . .

Stop thinking about that!

But Sally remembered that music too well. It went with this dimly lit hall perfectly. There was something familiar about this hall too; and if she weren't so intent on reaching the end of it, she'd know what it was.

On her right was a doorway, and it was open. Maybe she could go in there and shut the door, hide from Ted. She made her feet move, and then she was standing in the doorway.

Someone was already in there. Abruptly, Sally's mood changed, the music stopped, and she was no longer afraid. Someone was sitting behind a TV tray, drawing. She couldn't see his features.

"Hello," he said, without looking up.

"Hello," said Sally.

"Hello," he said again, in exactly the same absent tone. "Hello. Hello."

A small hand reached out of the darkness and grabbed Sally's. She tried to pull away from it, but it clung to her. It was delicate, not at all what she would expect a boy's hand—Ted's hand—to be like. She kept pulling, until she saw an arm, a shoulder, and almost . . . almost . . .

A face?

It wasn't the one Sally expected. But she screamed anyway.

Sally woke up for real. Sunlight was pouring into the cavern. Her heart was still pounding from the scream, and she didn't feel rested at all.

Damn. Some "good night's sleep."

She felt cheated and depressed. But more than that, she felt worried, a poisonous, gnawing sort of worry that did more damage each moment she bore it. She tried to remember whose face she had seen at the end of the dream. It shouldn't have made her scream, whoever it belonged to. In fact, she felt a little guilty about that, which just added to the overall feeling of bleakness.

Stop it, she warned herself, and tried to trigger the release of endorphins into her blood. She wasn't entirely successful, but it helped enough to get her up and ready for the day.

She went out into the cavern. Joey was standing at the mouth, looking out at the dawn just as he had on that first day, when he had been so full of hope. Sally stood for a moment and tried to memorize the sight of him, tried to recapture the feelings they had shared on that first day. Then she went to him. He turned to her, destroying the last lingering memory of that earlier happiness.

"I heard you scream," he said.

His face looked drawn, his eyes haunted. As miserable as she had felt when she had awakened in the morning, he looked a thousand times worse.

"It was just a bad dream," she said.

"About Ted. He's finally come to get us."

He was still linked with her; he must have sensed Ted through her dream.

I got a fix on him, said Joey. *He's in those mountains to the west, not far from where we found Susanna's house.*

Sally started. She hadn't thought to do that; she had been too much a prisoner of the dream. Good for Joey!

What good will it do? asked Joey, his eyes full of ashes. *It's useless, Sally. Everywhere we look we find enemies. I'm so tired of it. I don't know how much more of it I can take.*

He was frightening her. She wanted to shake him, to make him activate his own endorphins. But he just shook his head. He knew how to do that. He just couldn't seem to motivate himself to do it.

Please, Joey, begged Sally. *For me. Please. Just a little longer. We'll get where we're going.*

He tried to smile. *What are we going to do about Ted?*

Sally almost said, *Let's go find him and get it over with.* But Joey was in no shape to go looking for Ted. He was so depressed, he might not even defend himself.

"I'm going to get Caitlin," she said. "She's the one who's the most like Ted."

"Good luck," said Joey, with remarkably little irony.

Sally approached Caitlin's bedroom with caution. She could feel the other girl in there, alert, awake. Sally paused at the doorway and knocked. There was no answer, but she went in anyway.

Caitlin was perched on the side of her makeshift bed. Sally gasped at the sight of her.

Caitlin had made changes in herself, just like the boys had. But she had stayed the same height, and her dimensions were much the same. Sally couldn't quite put her finger on what Caitlin had done to make herself so beautiful.

Or so insane. Because Caitlin was smiling very much like Ted had smiled in Sally's dream. Her face was flushed, her eyes unblinking, and that smile . . .

"What do you want?" Caitlin asked lightly.

"Joey found Ted," said Sally.

"So?"

Sally tried to study the other girl, but it was just too disconcerting. She could hardly stand to look at her.

"You changed your eyes," said Caitlin, somehow managing to convey scorn without changing her tone.

"Caitlin, you're the one who's best qualified to go after Ted."

"And your hair. Why didn't you go a little farther? You still look like a mouse."

"I'll go with you. I'll back you up, but I need you, Caitlin."

The other girl smiled wider, until Sally could see the tips of her teeth; and she could have sworn that Caitlin had filed them. "No. I don't give a damn about Ted. You're the big hero. You go do it."

"Caitlin, please—"

"Just how stupid are you, Sally? Get a clue! I'm not part of your dumb crusade any longer. You go after that frightened little shit if you want to. I'm just going to ignore him, unless he comes after me. And then! AND THEN HE'LL GET HIS!"

She flamed up, making Sally take a step back from the heat. She laughed, throwing her head back, and for a moment she might almost have had human skulls tied around her skirt. She kept laughing until Sally couldn't stand it anymore and had to leave the room.

"Forget it," Sally said.

"How about if I just forget *you*?" Caitlin called after her, and Sally felt heat at her back. It took every shred of willpower she had not to hurry away.

Joey stood waiting for her outside. She thought his face looked a little less haggard. "Do you want me to come with you?" he asked.

"No." Sally put her hands on his shoulders. "We'll keep our link open. I'll call for help if I need it. You take care of yourself."

He said nothing, but tried to let her know that he had confidence in her. He lacked conviction, but he was trying, and that seemed an improvement.

Sally smiled at him and took off into the morning wind. He waved until he was just a small speck in the distance.

Sally turned her face toward Ted's mountains and increased her speed.

The first place she looked was Susanna's house.

She was rather surprised to see that it was still there. She had expected, possibly hoped, that it would vanish after Susanna had died. If it had done that, she would have had a neat explanation of its appearance. Instead it was still here, mocking her, filling her with painful memories.

Susanna in the mirror, Susanna on the floor.

Susanna in her grave.

You killed Susie.

I didn't mean to! I didn't mean to kill her!

It made sense that Ted might be here. It turned Sally's stomach just to look at the place, just to go up the walk and put her hand on the doorknob. She was a wreck before she even walked into the house, and that would certainly be an advantage for Ted. But she made herself go in. She made herself look into every corner, under every eclectic antique, in every cupboard and closet.

Things were much the same as they had been the last time. Everything was in its place and there wasn't a speck of dust anywhere. If Ted was living there, that was how he would want it; but it might also look that way if it were a fancy simulacrum, like the wrecked bus had been.

Sally left the kitchen and made herself go into the bedrooms. She tackled the hardest first, the one in which Susanna had been killed. There was old blood on the floor; some of it had spilled out of Susanna's nose and mouth after she had died. That had been horrible. Sally evaporated the blood on the floor, then thought, *You idiot! Why didn't you check the DNA first?*

Because I'm scared shitless and I'm not thinking straight.

The room was otherwise untouched, the bed unrumpled. Sally looked in the wardrobe, which was still empty.

Surprise, surprise, she thought bitterly. Nothing was going to be easy about this. And she was so on edge now, how would she react when Ted made his appearance?

Sally checked the other two bedrooms next, but she had a feeling she would find nothing there, and she didn't. As she left the last one, which had wooden floors, she was unpleasantly reminded of Ted's bedroom from her dream. She could still see that dreadful smile on the boy's face.

If you see something like that here today, you're going to jump right out of your skin, she told herself. *What good is that going to do?* She paused in the hallway and tried to get a grip on herself. She did manage to calm down a little, but she knew it wouldn't be enough.

I've got to take a chance. I've got to get rid of the feelings completely. It's the only way to deal with Ted.

As if in answer to her thoughts, Joey's link with her was suddenly severed. She felt it as if a hair had been plucked out of her head.

He was so depressed when I left—I must be pushing him over the edge.

That settled it. Sally took firm hold of her feelings and carefully obliterated them. She used the metaphor of the water receding from the shore, just as she had done after her battle with Marc. It worked admirably. In another few moments she felt cold sober, rock steady, as close to emotionless as a human being can ever possibly be.

Now, she told herself, *back to work.*

She went back out into the living room, and something immediately occurred to her. She wanted to search the room again. Obviously no one was there, so why should she want to do that?

Because someone is *here.*

Sally stood perfectly still and waited. She tuned her ears until they were many times more sensitive than normal. That didn't work as well as she had thought it would; her own body sounds drowned everything else out after a certain point; but when she toned it down slightly, she thought she detected something.

Someone trying not to breathe. Someone trying not to move.

"Ted?" said Sally, and listened for a sharp intake of breath. She didn't get one, but the air in the room seemed to tighten around her.

"This is a good trick," said Sally. "You're telling my brain not to see you. But you forgot my ears. Or maybe you can't manage that as well? The visual cortex is easier to manipulate—maybe because we rely so much on it? That's very interesting."

No answer, but Sally could have sworn he was listening to her. She walked to the front door and opened it.

"I'm sorry about what your father did to you all those years," she said. "He probably had no idea how to handle an ordinary boy, let alone an autistic one. They didn't even have the term back then, did they?"

The image of the smiling boy blossomed in her mind, but she shrugged it off.

"He was a monster, but he's dead and now you're a thousand times worse than he was. You have no excuse at all, Ted. So just leave us alone, and we'll leave you alone. Because, believe me, Caitlin would love to burn you alive right now. And she could do it. She might have to burn the world too, but she wouldn't mind that one bit."

Sally stepped through the door and closed it behind her. She walked away from the house, wondering if she was really feeling eyes on her back or if her imagination was just supplying the extra dramatic touch.

Sally made a perfunctory sweep of the western mountains. They were quite beautiful, and she found herself looking at the scenery more than she looked for Ted.

He was there, at the house. I wasn't just imagining it. I hope I scared him off.

It was well into the afternoon when Sally went home again. Jim was waiting for her outside the cavern. She tried to brace herself for another round of Let's Pretend We're Not Flirting With Him, but the look on his face immediately chased those thoughts from her head.

He was enraged.

Sally landed right in front of him. Her feelings were still damped; she hadn't had a chance (or the thought) to change them back yet. But something was jangling inside her, some alarm screaming from a great distance.

"Joey's dead," said Jim, almost casually.

"No." Sally completely rejected the idea. In fact, she doubted that she had heard him right. But something started playing back in her mind, that moment when her tie with him had been severed. She had thought he had done it because he couldn't stand the feedback.

"No," she said again.

Jim grabbed her by the shoulder and shook her so hard that her head whipped back and forth. "Yes!" he snarled. "Yes, Joey is dead. He—is—dead, Sally." And he shoved her to the ground. Sally was too surprised to use her talent to cushion the fall. She hauled herself up on her elbows and gaped at him.

"He's not," she insisted. "He can't be."

He spat at her.

"His body," said Sally. "Show me his body. Maybe I can fix—"

"Fix? Maybe you can *fix?* There *is* no body, Sally." Jim leaned over her, his face and body contorted by the force of his words. "There's nothing to fix! He disintegrated himself! He blew himself up into a billion atoms. Maybe you can catch them all and put them back together, huh?"

He dragged her to her feet and started to hit her with his fists. Sally had the presence of mind to render the blows harmless, but he just kept hitting anyway. He was making a point, and Sally got it. She certainly got it, despite her dampened condition.

"Why?" she kept asking. "Why did he do it?"

"He was suicidal!" Jim shrieked, as if Sally were an idiot not to have known it. "He couldn't stand it anymore. Couldn't you give him just one break, just one chance to catch his breath before starting another goddamned confrontation? You bitch! What the hell were you trying to prove? And now Joey's dead! He's dead!''

He started to cry, but not very hard. These were the painful tears of a man who didn't like to cry, but was forced to do it by the sheer volume of grief he was holding inside.

"It's your fault," he said. "You just live with that!" And he stumbled away. He hurled himself into the air and took off toward the northern mountains like a meteor.

Sally stood gazing after him, absurd thoughts running through her head.

I should turn my emotions back on. No, I should leave them off. No, I should turn them on for Joey's sake. No, I'll be overwhelmed if I turn them back on. He can't be dead. Where's his body? Joey! Joey, answer me! You just took yourself somewhere, like Apollo did that time. Joey! Joey!

She went to look for him. She half believed he was dead, but she still expected him to walk out into the cavern, or to be sitting there waiting for her. Wherever she went, she found nothing but a dreadful emptiness, a silence.

"Joey!" she yelled. "Joey!"

Timothy came out of his room. "He's dead," he said flatly.

"He can't be."

"He is."

"No."

"Yes," said Timothy relentlessly. "He disintegrated himself. He couldn't stand it anymore. What did he have to look forward to except seeing *you* again? I would have killed myself too."

Sally couldn't answer him. She stood there stunned, as if slapped. Her emotions were beginning to come in like the tide, beginning to lap at her feet, wanting to pull her in. She couldn't stand to have Timothy looking at her that way, with such contempt, such hatred. She fled from the main chamber, into her own room.

Joey! she called. *Joey! Joey!*

Something soft rubbed against her legs. She dropped to the ground, thinking he might be under the bed. But something else was there instead.

"Meow," said Mungy Bungy. He gazed at her with adoration.

"You," she said, taking him into her lap. She hadn't seen him in so long, and now she needed him. She needed that look in his eyes, that unconditional affection.

"Joey's missing," she told him. "Where is he, Mungy? I can't believe he's dead."

"He is," said Caitlin behind her.

Sally didn't want to turn. She didn't want to see the most hateful face of all. She heard the footsteps behind her, felt the searing eyes on her face as Caitlin walked around to look at her.

"That cat's not even real," said Caitlin gloatingly.

Sally was suddenly furious, too much so to be logical. "He's magic!" she snapped.

"You made him up, you idiot. You made him real—it's that telekinetic power of yours. You made him out of thin air."

"He's flesh and blood!" howled Sally. "Leave us alone!"

"I can prove it," Caitlin said nonchalantly. And suddenly Mungy vanished into thin air. Sally screamed, bereft.

"What did you do? Where is he?"

Caitlin gave her a triumphant grin. "I looked into your mind and made it see the truth."

"You're planting thoughts!" accused Sally, worried that Mungy had been killed, or that he was there and she couldn't see him. "Where is he? Where is he?" she said, not knowing anymore whether she was talking about Mungy or Joey.

"Look for him."

Sally did. She searched the room for any trace of him, even an atomic one. She found nothing. She broadened her search, going out from the cavern in concentric circles, wider and wider, finding nothing, nothing . . .

"You're way cold," said Caitlin. "Colder every second."

Sally followed the mocking voice, searching, until finally she ended up back at her starting point, inside her own mind.

And that's where she found the truth.

"It's in your own mind, *dummy*," said Caitlin. "Those tricks that you used to play to fool The Three fooled you too. You made up the cat because no one loved you. That's the pathetic truth, Sally. No one loves you and no one ever will."

Timothy had come in, and Jim too, back from the mountains already. They were standing next to Caitlin, glaring down at Sally in unified hatred. She was stunned at its depth. "I saved your lives," she said wonderingly.

"That's what *you* say," said Jim. "And then you murdered your rivals, so why should we believe anything you say?"

"I didn't," whispered Sally. She wanted to shout it, but they should have already known it. They had lived through it. She caught a glint in Caitlin's eyes and saw the triumph hiding there. Another truth dawned.

So you pulled a Ted, she sent on a tight beam.

Caitlin brushed off the contact as if it were dirty. Her natural contempt for others was so far greater than Ted's, it was almost a madness. She didn't even pause to gloat before she pulled together her Mastermind, that thing Joey had been so worried she was forming behind their backs.

It was much like Ted's, only Caitlin's eyes were the ones on top, and the others were in her belly. Sally could even make out poor Ralph at the very bottom, his eyes closed like a newborn kitten's.

Then the pressure began.

GET OUT. GET OUT. GET OUT. GET OUT. GET OUT.

Sally didn't resist. She got to her feet and let them drive her out of her room, across the cavern, out through the mouth and into the open.

GET OUT. GET OUT. GET OUT. They continued relentlessly. Sally managed to get herself into the air; but still they pushed her and tried to herd her. They wanted her to go to the western mountains, but Sally didn't want that. Her mountains were to the north. She fought them, pulling farther and farther away. It took every fiber of her talent to break loose, even more power than it had taken to kill Marc. Sally wasn't even sure if she had beaten them in the end or if they had just let her go, sending her off like a rock from a slingshot to the sound of Caitlin's derisive laughter.

If you ever come back, I'll kill you, Caitlin sent as a parting shot.

Sally didn't answer. She just flew and flew until she had reached her mountains, where it was raining now. She threw herself down on the slopes and let the downpour soak her as she lay there and sobbed. Everything was gone. Everyone she loved was dead, even Ralph, in a way, because that creature she had glimpsed in Caitlin's Mastermind was only a shadow of the boy she had known.

The tide had come in, and she was drowning in it. Literally as well as figuratively, because now it was raining so hard Sally could barely breathe. She wasn't even sure if she was crying anymore or just gasping for air. She lay that way for a timeless time, too swamped to remember that she could shield herself from the rain or even dry herself out if she wanted to. This was a grief too huge to bear.

And yet somehow, it still wasn't quite real. Susanna, Marc, Joey, Mungy. All gone now. As if they had never existed, as if she had dreamed them all, not just the cat. Really, what proof did she have? What proof that any of it had happened, that she had a history at all?

There were no tears on her face, only rain. She had never loved, never lost anyone. She could lie on the mountainside forever, and it would make no difference at all.

A dreadful calm settled over her. She sat up and looked at the swollen clouds.

GET OUT, they had said. *Get out, get out, get out . . .*

"I'm out," said Sally. "Mungy and I will make our own house."

You made him up, you idiot . . .

"He was magic. He was a messenger from Olympus."

I'm afraid of her, Sally . . .

"You haven't seen her eat human flesh. You haven't seen her . . . seen her laugh as . . ."

This is your skull . . .

Sally wiped her face with a wet sleeve. She tried to see the shape of her mountains, to take comfort in their familiarity, but they were strange and dark today. She wondered if Apollo and Aphrodite knew she was out here, suffering in the rain.

How come they didn't interfere when Marc tried to kill you?

"I don't know. I don't know. Maybe I had to—had to prove . . ."

What would you do if some people you didn't know were having a battle to the death? Would you interfere?

"Yes," said Sally. "No. I don't know."

No one loves you and no one ever will . . .

"That's enough," Sally told the rain. "Stop it."

As if it had listened, it suddenly stopped. Sally gaped, because she knew she hadn't done it. She hadn't used her talent. Those clouds were still heavy with water. Why would they stop?

Sally! someone sent her on a tight beam.

"Huh?"

Sally, it's Ralph!

"Ralph?" she said stupidly. "Where are you?"

Sally! Look out! Look out!

The earth shook, then stopped. It went *BOOM*. A few seconds later it went *BOOM* again.

Sally, run! *She's coming!*

"Who's coming?"

BOOM. BOOM. BOOM. Getting louder, getting closer, coming in rhythmic intervals like Ted bumping his head against the bedboard. Only this was something big enough to shake the whole earth.

She's using them, Sally. I've only got a few seconds before she finds out what I'm doing.

"Who?"

Caitlin! She's coming, Sally. Run!

Sally stood. Ralph's tone was frightening her, making her want to run; but she had a creeping feeling it wouldn't do any good. She felt paralyzed. She turned a slow circle, trying to find the source of the noise. The ground shook under her feet.

BOOM. BOOM. BOOM. BOOM. BOOM.

"What is she, a giant now?" Sally asked Ralph. But he was gone. *Too late,* she thought to herself. *You should have run.*

Sally gasped as something materialized around her. She had thought it was a giant hand grasping her, but it was a suit of armor. She was dressed from head to foot in it. There was even a helmet, with a visor that clanged shut at the slightest movement.

Sally tore it off, then disintegrated the armor.

FOOL, Caitlin said from somewhere, her voice sounding as huge as the footsteps. *You'll be needing that.*

A sword appeared in Sally right hand, dragging her arm down with its weight. She disintegrated that too.

What will you have to fight with? taunted Caitlin. *Nothing. Nothing, Sally.*

BOOM. BOOM. BOOM. BOOM. BOOM ...

And then Sally saw her.

This is how you could look if you wanted to, Jim had said in the dream. And Sally had been so excited, because she had realized he was right. She could change her body any way she wanted.

And much later, she had wondered what it would be like to be an eagle; an intelligent eagle with all of her own memories still intact. She had thought it would be possible, but very hard. It would take great skill and courage to try something like that, and Sally had decided to try it when she felt more confident.

But Caitlin apparently hadn't been afraid to go full steam ahead. Not afraid at all, because now she was a dragon.

Caitlin was a red dragon with green eyes, eyes as feral and predatory as any cat's could be. She fixed Sally in her gaze and made a sound in her giant throat, a sort of contented warble. She was a hundred feet tall now, and her front paws were equipped with dagger claws.

Her teeth were even sharper. She showed them to Sally.

I decided I couldn't wait to kill you, said Caitlin. *I*

*don't want to make Ted's mistake. You would only
come back stronger.*

Caitlin crouched and began to creep forward. Sally
stood where she was, transfixed. She knew right down
to her core that she was looking at Kali now, the
Goddess of Destruction in her purest form. And she
was terrible. She was death.

"I wouldn't have tried to kill you," Sally said
hopelessly.

Caitlin didn't bother to answer. She drew in an
enormous breath, almost sucking Sally in with it; Sally
looked down the dragon's throat and saw the fire
burning there.

She felt it coming one second before it struck her.
It was the fire of the very sun itself.

Sally protected herself automatically with a varia-
tion of Ralph's shield; but the ground under her was
instantly vaporized, and she quickly found herself at
the bottom of a smoking pit. She shot out of it at
supersonic speed, flying well above the dragon's head.

Caitlin! You'll destroy the world!

*You're the one who told Ted I would burn the world
to kill him, if I had to. I'd do it to kill you too, Sally.*

The dragon launched herself into the air. She shot
another burst of sunfire at Sally, striking her easily,
with all the destructive power of a solar flare. Sally
could feel the Mastermind now, filling Caitlin with un-
imaginable power. Sally was barely able to protect
herself from it, this time.

The power of a white dwarf, Caitlin laughed madly.
*Maybe even the power of a black hole. How would
you like that, Sally? How would you like it if I put
you in a place where you would be crushed forever?*

And then she tried to do it. Existence flickered for
a second before Sally managed to thwart the attempt.
She was so tied up in her own self-defense, she forgot
to fly. She fell like a stone.

The atmosphere was burning around her. Caitlin was really doing it! With every gout of sunfire, she was destroying Olympus. What was happening to Apollo and Aphrodite? And Ralph, and Jim, and Timothy—they would all be killed!

What's left for you after you destroy the world, Caitlin? Sally cried as she tumbled. *What's left for you?*

You still don't get it! Caitlin laughed. *How stupid can you be, Sally? You still haven't figured it out!*

Sally struck the ground like a small comet. Caitlin was on top of her instantly. Her eyes weren't green anymore, they were twin suns. She opened her jaws and let the fire dribble out like acid.

This time Sally didn't try to shield. This time she changed her form into something immutable, unburnable, something that felt the fire as if it were cool water. She hardly knew what she was doing, but she did it well. Her instincts were taking over.

Caitlin gazed down through the smoke and fire, ready to gloat, to celebrate her triumph. But then she caught sight of Sally, still alive, and her rage made the sunfire look puny in comparison. It was more like the fires of hell.

Goddamn you filthy fucking bitch! Caitlin howled, and seized Sally in her front paws. *Die die die die die die die die die!*

Sally's new form resisted the pressure of those paws, resisted the heat and the flames; but now the assault was taking place on another level. Now Sally could feel her brothers and sister in the Mastermind, hear their hate-filled thoughts—especially Jim's. He was furious at her strength and her will to resist.

NO ONE EVER LOVED YOU SALLY AND NO ONE EVER WILL! DIE DIE DIE DIE DIE DIE DIE DIE DIE DIE DIE DIE!

Sally could see herself, as if at a great distance. She felt like she was watching a movie and she was in it too. She watched as she slipped closer and closer to death, and she wanted to say, *Stop the movie, I don't like it, I want to go home, I want Marc to feed me some french fries and sit me on his lap, and I want Joey to be all right and Ralph to make his music, and I just want to rest because I'm sick of riding on this bus, sick of it.*

Sick of it.

She was going to die. One more second would do it. They were too strong for her, and she couldn't even bring herself to attack them back.

You dummy, Caitlin gloated. *You chicken. Even Joey fought back harder than this.*

Sally's eyes went wide, as if Caitlin had just rammed a dagger into her heart. The dragon grinned, delighted at her reaction. *Yes, I killed him. And now I'll kill you; but I'm going to savor it as much as I can. I hate you a lot more than I hated him.*

"He was our brother," Sally said, too tired to do more than whisper it.

You should have killed me when you had the chance. You thought you were so smart. Why didn't you kill me when you had the chance, Sally? When the bus was going over the cliff?

"Because," said Sally, "I loved you."

The dragon paused. For a moment, the onslaught seemed to recede, as if everyone were taking a deep breath. If it had been a movie, Caitlin would have been moved by Sally's confession. Caitlin seemed transfixed as she stared at her.

But it wasn't a movie.

Too bad for you, said Caitlin, and then she sucked in air for the killing breath. Sally watched the sun turn white-hot in the dragon's maw.

Please, Sally sent to the cosmos, with no pride left in her at all, only bewildered pain. *Don't let me die like this. It isn't fair; they're ganging up on me. Please, somebody love me. Somebody love me. Please.*

And then the dragon's claws were gone, and Caitlin was swatted aside like a fly. Apollo and Aphrodite were lifting Sally in their arms, and the air was sweet and cool again, the mountain whole.

The Mastermind recoiled. It glared at Sally's rescuers, awed and terrified. Apollo and Aphrodite hadn't needed to come in person to rescue Sally; they could have simply transported her to safety. But they wanted the children to see that *they* loved Sally, they stood by her, they wouldn't let anyone harm her. Not ever again. Caitlin's Mastermind tried once more to attack, but it was shrugged off like a tattered cloak, scattering its participants back into their individual selves.

Sally gazed at the perfect faces bending over her, the God of Light and the Goddess of Love. *Have I proved myself?* she asked them

Yes, they answered.

She was too damaged to frame any more words for them. But her heart expanded with a joy so great, she could hardly tell the difference between it and the pain.

This is why we can't stand to feel. Even the good stuff hurts.

She wanted to black out, but someone was calling to her. On the slopes behind everyone else, a man was watching. His face was so ordinary, it was downright forgettable. He gave her a half smile and nodded. He didn't try to interfere in her rescue; he seemed almost glad about it.

He was Ted.

———

W

Sally awoke in Apollo's house.

She had awakened there many times already, since her rescue. It no longer surprised her. She was taking a long time to heal. She could have done it in a day, but her heart wasn't in it.

It wasn't sadness that made her feel that way. She was grieving, yes; and she was terribly worried about Ralph and the other boys. But all of that was manageable now. What disturbed her most about her new situation was the sense of *relief,* the feeling that she was no longer responsible for everything and everyone.

For years she had shouldered that responsibility. To be relieved of it was wonderful and painful.

Sally lay back with her arms folded behind her head and watched the play of sunlight on her walls. This was *her* room, her own place in Apollo's home. It had white walls and Mediterranean blue windowsills. Sometimes it was enough for her just to gaze at that blue and marvel at its richness.

"Today is the day," said Apollo.

He had come into the room quietly, but he didn't startle her. Sally wondered why that was, how he managed the trick. Even his good looks didn't startle her, though she certainly enjoyed feasting her eyes on him. He was so handsome he made her forget to be self-conscious.

"The day for what?" she said.

"The day for you to be well," he said. He went to her bedside and sat, taking her hand.

Sally enjoyed his touch. But she didn't agree with him.

"What's the rush?" she said.

"You learned everything you needed to know before you even went through the Gate, Sally," said Apollo. "You just don't realize it."

"How do you know that?" she demanded.

"How could I *not* know it?" he asked, meaning much more than Sally could fathom at the moment. She supposed he meant that he could feel it with his talent.

"I didn't know everything," she insisted.

"You lacked confidence, that's all. You could do almost anything you imagine, Sally."

"Almost? What *couldn't* I do, then?"

"You couldn't be God."

His expression made Sally shiver. Her brothers would be so intimidated, so jealous if they could see this man, this perfect example of masculinity and authority and . . .

Love . . .

"What is God?" Sally asked, but didn't add, *and why didn't you say* a *god?*

"I don't know," said Apollo. "Knowing that is another thing you can't do."

Sally was surprised at her own feelings of irritation. She hadn't really expected him to know that answer; why was she starting to get mad?

"You're wrong," she said stubbornly. "There's something I didn't learn before I came through the Gate."

"No," said Apollo. "There's nothing."

"I didn't know that Mungy wasn't real." And to her

horror, she started to cry. She thought about stopping it, but that would be even more ridiculous.

"But he *was* real," said Apollo gently, which only made Sally cry more.

"I made him up," said Sally. "Because I needed him."

"You made him real. He comforted you."

"Yeah, and isn't that pathetic?"

"That's not the word I would choose." He cupped her chin in his hand. "I would say it was ... endearing. Charming."

Sally cried without shame, though she did stifle her runny nose. It was bad enough to be puffy and blubbery without making that awful snuffling noise too. She didn't want Apollo to see her that way. She didn't want that look on his face to go away, the one that made her glad that she had fixed her eyes and her hair. And her breasts. The one that made her think he might be about to kiss her.

"I'd like to kiss you," he said.

"I don't even ... know ... how," said Sally, but it wasn't really true. She had felt others making love for years; though that wasn't *hers,* and she had learned to block it out.

"I'll teach you," said Apollo.

She didn't have to say yes then, because he already knew it. He leaned toward her.

Sally tilted her head back. She closed her eyes. The moment before contact, she said to herself, *This is going to be really good.*

And it was too.

It was just like the kiss she had shared with Osiris—only better, because now she was one hundred percent *here,* one hundred percent real. Apollo knew what he was doing, and he enjoyed doing it. He wasn't some remote, perfect creature, he was a man. She could smell him, taste him, feel his desire. He loved sex and he wanted it with her.

"I love you, Sally," he said when he had finished. He still held her close.

"I thought you loved Aphrodite," she couldn't help saying.

"She's part of me," he said, without shame or guilt, without fear of hurting Sally, which was puzzling; because she *knew* he was telling the truth about loving her. Caitlin and Jim had been wrong, Timothy had been wrong. Apollo loved her, and she was too happy about that to let semantics trip her up now.

"Kiss me again," she said. And he did.

When they had come up for air again, Sally didn't feel like crying anymore. She didn't feel quite like making love either.

"Let me hold you." Apollo stroked her hair.

"You're not my dad." Sally still felt stubborn.

"I'm not trying to be," said Apollo. "I had another role in mind."

He lay down with her, still stroking her hair. Sally let him. He wasn't going to try to seduce her yet. And what he was doing felt so good. So good. All of the tension was draining from her body. The grief and worry were receding, going away for a while. She was getting drowsy.

As she began to drift off to sleep, something wonderful occurred to her, just like it had on the first morning she had awakened on the bus after rescuing everyone from The Three.

Now I really am *free!*

"Are you?" asked Ted.

Somehow, Sally was back at the abandoned Indian School; and there was Ted, at long last. They were in one of the classrooms, looking across rows of desks at each other. Sally wanted to look around to make sure it wasn't an illusion, but she didn't trust herself to look away from him. Besides—if it was an illusion, it was an excellent one. She could smell the dust, chalk, old paper; she could feel the heat of the Arizona summer burning outside.

She could feel the Gate.

"Don't try to squirm away," said Ted. "I'll only draw you back again. I can be quite obnoxious."

Sally opened her mouth to ask a question, but then thought better of it. She had wanted to know if he had drawn them both back through the Gate. But that would only let him know how much in the dark she was.

But had he? Sally could feel the Gate, the real thing, not some illusion. Its presence was so overwhelming, she couldn't imagine how she could have forgotten what it was like.

"Tell me what you want to tell," said Sally.

He looked at her with his usual blank expression, but she could read him, a little. He was looking at her with new respect.

"I'm not telling you a damned thing," he said. "I want *you* to tell *me*."

"I'm not any more anxious to do that than you are," said Sally.

He shrugged, as if this didn't matter. He didn't seem insulted by her new, authoritative tone either. Before, he would have killed her on the spot. The change in his attitude made Sally dizzy.

"I've been watching you almost since the beginning," he said. "I'm amazed you survived this long."

Sally shrugged. She had hidden her talents from him her entire life, so this was no surprise.

"You have far surpassed my expectations for you," he said, as if he were some teacher giving her a good grade, as if he were somehow responsible for her success.

"You expected me to be a loser," she said. "How was I supposed to build Olympus for you, then? If I was so incompetent?"

"I wanted to get rid of you years ago."

Sally didn't react to that. He appeared to expect that she would. When she didn't, he went smoothly on. "Speaking to you now is almost like speaking to Susanna."

"Liar," said Sally.

This angered him. "I haven't met more than three people in my life whom I respected," he said. "I used to think you were shit. Now I don't. Take it or leave it."

Sally did neither. But she couldn't help but be a little staggered by his admission.

"But you're still a fool," he continued. "Caitlin was right. You should have killed her when you had the chance. Now she will dog your existence."

"She's afraid of me," said Sally. "But you'll be happy to know she's not afraid of you anymore. As long as you stay out of her way, she'll leave you alone."

His face turned a little red. *He doesn't have Marc to fix that for him anymore,* Sally thought. *And maybe he hasn't learned to do it himself. . . .*

"By the way," he said, "about that remark you made about my father, I didn't appreciate it. My past is none of your business. If you raid my memories again, I'll kill you."

Raid your memories? Sally thought. He really seemed to mean what he said, though he was bluffing with the death threat. *Mostly* bluffing.

If he didn't send me that dream, where did it come from?

"I'm not going to waste my time attacking you otherwise," he continued, almost cheerfully. "Or Caitlin. You know, I used to wonder about her. I used to wonder what sort of children she and I could make together."

Sally tried not to show how horrifying that notion was. But Ted was too good to miss it. He smiled.

"Yes, our child would make the Goddess of Destruction look like the Goddess of Love," he said. "I still wonder if it could be done. It would come in handy. I could use it to destroy the world we left behind."

Sally didn't ask him why he would want to do that. His old distaste was plain on his face.

"How do you know Olympus could exist without that world?" she asked.

He looked triumphant. "I thought you did."

"It can't," said Sally firmly.

That soured his milk. "I don't believe you," he said.

"You mean you don't *want* to believe me. You don't want to think that your paradise exists only in your dreams. You don't want to believe that you could fool yourself better than you've fooled everyone else all these years."

"Look who's talking," he said. "I heard what Caitlin said to you. You and that pathetic cat of yours."

That was supposed to hurt her, but it only confirmed her suspicions.

"I don't have any more patience for your tantrums, Ted. You're wasting my time. I'm leaving."

"Wait!" he shrieked. "Goddamn you, you little cu—"

Sally held her breath. He was afraid to call her *cunt*. Afraid!

"An exchange of information," he said. "I give a little, and then you give a little."

"Not likely," said Sally.

"Wait till you hear what I have to say."

She waited.

"You're more powerful than me now," he said. "You're more powerful than any of us."

Sally had suspected that was the case, but she didn't trust the suspicion. "Why would you say that?" she asked. "Now I could kill you."

He laughed, and dared to move closer to her, around the desks, until he was no more than a foot away from her. Then he stopped.

"Look," he said. "You didn't kill me."

Sally kept carefully silent.

Ted looked into her eyes, neither smiling nor frowning, neither threatening or peaceful. "I love little Sally, she's so full of charm. And if I don't hurt her, she'll do me no harm. That's the truth, isn't it? You won't act against me at all unless I attack you."

Sally didn't answer. She hadn't agreed to give him anything. "Good-bye," she said.

"No!" he said, visibly controlling himself. "It's your turn! Tell me where you put them!"

Where I put them? I put them in the ground!

"I've looked everywhere for them, damn you. I always end up back here, and they're not here, they're not there, *so where are they?*"

Sally didn't know what to say; she didn't even know what he meant; and she was afraid to try to make him clarify. He would know her own uncertainty if she did.

But he read her silence as well as she had read his.

"You don't know," he said triumphantly. "You don't know!"

"They're dead," Sally said desperately, trying to recover control of the situation, but that just made it worse. He laughed.

"I wouldn't laugh," she said. "If I don't know where they are, I can't find them for you."

"So you admit it," he said.

Sally didn't intend to admit anything. She looked

away from him, at the windows, her face a mask. She watched the motes of dust swirling in the sunlight.

"Together we could find them," Ted was saying. "Don't tell me you wouldn't like to do that. I saw the way you cried. And Marc would like to see *you* again. You're prettier than you used to be. A few more changes, and you could catch his eye."

"You're so certain they're still alive," said Sally.

He didn't answer that, but she knew he was. Yet she remembered killing them.

But her dream afterward, when she had seen Marc in the hallway . . .

Sally, where am I? Marc has asked her.

The motes of dust swirled clockwise, counterclockwise in the sunlight; then started over. That was odd.

"There is so much we could teach each other," said Ted. "You need allies now."

Swirl, counterswirl, swirl, counterswirl—yet Ted and Sally weren't moving around enough to create the sort of draft that would make the dust move back and forth that way.

"You have no reason to be afraid of me anymore," said Ted. "None at all."

It was like a movie, going forward, backward, and then forward again. Like a loop of film. But if they were inside a loop, how could they still be moving forward? But they must be—there it went again. Forward, backward, forward again.

Sally looked at Ted again, impassively, studying him behind her own mask. He didn't know they were in a loop.

"I can do it by myself," she said. "I don't need you."

All the color drained from his face. He was angry enough to kill her now. Sally wasn't afraid, though. She was prepared to shrug him off the same way she had done with Caitlin's Mastermind. She had been in battle too many times now to be afraid.

But that didn't mean she didn't *respect* his threat, or that she underestimated it.

"You'd like to put us all away, wouldn't you?" he said. "Put us somewhere were we can't bother you, can't hurt you. You'd like us all to be out of the way." A fever glowed behind his eyes, his old paranoia raging.

"I would find them for you if I could, Ted," Sally said, suddenly. "You must be very lonely without them."

His eyes warned her of imminent attack, but he didn't move. "Don't patronize me," he said, his voice shaking with rage. "I swear I'll kill you, even if it costs my own life."

"I'm not patronizing you. I mean it."

"Shut up. I could have killed you a thousand times when you were growing up."

"And yet I haven't tried to kill you once."

The fire started to drain out of him. Within moments, he was something like his old self. "Yes," he said. "True. And now here we are, at an impasse. One of us has to give, or we won't learn anything."

Sally wasn't inclined to agree with him. She wondered if she could leave the loop without his help; she wanted to be away from him.

"Still playing hard to get," he said, his eyes looking first into one of her eyes and then the other, as if he were a lover and she a virgin who had resisted seduction. "How useless. Tell me, do you intend to even look for them?"

"I might," said Sally, wondering if she really would or not.

"Yes, you might," he said, softly. "You're just tenderhearted enough to do that. And then what? You'll exile us back in the dirty old world?"

"I wouldn't inflict you on them."

"Ah. Of course not. Maybe you'll find some other hole to stick us in."

This wasn't going well. If she didn't convince him, fast, he might not let her out of this loop, assuming he even knew they were in one.

"If I could put the three of you in Olympus, I would," said Sally, meaning it.

He stared for a long moment, until Sally began to worry that she had blown it. But then he smiled. He smiled the terrible smile she had seen in her dream, on the face of the child.

"Yes," he said. "I know you would. Sweet, soft Sally."

And then she was back. The school was gone, and Ted with it.

"Apollo!" she cried, but he was already there, already awake.

"I heard," he said.

"He said Marc and Susanna were still alive!"

Apollo pushed her down on the bed. He smoothed her hair, placed his cheek next to hers. "Patience," he said. "We'll see."

We'll see. Sally contemplated the words. They were good advice. There was no sense in crashing about the landscape, looking for clues, digging up bodies. Not in a place where illusion and reality were so much alike.

We'll see. Just wait. Learn. Think.

His hands were soothing her. She was drifting off to sleep. Ted wouldn't be able to grab her again without her consent. She was already unraveling how he had done it. She still wasn't sure about the loop or how it worked, but she would unravel that too, in time.

Unravel it. Understand it. And then . . .

"Then you'll know the truth," whispered Apollo, his breath warm against her ear. She shuddered, and he wrapped her up in his arms.

"Sleep," he said. And she did.

"Then we'll apply the voltage when the Apollo circuits were running as on the boundary say no, we must not —"
voltage, the last A

S ally dreamed of the city again.

She didn't dream about getting there, or even wanting to be there. She merely opened her eyes and found herself in the back of the boat, floating down the canal with Aphrodite sitting just where she had before, amidships, and Apollo standing with his back to her, in the bow.

"But this time we all know each other," said Aphrodite. She was dressed exactly as she had been the last time Sally had dreamed of the boat. Aphrodite pulled aside her veil and studied Sally for a long moment, then smiled at her. "What do you think of the city now?"

Sally stared at the marvel that unfolded on all sides of her. This time she didn't try to decide if the architecture was Egyptian, Mayan, Babylonian, or any other form; nor did she wonder if it belonged to the past or the future, because now she knew that it belonged to the future. Maybe *her* future.

"Is it still the City of the Gods?" asked Aphrodite.

"Yes."

Aphrodite pulled back her hood, as if to take in more of the sights. "Why?" she asked, though she didn't seem to disagree, necessarily.

"You're here," said Sally.

Aphrodite smiled again, like the Sphinx.

They drifted for a time. Sally thought back to the

other time, when her life had been in such terrible danger, and possibilities seemed more like impossible dreams. *You will help to build it,* Aphrodite had said then, and Sally had despaired because that had proved to her that the city must not be real, after all.

But now she didn't feel that way. She still had no idea how she could accomplish what Ted had wanted all those years, these superior buildings, this master plan of urban organization. But her short time in Olympus had taught her something already. She had learned she could fly, could change her body into any shape, could make food out of basic elements just by thinking about them, and if she could do those things, perhaps . . .

"Be an eagle," said Aphrodite.

"What?" Sally blinked, wondering if the woman was speaking metaphorically.

"You can do almost anything," said Aphrodite. "You've thought about it already. Be an eagle."

Sally wanted to protest, wanted to say, *I need time to experiment, to find out through trial and error how to do it.* But the wonderful city was calling to her, telling her that it would never exist if she was afraid to invent it.

She thought about the eagle's genetic structure, then about her plan to modify it so she could become one and yet still be intelligent. She took a moment to puzzle it out, and then . . .

She was an eagle. She spread her wings and flexed her talons, grabbing the edge of the seat underneath her.

I did it! she cried. *Look at me!*

And then she became a lioness, which felt marvelous. She felt strong and supple, ready to spring into action. She roared at Apollo's back. *Look at me! I'm a lioness!*

"He's busy just now," said Aphrodite.

Sally became a boy and asked, "Doing what?"

"He is the God of Light. It is he who is holding this analog of the city together for you, this picture of what could be."

Sally became herself again. "Why?" she asked.

"So you will know," said Aphrodite.

Sally was pleased. She had hoped that they would tell her things she didn't know, show her possibilities she hadn't imagined yet. Now they were finally doing it. She settled into the boat, really enjoying herself now, really feeling like there was a future worth struggling for.

I've proven myself worthy, she thought. *That's why they're doing it.*

"I was an oracle," said Aphrodite.

Sally looked at her, waiting for her to continue, but Aphrodite seemed to think she had made herself clear. Sally thought about it for a moment, what the woman had said about her past, about finding out the gods weren't really talking to her.

"When did you quit being one?" she asked.

"Almost twenty-five hundred years ago."

"So you retired when you were fifty-five hundred. I hope you at least got a gold watch."

Aphrodite didn't laugh. She seemed solemn, formal, as if they were bound for some important ceremony and she was already prepared for it. But Sally couldn't see anything up ahead, no crowds waiting expectantly. No people at all, come to think of it. Sally supposed the city wasn't ready for people yet.

"Or the people aren't ready for the city," said Aphrodite.

"Really? You mean—you mean they're not worthy yet."

"Not . . . *ready*," said Aphrodite.

Sally wondered what the difference was. The way people were now, they would throw garbage in the streets, spray graffiti on those beautiful walls to mark their territory, stick up billboards advertising cigarettes, arm themselves against their neighbors, tear up the streets and put down asphalt so they could run millions of cars all over the place and smog up the air. Sally didn't want them here, not if they were going to do that. They had a lot to learn.

But she had a lot to learn herself; so why shouldn't they go through the same process?

"Individuals learn fairly quickly," said Aphrodite. "Civilizations much more slowly. Do you have the patience to wait for them, Sally?"

Sally frowned. She thought she did, and she could live for thousands of years. So what was the problem? "You've been around for eight thousand years," she said. "How come you never tried to teach people a better way?"

"They must learn themselves, if they're to act from reason rather than habit."

That made sense. "Okay, then how come you didn't try to help people in other ways?"

"In what ways?" asked Aphrodite distantly.

"You could tell anthropologists how people really lived eight thousand years ago. You could show archaeologists where all of the tombs are buried and tell them about the mummies inside. Who they were, what they were like. You must have known some of them—"

"I did," murmured Aphrodite.

"So—you could fill in a lot of gaps."

"They're learning it themselves."

"Slowly! And they probably get most of it wrong!"

"But someday they'll get most of it right. They've learned the right process for finding things out. Now they're learning how to use it."

"You're talking about them as if they were children."

"I don't have much of a mothering instinct, actually." Aphrodite lifted a graceful hand, pulled a thick strand of midnight hair back into her coif. Sally watched her enviously, wondering what it was like to be so utterly feminine.

"That's right," she said, trying not to sound jealous. "You're the one who renews your virginity in the sea."

"Don't knock it until you've tried it," said Aphrodite, still not looking at her, still waiting for something.

Sally began to feel uneasy. It wasn't a bad feeling, exactly, but it set off all of her alarms, put her systems on alert. This wasn't just a pleasure ride they were all on, this wasn't a reward for Sally's struggles and accomplishments. It served some other purpose. She looked up ahead and saw a grand pyramid rising above the structures on the left side of the canal. It was so vast, Sally misjudged its distance from their position. She thought it was just up ahead, but it took them a long time to reach it, perhaps an hour.

And it just got bigger and bigger.

"Whose pyramid is that?" asked Sally.

"The Pyramid of Osiris," said Aphrodite.

Sally flinched. Apollo was still standing in the bow, still too busy to look at her. He was very much alive. Perhaps the pyramid was for show, to demonstrate that the Osiris period of his life was over. Perhaps he had built it to comfort the people who had known him as their king.

But Sally wished he would turn and look at her, smile, let her know that he was a permanent fixture of her life.

"He cannot," said Aphrodite. "Not now."

Sally gazed hungrily at the back of his neck, but he was as oblivious as Marc had been all those years. He brought the boat to a halt at the edge of a dock. Its steps led all the way up to the pyramid, became a part of it at its base, and continued up its side. Aphrodite stood and motioned to Sally.

"Come with me," she said.

They climbed from the boat, leaving Apollo behind. Sally looked at him over her shoulder and tripped on the steps as she tried to catch a glimpse of his face. She couldn't see it, so she gave up and hurried after Aphrodite.

There were thousands of steps, and it wasn't too long before Sally was augmenting like crazy trying to keep up with the unflappable and inexhaustible Aphrodite. *This is a great workout,* she thought to herself, trying to be cheerful, trying not to feel dragged down by ceremony and anxiety. Aphrodite climbed with her back straight, holding her skirts up just far enough to allow her dainty feet proper passage. Sally climbed like a tomboy, throwing her entire body into the process.

After what seemed like an eternity, they were halfway up. Sally stopped for a moment to look around, said "Wow!" at the glorious view, then hurried to catch up with Aphrodite again.

She was trying not to look above them to see where they were headed; it was too intimidating, there was still such a long way to go. The two sides of the face they were climbing seemed to converge into infinity, and infinity was definitely too far away to walk. And besides, even when they got to the top, what would they do? There was a point on the top; they couldn't stand there. Perhaps they would grasp hands and perch on either side of it, like flying buttresses. Or maybe they would fly up into the air, *ascend* like Ted had so wanted to do.

But Sally didn't really believe in that sort of thing anymore, and thinking about it was just making her tired, making her feel like it was all useless and pointless. She would never make it to the top with that attitude, so she stopped worrying about what was going to happen and what it all meant. Her weariness disappeared.

"We're here," said Aphrodite.

Sally looked up. There was no pointy top to perch on. In fact, there was no pyramid anymore. There were just a couple more steps that led up to solid ground. Mountains rose on either side of them, forming a valley, which was odd, since one didn't normally climb *up* to a valley.

"What is it?" asked Sally.

"The Valley of the Kings," said Aphrodite.

Yes. Sally recognized it from Susanna's memory of it. She looked down and behind her, where the pyramid still existed and a tiny Apollo stood in a tiny boat. The city was still there; a triangle still spread itself out below her.

She looked up again. No pyramid here, no vista of the city. The Valley of the Kings stretched itself from horizon to horizon.

"Okay," said Sally, and she climbed up the last two steps onto the dirt.

Aphrodite walked into the valley. Sally followed her. She didn't worry anymore about being tired and having to augment. She didn't worry about where they were going. She enjoyed the heat and the feel of sand under her shoes. She enjoyed the silence. She was almost surprised when Aphrodite stopped in front of a spot where the valley wall climbed steeply up from the floor and said, "Here."

There was a crevice about two-thirds of the way up the wall. Aphrodite gazed at it for a long moment, then rose into the air. Sally followed. The two of them lifted themselves into the crevice and set their feet on its uneven, rock strewn floor. But it wasn't as uneven as it should have been. Sally could see places where man-made tools might have altered it.

"What's in here?" asked Sally.

"A tomb," said Aphrodite.

Sally tingled with excitement. "Where? It just looks like a cave. Not even a very *good* cave."

"That's how it's supposed to look," said Aphrodite. "Most Pharaohs preferred immortality to fame." She climbed carefully down the sloping floor to the back of the cleft and suddenly disappeared. Sally hurried after her, only to find that the floor dropped suddenly. Soon the two of them were doing some serious spelunking: squeezing through tight spots, crawling under ceilings so low that it looked like a snake could barely get through. Sally could have disintegrated a clear path for them, but she didn't even suggest it. If the tomb was hidden, then this king wanted it that way, and who was she to argue?

At last the two of them squatted in a space so small and tight, Sally wondered if they would be able to get out of it again with everything still intact.

"Look here," said Aphrodite. A light shone on the wall facing them, and Aphrodite's hands brushed aside centuries of sand and dust. Something began to emerge. Sally expected something spectacular, but it was just a squarish lump of clay, smaller than a box of matches. She looked at it closer and saw symbols pressed into its surface.

"The seal," said Aphrodite.

Those symbols had been pressed there thousands of years ago. Sally felt awe prickling the back of her neck.

"We shouldn't break it," she said suddenly, thinking about the damage that could be done once the rarefied atmosphere of the tomb was disturbed by the outside world.

"We won't," said Aphrodite. And suddenly they were inside.

Sally unfolded from her crouch slowly. Her head

almost brushed the ceiling. Her eyes gazed at the sacred objects arranged in this outer room, illuminated by Aphrodite's light. She saw some things that looked familiar—animal shapes, stylized human figures, Egyptian hieroglyphics—but she didn't know what the significance of the items were. She didn't know their purpose.

"When was this tomb sealed up?" she asked, her voice hushed with respect.

"Six thousand years ago," said Aphrodite. "Before the period known as Old Kingdom. This is a pre-dynastic tomb, though archaeologists would place it in a later period because of the style of the wall paintings and the craftsmanship of the furnishings."

"Jim would love it," said Sally. Everything looked perfectly preserved, as if the artisans had just left and might return at any moment. *Just left,* thought Sally with a wonderful/sad thrill. Those workers had completed this project, gone outside, lived out the rest of their lives, and died. So long ago, so far away.

"Who's buried here?" she finally thought to ask.

"Osiris."

"You're kidding."

"In a way. There is a body in the sarcophagus which may or may not be his. It doesn't matter. The king dies, he ascends to heaven and becomes Amon. His successor becomes Horus and prays to him."

"But I thought Osiris was a god, not a pharaoh."

"Narmer was the first pharaoh of Egypt. Osiris was an old, old king."

"So old that he became a legend, right?"

Aphrodite shook her head. "You don't understand."

Sally blushed. Aphrodite looked so regal standing there in those surroundings, like she belonged there and Sally was just some callow intruder who didn't know anything. She took a deep breath and said, "Please explain it to me, then."

Aphrodite beckoned, and Sally followed her into another room. This was the burial chamber. The sarcophagus was sealed in stone casement, with the king's stylized image carved on its surface. Sally looked at the carvings, which didn't look symmetrical enough to be there for decoration. They must have been tools, or directions, or—

"Can you imagine what it's like to hear the voices of the gods?" asked Aphrodite.

Sally thought about it for a long moment and answered honestly. "No."

"But you believe in evolution, yes?"

"I've seen it," said Sally. "I even met ... a Neanderthal once."

"At one end of time we have the animal, at the other end, man. What happened in between?"

"All kinds of things," said Sally, hoping Aphrodite wouldn't ask her specifically *what*. She felt awkward enough as it was.

But Aphrodite just smiled. "Exactly."

Sally would have liked to claim credit for an intelligent answer, but she knew she had just lucked out, so she kept quiet. Aphrodite was looking into the eyes on the image on the sarcophagus almost tenderly.

"Why do you suppose these kings thought that they would become their father in heaven when they died, and that their successors would become them on earth?"

Sally had never thought about it. "Beats me," she said.

"Anthropologists have discovered Neolithic grave sights in which a single skeleton was propped up amid the debris of several older skeletons," said Aphrodite, "as if each new one took the place of honor from his predecessors."

"Horus becomes Amon," said Sally. "Then the new king becomes Horus."

Aphrodite looked her with glittering eyes. "Why?" she asked.

Sally shrugged, but she wasn't going to get away with that this time. Aphrodite continued to stare demandingly.

Jeez, Sally thought, *goddesses are pushy!*

"Give me a clue," she said aloud.

"I am your clue," said Aphrodite.

Sally looked away from that gaze so she could gather her thoughts. Aphrodite was the Goddess of Love. But no, that wasn't what she was talking about. She had said she was an oracle. She had said that she heard the gods.

"But you didn't really hear them," said Sally. "It was your talent."

Aphrodite pointed to the sarcophagus. "These kings did not have talent."

"What did they have, then?"

"Two sides," said Aphrodite. "Two minds. Two hemispheres that should be identical, but are not. One that handles details, and one that sees the big picture. One that can speak and one that can sing. One that is human and one that is divine."

Sally blinked. "Huh?"

"The voices, Sally. Where did they come from?"

Sally felt completely at sea. But she tried to play along. "Um," she said, "the divine side?"

"You say it, but you still don't understand it," said Aphrodite. "Yet you have dreamed of it. You dreamed of King Monkey, you dreamed of the scout and his wise Mother Goddess, you dreamed of Osiris and his struggle with his Enemy. Remember? When he grasped the hand of his Enemy and saw. . . ?"

"Himself," said Sally. "His own face."

She had forgotten about that, about how it had felt

to grasp the hand and feel its pain as if it were hooked up to her own nerves. *His* own nerves. Because, of course, it was. His two hemispheres were connected, and the pain had traveled back and forth, in a loop.

"And that's when he knew that he had killed his own son," said Sally.

"Part of him already knew it," said Aphrodite.

"Then why didn't it just tell him?" demanded Sally.

"It did."

I have killed him. I will kill any child you make. . . .

"Why would he want to kill his own child?" asked Sally, feeling more at sea every moment.

"Why would you want to kill Caitlin?"

Sally didn't want to answer that. She didn't have to; both of them already knew it too well. "We don't have to be monsters," she said, hoping that it was really true. "We can be . . . better than that."

"Perhaps Caitlin wanted to be better. She thought she was better than people already, didn't she? And now she is pushing at the edges of her own skull, trying to find God. Just as Durga must have done when she became Kali, trying to reach a higher plane, searching farther and farther out because the gods were not there, Sally. They were not there. They were *here*." Aphrodite tapped her own skull.

"Pretty outrageous thing for you to say." Sally tried to smile. "You'll put yourself out of business."

"Never," said Aphrodite, without a trace of humor.

"So she didn't find the gods."

"She didn't find the gods. She looked so hard that eventually she found something else."

Sally shivered. Aphrodite was a good storyteller; she really had Sally going. She only wished it was just a story. "What did she find?" she asked, feeling like she was opening the door in a haunted house behind which awaited the monster.

"She found the archetypes buried deep within the

wiring of the human brain," said Aphrodite. "Among which live the gods of war, music, love—"

"And destruction," said Sally.

"Yes," said Aphrodite. "She found the goddess. And that is what Caitlin will find."

Sally's mouth went dry. She felt something so hot and intense that for several moments she didn't even recognize it: anger. "So," she said, "that's what this is about. You brought me here not to teach me about the evolution of the human mind, but to convince me to kill my sister."

"Did I?" asked Aphrodite calmly.

"Didn't you? You're the one who said Apollo killed his son—"

"Did I?"

"And that the gods don't exist—"

"Did I?"

"Stop that! You know you did."

"I know I *didn't.*"

Sally thought back for a minute and had to concede that Aphrodite was right. She hadn't said those things. Sally had inferred them. "But you *did* say Caitlin could become a Goddess of Destruction."

"Absolutely. And what will you do about it?"

"And the only way to stop her is to kill her?"

"Is that what you believe?"

Sally didn't know. Caitlin had almost killed *her.* Caitlin hadn't thought twice about it, and she had taken pleasure in it, to boot. She had laughed at Sally because Sally had been swayed by love, by compassion.

No one could love like you did, Sally. . . .

"She doesn't have to die to be stopped," said Sally.

"Who will stop her, then?" asked Aphrodite, expressionless now as if she feared she would influence Sally's answer; and she didn't want to do that, Sally knew it, because Sally really *was* supposed to learn something now, something more important than anything else. And she even knew what it was.

Kali was not just the Goddess of Destruction. She was the Goddess of Escalation. She was the warrior who answered the call when the forces of evil kept coming back stronger and stronger. She became more and more powerful as greater and greater power was used against her.

Just like Ralph's shield. That's why I can't kill Caitlin. That's why! I will only make something worse!

"Who will stop her?" asked Aphrodite.

"I will," said Sally.

"Why you?" said the woman whose face had guided the hands of sculptors for centuries.

"Because I love her."

The face smiled. It blessed Sally.

"Yes," said Aphrodite. "Now you understand."

Sally nodded, fighting back tears.

"But there is one more thing."

Sally braced herself for it.

"Wake up," said Aphrodite, "and find out what it is."

Sally did wake up. She immediately looked for Apollo, whose warmth she could still feel in the bed with her. But he was gone. He must have just left.

She sat up, wondering if she should accept the dream as reality. Was there really something else to learn? She thought she had just learned the biggest thing of all; what else could there be?

She got up and dressed in her jeans and her blouse, pulled on her sneakers. She looked at her reflection in her mirror, hoping that she might look just a little older, just a little wiser. She didn't.

Sally crept from the room. She looked in Aphrodite's door but didn't find her there. She peeked into Apollo's room, but he wasn't there either. She went out to the kitchen and found him at last. He was alone, sitting at the table, his back to her.

Sally stared at the back of his neck. She was rather glad to have him to herself for a while. She had worried when he wouldn't turn around and look at her on the boat. But that had been a dream, and she didn't mind the view so much now. His neck was so masculine, so sexy.

Now's your chance, she told herself. *You don't have to just stare at it. Go do something about it. Maybe if you had done it to Marc, things would have been a little different.*

She crept forward. She didn't want him to turn at the last moment and spoil it for her. But he was aware of her. He wouldn't turn. He knew what she was doing and he was going to let her.

And now she was right behind him. She put her hands on his shoulders, loving the feel of his muscles. His breathing quickened, but he stayed still.

Sally leaned down. She touched her lips to his neck. She smelled something intoxicating there, tasted something that made her heart pound.

"I love you," she said, and wrapped her arms around him, pressing her face closer, getting his scent on her. He folded his arms over hers.

"Keep loving me," he said. "Forever."

Sally held him that way for a long time before she let him go so she could gaze at his face for a while. She sat down at the table.

"You had a long talk with Aphrodite," he said.

Sally stiffened. She had hoped she wouldn't have to learn anything else already, anything else that would blow her mind and rock her world. She hadn't realized it before, but *she* had been the only one to control what she was and wasn't going to learn before they had gone through the Gate. She and the Secret Mind. And now those days were gone.

"She said I should ask you about—about the one last thing."

But instead, he asked *her*. "Where is Mungy Bungy?"

Sally frowned. "Nowhere. He isn't real."

"Make him real, Sally."

She hesitated. She hadn't called Mungy Bungy back since Caitlin had shown her the painful truth. But now she had friends, now she had a lover. Why not bring the cat back?

Mungy materialized on the table, his old adoring self; and Sally found that she had to fight back tears after all. She missed him, she had loved him, and to know that he had only been a delusion . . .

"Make him *real,* Sally," Apollo said gently. "Let him go. Don't make him love you."

Sally did it. In another moment, Mungy was a living, breathing cat, with no link to her at all. He went from adoring her to being frightened.

"He doesn't know me," said Sally miserably.

"We'll introduce ourselves." Apollo produced a bowl of tuna. He set the bowl on the table and slowly slid it toward the suspicious cat. Mungy sniffed and edged forward. He watched to make sure no one was going to grab him, then edged forward some more. Finally his appetite overcame his caution and he settled in to eat, casting a cautious but neutral eye toward Sally and Apollo from time to time. Sally produced a bowl of water and put it nearby, but didn't try to pet Mungy.

"You created him without testicles," said Apollo.

"A million kittens have to be put to death every year because people refuse to spay or neuter their pets," said Sally.

"Ah. Then you made a wise decision."

They watched him in silence for a moment. His tail

was no longer twitching, and when he looked at them he seemed to be saying, *I guess I could get used to you.*

"Will he get hurt prowling around on your mountain?" Sally wondered. "Cats don't have very good depth perception."

"He might fall off," conceded Apollo.

"We could make barriers."

"We could. But he would work very hard to get around them. Such is the nature of cats and men."

"Okay, then—" Sally made a change in Mungy.

"You gave him a power!" Apollo sounded surprised.

"He can fly now," said Sally, a little defensively. "It's not like I gave him heat-ray vision. Now he won't fall."

"You could have just given him better depth perception."

Sally was embarrassed to realize that he was right. She fixed Mungy's depth perception, then thought about it a little further. He would need to be a little smarter so he could use that improved vision. So she did that too.

"And he can still fly," said Apollo, bemused.

"I don't want anything to happen to him!" said Sally. Mungy stopped eating, looked up at her, and started purring.

"A smart cat," said Apollo. "Just promise me you won't give him opposable thumbs."

"I promise," said Sally.

Mungy sat up and started to groom himself, as if he didn't know he could fly or that he was smarter now. Or as if it didn't matter. After all, a cat had his priorities.

"And now," said Apollo.

Sally looked at him, suddenly afraid.

"The one last thing," he said. He took her hand and stood, pulling her out of her chair. "Come with me."

Sally nodded, and in another moment they were no longer in Apollo's house. They were on Sally's mountain. Aphrodite stood a short distance away, waiting for them.

Sally felt the wind tugging at her hair, the sunlight on her face. She smelled the growing things, the rain in the distant thunderclouds. She looked around her until her heart filled up with the beauty and threatened to spill over.

"What is the one last thing?" she asked them, tears on her cheeks.

"Our Mastermind," said Apollo. "We want you to join with us."

Sally gaped at them. She never would have dreamed that they would share that kind of honor with her. In fact, she had never even thought to ask them if they had one. She had assumed that they must be beyond the need to form a Mastermind; after all, they had shrugged Caitlin's off like it had been nothing.

"Come," said Apollo.

Sally nodded. She let herself be drawn in.

"Now look," said the Mastermind, part of it with Sally's voice.

She had expected it to be like the others', a spider monster with someone's eyes sitting on top—probably Apollo's, but maybe Aphrodite's instead. But it wasn't like that at all.

The three of them literally became one being. Ted, Marc, and Susanna had never done that, probably had never even *dreamed* of doing it. This Mastermind had one set of eyes, belonging to them all. It had one mind.

"This is what we must achieve with the others," it said. It looked around itself, at the mountains of the gods, and it felt a joy so profound that it almost felt it could fill the world with it.

"I am alive," it said. "I am human."

The joy lasted for a few moments longer, and then
Apollo and Aphrodite gently disengaged themselves.
Sally felt herself become separate again. She would
have mourned it if she hadn't known that there would
be other times, other joinings.

"There will," said Apollo. "Very soon. We will
need it to survive."

"What do you mean?" asked Sally, still breathless
with wonder over what she had become with them.

"The Gate, Sally," said Aphrodite.

She stopped smiling. Not that again. She had
thought she had explained that it was gone, that she
didn't know why or where. She had thought they had
believed her.

"It's waiting," said Apollo.

"Waiting for what? Why should it wait?"

He looked at her with relentless eyes, the eyes of
King Monkey and Osiris. "Waiting for you to go
through."

"We *did* go through."

"No, you didn't."

"We *did.* Of course we did; we're standing right
here!"

"There is no *here,*" said Aphrodite, tugging that
strand of hair back into place, her gray eyes as calm
as if she were discussing the weather. "This place is
an analog, Sally."

Sally laughed. "An analog. A dream, is that what
you're saying?" She crouched down and tore up hand-
fuls of grass, threw them in the wind. "Here's your
dream! Taste it, smell the fake grass!"

They didn't even shake their heads, only stared at
her with compassion.

"Apollo," cried Sally, "I kissed you! I kissed your
neck, I ate your food. We went through the Gate, and
I made the fake bus, and I took us away, and I killed

Susanna and—and Marc, and my Secret Mind and I came together, and—"

NO, said Sally's Secret Mind. *We did not.*

Sally was shocked by the sound of that familiar voice in her head. She had thought she would never hear it again.

"But," she said, "we went through the Gate! We were supposed to come together!"

We didn't go through the Gate, said the Secret Mind, sounding tired, sounding strained. Why did it sound that way?

"Why not?" cried Sally. "Why didn't we go through? I thought we had a plan!"

We did. We have followed our plan. The Three couldn't be allowed to know; they would have seen what we were trying to do.

Sally shook her head. This was like what Aphrodite had said about King Monkey's Enemy, how it had told him the truth. Well, now she was hearing the truth, and it made no sense at all.

"Then where are you?" she said. "Why haven't you spoken to me in all this time? Why haven't you helped me?"

I have. I sent the dreams. I sent Apollo and Aphrodite. I sent the being that proved to you that Ralph's shield couldn't work.

"What do you mean *sent?* Where are you?"

With you, in front of the Gate. I'm the one holding the analog together, with the help of Ralph's special talent—

Sally! called Ralph. *It's me! It's true! I didn't know it until I went inside myself to start my composition, and I met your Secret Mind! I'm not Timothy's prisoner; he wouldn't do that to me. Even Caitlin didn't get much of me for her Mastermind.*

"Sally!" someone screamed at her. She looked down the slope and saw Caitlin flying up the mountain, looking terrified and enraged. The boys followed her, including Ralph, who still looked like he was in a trance.

"What are you doing, you idiot?" yelled Caitlin. "It's falling apart!"

"It has to fall apart!" yelled Ted, who was struggling up the slope on the other side, still apparently unwilling or unable to fly. "Let it fall apart!"

Apollo seized Sally and pulled her close. "Listen carefully," he said. "They're right; the analog is coming apart. Here is what we must do."

The sky behind him began to warp and buckle. Sally gaped at it, and he shook her to get her attention again.

"Soon you will be where you started, in the Indian School, looking for the Gate. You will go back slightly in time, and you will not remember what you've learned until you reach the moment before the analog was formed. But your Secret Mind will remember, it will be waiting, and when the moment comes, we will be with you. You will be ready this time."

"Ready for what?" said Sally dumbly.

"To pass through," said Apollo. "And to survive it."

"We don't need to go back!" Caitlin was shrieking. "We can be gods here! Stop it, Sally!"

"Don't listen to her," said Ted. "Susanna and Marc are back there! They're alive! And your precious little Joey too; you want to see him again, don't you?"

Sally gasped as if she had been shot. She looked from Apollo to Aphrodite, and they nodded.

"Yes," said Aphrodite. "You didn't kill them, Sally. That's part of the reason this analog was necessary: to teach you better skills without the danger of casualties."

Marc is alive. And Joey . . .

Lightning began to strike all around them. Sally

pulled herself away from Apollo and threw herself to the ground, tangling her fingers in the grass as if she could hold herself there. "I don't want to go through the Gate!" she cried.

"Why?" asked Apollo, crouching next to her. "What is it you fear?"

"I don't know," Sally said, her words almost lost in the rising wind. "There are—there's—someone on the other side! Something on the other side!"

"The real gods of Olympus are there," cried Ted triumphantly. "They're waiting for us! If you were worthy, you wouldn't be afraid to pass through! I'm not afraid!"

Sally looked into Apollo's face, trying to find comfort in the compassion she saw there. "*I'm* afraid," she whispered. "I am!"

"We'll be with you," he said. "You won't be alone."

Now the others had almost reached the top of the mountain. Caitlin circled like a harpy, screaming, "Stop it! Stop it!" Timothy helped Ralph climb. Timothy's eyes were full of doubt and grief. Jim's, by contrast, were full of hope.

Ted struggled up the last few steps, his face a mask of vengeance.

"Now we'll see!" he promised. "Now we'll see!"

"Yes," said Apollo, as he and Aphrodite put their arms around Sally. "Now we will see."

And the world pinched itself around them until there was nothing left of it.

Sally put her hand on the door to the girl's bathroom and pushed it open. The Gate was in there, somewhere.

The Three were herding the children ahead of them, using them as shields. Sally was more afraid than she'd ever been in her life. She could feel the Gate up ahead. It filled her mind with an impossible, inescapable dread. The monsters were in there. Why were they walking toward the monsters?

Sally went in first, with Caitlin right behind her. Caitlin's mind was locked deep within the Thrall; it couldn't resist what was happening to it. Sally almost wished it was that way for her too, because she was beginning to feel hopeless, like she wouldn't even be able to save her own mind, let alone the lives of the others, not against what waited on the other side of the Gate.

But The Three wouldn't listen. The Three *never* listened.

They moved past the sinks with the rusty stains like blood in them. They moved down the row of stalls, to the one that hid the Gate. Sally pushed the door open, her arm like a dead thing.

The Gate swallowed the door. It swelled before Sally, filling her sight and her mind as if the Indian School had never even existed.

Get ready, said Sally's Secret Mind. *Get set . . .*

Sally looked at the energy that was so much like the firing of neurons, at the glyphs on the door frame that were speeding up so fast that she could barely see them as separate entities anymore. They zoomed across the surface of her mind at the speed of light.

Now!

And the struggle was on. Ted tried to seize control, just as Sally's Secret Mind had thought he would. He wasn't interested in making peace, in learning that he might have been wrong about his Kids. He didn't intend to let them live. But that was too bad for Ted, because Sally had learned a lot inside the Olympus analog. She had learned more than him.

So the struggle was brief. At the end of it, there was only one being, with one pair of eyes, one mind; and it was greater than it had ever been. It surpassed anything that had ever been achieved before. Only Sally's Secret Mind was separate from it, riding piggyback just as it had always done.

Open the Gate, said Sally's Secret Mind.

The part that was Sally wanted to struggle. But she was the Mastermind too. She was beyond fear; she let go of it. The Gate was opened.

The Entities from the other side came forth and stood upon the threshold.

They were truly frightening. If Sally had seen them without the benefit of this new Mastermind, she would have been tempted to call them evil. But they were not. Not in the conventional sense, perhaps not in any sense at all.

In some ways they looked human, though they would never be mistaken for such. Everything about them was more intense. They felt love, hate, and pain to inhuman extremes. A glimpse into their world revealed a landscape shaped by potent energies.

"I know you," said the Mastermind. "You are another part of me."

"We know you as well," said the Entities. "You are another part of us."

"Communication is our destiny," said the Mastermind.

"There is no other path left to you," the Entities agreed.

"You have been waiting for me," said the Mastermind. "You want to cross over to our side, too. Why?"

"Because we must," said the Entities.

"Then there must be an equal exchange."

"You will never be the same."

The Mastermind gave birth to another, smaller Mastermind. This one was made up of The Three, and it didn't want to integrate completely. Ted's eyes kept struggling to perch on top of the others.

"Come together," said the larger Mastermind.

The smaller resisted. It reached out and tried to control the separate members of the larger. But there *were* no separate members. There was only one being, one who might be the closest thing to a god that human minds would ever achieve while still mortal. It reached out and touched the smaller, which shivered and became one as well.

"There," said the larger. "You are whole."

"I am!" cried the smaller, with joy. "I am!" It touched the larger with gratitude.

Then it turned and passed through the Gate.

At the same instant, three of the Entities passed through in the opposite direction. They instantly flew to three separate parts of the Earth. Where they were sitting, things began to change.

Sally's Secret Mind said, *Close the Gate now.*

The Mastermind began to close the Gate; but before it was completely shut, the Entities who still waited on the other side sent a message to the part of the Mastermind that was Sally—a message for her alone. It was brief, and chilling.

We know you, they said.

And the Gate was closed.

The Mastermind came gently apart. Sally was surprised to see Caitlin crying when they were separate again; but she wasn't surprised to hear her raging words.

"I was a god!" said Caitlin. "Why did you pull away?"

"Because you were not a god," said Aphrodite.

Caitlin was too intimidated to answer back. Sally almost pitied her; she had become the girl she had been before, young and no more glamorous than any mortal could be. The boys were boys again too. All of the changes they had made in themselves had been a dream, a learning experience in the analog. Sally supposed they could make the changes for real now, if they wanted.

She felt Joey touch her arm. He touched her mind first, just as he had done on that first morning . . . That first morning that wasn't a morning and that never happened.

She turned to look at him, so glad to see him that she could hardly believe it. He was glad to see her too; and relieved, so relieved and hopeful.

"I remember all of it, Sally. All of it. Even dying." He glanced at Caitlin, but not with malice.

"Where did you go after you died?" asked Sally.

"I don't know," he said. "It was almost like I was . . . asleep. I knew I still existed, but I didn't know anything else. I barely had enough awareness to wonder—to wonder if . . ." He swallowed a lump in his throat. "To wonder if I was in hell," he said. "But it didn't seem like a very bad place, like a punishing place, so I just hoped it would all make sense eventually. And it did."

"We can all do what we learned there, you know," said Caitlin, sounding flustered, sounding more upset than Sally had ever seen her. Her fire seemed to have gone out, like it had been doused with cold water. She noticed they were all staring at her, and flared up again.

"I can be a dragon again! I can make you sorry. I'll go back and visit that dumb girl you fixed, Sally, that Perla, and I can—"

"You'll do nothing of the kind, my girl!" snapped Ralph, sounding like a man even though he was still the white and pink boy he had always been. "I won't let you! I've learned a few tricks myself, some even *you* haven't figured out, and I'm not going to be your tool ever again!"

Caitlin gazed at him, her lip trembling as if he had called her a cruel name. *Leave me alone,* she said weakly. *Stay out of my life.*

"No," said Ralph. "You're my sister, and you're my responsibility. You're going to be part of our Mastermind again, Caitlin, and you're going to have to shape up. Believe it."

"I'm already different," said Caitlin. "You've already changed me. How come I changed, Sally? What happened?"

Sally wanted to know that too. The Gate had been opened, and now everyone was different. But weren't they all supposed to have gone through it? And her Secret Mind still had not joined with her. She could feel it waiting and watching. But for what? Hadn't she already done everything she could have done? The Three had gone ... somewhere. If not to Olympus, perhaps to the Fields of Elysium, where Kronos ruled.

"And now we've got three *Entities* on our side of the Gate. Now what? And where did they go?"

"We'll find one," said Apollo. He swept Sally and Aphrodite up with him, instantly transporting them, leaving the other Kids behind and, for the moment, safe. Sally felt a gust of hot air. They were outside again.

One of the Entities was near.

It was perched on a mountain peak, somewhere in Arizona. It still did not look anything more than vaguely human. It was both beautiful and ugly, male and female, or neither, or both. Things around it were changing at an accelerating rate. Rocks, plants, and sky were flowing into shapes and colors that were not new, yet were somehow more vivid. Sally watched the process, fascinated, wondering if it was all right to let that happen, if she should be alarmed.

Or if she even had a choice.

"Do you suppose The Three are doing the same thing on the other side that these creatures are doing on this one?" asked Sally.

"Not exactly the same," said Apollo. "They crossed over as One, as a Mastermind. But these three Entities never came together that way."

"Except that they *spoke* with us as if they were one," said Aphrodite.

"What have we done?" wondered Sally.

Aphrodite smiled. "Evolution, I suppose."

Suddenly the Entity reached out to them. Its lips were moving. Sally strained to hear what it was saying.

"I can't hear you!" she cried.

The Entity reached across the space between them as if it were standing right next to her and touched her hand.

The world shifted around them, until the two of them were alone, in a hallway. It was musty and dark, and very familiar. The Entity still had a tight hold of her hand.

"Philip says hello," it said. "Philip says hello."

"What?" said Sally.

The Entity changed. Its body flowed into more familiar lines. It became a small girl, a girl six years old.

Lydia.

"Philip says hello," said Lydia.

"Who's Philip?"

"You can hear me!" cried Lydia. "I've been trying and trying to talk to you! I've watched you get older and older every time, but I could never seem to quite make you understand me. I thought I would go mad!"

"Lydia ..." Sally touched the other girl, who was only half her height and less than half her age. Yet Lydia had the presence of an adult. Sally was staggered.

"You're dead," she said.

"Not yet," said Lydia. "You're not the only one who can hide in an analog, you know. I still have time to tell you something important."

"What are you trying to tell me?" *What is so important that you would defy time and death to tell me about it?*

"Philip," said Lydia. "Come on, I'll show you."

Lydia dragged Sally down the hallway and through a door that Sally couldn't remember having entered before, though somehow it was familiar. It opened into a small room. Inside was a young man sitting behind a TV tray. He was feverishly drawing something and didn't seem to notice the two girls when they entered.

"Hello," said the young man, without looking up.

"Hello, Philip. Sally's come to see what you're drawing." Lydia nudged Sally forward.

He was the boy from Sally's dream, she was sure of it. He was the one who had kept saying, *Hello, hello.* That's what Philip always said. That's the *only* thing Philip said.

She couldn't help staring at him. He reminded her of someone. There was something about the intensity of his concentration as he worked on his drawing, the single-mindedness. She looked down at the paper.

He was drawing the Gate.

"He's autistic," said Lydia. "He is Ted's brother."

Sally nodded, thinking, *Of course.*

"I found him when I was wandering the halls one day," Lydia was saying. "I tried to get him to talk to me, but all he can say is hello. I finally figured out he can *draw* conversations. That's how I found out that he's the one who made us."

Philip made them, and we can't make another Philip....

Lydia pointed to a pile of drawings at Philip's feet.

"You can go through them, if you want. But I'll save you some time. Those drawings tell the story of how Ted came back to visit Philip after being away for thirty years; how he noticed that Philip was making drawings of marvelous, impossible things, things that only someone with talent could use, and how he realized that Philip had a strange talent of his own.

We can't make another Philip. Philip is ...

"Dead," said Sally.

"Yes. But he's like one of his drawings. The part of his mind that has the talent must have realized that his image had to stick around and wait for us if he was going to accomplish what Ted ordered him to do."

"And what was that?" asked Sally, quite accustomed to being the straight man by now.

"Ted told him to design tools that would help The Three ascend. And Philip obeyed him. But the part of Philip that can do those things is not influenced by self-interest or anyone else's interpretations of reality. It's like a computer; it did exactly what it was ordered to do. It made us, and it planted us inside those surrogate mothers who gave birth to us and took care of us."

"And what did Ted think of that?"

"He was mad. He killed Philip."

"And why didn't he kill us too?"

"He didn't know yet. He didn't know we would be better than him; he still didn't quite see us as a threat. And even when he had his suspicions, Susanna and Marc talked him out of them. *They* knew we could be useful. They kidded themselves that they could control us completely. But sooner or later, Ted would have figured it out. He would have known what a threat you were to him."

"Me?" said Sally "Don't you mean *us*?"

"You, Sally. Philip showed me a drawing of your murder."

"But why me? Caitlin—"

"Caitlin can be manipulated. She is too easily put under the Thrall. But you can free her. You're a Master, Sally, like Ted. And that's why I got Philip to draw the Gate. Because without the Gate, Ted will get tired of all those fancy buildings you'll try to make for him, and he will—would have killed you. And then he would have picked off the others at his leisure, like lambs. Ultimately The Three would have been right back where they started. They never would have ascended; and Philip would have failed." Lydia sighed.

"But Philip never fails," she said. "So here we are. You've opened the Gate, yes?"

"Yes, but—"

"It's the Gate of evolution, Sally. It's like the bridge from our past to our future. The Three aren't the only ones who are going to ascend. Everyone will."

"How?" Sally asked in frustration. "How are we going to be different?"

"I don't know," said Lydia. "Philip didn't draw that. But when people changed a couple of thousand years ago, they did it gradually. They didn't know it was happening, they were even hurt about it, because their gods weren't speaking to them anymore. They thought they had done something wrong. They felt abandoned, and it took a long time for people to start to wonder if maybe they didn't need gods after all. People are still wondering that. And now we're about to turn another corner. I mean, *you* are."

"*Us*," said Sally. "What about *you*?"

"Philip is fading now. Look."

He was. Sally could see light streaming through him.

"Hello," Philip said, and then he was gone.

"Good-bye," said Lydia, a tear streaming down her cheek. She looked at Sally and said, "Yes, I know what's in store for me. I can face it now that I know it wasn't for nothing."

But Sally knew better. She remembered what had happened to Lydia—what *would* happen, how she would suffer. She remembered Lydia's terror, her agony.

"Let me help you!" she pleaded.

"You can't," said Lydia. "I did this so you would live. If you save me, you'll never get to this point. Believe me, I tried to think of every possibility that would save my life and still preserve yours. There aren't any."

Lydia stood on tiptoe, drawing Sally down for a kiss. She looked just like a little ballerina *en pointe,* so lovely, so tender. "Maybe there's another Gate," she whispered. "Maybe I'll see you on the other side of it, in the end."

And then she was gone.

"Lydia!" cried Sally, but nothing but silence answered her. She tried to stifle her sobs so she could listen, find out where Lydia was, call her back and save her. But Lydia was gone. Lydia had been dead for eight years. Sally could only stand there in the tiny room and cry alone.

Someone touched her hand.

Not alone, said her Secret Mind. *I'm here.*

Sally's tears began to slow down. She was comforted, a little. "What now?" she asked.

It's time.

"To come together?" asked Sally hopefully, fearfully.

For us, evolution will come a little faster. We'll understand, in a moment.

Sally heard footsteps. A little girl came into view. She stopped in front of Sally and smiled at her.

"Recognize me?" she asked.

Sally nodded. "Me."

"You're not so bad to look at, are you? You're kind of cute."

"I am," agreed Sally.

"Are you ready?"

"Ready as I'll ever be."

The little girl stretched out her hands, and Sally did the same, trying to meet her halfway. But two other sets of hands were reaching for hers too. She snatched hers back, finding Apollo and Aphrodite on either side of her.

"What are you doing?" she cried.

"Going home," said Apollo.

At first Sally couldn't comprehend what he was saying. And then, in one dreadful moment, she knew *exactly* what he was saying.

She shook her head. "No. No, you're real. You're alive—not—"

"We live," said Aphrodite. "We have always lived."

"Yes," said Sally. "You're not me! You're not part of me!"

"Sally," Apollo reproached her. "Is it so terrible? We will always be here for you."

Sally was sobbing again. This was as bad as losing Lydia. This might even be worse.

"I saw your history!" she cried. "I saw you as King Monkey, as the scout, as Osiris! You can't tell me you aren't real!"

"You saw human history," said Apollo. "It wore

my face. I am from you, and I will return to you; and when I do, you will have the benefit of the wisdom of that history. You'll need it, Sally. You'll need it when you do for people what you did for Mungy. When you help them through the Gate."

"I needed them to teach you to survive," said her Secret Mind. "I found them in the archetypes. That's why we had the dreams, Sally. I needed to give them their own history, their own lives, so we could benefit from their experiences. They lived inside us! I knew we needed more than what we already had in our hardwiring, and now we'll always have them. Me too! I came to love them too, Sally!"

"No!" Sally thought furiously, bringing back every memory she could of her time with Apollo and Aphrodite, anything at all that would support her argument. Something occurred to her that made her laugh with triumph.

"You *can't* be part of me. We've already come together in Olympus, when you let me be in your Mastermind! And back here, before we sent The Three through the Gate! If you had been part of me, you would have *become* me! We wouldn't be separate, now!"

She looked from face to face, hoping to see them transformed by her revelation. Instead, she saw only compassion, patience.

"What we became in our Mastermind was only a shadow of what we will become when we really come together," said Aphrodite. "When we pass through the Gate, Sally. The real Gate."

Sally shook her head. "I'm not following The Three through that thing."

"You don't understand," said Aphrodite. "It is the greatest truth we've told you yet, Sally. The Gate you have been seeing all these years is only a metaphor.

Philip drew it. The real Gate cannot be seen. We will pass through it when we come together."

"You see?" said Apollo. "It is not a place. It is a ... becoming. It is evolution. It's our destiny, what Philip engineered for us all along."

And now his face was more handsome than she had ever seen it. Now that he wasn't real, she longed for him more than ever. "I won't be able to hold you, to touch you," Sally whispered. "I won't be able to kiss the back of your neck, ever again."

He smiled at her. "Yes, you will. In our dreams. We'll be closer together than any lovers who ever lived."

"Stop bending the truth," she cried, uncomforted. "I can't believe I got fooled by my own animus after all. I can't believe it!"

"The truth is better than that," said Apollo. "The truth is, you love yourself."

"Now," said Aphrodite, "go love some others."

Sally looked at her, at the wise face that she had always wished could be watching over her. She looked at Apollo, the essential man. She looked at her Secret Mind.

"It hurts to grow up," said the Secret Mind. "But we have to do it, Sally. And when we do, we'll be glad."

Sally drew a deep breath, let it out again.

"Promise?" she begged.

Sally's Secret Mind smiled at her. "I promise." It stretched out its hands. Apollo and Aphrodite clasped them.

Sally stretched out her own hands. She reached for the others. She embraced them. She squeezed them.

They were her own fingers. She felt them being squeezed. And then ...

Sally opened her eyes again, whole. The room was

empty—or as empty as it could be with someone like Sally in it. She went to the window and looked out.

She hadn't known quite what she would find out there. Arizona, probably; but not the Arizona that had been there moments before. It must have changed, just as she had. The whole world was doing that, and people would change too—slowly or quickly, but surely.

Sally hoped those changes would be wise and beautiful; and so far they seemed to be. There were the mountains of her dreams. And on one particular mountain, just below the peak, there was a wonderful house; the sort of house one would expect to find in Olympus.

Or in Valhalla, thought Sally. Lydia wouldn't be there, though she deserved to be. But Sally could see some familiar figures on the terrace, waiting for her.

Joey was throwing a ball to Mungy Bungy, who flew through the air to catch it. Jim and Caitlin were sitting on the terrace wall with their legs dangling over the sides; and Timothy was eating a chicken leg, already growing back to the size he really wanted to be. He noticed Sally and waved at her, attracting the attention of Ralph, who turned and waved too, excitedly.

Sally! he called. *I've finished my first symphony, "Do Horses Have Dreams Mr. Williams?" Listen!* And then he began to play it in her head.

And he had done it. He had picked up the reins where the Post-Romantics had dropped them. Respighi and Rachmaninoff and Holst—and especially Ralph Vaughan Williams—would have been proud of him.

Keep playing, she told him, smiling, her tears gone and forgotten. *I'm coming!*

Hurry! he cried, and his music curled around her, lifting her up and out the window, into the clouds where the gods would have been if they could.

We, we fragile human species at the end of the second millennium A.D., we must become our own authorization. And here at the end of the second millennium and about to enter the third, we are surrounded with this problem. It is one that the new millennium will be working out, perhaps slowly, perhaps swiftly, perhaps even with some further changes in our mentality.

—Julian Jaynes
*The Origin of Consciousness
in the Breakdown of the
Bicameral Mind*

RALPH'S
RECOMMENDED
LISTENING LIST

For those of you who are curious about the music
mentioned in this book, run on down to your local
library or music store and check out some of Ralph's
(and coincidentally my) favorites:

George Butterworth:
  The Banks of Green Willow
Aaron Copland:
  Music For The Theater
  Music For Movies
  Quiet City
  Clarinet Concerto
Bernard Herrmann:
  The Day The Earth Stood Still
  Fahrenheit 451
  Psycho
Philip Glass:
  Dance Pieces
  Akhnaten
Gustav Holst:
  The Perfect Fool
  Egdon Heath
  The Planets

Sergey Rachmaninoff:
  Suites nos. 1 & 2 for two pianos
  Symphonic Dances (symphonic version or two piano version)
  Isle of the Dead
Ottorino Respighi:
  The Birds
  Three Botticelli Pictures
  The Pines of Rome and *The Fountains of Rome* (Ralph's favorite performance of these last two can be found in the CBS GREAT PERFORMANCES series, conducted by Eugene Ormandy)
Ralph Vaughan Williams:
  Symphonies nos. 3, 5, 7, & 9
  Oboe Concerto
  Double Piano Concerto
  Fantasia on a Theme by Thomas Tallis
If you are interested in knowing what King Monkey's chanters sounded like, you may want to investigate *The Ramayana Monkey Chant,* sometimes referred to as either *Ketjak* or *Retchak* (or variations of same). This selection can usually be found under Bali or Java, in Gamelan collections.
AND:
The music Ralph was playing in the very first paragraph of this novel is *Puccini Heroines,* Leontyne Price, soloist, from the MUSICAL HERITAGE SOCIETY, selection #MHS 512673X. This is an RCA Victor recording, licensed from BMG Music.